LENA'S HOUSE

Lena's House

AISLING MAGUIRE

Jasap Press

For my sister, Sabine, with love and gratitude.

All this is the person, that which is past and that which is future.

From the *Rigveda*

Chapter One

Well damn and blast Paddy anyway. I wouldn't put it past him to have sent his child on the evening train deliberately to make me drive through the rush hour traffic to fetch her. The Corkman's revenge on the Dubliner. And damn this rain too. I won't go so far as to blame that on the brother but if he could have arranged it he would. I'll never recognise her in this down-pour. The windscreen wipers sound as if they're going to expire under it. No doubt some bugger of a taxi driver will come along and tell me I'm blocking the rank. I'll have to do my deaf old bat routine. Paddy probably even knows first Friday is my night out with the Bagettes so he's made me good and late for that and my news will have to bake till then. Meanwhile the gals will have got a head start on the wine and gossip.

When did I last see this child and how old is she now? I'm her godmother so I should know. Yes, I remember, she turned twenty-one last year. Hardly a child any more but in my book she hasn't earned the right to be called an adult yet. Not after all the trouble she caused in college, getting her picture in the papers egging the Minister for Education. He probably deserved it for being an amadán but as a protest against the reintroduction of university fees it was self-defeating. Unless she really intended it as one in the eye for her father whose devotion to the party is obdurate and sentimental. Or maybe there is nobility in refusing to think ill of a once-cherished ideal, a yearning after old gods. But even Father, one among the vanguard in that brotherhood of heroes, lost faith in his latter years when the counter-jumpers began conniving their way through its ranks. Happy man that he didn't live to see Maid Marion take its reins.

Jean didn't come to Mother's funeral. I felt a mite sorry for Paddy then, with none of his kids there. Only Nóirín at his side, scowling like a bulldog. It wouldn't have killed the girl to come up with her parents from Cork. The older two were far too busy with their big careers, the Nora one sawing bones in America, and Pat chasing money in London. As for number three, Michael, my favourite, he fled to Korea the day after he graduated where he keeps himself in beer money by teaching English as a foreign language, which of course it is. No time for their old granny. Maybe I shouldn't have been surprised. Mother wasn't one of those little apple-cheeked, shawl-wearing, bootee-knitting grandmas of the story books. More like the wolf, with a glass of brandy in one hand and a cigarette in the other. We gave her a good send-off all the same, even without her unloving and unlovely grandchildren. A couple of the old guard came along, on day release from their retirement homes, remembering her and Father from those heady early days when God's own party applied a fig leaf of ideology to its organisation of the new State. One of the codgers gripped my hand and told me how lucky I was to be born into a free country. I know, I said, I know, and wanted to tell him I too had suffered and made my own sacrifice in its name, supposedly, but remained uncharacteristically silent. That must have been the grief, although I had yet to shed a tear. At the age of ninety-three Mother had done her time. Towards the end she said she wanted to go to Father, whether her own father, who had absconded when she was ten, my father, long departed, or God the Father, I wasn't sure, maybe all three, but one way or another she was ready to leave. She had lived through the first two years of a new century and did not want to make a century herself.

Interesting that Paddy didn't impose Jean on us when Mother was still alive. I know what he's up to now. Keeping an eye on me and the house, just as I'm embarking on my new life. He must have anticipated my reluctance to take the child in because he reminded me of his and Nóirín's hospitality to Muiris, and the other business, as he termed it, a full house played with all the skill of the keen poker player he once was, leaving me no option but to fold and assent.

Good God! What's that, tapping on the passenger window? The dreaded taxi driver? The Bride of Dracula? I open the window a crack.

Jean?

Yes. Where'll I put my bag?

On the back seat. But not on the dog's blanket.

What is she like? The size of her, the seat belt will never go around her. Chilly air gusts in when she opens the door, scattering cold drops over my hands and face. A damp smell rises off her black clothes.

Welcome to Dublin.

Thanks.

How was your journey?

Fine.

How are your parents?

Fine.

Hmmm. I turn my attention to the road, trying to nudge into the stream of traffic. Something flashing in the wing mirror catches my eye, headlamps switching from full to dim, the irate taxi driver telling me to get a move on. Let him wait. These fellows are a curse. And yes, I know, there's a female of the species too these days, but they're not much better if you ask me. They need to learn that the customer is always right and does not want to hear their state-of-the-nation jeremiad. There must be some kind of manual or induction course that teaches them how to aggravate their passengers, a half-baked version of 'the knowledge' in London but without any notion of local street names or directions. Maybe that's all about to change, however, with the influx of migrant workers. They at least have the merit of not knowing the lingo.

At last, a man in a silver beamer pauses to let me slide into the traffic.

You're a gentleman and a scholar sir. I wave my thanks.

What? Jean turns towards me. Her round face is whiter than alabaster and her lips and eyes are rimmed in black. There is a ring hooked to her snout.

Nothing. I was talking to the driver in the car behind.

The black eyebrows rise a fraction. Oh.

I'm going to drop you home but I have to go out this evening.

Okay. Whatever.

There's food in the fridge. I assume you know how to use a microwave.

Yeah.

Is there a want there or does she simply have no manners? She was an afterthought after all. Mother was quite shocked when Paddy announced that Nóirín was preggers again, as much a surprise to her at the age of forty as to the rest of us.

They should have some self-restraint at their age, she said. Like your father and me.

That was too much information for me, as they say now-adays, but I have to confess I was a little disgusted myself. Michael was eight when Jean was born so in a way she was an only child. An idle heap I'm guessing and probably pernickety as hell about what she eats with it. I hope she's not expecting me to pander to her foibles. Her head is nodding rhythmically to a beat only she can hear. Plugged into an iPod I suppose.

If I'm not going to get any chat out of her I might as well listen to the radio. . . . been told: put your money in crocOgold . . . The glic tones of that upstart little Liam Geraghty set my gnashers, most of which, bar a couple of crowns and a bridge, I am proud to say, are my own, on a razor's edge. Being the Taoiseach's lap-dog must get him a cut rate for the ads. Cross-subsidised by our licence fee. There's no avoiding him: he's either pestering us on the radio, smirking at us from a hoarding or prancing around on the TV like a dandified leprechaun. A twerp Father would have called him, with justification. An accountant turned investment guru he takes us all for fools but I warrant he's the knave. Now here's the Barcarole from Hoffman. Apt for the day that's in it. I could do with a gondola to navigate these streets. There seems to be more water in Dublin tonight than in all the canals of Venice. Hard to believe that only three years ago I was doing the rat run every day but it's a cliché to say the traffic is worse than ever. I'm struck by how quickly I have adjusted to slippered retirement mode. In the first few months of idleness, I snapped awake at six a.m. and was half way out of the bed before remembering I was no longer required at the office. Then, with diminishing tremors of guilt, I flopped back onto the pillow and slept until nine or ten. More surprising was the speed with which I detached from the work. The odd time that Myles, to whom I handed over my files, telephoned to check a fact or get a second opinion on a settlement offer I resented the intrusion although only weeks previously I had held a clear view of every case and its worth. I didn't dislike the work, on the contrary, I took pride in achieving a good result for a client. Even to this day, when I start awake in the black hours before dawn, all of a panicky swither with the fear that I am about to die, I prepare an account of myself for the recording angel, listing the prestigious cases in which I acted, on the off-chance that he doesn't take *The Irish Times* (not that I could fault him for not).

I went to one Christmas party after I retired and discovered I no longer had anything in common with the men and women whom I had hired and in whose company I had spent forty hours a week. They're all smart and decent people in their way but after eight months' absence from the firm and its ritual daily exchange of banter, in-jokes, confidences, gossip, anecdotes and searing anxiety about the government's desire to impoverish the legal profession, I felt like a recovering amnesiac trying to infer the meaning of the jargon and fumbling my grasp on the conversational codes. It is possible too that my hearing is not as acute as once but I think I had simply lost interest in all that had occupied and preoccupied me for a goodly part of my life. I pasted a smile on my face and reached for the wine. My erstwhile colleagues probably thought I was ga-ga. I still, however, have a stake in the firm, which retains Mossie's name, and turn up every quarter for a meeting with Myles, the new partners and the accountant. Although I haven't attended another Christmas party I continue to receive the card of the Georgian door, its fanlight painted a homely yellow and a luxuriant wreath sketched in beneath the brass plate: *M.Carmody, Solicitor, Commissioner for Oaths* but no scrawl inside, just the printed greeting and stamped copies of everyone's signatures. No doubt it will continue to arrive long after I'm gone. A cheap and phoney-looking production in more ways than one. The only time I hung a gorgeous wreath on the door it was fecked within a day so I never bothered again.

Surely that can't be the very same door on my left? Maybe I have gone ga-ga after all. I shouldn't be anywhere near Fitzwilliam Square. Is it possible to drive on autopilot? That's what I get for reminiscing. Passing the Four Courts must have switched me into my old route back to the office from a consultation or hearing. Just as well the creature beside me wouldn't know the difference.

That was my office. I take advantage of the detour to do my general guide routine. Any day now they'll put a plaque on the wall to commemorate the fact that Lena P. O'Neill dispensed sound advice there for forty-odd years.

Jean's head inclines to the left. Oh.

Dull. The child must be a dullard. I glance up. The lights in the reception area are off but some of the offices are still lit. Gratifying to see someone else working late for a change. The top floor lights are on too. Brennan, the caretaker-cum-delivery boy making his lonely tea. Myles wanted rid of him when I retired so that he could let the flat for a ridiculous sum but I put my foot down. Poor Brennan wouldn't know where to go or what to do with himself. That garret has been his home ever since Mossie took pity on his old school chum and gave him the sinecure with lodgings as part payment.

That was Mossie, an active, kind-hearted man. I never saw him defeated by a problem. He applied himself to each fresh challenge with vigour and a twitch of amusement as if it were a puzzle to which he need only find the key. When we got engaged his male friends affected to marvel at his courage but he laughed them off saying that a woman who spoke her mind held no fear for him. The truth was that they regarded me as tainted by my 'disappointment' but Mossie had enough self-assurance to rise above such pettiness.

My friends in turn marvelled at my luck in catching him, as they put it, on the rebound. But our luck was short, twelve years to be exact. Even at this remove, and with my sights on a new-old prospect, I crave his company.

Here is the news read by Eithne Reilly. Two US military aircraft were shot down today in friendly fire near Basra. President George Bush said there would be no withdrawal of troops from Iraq. A military investigation is underway to determine the cause of the attacks . . .

That man is a dangerous lunatic, I venture.

Yeah. And he wasn't even elected.

My God, the zombie speaks! A whole sentence. Well, half a sentence but that's better than dumb.

It shows who really holds power, I return the ball now that's in the air.

Crooks.

. . . crocOgold get your money on a roll . . .

Oh well, maybe I was expecting too much. What do I know any more about young people? One thing's for sure, however, this child is the classic antagonist of her father, which probably means that beneath the pancake make-up and the ugly clothes she is more like him than she wants to admit.

Paddy is a 'heart man' who features regularly on television and in the papers, urging the nation to keep its tickers tickety-boom. He pretends to laugh at himself, saying he's doing himself out of a job because if everyone follows his advice there'll be no more need for heart surgery. For him, the heart is a remarkable feat of engineering (God the engineer to be sure) and he a sophisticated plumber keeping the pipes clean. He is obsessed with this pump and thinks the rest of us should be too. He tells the nation to stop eating butter on its potatoes and then to stop eating potatoes altogether, trying to change the tradition of generations. A pity he wasn't around at the time of the Famine, I tell him. They must have had great hearts then.

His preaching may not have done him out of a job yet but despite his cant it scuppered his political career. Having followed Father into Fianna Fáil, he aspired to get elected to the Dáil or, failing that, to be given Father's seat in the Senate. The trouble was he reckoned without the power of the farmers. They didn't like his anti-butter campaign, especially when they were looking for European subsidies to continue producing mountains of the stuff while the market was falling. He ignored Father's advice and blundered on to his own detriment.

Father regarded Paddy as a bit of a plodder and suggested when he left school that he go for the civil service but Paddy was determined to impress him and surprised us all by slogging his way through to a medical degree. Nonetheless, Father refused to use his many contacts, professional, political and in the Knights, to get Paddy a job in his hospital, chiefly out of an exaggerated sense of honour, which, while commendable, was highly impractical, not to say deeply anomalous in a member of Fianna Fáil. No wonder he never got elected. For his service to the party, however, and specifically to the Taoiseach's son, whose squint he rectified, he was nominated to the Senate. There is a straw in the wind now saying Paddy wants to run for President. Nonsense of course but he has never stopped trying to prove himself to Father. Pitiful in its way.

Jean in turn seems to have reversed her father's advice. Maybe that's why he's offloading her. After squeezing consent out of me he claimed that she would be 'company' for me now that Mother is gone but I'm beginning to suspect he has developed a sense of irony.

I don't need company, I told him. I have Tanta.

Tanta is a dog.

That's why I like him. He doesn't answer back.

Unlike you, he answered back. Jean will look after herself. She'll be out most of the time anyway looking for a job.

Then she won't be much company, will she?

Look, Lena, she's your niece. It's a temporary arrangement. And, frankly, it's the least you could do after what, I mean to say she's the same age more or less you were when—

Yes, yes, I rush in. There's no need to rake all that up.

When she starts working she'll probably want to move out anyway.

I decided not to take offence at that remark. She can stay as long as she behaves herself. At the first sign of trouble I'm putting her on the express train to Cork, with all her bags and belongings.

Don't worry. She's learnt her lesson.

She'll have to pull her weight in the house.

Now that I see her I regret that choice of words. She's more likely to break the furniture than help to keep it clean. Not that she'll be required to get down on her hands and knees. Like all self-respecting Southsiders, I employ a Filipina cleaner, Felicia from Manila. Over the five years that she has been coming to me we have grown quite close. After Mother had her stroke and I was still working she came three days a week for a few hours and soon got the measure of that prickly woman, who came to depend on her. Felicia continues to come for two hours on Mondays and Fridays to 'do' for me. Aside from paying her well, I have funded her daughter's degree in bioengineering. Thus the social boundaries have shifted since Mother's day when charity to the 'maids' meant helping some of the greener sixteen-year-old girls from the country whose loneliness made them ripe for seduction in the city. They returned to us after their babies had been wrenched from them and sold to American families. 'Tough but fair' was how one described her to me years later. Maybe those should be my watchwords with this girl. She needn't think I'm going to run around after her like a mother hen, cooking and doing her laundry. I'll have to lay the ground rules from the get go.

If Paddy has sent Jean up here as a spy, his hunch is right— or more likely it's Nóirín's hunch—because my schemes for the house and for my private life would exacerbate the anger he already feels at Mother's not having left a will bequeathing particular items to him. He has always felt short-changed because he was born three years after me, as if, like someone invited to the 'afters' of a wedding, he was excluded from the main event. As against that, however, he was Mother's favoured child, bearing out the old belief that a mother will only give her heart to her son. I would have no objection in principle to giving him some of the paintings, furniture and Father's treasured Jacob Petit clock if he weren't so provoking about his grandiose entitlements. He has convinced himself that I told her not to make a will, which is laughable given my profession and our mother's intransigent nature. When, I asked him, was either of us able to influence her thinking.

As a child he had wanted to learn to play the trumpet, a notion inspired by watching the brass band play on the pier where we walked on Sunday afternoons, but Mother forbade it, saying it would distract him from his studies. He begged and pleaded, and whined and raged, saying it was unfair because I was learning the piano. When Mother explained that I was a girl and needed such accomplishments to enchant my suitors he asked me to intercede on his behalf.

He likes the idea of himself in the red uniform with all the gold frogging, like a British officer, said Mother, in a remark whose tone of contempt I should have recalled in later years. Besides, she added, I couldn't bear to listen to someone practising the trumpet and neither could your father.

Case dismissed. Father's authority was the final word, even when there had been no appeal to him. In the absence of a trumpet Paddy concentrated on developing a novel party piece: reciting the alphabet in burps. A resounding success wherever it was performed, including, I gathered from hearsay, medical dinners, or at least the ones that Nóirín didn't attend. Which goes to show that deep within the self-inflating layers of pomposity, the beloved giddy spirit of my little brother still dances. I'm not sure when he began to take himself so seriously but it coincided with a growing piety, when he gave up the booze, for the good of his heart, he said, a concept that Mother greeted with an exasperated grunt and eyes rolling heavenward. Indeed she had been the first to spot when he began drinking by observing that the nicotine stains on his fingers had shifted from his right to his left hand. Not that she objected, how could she? When he went on his sobriety kick she took to calling him 'poor Paddy'. Drinking, after all, didn't create as much noise as the trumpet or so she liked to pretend, ignoring her nocturnal rows with Father.

So now, in his self-righteous plumage, Paddy the pump-man and paterfamilias was insisting that Father would never have wanted him to be cut off.

It's not a question of being cut off, I said evenly. Father died twenty years ago. He left what little he had, and it was very little, to Mother. But for me she'd have been on the street. Remember this is my home. I bought it. Besides you already have two homes.

I wouldn't call a cottage in West Cork a 'home'.

That just shows how far we have advanced beyond the peasant class.

It's not a question of money, Lena.

What is it?

Heritage, my birthright. My children's birthright.

Bollocks.

That kind of language may have intimidated the men you employed but it doesn't intimidate me.

That wasn't my intention. I simply don't believe that sententious claptrap.

You haven't heard the end of this.

A week later he phoned with his suggestion about Jean and called in his debt. He's mistaken if he thinks the child's presence will put a stop to my plans. Muiris is coming over tomorrow morning to look at the site.

The cuckoo here beside me needn't know a thing about it.

Well, Jean, I shout this time. What do you make of the Big Smoke?

Cork is a city too.

So your father would have me believe. Have you any plans?

Look for a job I suppose.

What did you do for your degree? I forget.

Communications.

Stupid question. The girl might look moronic but as I recall she did quite well in her exams although that may simply be a sign of the drop in educational standards, a decline I had noted in recent years of recruiting young solicitors. They could not spell, thought an interlocutory injunction was a medical complaint and found it hilarious that I referred to the midday meal as luncheon. Some even thought I had invented the word. No wonder they called me a stuck-up cow behind my back. One of Old Brennan's jobs was to do a little discreet spying for me, so I knew from the start whom to watch and whom to trip up.

Damn and double damn Paddy, damn this rain and damn this traffic. I cannot understand why people say the pace of life has accelerated when it takes an hour and ten minutes to do a journey I used to do in twenty minutes. It's not that the pace has picked up but that the time available to enjoy oneself has shrunk so we have to rush our pleasures. Where did all these people come from? Not so long ago a child like Jean would have boarded the first plane off the island. Instead, here she is in the glossy new world of 2004 confident that she can afford to be choosy about her job.

What's your father up to these days?

The usual. Talking about retirement. Jogging every morning with Mimi and Rodo. Telling Mum to stop smoking.

He'll kill those dogs.

Or himself.

What'll Nóirín do when the smoking ban comes in?

She says it'll never happen and if it does she'll go to live in London with Pat.

Interesting, I think. Maybe she's looking for an excuse to leave Paddy.

I suppose Pat's still making boat loads of money.

Yep. He and Mandy have just bought a new house. Dad is at them to get married.

What about the other two?

Nora's on maternity leave and Mick's thinking of moving from Korea to Japan.

So much for Paddy's guff about their birthright. That lot wouldn't give tuppence for the house or its contents. Cash is all they want and they seem to have plenty of that. Bar this lassie.

And have you no plans to travel beyond Dublin?

Not yet. I need to earn some money first. I'm the black sheep of the family.

You sound proud of it.

Every family needs one.

A glimmer of wit. Maybe we'll rub along well enough after all. Not that I'm a black sheep, more like a grey one. After all an affair of the heart can hardly be deemed a crime or even a misdemeanour despite what the bullies who picked on me, in the guise of patriots professed to think. None of which a child like Jean would understand, which is progress.

. . . don't be fooled put your money . . .

The windshield wipers sound as exhausted as I feel. Another news bulletin already. I'm growing old just sitting in this car. . . . The Taoiseach, Mary Lacey, said it was time for both sides of the dispute in the Middle East to come together and negotiate a settlement. She offered Ireland as the ideal location for such talks. . . . That Lacey woman is cracked. She has neither style nor sense. An apt reflection maybe of the state of the nation.

A bit big for her boots isn't she?

Who?

Lacey, the Taoiseach.

Jean nods vigorously, whether to the music which she can still hear through one of her ear buds or in agreement with me. Just because she's a woman doesn't mean she's good.

Exactly. What does your father make of her?

Not much but he has to be nice to her if he's going to get the nomination.

Nomination for what?

She pauses, presumably to attend to the music in her other ear then says simply, President.

What? I all but run a red light in shock.

He wants to be President. He says.

I see. I try to remain calm. And did he say why?

Something about serving the nation I think.

That's absurd.

Yeah. I suppose.

Trying to please Father again, poor man. Or to outdo him. But he lacks the sheen of Father's heroic past. A time we knew little enough about because he never spoke of it to us. Mother had revelled in his later Roman title and continued to use it long after his departure from the Senate. When challenged by a garda for parking illegally she would say Do you know whoooom I have in the car? The misfortunate garda would shake his head. *Senator* Patrick O'Neill. She would tilt her chin defiantly but the garda would remain nonplussed, being too young and too indifferent to know the name. Paddy, it would appear, has inherited some of her notions. So far, however, his contribution to the body politic has been as a member of the party to tap his medical colleagues for money to keep its leaders in the power and luxury they arrogate as their right, winning them in turn a few concessions on mixing public and private practice, along the way. At least he lacked the guile, overweening egotism or cynicism to get right in on the inside, deal-making track which keeps his hands clean, unless one accepts the principle of guilt by association. He is not a bad man, just sorely deluded. What precisely he imagines he can achieve in the Park it's hard to imagine, apart from a slow death by inanition. Not that he has a hope of getting there. Unlike me, he's not one for retrospection or what-ifs but it's an awful pity Mother never let him play the trumpet. He might be touring the concert halls of the world now tooting for Ireland.

. . . make your money safe as houses . . . That blasted leprechaun again.

Good job we're home but what's this? My neighbour Bernie 'Murphy-Benz' has parked in my spot again. Botheration. Just what I need after battling rain and rush hour traffic. I'd let the air out of her tyres only she's a decent sort. She was barely in the house a wet week when Mother died but next day she landed in with home-made chicken à la king, she even came to the funeral and continues to deliver a loaf of her high-fibre multi-seed HRT bread to my door every Thursday. Hard to imagine bird food will stop the hairs sprouting on my chin. I haven't the heart to tell her chewing it is too much like hard work for my taste. Reminds me of the black bread at Lough Derg. Maybe I could offer it to the singularly unhealthy-looking lump beside me.

Nothing for it now but to park in the lane and get soaked walking around the corner to the house. And yet, and yet . . . why not put the child to use? I pull in to the kerb opposite the house and hand her my latch keys. You can hop out here, I say then direct her to the kitchen door and the back gate. Don't mind Tanta, I add. He'll yap his head off but he won't bite.

Although sea and sky are a moil of grey obscuring Howth she nods and pulls up the hood of her ghastly black garment. When she opens the passenger door wind slices through the fug in the car speckling the dashboard and my cheeks with rain. Another blast of damp air whips across the nape of my neck when she retrieves her bag from the back seat. Then she is gone. In the rear view mirror I watch her cross the busy road before I merge with the stream of cars. She's not such a bad kid after all. No doubt she has as many reservations as I do about sharing my home but it may be a relief to her to get away from her parents.

The lane running behind my house, and the terrace of which it forms one end, was once the access to stables for the coaches and horses of the 'gintry'. Fallen out of use, it was throughout my childhood the ill-lit lair of bogey men, later to be made flesh in the mask of gallus heroes. Today the lane is paved and lit to facilitate entry to a hodgepodge of mews, garages, offices and teenagers' dens soon to include— the dopes in the planning office permitting, sans baksheesh— my own bijou dwelling. As I guide my carriage into the lane the headlights pick out Feargal Murphy-Benz sheltering under the purple and white dome of a golf umbrella emblazoned with the name of his business, Murphy Motors, and the Mercedes logo. Terror jolts me as a second figure detaches itself from the lee of the wall. I draw up and cut the engine but remain in the driver's seat, my hands on the wheel. Inhale. Exhale. Slowly. Deliberate breaths. How swiftly old fears reassert themselves, against reason, and erasing time.

I watch as the stranger, a lanky fellow, canted to one side, moves under Feargal's gamp and begins describing jagged shapes on the air with the beam of a torch. Curiouser and curiouser. Feargal stays the man's hand, however, and ushering him back into to the shelter of his gateway approaches my car motioning me to roll down the window. With him too I must be gracious in deference to his generous trade-in on my last car. Such are the transactions of good neighbourliness: meals and wheels.

Sorry, Lena, he says. I know Bernie has done it again. She was in a hurry with the kids and someone else was parked in her usual spot. Taking his mobile phone from his pocket, he offers to call Bernie and tell her to move her car.

Don't worry, I muster a nonchalant smile. I've sent my niece to unlock the back gate. Rain is good for the complexion they say.

Very well, he bends to open my door. I'll wait with you till she arrives.

Maybe we need a multi-storey car park back here, I quip, easing myself out of the seat into the shelter of his brolly, with a bridge to the houses.

It could be an effect of the yellow street lamp but a queer expression seems to cross his features as he half-laughs, yes. That would be just the job.

Before I can wonder further why he and his friend are mooching around the lane in a downpour I hear Tanta yap ferociously while the gate scrapes open and Jean appears, a bedraggled and unlikely porter.

Chapter Two

They grab me from behind. Again. Pawing my breasts, bruising the soft flesh. Stubble grazes my cheek, too close and intimate. Traitor, a voice rasps in my ear. We'll show you what happens to traitors. I'm scrabbling at the hands. Get off me. Go away. More hands grab my wrists. Let me go. I'm shrieking. Out of breath. Struggling. Panicking. Fear is plunging through me. Ice cold. In the dim light their faces are grotesque masks. The more I writhe the deeper the pain of their grip. Hold still you bitch and take your punishment. Yanking my hair making tears spring from my eyes. Sneering. Tar and feathers'd be too good for you. A sharp kick to my shin. Pain bolts through my marrow. Let me go. Leave me be. Leave me.

Over the sound of my own screams, gathering volume like an approaching train a different noise shrills through my head. Rrrring-Rrring. The nightmare pours away, down a sinkhole to the past leaving pain to ring my head. Rrring. Shuddering in my bones. Rrrring. I lie still. Take my bearings. In the bed. Thanks be. Rrring. Shudder subsiding. What did I drink last night? Not much I don't think. A dirty glass no doubt. Rrrring. Will it never stop? My eyes slide effortfully to the right and light on the phone, its little red eye winking in time to the ring-ring-ringing. Persistent bugger.

Whatever the time of day it's too bloody early to be talking but I pick it up in a reflex.

Yes.

Lena?

I think so.

Did I wake you?

Of course you did. Don't tell me: you've already jogged five miles with those misfortunate dogs and eaten your porridge.

Yes, as it happens. The dogs are perfectly happy. And healthier than that dog of yours.

Did they tell you that themselves?

May I speak to Jean?

Is she likely to be awake at this ungodly hour?

No, but I don't have all day.

I move slowly, working my limbs against the ache that seizes them every morning, and fumble for my slippers. Tanta remains snoring in the nest he has made at the corner of the duvet. Pulling on my dressing-gown I shuffle down the landing to knock on the door of Paddy's old room. No response of course. I push it open. A trail of black garments leads to the bed where a shadowy mound rises and falls with the rhythm of loud snores.

Jean, I call. Jean. Your father's on the phone. You can take it downstairs.

Back in my room I crack open the curtains to see what the day is doing. The rain appears to have stopped although drops run off the gutter, and a watery sun seeps through the clouds. Everything in the garden sags under the weight of last night's deluge. I roll into the bed although I know I won't get to sleep again. Tanta stirs and yawns. I pick up the receiver gently – just checking whether Jean has heard me and gone to the phone. Truly. Honour bright and all that.

. . . last night?

Had dinner. Watched TV.

How does the house look?

Fine. The same.

What about the paintings?

What paintings?

The Hone, the Henry, the Keating.

The so-and-so *has* asked the child to spy on me. In my annoyance I kick out under the bedclothes disturbing Tanta who yaps.

. . . only just arrived.

Do it today.

What do they look like?

Awake now, Tanta barks urgently, requesting outies.

Lena should discipline that bloody dog.

Ha! I could say something about the way he brought up his children.

I told you already. The cows, the cottage, the turfcutters—

Yeah, yeah, I remember now. I'll look later when I—

Wait a minute. Lena? Are you listening to our conversation?

The damn dog has given me away. Yes, as it happens I am. But don't mind me. It's very interesting.

It's none of your business.

Au contraire, mon frère. It seems to be very much my business and actually not much of yours.

Dad, Lena. I'm going back to bed.

Good idea, Jean. Now Paddy, what exactly do you mean by sending your child to spy on me?

You know what I mean. Those paintings are part of my inheritance too.

Do you think they'd look nice in the Áras?

What are you talking about?

I think you know but I'm too tired to argue with you now.

Or too hungover?

I don't want a lecture either. Good bye.

I slam the phone down. If ever I die of a heart attack it will be after talking to my brother the heart surgeon. I get up to let the dog out but discover it's too late. He has performed a protest pee which has not only soaked the carpet inside the bedroom door but is also spreading across the cotton sole of my slipper. God be with the days when I could clatter around the house in mules – now I'm reduced to flat yokes that make me feel frumpy and stumpy.

Tanta, what will I do with you?

The dog's eyes fill with scorn.

Oh Lord, does no one love me? My brother, my niece, even my bloody dog are at loggerheads with me. I step out of the damp slippers, dab the stain with some tissues, pick the dog up and descend barefoot to the kitchen where I open the back door and release him. He hesitates before advancing gingerly onto the wet grass then, catching a scent, presses his snout to the ground and zig-zags away towards the rockery. The chill rising from the tiled floor through my bare feet numbs my legs. I go into the utility room to get my gardening clogs. The cramped space is still cluttered with Father's old shooting and fishing gear, wax jackets, rods, reels, waders and picnic baskets. I slip my feet into the clogs whose hard plastic is at first creepily cold to the touch, and return to the kitchen. Might as well put the coffee on, although a shot of whiskey would banish the cold and the demons more effectively. When I go to the sink to fill the coffee pot I am startled to see a dirty dinner plate and cutlery resting there. The lodger. Well she needn't think I'm going to wash them for her. Some house rules will be necessary if we're going to get along.

After pointing her towards the ready-made meals I had bought for her (one vegetarian just in case she was a crank) and to the microwave and television, I had taken a taxi into town for dinner with the Bagettes, my school friends Dorothy and Claire, all three of us old bags getting drier and crustier with every passing year. After the night Claire overshot her own gate and, instead of reversing to it, attempted a three-point turn and backed into a lamppost, we decided it was foolish to drive on these occasions. Now we share a taxi home. To get there, however, I normally take the bus or the DART, using my free travel pass, that boon of age but, thanks to Paddy, I was running late last night. Maybe I'll send him the bill for the taxi fare.

We have been meeting for dinner on the first Friday of every month for the past eighteen years. The choice of date is a hangover from schooldays when First Fridays were marked by a special ceremony in the school hall. Claire, whose mother had been a head girl, was one of a handful of girls invariably chosen to lead the procession to present the 'lilies of our hearts' to Our Lady, and to play Mary in the Christmas play. She also made a superb Gwendolyn, a theatrical talent she has continued to nurture in her amateur drama group, moving from Kate Hardcastle and Ellie Dunn to Pegeen Mike and Blanche Dubois. Dorothy was a natural sportswoman, her prowess on the netball and tennis courts endowing her with heroic status and magnifying the honour and glory of the school, all of which went some way to redeeming, in the nuns' eyes, the shame of her father's being a publican. On entering the school she and her sister had been warned not to say what their father did for a living but merely to describe him as a 'businessman', otherwise they would be asked did they live over the pub. By contrast, I, whose father the nuns exalted as a 'great man', was a sorry disappointment to them, my boisterousness unbecoming in one with such a proud escutcheon and my character too wilful to amount to any good. Polite but insubordinate, Mother Ryan, the headmistress, had written in her mincing script on my last school report. Not quite an oxymoron but confusing all the same.

Once, we three had been a tennis foursome, playing genteel doubles every week until our friend, the energetic Avril, succumbed to breast cancer. Before we could find a new fourth I retired from the game proposing that we make a regular dinner date instead. Dorothy and Claire, the stronger players, found two new partners from the old school network and continue to play on Monday nights in defiance of rickety knees (Dorothy's) and sciatica (Claire's). As each winter approaches Claire protests that she is just not going to play any more in the cold and the dark forcing Dorothy to cajole her back onto the court. Dorothy had been my tennis partner and Claire was Avril's. Claire and I were Dorothy's bridesmaids, Dorothy and Claire were Avril's, Claire was mine while a heavily pregnant Dorothy was my matron of honour. Happily for Claire, on whom decision-making has the effect of headlights on a rabbit, she has two sisters and so was spared the swither of choosing between or enlisting all three of us to do the bridesmaidenly honours. Just as well because none of us cared for her husband, Eamon, who had a fondness for check suits and, like many short men, carried a large chip on his shoulder. Avril thought Claire was in too much of a rush to get married and so was easy prey for Eamon's sales patter and big promises. Checks and chips notwithstanding, Dorothy and I privately aver that it was no wonder Claire, with her indecisiveness and tendency to indolence, lost him twenty-five years ago to a nimble young ski teacher. Which leaves Dorothy, alone of we three, still contentedly married, to Ken, her mixed doubles sweetheart. Claire and I believe that regular sex is the key to her perennially youthful looks. Appropriately, she gave birth first to boy and girl twins, a ready-made mixed doubles pairing, save that neither of the kids was sporty, unless you count the boy's undergraduate poker habit. Having mastered that compulsion, however, the lad now designs software for the stock exchange while his sister, my god-daughter, is a rising civil servant. There followed two more girls. Dorothy, once also a solicitor, stayed at home to raise her children, and now devotes much of her time to charitable work and caring for their children. As for what Dorothy and Claire say about me, I imagine that it mingles sympathy with my misfortune (Mossie's untimely death) and irritation at my pigheadedness (rejecting the single men, many trapped in the closet, or widowers, mostly looking for carers, whom they lined up for me after Mossie died; returning to live with Mother against their advice) and, maybe, respect for my successful career. When a year's decent interval of mourning had lapsed, Avril's heartbroken husband, Brian, began to invite me out for dinner. I accepted in a spirit of friendship, dressed up with my usual flair and tried hard to look interested as he worried about whether to allow the accountancy firm established by his father merge with a large international group. While I hadn't the heart to say so, it was soon apparent that the only chemistry between us was in the several bottles of claret followed by crème de menthe frappé that we consumed. After a few of these dinner outings he and I went our separate ways. Next I knew his firm was swallowed by the big fish from overseas, creating a new entity whose acronym employs half the alphabet, and he had married a widow from Sutton who made him defect to the Northside where, apparently, he is happy if invisible to our social circle.

At last, after thirty years of being more or less alone, if not quite celibate, I had a snippet of news to surprise the Bagettes but was about to be upstaged by Claire. They were already half-way through the first bottle of wine when I arrived. Claire was in possession as usual, Dorothy nodding sagely while she listened to our friend's latest calamity.

We didn't want the wine to get cold, Dorothy laughed as I took my seat.

Not to worry. I knew you'd have got a head start on me so I had a stiff G and T before I came out. To restore my equilibrium.

Claire poured, her face a study in solicitude.

Dorothy ordered another bottle.

I drank deep, defying the oenophile snobbery about sipping and savouring. By the time the soi-disant connoisseurs get to their third bottle they wouldn't know the difference between vinegar and a good vintage.

Are you all right? Claire asked as I lowered the glass to the table.

Fine except for bloody Paddy.

Ken warned you he'd make trouble about the house, said Dorothy.

Yes, well, he's sent his daughter up as a wedge to keep the door open, although I don't think she could care less.

Maybe he thought you'd like the company, Claire mollified.

Hah! She's not exactly a sparkling conversationalist. But never mind, I have other plans. I tapped the side of my nose. Right now I'm ravenous so let's order first. I picked up the menu which was bound in faux tooled leather and had the heft of a dictionary.

You didn't have to take her in, Dorothy pointed out sharply. It's difficult enough having one's own grown-up children in the house but having another person's kid around the place could be a nightmare.

We'll see, I conceded. Blood is thicker and all that. She'll be on probation for a few weeks.

She wagged her forefinger. Deep down you're a softie.

Soft in the head I suppose. I brushed her skewering insight away. Dorothy knows me too well. She had seen through my carefully mounted armour to the twinge of loneliness I refused to acknowledge to myself.

Happily Claire's neurosis banished that pinprick moment.

I wonder what the 'whipped 36-month aged parmesan' is, she frowned over the top of her tome.

Stale cheese they're trying to flog to the unquestioning customer, quipped I.

Doesn't sound very healthy.

Don't mind Lena, said Dorothy. Its probably just a cheese soufflé.

It's the whipping I'm worried about.

Maybe we should call Cheeseline.

I think I'll just have the roquette salad and a steak.

You're not worried about mad cow disease? I asked.

Dorothy glared at me.

That's a good point, Claire opened the menu again. I'll have the salmon.

I thought of the article I had read recently about salmon farming and the accompanying photos of sadly deformed fish but decided not to mention it or we'd never get fed.

The restaurant was Dorothy's choice. We take turns choosing, which gives each of us a chance to indulge our tastes. At the rate restaurants open and close in this town we could go to a different one every month for five years without visiting the same one twice. Last time around Claire chose a Japanese place where the drinks were served by robots. She and I each wanted to take one home then fell to giggling about what other services it might render while Dorothy feigned disapproval.

For last night's dinner she had chosen a mock Parisian bistro, where the waiting staff wore long starched white aprons, the food was served in miniature frying pans and copper sauce-pans and the condiments sat in brown paper bags, their tops 'artfully' rolled down like sacks. I suffered a momentary pang of conscience for Jean alone in the house heating her mush in the microwave but it would have been against all our rules to bring her along.

Before you came in, Claire eagerly resumed. I was telling Dorothy about Eamon.

Is he dead?

No. But he's dying.

About time.

He's not dying, Dorothy corrected her. He's ill.

Let me guess: Miss Meribel 1979 wants to offload him now that he's old and sick.

Sort of.

And he wants to come back to Claire, Dorothy added.

What's wrong with him?

Parkinson's.

You're not taking him back?

I really should.

Don't be ridiculous.

That's what Dorothy said.

He's just preying on your kindness.

He's still my husband.

You could get a divorce in the morning. We told you that years ago.

What's the point at my stage in life?

I don't think that's the issue now, said Dorothy.

Where else can he go if he doesn't come back to me?

That's his problem, not yours. Have you told him already that he can come back?

Claire nodded. He's arriving next week.

Next week! cried Dorothy losing her mediating cool. How are you going to mind him? You'll need help at least while you're out at work.

I'd rather not have someone coming into the house.

That's daft, I said. There's no prizes for martyrdom. And none of us're getting any younger. You won't be able to lift him off the po'.

I . . . well I don't think he's that far gone. I'd never forgive myself if I didn't at least try to mind him. You looked after your mother.

She was old but not ill until the last few months and then I employed agency carers, and Felicia came in three times a week, I said. If it's a question of money, I can help you.

No. Claire looked affronted but her work as a doctor's receptionist is only just enough to keep her head above water. I had compelled Eamon to provide money to help her raise their four children which he did grudgingly and with many delays until they were finished their education. Two of the children are still in Dublin but both have jobs and kids. There will be no help from that quarter to nurse their opportunistically repentant father, assuming they would want to. Claire retains an admirable faith in people's essential goodness which might explain why she still claims to love the creep, despite the trouble and hurt he has caused her, and he probably knows that. I was tempted to tell her about the time he made a play for me after Mossie died, thinking that because I was free I was also easy, and desperate. In response I ground my high heel into his foot and walked away.

Lena's right. We can both help you financially.

That's kind, thank you, but I'd like to at least try to do it myself. If I can't I'll take you up on the offer.

Fine, I shrugged. I just hope he appreciates what you're doing.

He will.

We lapsed into silence as the waiter cleared our starter dishes, rattling the empty shells of mussels and snails. Sorry, moules and escargots.

When he was gone Dorothy turned to me, You said you had plans.

I do. But first I need a top up. I tendered my empty glass, knowing that I would need fortification against my friends' reaction to the news that I had invited Richard to come and stay with me.

Drip. Drip. Drip. Yappety-yap-yap. Drippety-drip. Yappety-yap. Tanta adopts an indignant tone when he wants in from the rain and fed. I'm sorry, Sir, I say as I open the door and fling an old towel over him to prevent him shaking his wet coat in all directions. The sound of kibble pouring into his bowl makes his eyes shine and his tail wag. Happy creature. There are days I wish I could swap places with him. My brother's whingeing about his birthright has got this morning off to a bad start.

It was Mother's sale of a Yeats print that first betrayed the parlous state of her finances. When, on noticing the bright square in the otherwise faded wallpaper, I asked about it, she said she had got tired of it and put it away. I had seen better acting at Claire's amateur theatricals and in time she yielded to my questions, saying she needed the money.

But what about Father's pension and investments?

Gone, she shrugged.

Loath to criticise him now that he was dead, she eventually told me that he had got bad advice from a friend in the insurance business. It hadn't gone by Mother, however, that the same man's widow was left well enough set up to take a Caribbean cruise every winter. Father's investments had been misguidedly patriotic and disastrous, among them Shanahan's Stamps and a thimbleful of oil extracted from a stony field in Connemara.

Selling your possessions won't keep a roof over your head, I told her. Let alone keep you in brandy, I thought. You need to sell the house.

And then what? Go into a home to rot? I'd rather be dead.

We could buy you a bungalow or a flat. They're building some nice apartments now, with all mod cons.

I don't care what 'mod cons' they have, you might as well put me straight into the box, she tossed her head defiantly.

You don't want to end up like Mrs. Crawford.

She had no one to care for her, Mother said starchily.

So it's down to me and Paddy to bail you out.

Not poor Paddy, with all those children. Jean is only two. But you could sell your house and come back to live here.

Winded with surprise I opened my mouth then closed it again, not knowing what to say.

Don't look so horrified, she chided.

When I had recovered my senses I protested, But I like my own home. And it's Muiris' home too.

Very well then, she turned haughtily from me. I thought you had more heart.

Don't play the victim, I sighed. I'll think about it.

I glanced around the room which Mother had once decorated all in black, Princess Margaret's chosen style. It was a fine room but in need again of redecoration. The same was true of the whole house, from the roof down. And there was the rub, in need of major remedial work it would have fetched little in the depressed market of the 1980s.

As ever, Mother got her way. Some weeks after that conversation she collapsed and the housekeeper found her lying on the floor of her bedroom. Malnutrition was the diagnosis. Sure enough, the kitchen cupboards and the fridge were bare. Not so the drinks cabinet. False economy. When she came out of hospital Muiris and I moved in for a few weeks to mind her and restock the kitchen. The few weeks turned into a couple of months. She refused to accept meals on wheels, insisting that she was not a charity case. None of the live-in housekeepers I subsequently employed to care for her lasted more than three months. One she sent packing because she was too forward, another left in tears when Mother castigated her for failing to take all the eyes out of the potatoes and a third liked to smoke in the kitchen, which, although herself a smoker, Mother detested. And so, in a compromise, I remortgaged my own home to finance hers and stayed a couple of nights a week with her. When she had a mild stroke seven years ago I moved in full time, imagining that she had not long to live but reckoning without her determination. Soon, maintaining the two houses became a burden, even when I had let my own and, with retirement in view and prices going up, I sold it four years ago. Mother thanked me once but took the good out of that by quickly adding that I had got a fine investment. While the comment hurt, time has proved her right because today it's a crock of gold. Hence Paddy's, or more likely Nóirín's, acquisitive antennae are up. Not that he was left in the ha'penny place. He received all Father's personal possessions, signet ring, cufflinks, tie-pins, watch, fountain pen, silver ink well, the set of Malton prints that had hung in his consulting rooms, and the medical reference books.

I had fully intended to give him and his offspring some of the paintings but after this morning's aggravation they'll have to wait till I'm in the ground. I might fob him off with the portrait of Mother. And throw in mine for good luck. Would that it and not I were acquiring the worry lines and crow's feet. I should have stuck to the Pond's Vanishing Cream. Too late now. It's Polyfilla I need these days. Richard probably won't even recognise me. He looked quite like himself in the picture I saw recently. Probably an old file picture. On seeing it I had pulled out the photograph taken the night we met. How almost childishly young we looked, also how remote and quaint in our evening attire, although at the time we imagined ourselves the acme of sophistication.

Riiiiiiinnnnnnngggg. What now? Forget Dorian Gray. I'm beginning to feel like Quasimodo today. This time it's the doorbell and it draws Tanta yapping into the hall, whither I follow, shushing him as I go. A yellow flyer peeps from the letter box suggesting that the caller was a salesman. I yank it free and spotting the gaudy rainbow rip it in two. I'm tempted to send the torn pieces right back to Mr. Geraghty, and tell him to stop wasting paper, ink and my time. I stuff the paper into my pocket and am about to return to the kitchen when the bell goes again. Hell's bloody bells. I have my hand on the doorknob ready to give the salesman a piece of my by now very irate mind when I remember that I am still in my dishabille so open the peephole instead.

A blast of colour resolves to a bouquet of flowers. Muiris. I had forgotten our arrangement for this morning.

Am I early or are you ill? He puzzles on seeing me.

Neither. I step back to let him into the hall then reach up to press my cheek to his. You're on time as always and I'm fine. All the better for seeing you, my dear. Just a bit behind schedule.

My heart wells up every time I see my beautiful son. At forty he is only a year younger than Mossie was when he died and he grows more like him every day, stirring my old, irrational but ungainsayable fear that he too will be taken untimely from me.

The moment he is in the hall Tanta starts to nuzzle his shoes and hug the hem of his perfectly cut trousers. Down you beast, Muiris scolds.

Don't speak to him in that tone of voice.

He shakes his leg to loosen the dog's grip. He's spoilt.

Don't you start, I say. I've already heard from Paddy on that matter this morning. Wresting the dog from Muiris's trouser leg without causing expensive damage is a challenge but with a little cajolement and negotiation I succeed.

Is he here? Muiris glances around.

No but Jean is. I say, pulling a face.

She can't be *that* bad, Muiris grins. I forgot she was coming to stay. Of his cousins only Mike was close to Muiris and Jean was always viewed as a baby.

I flap my hand at him to get him to lower his voice then say loudly, breezily, Go on down, there's fresh coffee in the pot. Thank you for these, I lay the bright bouquet on the hall stand. I'll put them in water when I'm dressed. Bundling Tanta under my arm, I climb the stairs to my bedroom.

I'll wait in there. Like a homing pigeon he makes for the drawing room, the place where he had spent many contented childhood hours with Mother, she having collected him from school and brought him here, while I was at work, to have a snack and do his homework.

I still half-expect to see Gran there, he says when I join him in.

I follow his glance to the fireside chair whose lumpy cushions seem to retain the contour of Mother's body. Yes, I say. I rarely sit here now.

He had formed a close bond with Mother, such that sometimes seeing them together, heads bent over a jigsaw or the draughts board, or picking out a tune on the piano, I felt excluded and not a little jealous, as I had when Paddy was a child. Eventually, it was she who articulated what I had understood but dared not name when, in his teens, Muiris became by turns withdrawn, refusing to speak to me for several days, and vituperative when he did speak, unleashing confusion about his own nature in torrents of rage. I longed then to enfold him in my arms and soothe his troubled heart as he had allowed me to do in the year after Mossie's death, when, only ten years old he had been bullied by his classmates who were quick to find his softness and vulnerability.

So what's this mysterious project?

I want you to design me a new house.

What do you mean? He twitches his head as if he has not heard aright. Where?

For the past year he has reprised my old line with Mother, suggesting that I move to a townhouse or apartment but much like Mother I have rejected those I have seen as being too small or having the wrong aspect.

I go to the window and point. There, I say.

In the *greenhouse*?

I raise a finger to my lips and then point at the ceiling, mouthing the name, Jean and whisper, Paddy has sent her to spy on me.

Oh Ma, that's childish. A look of Mossie flits across his features as he echoes his father's impatience with Paddy's and my bickering.

I tell him about the telephone call but he remains impassive. Just give him one of the bloody paintings.

He'll only sell it to raise money for his presidential campaign.

He laughs, That's absurd.

Truly. I had it from Jean last night.

What was she on?

Chewing gum. Leave it be now, I sigh. Let me tell you about the new house.

I unfold my idea of building a small modern home, a mews, in the back garden, using the access from the back lane, and selling the main house.

He nods pensively, scanning the mucky lawn, the semi-neglected rockery, the shed, vegetable patch and green house, some of whose panes shattered in a recent storm. It's doable, he nods. I suppose.

I take a deep breath and, keeping my eyes on the garden, say, It'll need to be big enough for two.

You and Jean? He asks, incredulity straining his voice.

No, I pivot to face him, frustrated by his obtuseness. Me and someone else.

Oh, his eyes widen as he takes in my meaning. Who is he? At least I assume it's a he.

He is, I watch him absorb this information.

And do I know him? He tilts his head coaxing the information from me.

No. He's someone I knew a very long time ago. Before I met your father. He just turned up again recently.

Turned up where? Here?

I shake my head. He lives in Cardiff.

On the internet? You mean you went looking for him?

It wasn't quite like that.

His smile falters as a new thought occurs. If you knew him before Dad, does that mean Dad was, like, second choice? Were you still holding a candle for this other man? Or did you . . . ?

Absolutely not, I flash indignantly. Your father was everything to me. I loved him utterly. Completely. Mossie steadied me. I was only twenty when I met Richard. Young, flighty, filled with romantic notions and . . . well . . . I suppose I allowed myself be swept away by him. Trouble was, he was British, which made for difficulties at that time. Too many finally. I neither saw nor heard anything more of him until about a month ago.

And now he's coming to live with you? Isn't that a bit hasty? My son's expression hovers between amusement and concern.

Not necessarily. I don't know. Maybe in time. We'll see. No harm to have the space anyway. I don't want to be boxed in, like in those apartments where the doorknob gets into bed with you.

Muiris laughs, Well I can understand you'd rather have something warmer in the bed but don't do anything rash. I'll have to approve him first, he puts his arm around my shoulder. Come on, let's walk the land.

Like Muiris, the Bagettes had voiced mixed reactions to my news, seesawing from indignant incredulity (Dorothy) to encouraging enthusiasm (Claire).

Why on earth would you want to have anything to do with that bounder? Dorothy scolded.

He was attractive, Claire countered. I can understand it. Although it's true he wasn't very nice to you in the end. But it was a long time ago. We're all older and wiser now.

Older is all, Dorothy shook her head in exasperation. You've just told Claire she's mad to be taking Eamon in, now look at you.

That's different, I began to backtrack. I won't have to care for him and if he expects me to wait on him I'll show him the door. We have resumed contact and maybe that will lead to more. There's nothing definite or permanent yet. It's only a visit, he'll be on probation, like Jean. Which is really why she's a problem.

You could go to him. Or you could go away together.

He didn't invite me. Anyway who goes to Wales on a holiday? I pull a face. And going somewhere else wouldn't be real.

Granted, she said, except for rugby.

Anyway, said Claire, He should come to Lena. That way you have more control too, she turns to me. It'll be like old times.

They weren't such good times, Dorothy frowned. But I give up. You're both crackers.

As we pass through the hall I pick up Muiris' bouquet and, holding it before me, say, I feel like a bride.

Bags I be the bridesmaid, my son grins.

Sensing an outing, Tanta scurries ahead of me down the stairs but pulls up inside the kitchen and begins to bark hysterically. It's the fuss he usually makes when he sights the Kiely's cat outside the window. But this time I find him bouncing furiously on the threshold of the breakfast room, hackles raised, halting every few seconds to renew his racket. There can't be a cat in there. I advance slowly hoping it's not some other furry creature and shushing the dog as I go but when I reach him the shushing stops and I stand and gape, dumbfounded.

Chapter Three

The Parents, wearing dressing gowns, sit in their usual places at the table, looking out to the garden, and my heart quails.

Mother? I venture.

The head turns to disclose a white face framed by jet black hair. Hi Lena, says Jean. I found these in Gran's room. It was too cold to come down in just a teeshirt.

I see, I say, not sure at all what I'm seeing.

A red pony tail straggling down the back of Father's gown confuses me further.

And who is this?

Oh, that's Pól.

Hi Lena. The stranger glances over his shoulder, revealing a beard that matches his red locks.

Although my dealings with the new generation of barristers and apprentices in the office have inured me to slipping standards I cannot help being offended by a man who does not stand up when a lady comes into the room, all the more so when I am the lady in question and the man is young, a stranger and seated at my table in my father's dressing gown. I begin to understand how the three bears felt.

Good morning, I respond. Pól who?

MacCártaigh. The youth half twists around again to reply.

Another refugee from Cork I take it?

No. Or yes. Not exactly. I'm doing post-grad research here. Peace Studies.

Never heard of them. Sounds like an excuse for idleness to me.

At this he swivels completely on his seat which causes Father's plaid dressing gown to fall open, baring washboard ribs and a pale chest lightly coated with more red hair. I wish, he grins. It's an interdisciplinary subject. You kinda have to know some history, some philosophy, some politics, economics, law—

Yes, yes, I cut in. Exhausting I'm sure. In that case, no doubt you need to return to the library now.

Not today, I've to go to work soon, he says. I'll just finish my coffee.

Pól works in a posh restaurant, Jean jumps in to defend this hairy upstart.

Good. He can get a posh cup of coffee there. No need to delay himself here.

Aware that Muiris is hanging fire behind me I turn on my heels and, meeting his raised eyebrows with a brief shake of my head, lead him through the kitchen to the utility room. There he pulls on a pair of Father's old Wellingtons, being careful to fold the crease of his trousers inside them. I pull on my gumboots and a rain jacket and together we step out to the garden.

My cousin I presume, he says as soon as the door shuts behind us.

Yes. I lift my face to the drizzle and inhale, welcoming its cool soothing touch.

And Ghandi?

No idea. Paddy never mentioned him which means one of two things: he doesn't know about him, or he does and the lad's a troublemaker.

The perfect irony.

Peace studies indeed! A good kick in the pants is what he needs. If he's wearing any.

I move briskly along the gravel path towards the end of the garden. Fast as I walk, however, I cannot shake off the disconcerting sensation produced by half-seeing my parents' ghosts. Now I hear the slow steps of a queer little procession approach and my eighteen year old self overtakes me, training the beam of a torch on the path. Behind me comes Father bearing the corpse of a dog wrapped in a blanket, and after him Mother and Paddy, our sobbing breath forming sour clouds in the chill November darkness.

I had returned late one night from a party and descended to the kitchen for a glass of water. In the darkened house a thread of light gleamed under the door and a muffled hiccupping sound came from within. Assuming that it was one of the maids and that maybe, against all the rules, she was entertaining a 'follower', I drew myself up imperiously and swung the door wide. My haughtiness faltered, however, when I crossed the threshold and found Father sitting on the floor, in his pyjamas and dressing gown, with Bran, our sheltie, on his lap. A series of short sobs stuttered from him as tears slid down his cheeks. Seized by fear I stepped back, uncertain what to do.

Get your mother, he said.

What's happening?

Bran . . . he raised his hand from the dog's shoulder, palm upraised in demonstration.

Is he—?

Not yet. Go.

I ran up the stairs and without knocking on the door burst into the Parent's bedroom. Mother, Mother. You have to come. Quickly.

She moaned in her sleep and turned over.

I went to the bedside and shook her gently. You have to get up, Mother. It's Bran, he's sick.

Now she rolled over and opened her eyes. What? What are you saying?

Bran. He's downstairs. Father is with him. He says you're to come down.

In the shaft of light from the door I saw her expression shift from annoyance to fearful comprehension. She flung back the bedclothes and snatching her robe from the back of her door, hurried onto the landing and down the stairs.

Following her I hesitated for a moment at Paddy's door then knocked and pushed it open.

Paddy, get up, I said urgently.

Go away, he muttered.

No. Come on. You have to come downstairs. Bran is dying.

Shag off, he grumbled.

No. Didn't you hear me? Bran is dying. Really. Really he is. My voice rose and tears brimmed in my eyes. Father says so.

I left the room and a moment later heard Paddy's tread behind me.

When we reached the kitchen poor Bran was gone but with no mark of injury or illness, his coat still fluffy from his recent grooming.

Mother knelt beside him, weeping and canting her body back and forth. Father wrapped his arm around her shoulders and drew her to him, pressing his lips to her hair. She acquiesced in his embrace, leaning her body into his, her sobs deepening. I looked away embarrassed by this glimpse of their intimacy.

I heard him whining, Father explained softly, so I came down to let him out but he didn't even stand up when I opened the door, just went on whimpering. It was his heart. He knew he was going. All I could do was stroke him and talk to him.

Paddy stood beside me staring down in disbelief.

Poor Bran. I crouched beside Mother and seeing our tears gleam on his hair smoothed them away. His little body was still warm.

He looks like he's asleep.

Yes.

Bran had been part of our family for most of my life. The Parents had brought him home after a weekend in Muckross House with Lord Castlerosse, a parting gift from their host who bred shelties. I was seven, Paddy four, and, as was usual on the day of the Parents' return from holidays, we had been scrubbed and dressed up by our aunt Sarah, Mother's elder sister who stayed in loco parentis when they were away. We sat in the drawing room, ready to greet the Parents on their arrival, a ritual we detested because it kept us from our toys. Sometimes we entertained ourselves with trying to guess what gifts they might bring us but that game never stretched to the prospect of their arriving with a six-week-old puppy curled into a fluffy ball in the corner of a perforated box. It was a better surprise than any conjuror could have produced and the puppy became for a time the centre of our games before settling into the role of frolicking companion, always happy and eager to please. Mother sometimes entered him in dog shows and then it was his turn to have his hair washed, brushed and every last strand combed into place. He pranced around the ring as if born to it and Mother preened when she took home rosettes and cups. Some compensation maybe for our lack of trophies and prizes. We brought home only scraped knees and indifferent school reports.

Once past the 'age of reason', Paddy and I were discouraged from physical displays of affection toward anyone. The Parents in turn rarely touched one another in our presence. But there was no embargo on caressing Bran who provided the creaturely warmth we still craved from time to time. He seemed to know, too, if one of us was sad or upset and would sit pressed against our legs, head tilted back, trusting brown eyes fixed quizzically on ours. Now there was no cold nose and soft body to comfort us and we could not bear the sight of one another's distress.

At length Father turned to me and Paddy and said, I'll look after this. You go to bed.

I shook my head slowly, too weary to move or think.

It's all over, Kathleen, Father said softly. There's nothing more we can do for him. Tightening his hold on her waist, he encouraged her to sit in a chair.

I need a drink, she said, coming back to herself.

Put on the kettle, Lena, Father directed.

A real drink, Mother snapped. Dragging herself out of the chair she moved to the door and we heard her mount the stairs.

Father bowed his head, defeated.

Shaken out of my paralysis I rose to fill the kettle.

Paddy crouched beside Bran allowing his tears course down his plump cheeks as he kept his back to us.

Sit down, son, said Father.

Paddy shook his head.

Father, who had seated himself at the table, scraped back the chair impatiently and stood up saying, We'll have to bury him. He went into the cloakroom and returned moments later, pyjama legs tucked into his wellies, a raincoat dragged on over his dressing gown and carrying a picnic blanket which he spread over the dog's body.

Can't we wait till morning? I asked.

No. It would be too much of a shock for the girls when they come down.

They'll miss him anyway.

Now is as good a time as any, he snapped. You can go to bed if you like. Paddy and I will do it.

Paddy, who was still kneeling beside Bran's body, glanced around. In the dark? He asked, childish fear blenching his tear-streaked face.

Just then Mother reappeared in the kitchen, a snifter of brandy in her hand. She darted a questioning glance at Father.

We're going to bury him, he said.

Silence as she swigged deeply from the glass, eyes closed the better to savour the hit, and opened again to fix on Father, Where exactly?

In the corner next to the rockery, he suggested. Unless you prefer to put him somewhere else.

Glancing down at the tartan rug where the outline of the little corpse bulged in relief, she said, I'm coming with you, went into the cloakroom and emerged wearing boots, mac and hat, and carrying two torches, one of which she handed to me.

Thus we proceeded to the garden. A fitful wind set shadows dancing in our torch beams, while beyond them darkness mustered like a rising tide. Moonlight struck lustre from the marble birdbath, relic of a Cromwellian estate in Wexford, now a stump shrouded in woodbine and bindweed. Father once told us that the ancient Celts believed we leave a trace of ourselves on every boulder, rock and stone we pass, carbon signature of our souls, like an invisible graffito. Perhaps there is some truth in that I reflect as, passing it now, I am elbowed aside by our revenant selves.

When Mother cried, Stop here, we halted and Father laid Bran on the ground. From the shed he brought a spade and a fork which he handed to Paddy telling him to break up the surface of the soil which he then commenced to dig. Mother and I trained our torches on the designated place. The only sounds were Father's and Paddy's labouring breath and the rasp of their implements in the soil. Exhaustion shuddered through me and I no longer knew whether I was awake or caught in the warp of a grotesque dream.

That's enough, Father said, straightening up.

I watched as he laid Bran in the grave. Mother's sobbing started again and she knelt on the turned up soil reaching into the hole and tucking the blanket around the dog. Taking up a fistful of the earth she tossed that in on top of him, rose and turned back towards the house. I waited until the hole was filled and the surface tamped down, then lit the way for Father and Paddy.

A couple of days after we had laid Bran to rest Father planted a rowan tree to mark the spot. That way he won't haunt us, he said but when the berries swell and ripen they appear to me like drops of blood. Maybe I should have planted a rowan tree on the Parents' grave.

I watch Muiris pace and crouch to take measurements and I move to the centre of the space where I imagine my new living room will be.

It'll be tight but I think we can do it, he says.

Good. I spread my arms as if to touch the walls that will house me and feel an access of fresh energy at the prospect.

Coo-eee! Yoo-hoo! A woman's voice breaks over us suddenly.

Startled, Muiris and I spin around simultaneously to see Bernie Murphy-Benz grinning from above the garden wall.

I was emptying the compost bucket and heard your voices, she explains. Sorry about last night, Lena. Feargal said he met you in the lane.

Not to worry. A bit of rain never hurt anybody.

Yes well I – we really – want to have a chat with you about our plan. That's why Feargal was out there.

Waiting for me?

No, no, she laughs, teeters, and with a yelp, vanishes.

What happened? I look from the empty space to Muiris who is running towards the wall calling, Bernie? Are you all right?

I think so, she replies through the crumbling mortar, a chirpy modern Thisbe. I turned the compost bucket upside down to stand on but it slipped.

Maybe you should come into the house and we can sit down and talk over coffee, I suggest.

Good idea. I'll clean myself up and be around in two minutes.

Back indoors I am relieved to find that Jean and Pól the peacemaker have vacated the breakfast room but less than pleased to see that they have left their dirty mugs and bowls on the table.

As I see Muiris out at the hall door I spot Bernie coming through the gate and spy Pól in the distance strolling towards the DART station. No hurry on him to get to work.

Not staying for coffee with us girls? Bernie calls to Muiris. I have lovely fresh scones here, she holds aloft a plate covered with a gingham cloth.

'Fraid not, he says. I'm meeting some other 'girls' in town.

You'll miss all the best gossip, she laughs.

Lena will fill me in I'm sure.

I am never quite able to fix Bernie Murphy-Benz's age. There are more crow's feet around her eyes and commas around her mouth than one would expect in the mother of two small children. I have a notion that Feargal is a few years younger than her which makes me think she was a late convert to marriage and motherhood, after abandoning her career in the civil service to establish a suburban boutique catering to other suburban women of independent means. And, yes, I do shop there. This morning she is, as usual, perfectly turned out, in natty boots, neat jeans, a floral blouse and rosy pink cardigan. Her hair, shaped like a golden bell, gleams, as does her make-up. Her fingernails match the pink of her cardigan. She must rise before dawn to do the exercises that keep her so slim, and to co-ordinate her outfit for the day. Holding back the years is hard work, which is why I gave up, despite Dorothy's efforts to get me doing yoga and drinking green tea. Those fads were all very well when we were young and idealistic members of the Women's League, wearing our black leotards, walking around with books on our heads, trying to stand on one leg, or sitting in a circle on the floor to gaze at a candle flame, suppressing fits of the giggles. But too much exercise can cripple a person's sense of humour. I've yet to see a happy jogger. Look at Paddy: tedious as a long drink of water. I prefer to take my ease. When

I'm let. Today the fates are ganging up on me. It's only half eleven and Bernie is busying herself in my kitchen with her plate of home-made scones and crab-apple jelly, chattering about the discovery of a young woman's body in the Djouce Woods. By rights I should be just rising from the scratcher now. Instead, I feel as if I'm on a hurdy-gurdy and need a stiff gin to straighten me up but coffee'll have to do for the moment.

The corner of a glossy yellow brochure pokes out of Bernie's back pocket.

I see you got one of those stupid flyers too, I say to divert her from the upsetting details of the murder. Time to put up a No Junk Mail sign methinks.

Sorry, she tosses her head as if recollecting herself. What flyer?

I point to her rear end.

She reaches around to take the offending page from her pocket. Oh this. I found it stuck in the door when I was coming out.

It looks more like an ad for butter than for money. I watch her smooth the page on the table.

I never thought of that, she laughs. Spread it around!

That's good but I don't think that's the intention.

She purses her lips. He's offering a good return.

He could offer the moon. Could he deliver though?

Mary Lacey seems to think so.

I wouldn't mind her.

Talk about Molly Hick, Bernie grins. I'd love to give her a make-over.

That would be a challenge, I bite into one of her scones and say, These are delicious. You said Feargal was waiting for me last night?

Yes, well, she pops her eyes and pauses meaningfully. Not exactly waiting for you. He and Phil were scoping out the space back there for our project.

Which is? I mute my curiosity suspecting I'm not going to like what I hear, mainly because I didn't like the look of Phil.

A nursing home.

I'm not that doddery yet.

Not for you. Of course not, she shakes the golden bell. This is a business proposition. We're thinking of building one behind our houses. As she straightens up proudly, preparing to elaborate her vision, I see the zealous entrepreneur emerge from the fuzzy pink cocoon of the model hausfrau. The back lane is quite wide and our gardens are long and need a lot of upkeep. If between us, *you*, and me and Feargal, we cut, say, a third off our gardens and take in part of the lane we'd have space for a decent-sized nursing home.

But why?

Because it's the sweetest little investment around. There are lots of people like you who have lived in this area for most of their lives and don't want to be shipped out to retirement homes in the sticks, when that time comes.

At her words the lump of scone and jelly in my mouth turns sour and a tawdry red-top saga unfolds in my mind's eye:

SCONED TO DEATH
Old Lady's Neighbours Steal her House and Lock her Away

Neighbour-from-hell, former clerical officer turned business mongrel, Bernie Murphy, slowly poisoned an old lady, , sister of famous heart sturgeon and presidential hopeless, PloddyO'Neill, with scones and jam till she went off her crocker. Then, adding injury to inslut the the monsters stuck the bemildewed old bat into the old folkes home they bilt on her land, sold her house for a cool €3.5 mill and bought themselves a ritzy Palace on the Med.

I'll have to think about this, I say, but my mind is filled with the lurid pictures that would accompany the tabloid tripe: cameos of me wild-eyed, my hair astray; Bernie in strict suit, taking advice from some of my erstwhile colleagues; Paddy looking portentous and indignant at being dragged into the quagmire of what he would no doubt term my wilful foolishness; all surrounding an aerial view of the ochre-roofed, neoclassical pile in Cap D'Ail, accented by cypress trees, the turquoise lozenge of its swimming pool flashing like a pendant on the warm green bosom of its lawn.

It would diminish the value of these houses, I venture returning my gaze to the jam smeared plate on my kitchen table.

Not much because the beauty of them is the sea view. Nothing can interfere with that. Besides we'd make a fortune on the nursing home.

Our neighbours would object to the noise of ambulances and so on disturbing their peace.

The traffic is loud here anyway. Double-glazing would help soundproof their houses and reduce their heating bills.

I'll have to try another tack with little Miss Answer-for-Everything. I suppose I'd be entitled to priority booking in the home.

Of course, Bernie nods, as much as to say now you're getting the idea. Not that you'll need one any time soon, she adds hastily. But this house must feel very big for you now that you're alone.

My niece has moved in for a while, I say, grateful now for the cover Jean's presence provides. So who's Feargal's pal? I divert Bernie's attention from me. Another investor or the architect?

Architect. Best not say anything to Muiris. I wouldn't like to offend him but it's not really his type of project. And Phil was in school with the planning officer on the council.

Covering all the angles.

It pays to be realistic, she shrugs then darts her head forward like a bird that has spied a worm. I hope I didn't distract Muiris from his measurements.

What? I try to follow her leap.

Just now, in the garden, he was measuring something, she prompts, barely concealing her curiosity.

Oh that, I play for time, marvelling at her stealth. She must have been watching us for a few minutes before hailing us. I want him to do something with that corner, get rid of the greenhouse, maybe put a pavilion there where I can sit in the summer.

That's a great idea. We could put one beside the nursing home.

Ha. Yes, indeed but I'll need to see some figures and an outline plan before I make a decision on that project. What I really need is to get Bernie and her scones and jam and her loony scheme out of my house. I cast my eye at the clock and exclaim, Look at the time. I'm sorry, Bernie, I have an appointment at one.

Ohmygod, she yelps. I didn't mean to stay so long. I'm due in the shop now. Up she springs and begins stacking the coffee mugs and plates.

Tanta, who has been snoring under the table all this time, bestirs himself at the sound of plates being scraped and noses forward in search of crumbs.

Don't worry about those, I take the crockery from her and place it beside my lodger's dirty dishes in the sink.

Thanks. I'll leave the scones. You can drop the plate back when you're finished. By then I'll have some plans I can show you.

Thanks. Jean might like one.

Ah yes. The red-haired girl.

No. The red-haired one is her boyfriend. Apparently.

The crow's feet and the commas on Bernie's face crinkle up with laughter. Oh Lena. That's funny. We must both be getting old!

Well *that's* certainly not funny, say I, ushering her out of the room.

When I return to the kitchen I throw out the remaining scones and jelly, not that I seriously believe they are laced with strychnine or arsenic, or Epsom salts, but because they have the whiff of the Trojan horse. What, I wonder, will happen if I refuse to throw in half of my back lot with the Murphy-Benzes? Will they take the same proposal to the Kielys, the neighbours on their other side, leaving me to shiver in the shadow of the institution, its melancholy occupants haunting the windows, their lost stares infiltrating my rooms and my dreams until one day I find the same uncomprehending eyes and trembling lip facing me in the mirror. Suddenly, and for the first time since the years immediately following Mossie's death, I feel utterly alone and bereft. It's a measure of my desperation that I have a fleeting impulse to pray or light a candle for guidance, a habit I had thought long atrophied, and irrelevant as my vestigial tail.

Chapter Four

Muiris was close to the mark when he charged me with going in search of Richard. I had intended to explain how we had rediscovered one another until the moment of disclosure came and then I felt shy as a teenager bringing home her boyfriend for the first time. Now I wonder at that inhibition, first inkling of our roles reversing. Strange to report, were it not for Paddy I might never have found Richard again. It was the week before Christmas when, before delivering Old Brennan's bottle of seasonal cheer, I ran the gauntlet of Grafton Street to buy a gift for Dorothy and Ken who had invited me to join them for the festivities. In Mother's latter years she and I had spent the holiday at various country house hotels, reading and exchanging courtesies with other elderly refugees from the culinary and social obligations of the festival. Sometimes Muiris joined us but more often he liked to go abroad to a place where he could sail in the sun. Paddy's house was always full of his emigrant children and their various appendages but that first Christmas after Mother's death he and Nóirín were going to Philadelphia to spend the holiday with their daughter, Nora, and her family. I continued to observe the Christmas rites although my heart was far from in them. Bernie and her kids came in as usual to help decorate the tree, she applying designer flair, the children enjoying the rummage through our boxful of ornaments, some harking back to Paddy's and my childhood, others to Muiris', their gilding and glitter, like their promise of magic, a little jaded. Fruits of memory nevertheless, they deck the tree and pierce my heart betimes.

Grafton Street was aswarm with youths in Santa hats, carol singers, volunteers shaking collection boxes, shoppers hefting large carrier bags, parents hefting, pushing or towing small children whose cheeks and eyes shone in wondering antici-pation. It was easier to move with the crowd than to carve a way through it so when it paused and eddied around a circle of spectators I halted too, and gawked with them. A group of street artists had set up a Nativity scene: Joseph and Mary, draped in white to resemble marble, watching over a plastic infant, also in white. At the jingle of money in their collection plate, however, their haloes flashed in neon colours and a blast of Handel's *Halleluiah* chorus issued from somewhere in the region of the babby's arse, resulting in applause, laughter, more coins, lights and Handeluiah until the arrival of two gardaí on horseback dampened the hilarity and the crowd drifted away.

In need of refreshment and a rest after I had done my shop-ping, I turned left through the concrete 'way' carved out of the old Hibernian Hotel. Fadó, fadó Mossie and I liked to dine in its Lafayette Room, relaxing in its unhurried hush and unctuous-ness. Over-swagged and over-priced it may have been but it had more style than the fly-by-night franchises favoured by our modern Jacobins.

Good old times. Gone now, I murmured to myself, nodding in imitation of the old man Mother and I had encountered on one of our Christmas trips.

We had broken our journey for a cup of tea and a pee at a commercial hotel in Cavan. The front lounge was cold, its ersatz gas fire unlit. A fake Christmas tree tilting over the reception desk like the last drinker at a bar failed to cheer the gloom. I banged the bell on the counter before following Mother to a table at the window where we waited to be served. Enter an elderly waiter all got up in a shiny black suit, white shirt and bow tie, a tea cloth folded over his left forearm, bearing two menus. Using his sleeve he wiped the laminated cards before proffering them but I waved them away saying we would simply like a pot of tea.

Very well, tea for two. He leant in to whisk the cloth at some crumbs on the table then hitched himself upright to ask, Would Madam like biscuits with her tea?

As I studied him for a moment wondering was he mocking me I felt an improbable twitch of recognition. Yes please, I said.

I hope someone gives him a pair of socks for Christmas, said Mother, referring to the threadbare heels we saw slip out of his shoes as he hurried towards the kitchen.

I think I know him.

By his socks?

No. Something about the way he stands.

When he returned with our order I watched him arrange the tea things on the table. Will that be all, Madam? he stepped back, folding his hands at his waist.

Then I had him. Yes, thank you, I smiled. But haven't we met before? Usen't you work in the Hibernian Hotel in Dublin?

At my words his expression flickered from professional impersonality through surprise to an awkward feint at recognition. Yes, yes. It's Mrs. . . . . ah . . .

Carmody. My husband and I dined there quite regularly, I nodded encouragingly. Maybe he remembered Mossie.

Quite, Mrs. Kearney. Good old times, good old times, his face drooped alarmingly. Gone now. Progress. So they say. He sighed then hitched himself up again. Are you visiting the area Mrs. Kearney?

My mother and I are just passing through.

We get a lot of passing traffic. Quiet today but. He glanced wistfully past us through the window to the desolate street.

Yes, well we'll be off as soon as we've had our tea. What do I owe you?

Ah, yes, to be sure, he stooped over the table and with an unsteady hand filled our cups. Including the biscuits that'll be seven euro and fifty cents.

I handed him a tenner telling him to keep the change.

Thank you, thank you, he took my hand and pumped it. Good old times Mrs. Kearney. We won't see their like again.

Happy Christmas, said I.

As soon as we were outside, walking towards the car, Mother said, For a moment there I thought you were going to invite him to join us for Christmas dinner.

Halting, I said, Maybe I should.

Don't be absurd. Apart from anything else he's an old phoney. He never worked in the Hibernian in his life.

What makes you so sure of that?

He didn't know how to serve the tea. The pot was on the left hand side of the tray.

I hadn't noticed, I laughed.

I know that. You were too busy chasing the butterflies of the past. You can't bring Mossie back, any more than I can bring your father back.

Sometimes even I found Mother's perspicacity unanswerable. Lately, however, far from chasing them, I am overtaken by scenes from the past. They arrive unbidden and impinge on me with greater clarity than present ones, which may explain my response to tidings of Richard.

As I passed through the bleak arcade I stepped into a newsagent and ran my eye along its display of titles, bypassing the local broadsheets in search of *The Daily Telegraph*. These days I can't open *The Irish Times* without seeing the brother's name attached to some new prescription for the health of the nation. As if that isn't bad enough the nation has to suffer his aortic evangelism on the radio where he has become a useful source of filler between point-scoring politicians and goal-scoring Ga players. I could swear I heard the presenter refer to him one day as Mr. Padding O'Neill.

We've only what's there, the desultory assistant when I inquired.

I moved left and bought *The Guardian* instead.

Making for the Shelbourne, another sanctuary of memory, I was poised to cross the top of Kildare Street when the red man turned green but a bus, emblazoned with seasonal crocOgold advertising – the leprechaun got up as one of Santa's elves – lurched forward. I jumped back, apologising as I collided with a young couple who parted to flank me protectively.

Are you hurt? The woman asked, stricken with concern.

Fine, thank you, I smiled. It would be too demeaning to be knocked down by the leprechaun bus.

Topple o' the day, her companion grinned.

The last car through before the green man reappeared was a black Mercedes with darkened windows which drew up out-side the hotel. The doorman beetled towards it, tipping a fore-finger to his top hat, and passers-by paused to stare. A short, trim-figured man with a familiar but not distinctive face got out of the car and moved briskly up the steps acknowledging the onlookers with a curt wave.

It's Tony Blair, said one.

No it's not. It's your man off of *Coronation Street.*

Don't be an eejit. It's Chris Tarrant.

Someone next to me began to hum 'Who wants to be a millionaire?' Like a spell, the old tune transformed me into the young woman who wouldn't miss a hunt ball or swell affair for all the world. Seized by the fleet eagerness of youth I climbed the steps to join a knot of people who, forced to stand aside while the mysterious celebrity entered the hotel, goggled im-patiently at the revolving door. The instant an opening ap-peared we surged forward into one of the glass wedges where the crush was such that my feet rose off the ground and the breath flew out of my lungs. Spun like a bottle I came to rest in front of a stranger who said with a laugh, Shall we dance?

When I can breathe again, I panted, recalled suddenly to my mature and creaky self.

Re-established on my two sensibly but smartly booted feet I elbowed and squeezed and excuse me'd a path through the busy lounge until I found a vacant seat in a corner. Its faded cushion felt like home as I eased myself down and beckoned a waiter to bring me a gin and tonic. Sitting back I sighed and shut my eyes absorbing the relief of coming to rest and letting the hubbub recede.

The joyful tinkle and fizz of ice in a glass heralded the arrival of my drink. I straightened up and gratefully brought the tumbler to my lips. The tang of the sharp, clear liquid burnt through the flurry and distraction of the day and I held it on my tongue a moment before the alcohol lit through my veins. Another sip kindled complacent wellbeing and I shook open the paper. The big news that day was the capture of Saddam Hussein, found in a foxhole, haggard and bearded as a hobo. I leafed through the pages, past the many variations on the headline story, to scan the contents, or more accurately the malcontents of old Blighty: a couple on trial for the murder of two schoolgirls, a supermarket takeover bringing job cuts, departure tax in the air and more quibbling over a European Constitution, which, foreshadowing a united states of Europe, strikes comical fear in the hearts of the Brits (we'll lose our Queen) but is music to the ears of our fresh-faced 'new' Europeans, poster-spawn of Ms Lacey and her many fans. (Some joke considering we can't unite our own four scutty green fields.) They're gunning for her as president, queen even, of the USE, a wrinkle Paddy hasn't thought of. Yet.

Past all that clamour, I came to the pedantic columns of the opinionistas where my skimming eyes halted. Blinked. Popped open. Looked again. Narrowed with concentration.

And, confirming that my initial quick impression was not an illusion, a self-conscious tingling crept up the back of my neck coupled with a girlish flush of desire in my limbs. For the first time in almost fifty years I was face to face with Richard or more accurately, Major-General Richard Arthur Davies KC (Ret'd) of the 2nd Queen's Dragoon Guards.

So there you are, I whispered, with the rewarding surprise of finding something so long lost that I had almost forgotten about it. Time was when his comrades on the streets of Belfast and Derry were daily fare on the TV news and in the papers and I found myself occasionally scanning the grainy images, wondering if he was among them. Father had been right in his prediction that the treatment of the Catholics in the North would lead to further conflict there. He had intended it in part as a warning or deterrent to my romance with Richard, knowing that the army would likely be sent in which would invidiously divide my loyalties. I would not have conceded it to him but had to acknowledge silently that even as I searched for Richard's features behind the camouflage I sensed an incipient and treacherous division of myself.

To judge by this photo he had aged well, his features still lean, if somewhat lined, the cleft in his chin more pronounced, his once chestnut hair now white. The picture accompanied his by-line on an article condemning the British Government's failure to plan for a post-war settlement in Iraq. Reading it I heard his voice project with confident logic the dissolution of the war into a counter-insurgency that would mire the troops for years to come in Baghdad and Babel. Maybe it was the coincidence of seeing his image in the Shelbourne, where we had first met, or maybe it was the effect of the day that was in it, but the hazy print resolved itself into a living form who strode clear of the intervening years. I sensed his presence closer to me than my own skin, the sound of his voice, the citric scent of his aftershave mingled with cigarette smoke, vivid and warm. The scarlet sleeve of his service dress brushed my shoulder again. By rights, that officer's uniform should have signalled taboo on our first encounter but there was a challenge in his eyes and sceptical expression that took all my attention.

It was Horse Show week 1957, a time when an influx of jovial aristocratic continentals, astride Irish-bred nags provided the colourful pretext for a string of parties and balls. In addition to those exotic visitors it drew the old ascendancy boys and gals from their crumbling houses around the country, along with second division socialites from England, relishing their putative superiority and our unfettered hospitality. We, in turn, found these double-barrelled chinless wonders diverting but hardly worth serious consideration as suitors. Escorts for the week but no more than that. Some of them made the mistake of trying to impress us with their connections to the Plantagenets and were roundly scolded. They seemed oblivious of the fact that we were the first generation in eight hundred years to be raised in an Ireland released from their country's tyranny, or, if not oblivious, merely ignorant. Ah yes, we were the fresh heirs of freedom, the princelings and princesses of new dynasties. Forget the mouldy Tudors and the Saxe Coburg and Gothas, lately Windsor, and all hail good Irish names like de Valera and Fitzgerald.

The Cavalry Ball was always the most colourful of the week where the women's bright dresses were eclipsed by the uniforms of the men. I was at a table of what our hostess, Mrs. McNally, chirpingly dubbed 'young things', clustered around her son, Gerard, for whom she hoped to snag a well-connected Dublin wife to guarantee the survival of their estate in Longford. Sadly for her and for Gerard, most of the female 'things' at the table had eyes only for the Italian riders, who included a dishy scion of the Medici family, in a pink hunting jacket, accompanied by his wife, smart woman. Gerard was rather sweet, like a puppy, and winced every time his mammy talked him up.

I had no alternative but to cast my eye about the room and it wasn't long before it fell on the table from the British embassy, and the man with the laconic smile. When Gerard, at his mother's prompting, asked me to dance I accepted with alacrity, purely to have the opportunity of brushing close to the table where this Adonis sat. Earl Gill's band played some lively swing tunes and I encouraged Gerard to jitterbug but he stumbled and looked blushingly confused so I had to slow my tempo. I managed a serpentine shimmy of my hips all the same for the British officer's benefit. When I glanced around to ensure he was watching I caught the flick of his head towards the woman seated beside him who kept her hand on his arm as she spoke and I knew that he had indeed been watching me covertly. I laughed. The game was on. When the tempo dropped again to a waltz I moved in close to Gerard rendering the poor lad's embarrassment complete.

You're a great dancer, he panted over my shoulder, holding his head stiffly away from mine.

It's good for the digestion, I quipped.

I must try it again so instead of the liver salts. But I think I have two left feet.

Not at all, said I.

Taking his hands I guided him through the steps until we made a passable show of dancing, with me leading. By now I could feel the British officer's eyes burning into my back and consequently ignored him, conniving flibbertygibbet that I was. Only when I returned with Gerard to the table did I realise what a mistake I had made for Mrs. McNally stood up to embrace me, evidently assuming that it was only a case of calling the banns before I became her daughter-in-law. Panicking, I grabbed my clutch and fled to the Ladies' room. There

I sat at one of the dressing tables and smoked a cigarette, pondering my next move. He smoked too. Ask him for a light? Too obvious. Continue to ignore him and wait for him to come to me? Very risky. Ask him to dance? Far too forward even for me and likely to lead to humiliation. He looked like the type of man who cherished the mystique of aloofness and didn't condescend to dance. I could simply forget about him altogether and cosy up to the Italian riders with Claire but the challenge held charms. I crushed the cigarette in the ashtray, refreshed my lipstick and eyeliner, plumped my breasts up inside my brassière and straightened my stockings, girding my lingerie for battle, then set forth, determined to make the proud officer stoop at my knee. I swung open the door of the powder-room and walked slap into the man himself almost blacking my eye on his brass buttons.

I beg your pardon, he took a step backwards. I was looking for the Gents.

You're in the wrong shop so, said I and, leaning forward a fraction more than was necessary, pointed down the corridor, It's that way.

Thank you, he said without budging.

This must be your first time here.

Where? In Dublin or in this hotel?

Either or both.

It is actually, he nodded. In fact.

Oh God! Was it possible that he was a bore? I bit my tongue rather than ask the obvious next question about how he was liking it, remarking instead, You'll find your way around soon enough. In a feint at passing him and quelling the burst of desire that would have crushed him to the wall and drowned him in kisses, I said in my glassiest convent-bred tones, I had better not detain you. I hope you enjoy your stay.

You are charmingly eager to return to your beau, he said.

My who?

The young man you were dancing with. Your fiancé I presume. His eyebrows rose above a teasing smile.

Gerard? You must be joking, I laughed. He's only a poor eejit. Well, actually, a rich eejit. In fact.

We can't all be perfect.

I never said . . . There's no harm in him. Besides he probably has a good country girl tucked away somewhere in the bog.

Which leaves you where?

Right here, free as a bird, I chirped. And ready to tread another measure or four.

In that case I shan't hold you up any longer.

Would that you would hold me I thought as he clipped his heels together and bowing stood aside to let me pass. Good evening.

I nodded and moved on towards the ballroom, making sure that the hem of my dress swept the crease in his black trousers. Really it was all I could do not to laugh. That skirmish had piqued his interest. Now I needed only to continue flirting with others to win the sultry officer's attention.

Gerard leapt to his feet as soon as I returned to the table and held my chair until I was seated. He was well brought up, I'd give him that. Mrs. McNally immediately turned to quiz me about my studies. I replied with more enthusiasm than I felt, hoping that she might write me off as too much of a career woman for her darling boy.

You must come and visit our tigín, my dear, she said. Gerard is a fine horseman. He'd be delighted to bring you out for a canter. Isn't that right, Gerard? She simpered at him.

What's that, Mammy?

You'd love to take Lena out riding wouldn't you?

I would but only if she'd like to come.

Yes, I know, it's not a conversation one could hold nowadays with a straight face. Back then we were innocent. Or mostly so. I doubt I could have had that exchange with the British officer and refrained from grinning. A dart of red at the corner of my eye alerted me to his return and I could tell by its direction that he had not rejoined his table but was mingling with a group standing at the edge of the dance floor. I wondered if he was asking about me. Meanwhile, Mrs. McNally talked on about her 'tigín', the farm, their famous herd of Herefords and prizewinning bulls, calling on her husband every now and then to confirm her portrait of their bucolic idyll. He, a courteous, docile man with the strong calloused hands of a farmer, nodded and said I should come to visit them in spring to see the calves, and their champion sires, Mars and Jupiter. I should also admire Mrs. McNally's walled vegetable garden, which she had restored to its original abundance even to planting old varieties of fruit. She dispraised this suggestion saying I would prefer to meet some of the neighbours for card games or croquet and lemonade. I smiled and murmured assent with a pretence of interest while my attention drifted, a skill I had perfected during the tedious processions and ceremonies at school. But I did not deceive sharp-eyed Gerard who interrupted to say, Mammy you're boring poor Lena.

Not at all, I demurred without a shred of sincerity, and seizing the moment, added quickly, I'm sorry, can you excuse me? I see someone over there I must say hello to.

Gerard stood up again and bowed as I left the table. I tipped him a wink to which he responded with a smile. Not such an eejit after all, I thought. It wouldn't have surprised me to find that he did have a wench hidden away down on the farm. Nevertheless, I felt a quick stab of guilt when I saw the dashed hope in his parents' faces and wondered briefly why they were so anxious to pair him off. I moved across the room as if going towards the table where Dorothy and Ken sat with his crowd, keeping my eyes carefully fixed in that direction. A tap on my shoulder, however, caused me to swivel around and I knew before I did so that it was him.

Miss O'Neill, he said. May I trouble you for a light?

Of course, I scrabbled in my clutch for my lighter. As he leaned forward with his cigarette I said, And may I be permitted to know your name?

He straightened up and all but saluted, Captain Richard Arthur Davies, Queen's Bays, 2nd Dragoon Guards, at your service.

Queen's what's?

Bays. Horses. Rhymes with neighs.

Oh. Of horse.

He laughed. We're the ones who routed your lot at the Battle of Aughrim.

Really? I strove to recall something about the Battle of Aughrim but could only come up with the song 'The Lass of Aughrim', which was no relation. Our history lessons at school had got bogged down in the many wives of Henry VIII, a story that Mother Connolly relished. The nearest thing to a bodice ripper she knew.

Knocked poor old General St. Ruth's head off, and that was it.

I tilted my head quizzically unsure whether he was just making conversation or trying to get a rise out of me. As chat up lines went it was novel. Better than the one about the Plantagenets. Wondering how a female saint came to be on the battlefield I was spared trying to think up a witty response by a dazzle of light. For an instant I imagined it was the coup de foudre but no, it was the flashbulb of the photographer from *Social and Personal: Ireland's gayest society magazine* who stepped forward to take our names.

Such a pity the picture won't be in colour, the man said. The Captain's scarlet and your royal blue make a perfect contrast.

We planned it that way, we said in unison and laughed.

Lena? Lena O'Neill that was? A jovial male voice tugged me back to the present as if out of a deep dreaming sleep.

I swung my head from side to side feeling like Cinderella at midnight, back in her rags at the cold kitchen range. Am I right? Rubicund jowls hovered inches above me and a pair of slightly bloodshot eyes came into focus beneath a jutting grey fringe that failed to reclaim a long lost hairline. Tim, the man grinned. Tim Gallagher. His right hand shot forward.

Tim. Yes, I took the hand while trying to align my memory of Paddy's old school chum with the figure before me. As I did another image slotted into view, of vinyl records sliding from the backcarrier of his falling bicycle shattering on the ground rough hands tightening on my wrists, a voice rasping in my ear traitor hoor traitor big Tim running with a pitchfork. How are you? I managed to say, shaking myself back to the present hubbub. PLOT wasn't it? I smiled vaguely.

You remember! he laughed. Only myself and the brother left of our little gang of four. How is the old rogue?

Paddy, Larry, Owen and Tim. Four inseparable friends the acronym of whose names led to jokes about thickening, twists and turns, until TB killed poor Larry at the age of twenty-one. Then, as some of their crowd said, things went to POT. Certainly they did for Paddy, grief so unmooring him that he wanted to give up his medical studies. Cracking black jokes about cadavers in the anatomy lab was too close to the bone after seeing his best friend laid out in his rugby club blazer and tie on the family's dining table. Mother, ever haunted by the loss of her brother at the Somme, sat with Paddy's hand in hers silently trying to absorb his grief. Finally Father reasoned him into agreement that abandoning his studies could not help Larry whereas pursuing them might give him the opportunity of saving others. As for Owen, a rare blood disorder killed him at forty-seven.

No improvement, I told florid Tim, thinking however that he might benefit from a smidgen of Paddy's advice.

I see him on the box from time to time. He's wearing well. Is he ever in Dublin these times?

Not since Mother died. He's been well and truly corked by now.

Ruined his career going down there. I told him that at the time. Could have got the big job here. Transplants. The lot.

He always knows better than anyone else, I shrugged. What about you? Enjoying a well-earned retirement I assume?

Yes and no. They put me out to grass two years ago but I've been doing locums in Dubai. Handy pin money, he jingled small change in his pocket and winked. Tax free. I have new responsibilities now, you know. With a sheepish moue he gestured towards a group of men and women waiting to be seated. One of the women, well advanced in pregnancy, smiled and approached. She looked to be at least thirty years younger than him. It came to me then that I had heard of his remarriage a year after his first wife, notorious for her 'problem', had finally obliged him by drinking herself to death. He had missed Mother's funeral through being on honeymoon in the Seychelles or the Maldives. The new Mrs. Gallagher had been his registrar and the story went that they had fallen in love when rehearsing a panto for the patients, she Jack to his giant. Fee Fi Fo Tim.

He curved his arm protectively around his wife's hips. May I present Fiona.

Hello, I reached out to shake the young woman's hand, feeling like a dowager at a court ball.

This is Lena, sister of one of my old school pals, Paddy O'Neill.

The Paddy O'Neill? She said brightly. The cardiologist?

The very one, I replied, hoping that my wince would be read as a smile.

He's a brilliant surgeon.

So he says.

A friend of mine worked with him and sang his praises. I always read his columns in the paper.

Well the world is full of wonderful surprises indeed. Good, I said. Delighted to have met you. I really must be going now. Why don't you take this table? You should sit down my dear.

Oh no, that wouldn't be right, she protested.

I have a better idea, Tim intervened. Lena can join us for a drink, and that way we'll stake a legitimate claim to the table.

No thank you. I have an appointment.

Ah you'll have one. For old time's sake.

Really, no thank you. I must be going, I began to pull on my coat.

I insist, One for the road. He looked around for a server, waved urgently at one then turned back to me. Do you remember the night we serenaded you? 'Mona Lena, Mona Lena . . .' he began to croon. We were on our way to a Hallowe'en fancy dress party. Isn't that right?

Yes. I remember, I smiled faintly.

You won't believe it, Fifi, the big man laughed, riding the wave of memory, but your esteemed Mr. O'Neill was got up as Harvey the Pooka, a giant rabbit in green pyjamas and a giant pair of cardboard ears, also green.

What was that all about? Fiona turned from Tim to me. Who's Harvey the Pooka?

That was the best bit, Tim wobbled with laughter. He was an invisible rabbit. In an old James Stewart film. They say he was never the same after making it. Amn't I right, Lena?

I nodded, Yes. A very old and very silly film.

I remembered. I remembered, gently applying make-up to my brother's face to cover the cuts and bruises he had acquired for my sake.

He winced when I touched them.

Sorry, I said. I'm so sorry. I began to weep.

Go on, he insisted, clenching his teeth against the pain. Cover my whole face and neck and paint on whiskers to cover the cut on my lip.

I continued cautiously, gingerly, lovingly, spreading the disgusting green greasepaint over his cheeks and brow, wishing that instead I could rub away the wounds and the hurt, my tears undoing some of my handiwork.

It's all that fellow's fault, he said tersely as I repainted the teary streaks.

What fellow? I addressed his face in the mirror.

You know who, he scowled. The Brit who's never here but has you all dreepy and moony. Mammy says it's not good for you to be left like that.

I love Richard, I protested.

Well just . . . just . . . unlove him, burst my little brother with the wisdom of seventeen years. Here, tie these on would you? He handed me the ears he had made himself and I fumbled with the elastic that hooked them to his head over my green bathing cap which concealed his hair.

Thanks, I have to go, he stood abruptly. Only his eyes betrayed his real self beneath the make-up and they were hot with tears

I smiled at his get-up and said, You look great. It's a pity there's no film left in your camera. Enjoy yourself.

As he made to leave the room I stopped him. Wait. You're missing something, I grabbed a downy powder puff and some safety pins from my dressing table and attached it to the seat of the pyjamas. Now you're right.

He moved his hand around to feel his tail. Perfect, thank you, he laughed now, ready for merriment.

A waitress appeared bearing aloft a tray laden with dirty glasses.

What's that you're having, Lena, said Tim, G and T?

I nodded on a reflex.

Make that two G and Ts and a fizzy water for the missis and for the love of God find us another chair before she goes into labour on the spot.

I stood buttoning my coat and said to Fiona, Here please take my chair.

If you insist, thank you, I think I will, she sank gratefully into the chair. Looking up at her husband she asked, And who did you go as?

Me? He pulled a large hankie from his pocket and mopped his face. I was Frankenstein's monster. Uncertainty shaded his expression as he glanced at me.

It was very effective, I said. His face was like a patchwork, all stitches and a box on his head with hair painted on. A ringer for Boris Karloff.

Fiona shook her head. That's pretty incredible too.

It was, I smiled keeping to myself the knowledge that her husband's costume, like Paddy's, had been designed to conceal the marks of a fight.

Didn't you go to the party too? Fiona asked.

No. I wasn't invited, I said.

Lena was indisposed, Tim's head swivelled back to us. A bad business, he addressed me in a serious tone. Often wondered what happened those bastards, his lip curled with contempt.

The waitress returned with the drinks.

Tim handed me a glass and despite myself I drank to quell the burn of shame that had begun to spread in me at his words.

No chairs? He looked from the tray to the young woman, eyebrows raised.

They're all taken, she shrugged. You'll have to fight for them.

I don't need one, I said firmly. I'll be off.

Catching the severity in my tone, Tim tried to restore the jollity. Ah don't be like that, Lena. We have to toast absent friends. I miss the brother. His glass chinked on mine and his eyes meeting my reproachful look he quickly bowed his head.

Well, I sighed, Cork isn't exactly Kathmandu.

You can say that again, he laughed.

Is it true, Fiona cut in, that Mr. O'Neill is going to run for president?

President of what? Tim looked at her in surprise.

Ireland, she said.

Not political enough, said he dismissively.

Which might be a blessing, I said. I think it's Harvey that's running, I added, keen to scotch the growing rumour.

That's a good one, Tim spluttered. He'd be the right one for the job though. A Pooka in the Park.

I'll be off, I drained my glass and placed it on the table. Thanks for the drink. Turning to Fiona I smiled and said, It was nice to meet you. Good luck.

Thank you, she caressed her swollen belly, only six weeks to go. I hope we meet again. Meanwhile don't forget to tell Mr. O'Neill he has a fan club.

I won't. I gave a little wave and began to weave through the noisy throng. Night had fallen and the blackness pressing against the tall windows seemed to intensify the hysterical revelry in the lounge. Old melancholy began to creep over me as I moved towards the door and prepared to face the cold, dark street. Once, I would have known half the people in the room and could have passed airily from group to group savouring the nectar of gossip and laughter. Now I felt shrivelled and unwanted. The two-drink blues. A third might have borne me through that shadow to a sense of possibility and potency. Maybe Old Brennan would offer me a glass of Old Grouse to light me home. With that thought I realised that I had left his Christmas package and my newspaper at the table. I swore inwardly as I looked back across the crowded room to the corner where I had sat, my heart misgiving me at the prospect of burrowing all the way back there and having to re-extricate myself from Tim's nostalgic ebullience. I decided to abandon the bag and its contents and buy replacements in a Spar. I had only got as far as the Huguenot Cemetery when a hand grasped my shoulder. I started and spun around to find Tim dangling the carrier bag before my eyes.

Did you leave this behind? He cocked his head. Fiona found it beside the chair.

Yes, thank you, I gushed with relief. I must be getting forgetful in my old age.

Not at all. You're looking fit and well, he handed me the bag then hovered for a moment. I'm . . . eh . . . sorry, he began to gabble. If I, you know, overstepped the mark there when . . . well, you know . . . I never . . . I wouldn't say anything to Fifi about it.

Don't worry, I said, certain that Fifi would know all before the hour was out. It was a long time ago. I am still in your debt but for me now it is a closed chapter, I lied.

Oh don't mind that, he waved away my gratitude. You're right though. Water under the bridge and so forth. In the end it was for the best.

I'm not sure I understand. I peered up at him, unable to read his expression in the streetlight.

He shifted edgily from one foot to the other. Ah, nothing except that you got a better man out of it. Irish too.

Yes well goodnight, and thank you. I raised the bag.

Goodnight so. With an apologetic look he leant in quickly to kiss me on the cheek. Happy Christmas to you and the brother. Shivering slightly and pulling his jacket tight against the chilly night air he hurried back to the genial glow of the hotel bar.

Chapter Five

As I waited in the perishing cold for Old Brennan to make his way down three flights of stairs and open the hall door I reflected once again that this was no longer a practical arrangement for an elderly man whose joints, like mine, must be rusting by the day. Myles has a point about renovating the flat, and calling it a penthouse apartment to bring in a market (exorbitant) rent which would more than cover a comfortable alternative for Brennan and leave spare change for the office. Maybe the time has come, I thought, to propose, delicately, that he move. My hesitation is born of fear that the upheaval would plunge him into a nervous crisis and I confess I am emotionally attached to the idea of his being there, as if he were a flag planted at the top of a mountain declaring my proprietorship and retaining a link with Mossie.

A glow suddenly illuminated the fanlight and after a few moments the door opened to reveal Brennan in a faded plum-coloured smoking jacket, one of Father's that I had passed on to him, and, crowning his bald head, a moth-eaten astrakhan hat.

Come in, come in, he urged, before you catch your death.

I stepped into the hall through which I had passed several times a day, almost every day of my working life and stood aghast. Before I could speak the light switch timed out and in the dark hiatus I offered a silent prayer that when light returned the horror I had glimpsed would have vanished. Brennan pressed the switch and lo! the abomination leapt into view again. I blinked stupidly, breathless with disbelief.

Whereas in my day the walls of the elegantly proportioned Georgian hallway had been painted in two restrained shades of green above and below the dado rail, there was now a shiny wallpaper of blue, black and silver stripes below and another of giant flowers in the same colours above. The anaglypta tiled floor which I had softened with a Turkey rug was hidden by a vile indigo and lavender carpet. The seats of the two Hicks chairs flanking a matching hall console had been covered in lilac velour, and two glitzy modern chandeliers replaced my antique bowl and chain light fittings. In the large gilt-framed mirror above the console I saw myself and Brennan dwarfed by the grotesque decor, like figures in a convex fairground mirror.

What happened? I squeaked.

Ah, yes. Hah, Brennan turned a pained look on me. A bit of redecoration. Yes. Maybe I should have told you?

I shook my head, Nothing could have prepared me for this vandalism.

Yes, well, Myles . . . Myles . . . he spread his arm wide then let it fall hopelessly.

I raised my hand to spare his distress, Say nothing. I know exactly what happened: Myles' wife did an evening course in interior design and he let her loose in here to experiment.

You're not far off, he giggled. But the lady in question wasn't exactly his wife. So to speak.

Not *exactly* his wife?

Brennan shook his head which caused his cap to slip sideways.

His mistress? I raised my eyebrows.

Hah. A lady friend. Yes.

The dog. She must be a bit of a slapper to judge by her taste.

Not at all. Mousy, I would say.

Myles and his mousy mistress. That sounds like the title of a third-rate play.

The Mousetrap, Brennan half-winced, half-grinned.

Don't tell me they have assignations here, I said, as a new, distasteful, thought dawned.

Well, he likes to burn the midnight oil so to speak.

Stop. I don't want to know.

No. I . . . No. It does him no credit. An insult to you and to Mossie's memory. And Mossie's name still on the door. Still on the door. He glanced sorrowfully at the door, through which his friend would never step again.

For a moment I too sank into the gloom that only Christmas, with its exhortation to jollity, induces.

Brennan had arrived in our life like a hurricane, heralded by a ferocious hammering on the front door and cries for help, a racket that woke us at two a.m.

What the hell is that? Mossie grumbled coming slowly to consciousness.

Some drunken eejit who's lost his way home? I speculated.

He can go to hell. Mossie crossed the landing to shout at the noisy drunk from the window of the spare room. But instead of doing that and returning to bed he ran down the stairs shouting something incomprehensible as he passed our door.

Pulling on my robe I stepped out onto the landing and stood at the top of the stairs while Mossie opened the door to admit a dark jabbering bundle that staggered into the hall and dropped on all fours. What is it? What is it? I called, seized with panic.

It's fine, Lena, Mossie said quietly. It's only Ned. I'll be up shortly.

I had last seen Mossie's schoolfriend almost a year previously at his mother's funeral. That day the poor fellow had been distraught, leaning so perilously into the grave that

Mossie and another man had to take his arms and guide him away. Since then Mossie had travelled up and down to Arklow frequently to visit him and help sort out his mother's affairs. That included selling the petrol station and shop she had run for over thirty years because while Ned had happily served the customers and engaged them in chat he lacked the nous to run a business. Much later that night, or early morning, when he finally returned to bed, Mossie told me that Ned had taken a bus to Dublin and gone on a binge but had retained enough sense to decide when he was down to his last couple of quid to take a taxi out to our house.

We'll let him sleep it off, he said. Then we'll decide what to do about him.

There was no decision to make about Ned. He became our responsibility because, as Mossie said, no one else gave a tinker's curse about him. The few lost cousins who materialised at Mrs. Brennan's funeral vanished when Mossie told them, with some pleasure, that they had no claim on the old lady's will. Her Northern Irish family had ostracised her when she moved south and converted to Catholicism in order to marry Ned's republican father, whose family in turn did not hide their dislike of her. She had enlisted Mossie to secure her will against these hostile relatives and to protect her only remaining child, a girl having died in her teens of TB. Ever after that Mrs. Brennan had depended emotionally on her son, by turns mollycoddling and dominating him.

For a couple of weeks Ned soared, gabbling about being free at last, making and rejecting wild schemes for his new life, reminiscing about schooldays, staying up all night against Mossie's best and sternest efforts to get him to rest, singing to himself and looking for the drink that Mossie had stowed in the attic. One Saturday night, when he came home pie-eyed from the local pub, he worked himself into a rage cursing Mossie, calling him a jailer, saying he was a free man and could do as he pleased. Mossie remained calm, telling him he could walk out the door whenever he liked but Ned didn't want to hear. Swollen with angry frustration he danced in front of Mossie, spoiling for a fight.

I hate you, Mossie Carmody! He raged. You were the only one. A god on the pitch. Ha! A cruel god, Moss. A cruel one.

That's enough, Ned. It's time to forget all that, Mossie's voice was colder now. Come on, man. You need to rest.

No orders, cried Ned, backing away. I'm a free man. A proud soldier of Erin. He stood to attention, as best he could, and saluted.

Yes but even free men need their sleep.

No. No. No. I refuse. Non serviam. Orders. All my life. First Daddy then Mammy. Do this, do that. Ned put the cat out. Ned bring in the coal. Ned put on the kettle. No more I say. Ned says no.

Clamping his jaw in defiance he lunged suddenly and swung his fist but Mossie seized it before the punch landed. That's enough, Ned, he said. I'll have to call the guards. Then you'll really know what jail is like.

Ned's face bulged and reddened till I thought his veins would burst and the blood spring from his temples. An old horror convulsed me and I shouted at them to stop, cried and begged of Mossie to come away but neither man heard me, so tightly were they were bound in their tussle. Suddenly Mossie had a grip of Ned's arms and was hissing at him to leave it be leave it be that's all over now over leave it be. Ned cast him a fearful, chastened look and crumpled, the fight draining from him, as he dropped backwards into a chair, and, engulfed with heavy sobs, begged Mossie to help him.

He slept for three days after that during which time Mossie spoke to a psychiatrist recommended by Father. When he came round Mossie began the difficult negotiation to persuade him to visit this doctor.

He mounted the stairs ahead of me, pressing the light switches on each landing as he went.

Passing what was once my office I had a flashback to quiet lunchtimes when Mossie and I locked the door and availed of my deep leather couch for a brisk roll and shared a post-coital cigarette. It galled me, perhaps unreasonably, to think of Myles and his tasteless mistress indulging in like pleasures there now, minus the fag. Hot on the tail of that grudge came an insight into Myles' plans for the top floor flat. I promptly revoked my decision to move Brennan out. Let him stay till he drops, I thought. Indeed, the mousy decorator's wand had by-passed his flat, which is so full of fusty pictures and oversize furniture from his family home that, were it not for the piles of yellowing newspaper stacked on every surface, it could be an antique shop. (I concede Myles' point about the papers being a fire hazard.) With the gas stove lighting and the curtains drawn, however, the place is snug if stuffy.

A deafening jabber from the large TV in the corner re-solved into Liam Geraghty talking up his crackpot investment scheme.

Will you be putting your savings in crocOgold, Ned? I asked, pointing to the screen. For all the oddness of his manner Ned is sharp enough when it comes to current affairs and money.

Are you codding me? That jackanapes is too much of a showman. I wouldn't trust him an inch or a mile.

Nor I.

It's all payback and you scratch my back, I'll scratch yours. That's what it is. He shook his head impatiently and muted the sound on the TV. Too cosy with her Laceyship. Bad history there, he muttered.

Geraghty mouthed on, dumb as a goldfish, beside clichéd shots of a tropical beach, some dubious Shangri-La he's flog-ging, if only one could find it on a map.

To fill the silence Brennan moved to his gramophone and, in an obsolete ceremony, set a vinyl record spinning on the turntable before dropping the needle into one of its grooves. The voice of Richard Tauber crackled around us. Some day the needle will puncture the groove so often has the record been played. One Christmas I had given Brennan a CD player along with digitally remastered versions of his favourite LPs, but they remain sealed in their wrappers because he can't resist the nostalgia of that old time sizzle. That was the background music to the respite he and his mother enjoyed from his brutal father who, along with his so-called comrades in arms, spent the Emergency in the Curragh. Local gossip had it that, for all his boasts, ('The Brennans are a proud people', 'The Brennans bend the knee to no man') Old Man Brennan had run away from the scene of an ambush. Being locked up by the Free State government saved him from execution by the comrades he abandoned, or those who survived at any rate. Besides, for a man like him it was a badge of honour, which he lived off to the end of his days.

The old ones are the best, isn't that right? Ned smiled as the Austrian serenaded his heart's delight. He knows all the words to these corny songs and, when his mood is up, sings, hums or whistles them incessantly, a habit that became a feature of life in our office, disconcerting at first for newcomers until they settled in and accepted it as part of the environment, like the gurgle of water in the old radiators and the rattling of the sash windows on a blustery day.

Yes, I nodded, indulging a brief nostalgia of my own, recalling Mother picking out the melody on the piano to accompany a warbling guest at a dinner party. But what were you saying about Geraghty?

That scut. His father, they say, was a garda up in Laceyland. Got himself promoted to superintendent very quickly. He tapped his nose significantly before handing me a tumbler of whiskey. I took a warming sip while he cleared a bundle of papers from one of the armchairs for me. With a flick of his wrist he despatched a large calico cat from the other chair and sat in its place, raising his glass in a toast, Your health. The cat sprang onto the chair back and blinked balefully at me.

He's a mountebank with no money in the bank if you ask me. As for herself I wouldn't give you tuppence for her. What happened to honour and *gravitas*? Men like your father. They had dignity. Geraghty's father has the goods on Clan Lacey. No strangers to cross-border trade. He's been in here you know.

Who? The father?

No, no, no. Brennan shook his head vigorously. Himself. There's a tie-up there, so to speak.

Who's tied to whom? Or what?

Myles' wife's half-brother-in-law is Geraghty's right-hand man.

Hold on, I said, feeling my brain go fuzzy. That's quite a tangle. Which half of the brother-in-law?

Hah! Brennan giggled. He's married to Rosemary's half-sister. Comes in with Geraghty. Burly fellow with a beard.

Maybe he's Geraghty's bodyguard.

He might be needing one to fend off angry clients. That or he'll take refuge in the Áras.

What do you mean?

They say herself has plans for him. It was in one of these papers, Brennan made to rummage through the pile nearest him on the floor.

Don't bother looking for it now, Ned, said I, having heard enough on that topic for one day and thinking he'd be a poor type for Paddy to lose to. I stood and pulled on my coat and scarf, saying I really must be off. Besides, I had a newspaper of my own burning a hole in my bag.

Although it was almost midnight by the time I got home I poured myself a G and T and went straight to the computer where I googled Major-General Richard Arthur Davies KCB. I watched the cyber wheel spiral while the search engine foraged silently in its files, rewinding my life towards the moment when Richard and I had just met.

Throughout the rest of that evening at the hunt ball we conducted a dialogue of arch glance and gesture across the room. It was easy to keep him in my sights because while he was not the only British officer there he had a way of standing slightly apart from the throng. I danced my heart out, Salome of the Shelbourne.

When the ball had ended and the crowd lingered in the foyer in a flurry of farewells, last minute quips and arrangements to meet again, Richard brushed past me, forcing me to meet his eye.

Good night Miss O'Neill, he said.

Good night Captain Davies, I replied.

His red jacket blazed briefly on the doorstep then was gone into the night. In a surge of panic and dismay at the realisation that I might never see him again I tacked around the chattering clusters of friends mouthing apologies, begging pardon, promising to telephone this one and that one, waving goodbye until at last I gained the door only to bounce off Gerard Mc-Nally triumphing that he had secured a taxi in which to escort me home.

You're too kind, I said. But I'll be perfectly safe on my own. Thank you, I held out my hand to shake his.

But Mammy insists I see you home.

I'm sure you don't always do what your Mammy says.

Not always, he tittered. Only she'd never forgive me if anything happened you.

Glancing over Gerard's shoulder I caught sight of Richard halting beneath a street lamp to light a cigarette. Nothing will. I promise, I reassured him, hoping I was wrong.

Grand so.

Good night. I kissed him lightly on the cheek and stepped into the taxi.

Good night, he said, shutting the car door. I enjoyed dancing with you.

I directed the taxi driver to follow Richard and to slow when we drew level with him. As the car crawled beside the footpath I rolled down the window and offered him a lift.

No thanks. I'm glad of the walk, he said and motioned the taxi driver to move on.

Are you sure?

Quite sure.

Ah sure a walk would do me no harm either, said I, wincing at the oirishness that a British accent brought out in me. Can I join you?

If you insist, he said. As long as you don't complain about your shoes and expect me to carry you.

Don't worry, I replied. I'm tougher than I look.

That's saying something.

As I was getting out of the taxi the driver commented, He should be chasing you, Love, not the other way around.

Mind your own business, I snapped, knowing he was right. You may keep the fare. Gerard, ever the gentleman, had pre-paid the man.

Trying to buy me silence, the driver laughed darkly. Don't say I didn't warn you. He's a Brit and they never respected our women.

I got out of the car and slammed the door as hard as I could. I tried to fall into step with the Brit's stride but he wasn't making any compromises on that score for me. We strolled around the city for an hour then turned towards Ballsbridge and the sea, encountering other late night stragglers, fellow wayfarers in the no man's land between night and day. Only as we approached the suburbs rich with shrubs and late summer blooms did we kiss, dallying in the cloak of shade they provided against the coming dawn.

By the time we reached Seapoint the milk dray and bread van were on their rounds. At the gate of our house Richard kissed me again lightly on the forehead. Once inside I ran up the stairs and opened the curtains on my bedroom window to watch him stroll along the seafront towards the city. When he reached the Martello tower he turned to look back and seeing me, half-saluted. I waved and watched until I was not sure whether the dwindling figure was him or a trick of the light which had begun to flare along the horizon and gild the indolent sea. Leaving the curtains open I stood before the cheval glass and slowly removed my dress, letting its blue folds pool on the floor around my feet. Then, still watching myself in the glass and imagining Richard's eyes on me I drew my slip over my head and let it too slither to the floor. I stooped to unsnap the suspender on my right thigh, bent my knee till my leg balanced on the tip of my big toe, rolled my stocking down and shook it free of my foot. Dipping to the left I removed the other stocking with the same deliberation. Under his imagined gaze my limbs grew warm and heavy. I unhooked my brassière and dropped it. Relieved of that constraint my breasts softened and swelled, longing to be touched. I cradled them in my hands and inhaling drew them up and forward till the nipples tensed exquisitely. As I exhaled I pressed my hands down over my ribcage and belly to the waistband of my smalls which I peeled away and, flung aside. Taking the hand mirror from my dressing table I summoned my rear view in the cheval glass and found it a pleasing sight, the flesh made rosy by the rising sun. My spine curved deeply above my buttocks and where my hips flared dimples sat like quotation marks, indicating the space that awaited the imprint of Richard's kisses. Reflected there too was the ugly statue of Our Lady which had watched over my sleep since earliest childhood, her eyes expressionless, her foot not quite crushing the head of the serpent.

Feverish with excitement I got into bed naked and moved my hand down between my legs parting the delicate hidden lips to touch the nexus where the desire that branched and quickened through my body converged.

The whirling wheel vanished from the screen to be replaced by the first batch of 8,305 references to Richard Arthur Davies and strangers with permutations on his name, including an attorney in Cincinnati, a singer with an Australian band, an estate agent in Swansea and a man accused of leaving his baby in a car while he went on a binge, which I must confess gave me pause. When I found the real Richard's name in this list of homonyms I hesitated to click, halted by the uncomfortable sensation that I would be spying on him, as though I were reading his diary and he would learn of my trespass. Absurd scrupulosity because all the information was official or linked to articles that he had penned. Another swig of gin emboldened me to open one of the sites that contained the name of my long-ago lover. There I read the impersonal narrative of a soldier's career encompassing tours in Germany, Borneo, Northern Ireland, Aden, training at Catterick, Northern Ireland again and peacekeeping in Lebanon, until he became a member of the Commonwealth Monitoring Force in Zimbabwe, and later an advisor to the Ministry of Defence, and now to the UN. Once, with the bravado of youth, he had told me he'd prefer to take a bullet than be trapped behind a desk. At the time the comment pierced me with a naive thrill of fear and respect. Now I applauded his survival. Reading this list of tours I see rewind before me the life that Mother warned me of, the long days, weeks, months of lonely apprehension and dread as I waited for news, punctuated by the intervals when he would be returned to me and the family I once fancied we would have, followed by the wrench of his fresh departure. Reviewing that condensed account of the nerve-wracking life I might have lived I understood too what Mother had been trying to tell me. While, astutely aware that prohibition would act on me as a spur to foolhardy defiance, the Parents would not forbid me outright to see Richard, they would have cut me off had I married him. That was the isolation Mother had once forecast for me. They could not have borne that intimate connection to what for them had been an occupying force in our country.

As to what prompts my pursuit of Richard now for friend- ship and maybe more as they say in the personal ads, is it curiosity, nostalgia, a sense of something unresolved or incom- plete? Or am I after all just another lonely heart huddling up to memory and fantasy for comfort? When Mossie died I felt as if I had been flung from a train, abandoned at a disused station, its little sign, Widowhood, creaking in the wind. He is even absent from my dreams, which deepens my sense of loss.

In the year following Mossie's death I would sometimes drive around the city until the small hours finding perverse consolation in its desolate rain-slicked streets. The mechani- cal business of driving pushed the 'Why me?' that turned in my head, like one of Brennan's records, into the background. The only other people about were the drunks staggering home from the pubs, taxi drivers on the hazard, prostitutes on the beat trying to keep warm and occasional students unsteadily cycling back to their digs in Rathmines, each of us cloaked in the silence and solitude of anonymity. On one of those nights my route took me into Fitzwilliam Street East, across Baggot Street and on to Fitzwilliam Square where, at the sight of a fox darting across the road from the park I slammed on the brakes. I waited a moment watching the fox slip between the area rail- ings of our office building and in the same moment the front door of the office opened and a woman in a red coat stepped out. A cheery exchange of banter was followed by a final good night before the door shut and the woman descended to the street. Transfixed by this synchronicity and the glimpse it afforded of Brennan's secret life I was startled by a tap at the passenger window. The woman looked in at me with what I suppose was intended as a fetching smile, one that swiftly curdled when she realised I was not a potential client and fleetingly her poise tottered to reveal the uncomfortable man beneath the heavy make-up. Wait a minute, she called through the glass while fumbling in her fake ocelot bag. Producing a pack of cigarettes she shook one free and bending again to the window she held it up, pincered between her fingers, Gotta light? With a sense that some contract had been established between us by my catching her momentary slip out of character, I leaned over to roll down the window and handed her my lighter. Thanks, she said gruffly, then nursed the flame which cast a seductive half-light over her features. Her hand encased in a red leather glove appeared beside me returning the lighter. Keep it, I said. She tilted her chin up in acknowledgement and dropped the lighter into her handbag. I rolled up the window and put the car in gear. Through the rear view mirror I watched the stranger wobble down the street in ludicrously high plat-form shoes. Above us the light in the window of Brennan's flat winked out.

I drained my glass. The sharp taste set my drowsy senses aquiver and fired by the alcohol I began painstakingly to trawl through the sites containing Richard's name until just as my eyes began to droop again I happened on a short news-paper report of his KC. According to the item, his daughter Anne accompanied him to the ceremony because his wife Bronwen, herself the daughter of a decorated brigadier, had died three years previously. Maybe it was the effect of visiting Old Brennan, islanded in the furniture of his childhood but I pictured Richard now in a threadbare wing chair chewing his lonely supper at a card table in front of the box, a grizzled lab stretched at his feet. Or maybe he whiled the nights away at the retired servicemen's league repeating the conversations and one-liners of last night and last week. Both scenes struck a gloomy chord summoning a pang of pity for him but before that had fully taken hold Tim Gallagher's rubbery face rose up from the haze of the previous evening with a leer of triumph in his new, young, pregnant wife. The image wavered and gave way to Richard's features, stirring a flap of panic in my chest. If garrulous Tim could snag a young bride then so could taciturn Richard. It seemed suddenly urgent that I speak to him again. Scrabbling at the page where his article appeared I noted, at the bottom of the last column, an invitation to comment on its contents and an email address. In my panic even an email seemed too dilatory a means of communication. I needed to speak to the man, to find a way back through the years, to understand what happened. I would telephone the night editor who would surely provide a number when I told him it was an emergency. I tore at the paper seeking its contact details. Preparatory to dialling I wet my whistle with another dose of G and T. My call was answered by a machine informing me that the offices were open between 9 a.m. and 6 p.m. and that if I needed to contact the night editor I should dial another number which I transcribed onto a corner of the page in front of me. A friendly cockney voice greeted me on that line. When I asked for Richard's number, however, the voice turned stiff and pompous saying that it was not newspaper policy to disclose personal details of staff or contributors.

But this is urgent, I pressed.

Not my problem, the cockney snapped.

You don't seem to understand, young man, that I am a friend of Major General Davies and need to speak to him on an important matter.

If 'e's such a good pal 'ow come you don't 'ave his number?

As it *happens*, even though it's none of your business, I mislaid my address book.

That was a bit careless wannit? said the Oscar Wilde of the East End.

How dare you! I am meticulous and punctilious but those words probably have too many syllables for you to understand. I assure you I am anything but careless. I am a model of—

Listen darling, I couldn't give a stuff about you or your syllables even if you are a model. I 'ave work to do. That's a four letter word and there are more where that came from. Goonite.

Cheeky little bugger, I addressed the receiver although the line was dead but I was damned if I was going to be thwarted by his like. I tried directory inquiries where I was told I needed an address. Email it would have to be. Another swig of gin would guide my hand. Tone was the problem: how to strike the right note, to be friendly and casual as if it were only weeks since our last encounter but at the same time not to seem too anxious. I did not want to invite recriminations or accusations. I needed to make it easy for him to respond. Later there would be time for questions and explanations. The register had to lie somewhere between fond reminiscence and flirtatious suggestion. Even the salutation was problematic, 'Dear Richard', 'Hello Richard', 'Hi there', 'Richard', . . . all the traditional greetings looked formulaic and impersonal. Email is funny that way. Had I been writing a letter I wouldn't have hesitated to open with 'Dear Richard' but the electronic format seems to demand some more spontaneous form of address. 'Yo' or 'Hey' isn't that what the kids say? Do Jean and Pól and their pals have an acronym to cover the situation? After some thought and a little more gin I opted for 'Hello' then segued into my surprise at seeing his name in print, not that I am a daily *Guardian* reader, which inspired me to make contact and wonder how he was, adding that if he ever chanced to be in Dublin it would be a pleasure to meet. Signing off was an even more delicate problem than opening. 'Love' was out of the question, 'Regards' too formal, 'Best wishes' too birthday cardish, 'Warmly' and 'Fondly' might scare him off. I had to acknowledge the possibility that he would not remember me. Finally, I went for 'Cheers' as being anodyne and undemanding. Long years of legal correspondence had taught me to put nothing in writing that could be misconstrued or misused by an interested or jealous third party. Away the message flew into the pulsing ether of satellites and electronic gossip and a moment later the first bird summoned the dawn.

Chapter Six

Let me get back to this morning which has been sabotaged by multifarious interruptions, starting with Paddy's phone call about the paintings and ending with Bernie's grand projet. Piranhas all around. Time to resume my own pace and pursuits starting with a shower. That might wash some of the irritations from my mind. I take off the clothes I had scrambled into when Muiris arrived but now that I am naked am overcome with the urge to lie down.

On my back, staring at the ceiling, I am possessed by tremors that rattle every nerve and sinew in my body like a palsy. When I shut my eyes my head swoons, plummeting down a long dark shaft. My hand flails for the radio in search of distraction.

. . . riches untold . . . crocOgold . . . crocOgold . . . Coming up in the next hour investment guru, Liam Geraghty, answers your personal finance questions and talks about his presidential ambitions. That's all to come on the Didi Doherty show.

Brennan has his finger on the pulse to be sure but mine is on the on/off button.

The isle is out of joint and going down the tubes to the dogs, pigs and whistles. But whisht, is that the bloody doorbell again? Impossible. I refuse to answer, for anyone, no matter what telecom deals they are offering or charity they are begging for. I roll over and draw the duvet tighter around my head but the infernal bell won't let up. At last, yielding to its summons, I haul myself off the bed, drag the dressing gown on and descend the stairs ready to run the blighters with the sharp end of my tongue. A peek through the spy-hole, however, reveals Dorothy raising her hand to press the bell again.

Hold your horses, I call as I open the door. Come in.

You're not dressed yet, she says.

Half. But what's the matter? This isn't our meals on wheels day. It's your golf day.

Yes I played this morning. It's afternoon now, Lena.

I glance at the grandfather clock which seems to reproach me, its hands pointing to twenty to two, So it is but you wouldn't believe the morning I've had.

You can tell me about it in the car.

In the car? I'm going nowhere except back to bed.

You can't've forgotten already: we offered to help Claire set up a room downstairs for Eamon. She inhales significantly and folds her arms. She will brook no protest or delay.

Okay. I just didn't think it was so urgentissime, that we were absolutely going today.

(I also don't believe I drank that much last night but I'm worried about people asking whether I've forgotten something. The marbles, I fear, are slipping like quicksilver through some crack in the grey matter.)

She rang me this morning to ask if she could take us up on the offer today because he's arriving next Wednesday and she'll be at work on Monday and Tuesday.

So the marbles haven't deserted me yet, No one told me about the plan.

I rang and left a message with Jean.

Aha! Another instruction to give the girl, She didn't pass it on. I must have been in the garden with Muiris at the time.

I left a message on your mobile too.

Oh I see, I say, wondering where I left the phone, I'll just go and dress. Two ticks.

Half-way up the stairs I pause to call over my shoulder, I hope she's not expecting us to move furniture as well.

No. Her son-in-law and his brother will bring the spare bed downstairs tomorrow.

Why not leave it where it is and hope he falls down the stairs?

Stop it. Get dressed.

When I reach the bedroom I sit for a minute on the side of the bed. Tiny lights flash before my eyes and my ears ring. I haven't felt this dizzy since one madcap night, not so very long ago, albeit in the last century, when I climbed aboard a hurdy-gurdy at a Brussels funfair with some of my European lawyers' association colleagues. We whirled so fast I was sure I'd be catapulted into mid-air. It took the strong arms of a handsome Dane and a somewhat over-amorous Luxembourger to keep me upright when the thing stopped spinning. Where is the strong arm to support me now? Or the pragmatic voice to chivvy me along with the promise of a fire, a drink and a listening ear when I come home? Who will comfort me, Moss? I ask of the smiling face fixed in a silver frame on my bedside table. I miss you. It doesn't get any easier, making myself busy in a void, staying ahead of the shadow that creeps in like spilt ink, devouring light. Maybe deep down I envy Claire the return of her errant husband.

Are you nearly ready? At Dorothy's call Tanta springs off the bed and stands growling at the door.

On my way, I reply, smothering the growl that rises in my throat. Reorganising Claire's chaotic house had not been in my plan for the day. I pull on my oldest pair of jeans, then rummage in a drawer for a scarf to protect my hair.

When Eamon and Claire bought their house in Templeogue, it seemed like the other end of the earth but nowadays the once-distant suburb is billed as a stunning location, close to the city and with all the adjacent amenities the heart could desire, including a synagogue and GAA grounds. Eamon, a quantity surveyor, talked of one day building a large Californian style home in Howth but decamped to the Alps instead. Now, while her neighbours extend, revamp and upgrade their homes, or simply sell up and retire to the Costa Brava, Claire can't afford to replace her rotting window frames. As I have tried many times to tell her, divorcing the blaggard would force a sale and divvy up of the spoils and she could buy a decent apartment close to town. Her last state is worse than her first because her returning hero won't come bearing loot. As far as we know he earned his keep by tending the bar of the hotel owned by Miss Meribel's family where he chewed the ear off anyone who would listen with a discourse beginning 'The trouble with Ireland . . .' and proceeding to his big schemes for the modernisation and marketing of the hotel, all the while topping up his tumbler of Pernod.

By the time we reach Claire's house I have given Dorothy a synopsis of my morning and she has pronounced Paddy's interest in the Parents' paintings understandable, my mews house not a bad idea and the Murphy-Benz's plan unworkable.

Can't you just let Paddy pick one or two paintings? After all, they were part of his childhood home too.

I would but he wants the lot. Probably to sell. It's this business of getting Jean to snoop around that I object to.

All the more reason for you to be upfront.

I'll think about it. Mother gave him some items over the years but Paddy has felt hard done by since the day he was born and Nóirín has a mega-chip on her shoulder so there's no pleasing either of them.

You're both obstinate as mules. That's the real problem. She presses her lips together, drawing a firm line under that statement.

Claire is brandishing a china vase when she opens her front door.

Hi, she beams, You're really kind to do this. I made a bit of a start this morning. God! I didn't know I had so much *stuff*! She hoists the vase, which is in the form of a squinting squirrel gripping a tree trunk as if she's about to drop and break it but sadly instead sets it on an already cluttered hall table, Wedding gift from Eamon's Auntie Marjorie, she explains, pulling a face, Hideous I know but he'll be pleased to see I still have it.

Would the bugger even notice?

At the centre of Claire's living room stand a couple of grocery boxes half-filled with books and bundles of the fabric remnants she uses for her quilting. One end of the couch has been dragged out at an angle, revealing spots of mould in the corner and a wedge of carpet bright and clean as a putting green against the stains and fading of the exposed area.

I found an old penny on the floor there, Claire laughs, I'm thinking of sending it to the museum. She takes the large coin, stamped with a fat feathery hen, from her pocket.

How did we carry those big yokes around in our purses? Dorothy shakes her head.

We had fewer of them, say I.

Yes and the ten bob was a note, adds Claire.

Remember the florin.

And the half-crown.

For a moment the three of us stand contemplating the small change of our youth.

But no crown, Dorothy raises an admonitory finger, Put the penny away, Claire, and you and Lena finish filling that box while I start on the next one.

Yes Chief, we chirrup together.

The jaunty ring tone of a mobile phone halts us before we begin. Like a baby's cry it refuses to be ignored and we glance from one to the other, wondering whose it is. I'm sure it's not mine but I have a niggling concern that I might have become like the woman I read about who put her phone in the fridge and a half pound of sausages in her handbag. I keep my bag firmly shut.

It's probably mine, says Dorothy, rootling in her bag.

It's probably Ken, say I.

She nods agreement, rolling her eyes, as she answers the phone and steps out of the room.

Winking at me Claire pushes the door closed behind her, seizes my hand and draws me onto the couch, Quick, before the slave driver comes back, she laughs, You have to see these old photos. She lifts an album onto her knee. Part of its brown cardboard cover is torn away and gives off a dampish smell. She turns the thick charcoal grey pages, on which the photographs, captioned in white ink in her neat roundy handwriting, gleam like ore of dubious value, glimpses of ourselves when young.

Look, she jabs her finger at one of a group on bicycles strung across a sunlit country road. Although the image is black and white I see it in colour, even to the summery print of my frock. The men are in shirt sleeves and we all smile with the certainty that the road ahead is smooth and straight.

There's Richard, Claire points to the figure astride Paddy's bike, lent after some negotiation and bribery on my part. One hand rests lightly on the handlebar, the other dangles at his side, a cigarette clipped between the first two fingers, its wisp of smoke blurring the air. The bike is too small for him, giving him a slightly clownish appearance. His head is half-turned over his shoulder and I hear him calling me a slowcoach.

It was the day we cycled up to the Featherbeds, Claire's voice pulls me back to the present.

I remember, I nod, Richard was highly amused by the name. He thought I was propositioning him.

And you weren't? Claire raises her eyebrows.

I told him not to get carried away that it was more bog and forest than feathers. He said, Leaves make a fine mattress. We'll see, said I.

What we saw was the carpet of scrubby grass, rock, bog and gorse vivid with nut-scented blooms, that covers our low mountains and below, the haphazard geometry of our tiny city fringing the bay. I saw too that Eamon, who was less fit than the rest of us, and had puffed and panted his way up the hill, his face turning puce with the effort, felt disadvantaged and tried to overcompensate by being a smart arse. He began by playing with Richard's name, calling him Dick then Dickie and Davy Dicks. On his second beer he asked Richard whether he regarded himself as Welsh or British.

Richard frowned for a moment before saying, That depends who I'm talking to.

Or fighting, Eamon shot back.

Or playing, Ken headed him off. Who has the better side this year, do you think?

Grateful for the intervention, Richard moved into analysis of the line out for Wales.

Meanwhile, Claire put her hand on Eamon's sleeve and flashed him a quick pleading smile.

He pulled his arm away, shrugged and entered the rugby conversation, which Dorothy had also joined.

As broad mauve clouds crossed the sun we began to pack up our picnic wares and replace them in our baskets. Richard moved away to, as he put it, see a man about a dog.

I might do the same, said Eamon bustling after him.

I could tell by the set of Richard's jaw when he returned that something was amiss.

We mounted our bikes and freewheeled most of the way home, Ken, the only one among us who could carry a tune, breaking into a rendition of 'Summertime', the rest of us joining in less tunefully.

Back in the lane behind the house, Richard held the bikes as I opened the gate and the shed.

Tell Paddy thanks for the loan, he said, wheeling the bike into place.

Come in and you can thank him yourself, I suggested, The Parents are going out.

Richard and my parents had met a couple of times, with reservations on both sides, he somewhat terrified by Mother, while she and Father, although politely hospitable, were unable to disguise their concern for me.

No, he said, wrapping his arms around my waist and kissing me on the forehead. I don't think that's a good idea.

The coast is clear, really.

Releasing me he stepped back and said, Maybe in fact none of this is a good idea.

What do you mean? Fear clenched my gut.

Us, he shrugged. Look at what happened today. Eamon's probably not the only one who dislikes me.

I don't think he dislikes you. He's stupid, that's the problem. He thinks it's smart to get a rise out of you. Make himself look like the big fellow.

He told me to leave you alone. To go with my 'own kind'.

Ah, that's why you looked so put out coming back from the bushes.

Yes. But it's not just today. I don't think he's alone in feeling that I'm trespassing. I sense it in your other friends and your parents, even if they're too polite to say anything about it.

I don't care what they think, I protested. The only thing that matters is you and me.

It's not fair to you when I'm away. You're alone, people might begin to shun you.

I tilted my head, catching another meaning behind his words. That's different. I cried. Are you trying to tell me you don't want to see me anymore? Because if so you should at least have the guts to say it outright, instead of pretending that it's for my good.

As you put it that way, yes, I suppose so, his head drooped and he studied his shoes.

What's changed? Why now all of a sudden? Tell me the truth. What's up?

I just think it's difficult – for both of us.

I can manage it. Why can't—

I know you can, he cut in. And you go out with other men. But it's not easy. For either of us.

That's different. It's light hearted, just going to a hop or the flicks. For all I know you see other women. I know what soldiers do. I'm not naive you know.

He balled and released his fists a couple of times before responding. For a moment I feared he might be restraining an impulse to swing at me, after being needled by Eamon. I stepped out of the shed, tightening my grip on the picnic basket as if it could shield me.

That's not the point, he loosened his hands and plunged them into his pockets, I just feel this a wave of resentment. People here are still angry. I understand why, truly I do but that wasn't my war and I'm not going to stop doing what I do because of it. Blame history, he tried for a nonchalant tone, as if to wash his hands of responsibility for ditching me.

For God's sake, I fumed. History is yesterday. We're here and now. We'll be tomorrow's history. A different story. I know your father was a prisoner of war in Germany and he probably hates the Germans but are you going to spend your life hating them too? You'll be making the world a very small place.

No. I don't suppose I shall, but I probably won't fall in love with one.

His switchbacks were dizzying. I took a deep breath and asked was he really in love with me.

Yes, I believe so, he said with a troubled look.

Then what's the problem? I put down the picnic basket which had begun to give me a cramp and hooked my arms around his neck.

I don't know, he smiled and held my wrists. It's just when I'm away it's very difficult. I try not to think of you and when I do I feel a dread that we won't be able to be together. That your parents will prevail over you.

Is that why you don't write often?

Partly. Also it's not that easy to write a letter when you're in a foxhole.

You think it's easier to reject me than to be rejected.

He let his hands fall to my waist and ran them over my buttocks, All this deep talk, he said. It's complicating. It makes my head go fuzzy.

War is easier than love, is that it?

I don't know any more. Just kiss me and we'll forget it all.

I complied readily and taking his hand drew him up the path towards the house.

So you've been skiving in my absence, Dorothy comments on returning to the room.

Claire and I jump and Claire slams the album closed blushing like a schoolgirl caught with *Forever Amber* inside her history book, Just some photos I was showing Lena.

Was Ken missing you already? I ask in order to deflect the attention from us.

Yes but the pretext for the call was that he wanted his sister's phone number.

Surely he has his own sister's number. Paddy has mine, more's the pity.

You've obviously forgotten what it's like to live with a man: compartmentalisation and delegation are their preserve. Telephone numbers, birthdays and other trivia are ours.

Eamon kept my number. Our number.

Because he knew he'd need it some day.

Dorothy silences me with a look then says, Let's get to work here. Where are you going to put the bed?

In this corner. That way Eamon can see the TV and he'll be able to chat to me through the door when I'm in the kitchen.

In other words she knows he's not going to let her out of his sight, I think.

I'll use a baby monitor at night, she continues. Her smile, half-fond, half-rueful, fends off her own apprehension and our scepticism, Eamon always knew how to make me laugh. And I still have our old Scrabble board. She pulls the dusty green box from under a pile of magazines on the shelf she has been clearing. I'm sure there are some letters missing but we'll manage. Eamon invents words.

I stifle the impulse to say that's probably because he can't spell and say instead, That makes it more challenging.

Yes, she nods staring at the box, I'd forgotten it was here.

Fleetingly, I see Claire as a stranger might. She looks old and tired and brave, far from the blithe and pretty girl in the photograph. Richard would scarcely recognise her. As long as he recognises me in the line-up at the airport we'll be all right.

It had taken him a couple of weeks to respond to my email. After the first week of checking my inbox and answering machine every hour just as once, decades ago, I had watched for the post morning and evening, and badgered everyone in the house to know if it had arrived and whether there was a letter for me, I gave up on him and reproached myself for being such an eejit as to think he would bother replying. When the call came it caught me in the middle of watching the Nine O'Clock News and for a confusing moment Richard's familiar, if now slightly gravelly, voice, overlaid a Sinn Féin spokesman's priesteen pedantry about decommissioning.

*Hu*llo. *Hu*llo, Richard boomed. (His hearing was obviously shot.) Is that you Lena?

Yes, yes, I laughed as I zapped the Shinner into silence, It's me. This is a quite a surprise.

Communication had never been his strong suit. Indeed I was the most surprised of all when he made his first return visit to Dublin. At the final party of Horse Show week he had told me he was leaving the next day. His regiment was about to be deployed overseas. He left me so winded with shock that I could neither cry nor speak.

I'll come back, he said, when I can.

I shook my head refusing to listen to what he was saying. We had scarcely been apart since the night of the ball where we had met.

Soon, he caressed my cheek.

Please, I breathed, seizing his hand and pressing my lips to his palm.

After he left I had moped, unable to concentrate on lectures at college and impatient with my friends. I continued to join the Grafton Street Parade although I was no longer eyeing up the fellows and didn't care if they eyed me up. When I joined the college crowd in Roberts Café I had no interest in the gossip about who was doing a line with whom, or in earnest discussions about the end of the Korean war, Khruschev's ascent to power or whether Ireland should join the UN. I was preoccupied with wondering where Richard was and whether his life was in danger, fear squirming in the pit of my stomach. I even fished my pearly rosary beads from the bottom of my jewellery box where they had lain idle for several years. Mother chid me for not eating. I sat for whole afternoons with Dorothy in the DBC tea room, speculating about when and how Richard might contact me, until the pain in my heart, combined with the willow pattern décor, made me feel like bursting into a few bars of 'Un bel di vedremo'. For a time Dorothy listened tactfully but after three months had passed with no communication she told me he was a 'bolter'. The word sounded to me like a Ken-ism and I told her so, adding that I didn't appreciate her discussing my affairs with Ken and that neither he nor she could possibly understand what Richard and I felt for one another. We didn't speak for several weeks after that conversation. I stewed with resentment chiefly because in my rational moments I feared she might be right. Then, suddenly, the following May, he turned up, with no advance notice just a telephone call to know if I was free that evening to go to the cinema as if he had never been away. He brushed off my questions about why he had not written to me with the comment that he was not a great hand at writing and he had nothing to say.

But didn't you miss me? I had whined.

Of course I did, he smiled, but writing to you wouldn't have changed that.

I'd have written back. That's what people do when they're apart.

It wouldn't have been the same as this, he had mumbled pulling me to him.

In the Shinner-free silence he explained that he had begun to write an email, but then thought why not just pick up the ruddy phone and talk.

Good thinking, I said. I tried to get your number but some guttersnipe at the paper refused to divulge it.

Poor chap! I'm guessing you gave him what for.

Of course I did. He didn't have a very good grasp of the English language.

It's not a pre-requisite for journalism.

What made you take up the pen?

Just the occasional op-ed. The pen isn't actually mightier than the sword but it's a useful alternative especially now that I'm semi-retired. What about you? Have you been put out to grass?

Yes, like you I'm mostly out there, for the past couple of years.

It must have been hard for you to keep going when Mossie died. I thought of writing to you but decided you mightn't appreciate hearing from me.

The sound of Mossie's name on his lips was almost as disconcerting as the fact that he knew all about him, But how did you—

Our spies are everywhere.

That's creepy.

I wasn't tailing you. I did two tours in Northern Ireland and made a couple of trips to Dublin. Ran into one of your old chums one day. The mouthy little fellow with the loud suits – Eamon, was that his name?

Poor you.

Yes, he's a bit of a bastard but he seemed genuinely touched by your plight.

That must be why he touched me up when I was still in my widow's weeds.

Black becomes you.

Not any more, I laughed.

We chatted for another half an hour, quite like old friends, and arranged that he would come to Dublin in March, when he had a break from travelling to do his UN consultancy work, and give lectures. Only when I put the phone down did I realise that I was trembling from top to toe. I was twenty years of age again, vacillating between fear at what I had started and eagerness for its consummation.

Once again the ringing of a mobile phone claims our attention. Claire and I look at Dorothy who shakes her head saying, That's not my ring tone.

Claire goes into the kitchen and returns holding her phone which is dark and silent.

It must be yours, Lena, says Dorothy.

What? Oh yes. Must be, I open my handbag, tilting it towards me so that the other two can't see its interior. Reassuringly, it is lit by the blue glow of the phone's miniature screen. So I didn't put it in the fridge after all. And the sausages, I presume, are where they should be. Of course the ringing stops as soon as I take the phone in my hand but I see a message telling me I have two missed calls. The first message is from Dorothy reminding me of our promise to Claire and telling me to be ready when she calls at one thirty, the second is a fractured gabble in which I can make out only the names Paddy and Jean. When the blather finishes I return the phone to the bag and shrug, It was Nóirín. But I've no idea what she's saying.

You'd better call her back, says Claire.

Hmmm. Maybe, she doesn't phone me as a rule. I step out of the room to the hall and pull up Nóirín's number which I have filed under Gorgon.

She answers immediately, Lena? Did you get my message?

Yes but I couldn't make it out.

It's Paddy. He's had a heart attack.

He's *what? When?* I was talking to him only this morning. I grasp the banister for support as my legs crumple and, before I fall, twist myself around to plump down on a step.

A shadow closes over me and a muffled cry seems to come from a long way off, It can't be true. It can't be true. I'm doubled over, gripping the phone like a lifebelt. A babble of accusation in my head drowns out Nóirín's voice. In a flash I see Paddy stretched on the floor after his morning call to me, his arteries slamming shut. I close my eyes and try to inhale deeply, to summon calmness.

Finally Nóirín's voice comes through with her nurse's composure giving me the clinical details, He's in the Mercy, she says, I'm going back there now. Will you tell Jean? She didn't answer her phone and I didn't want to leave a message. I think you should both come down.

Yes of course.

Thank you. She hangs up.

I remain seated, my head pressed against the wooden stair rail at eye level with an ugly vase. Why does it look familiar? Slowly the picture forms in my head of Claire holding it when I arrived here. My hand itches to reach out and smash it.

The sitting room door opens and Dorothy's head appears, angled quizzically, eyebrows raised. Seeing that I am not on the phone she steps forward and touches my shoulder. What's up?

Paddy's had a heart attack.

She pulls back, startled. Where is he now?

The Mercy. In Cork. I need to find Jean and get us both down there. Saying it seems to draw some of the harm out of the crisis. The shadow lifts a fraction and I try to stand up.

I'll take you home.

Thanks. A spasm of dizziness rushes me and I sit again. I pause and shut my eyes.

You'd better come back inside for a minute. Claire is boiling the kettle. I'll help you up.

Jean may not be at home, I say, recalling the open door and darkness of her bedroom when I was leaving the house. I'll have to phone her, tell her what's happened and find out where she is.

Dorothy has her arm around my waist now as she guides me into the sitting room. Don't worry, we'll sort it out. I'll take you to collect Jean then bring the two of you home.

Thanks, I start to weep, partly with the relief of handing over to someone else. Bloody Paddy. Ironic, isn't it? I force a laugh past the tears. Probably did it deliberately to punish me.

That's a stretch, Dorothy smiles. Maybe he wasn't feeling well this morning and that's why he was bad-tempered.

He wasn't lacking in fire power.

Here, Claire hands me a cup of tea. Don't worry. He'll get the best of care. The nuns down there probably worship him.

I sip the hot sweet drink, wishing it was gin and say, Yes they'll be fussing over him like mother hens.

We're on the road to Pól's place which Jean has told me is in Poppintree. Injun country but Dorothy negotiates the network of streets with a confidence she attributes to the fact that it is Ken's VdeP chapter and she occasionally helps him with it.

Here we are, she announces, pulling up in front of a surprisingly trim townhouse. I open the car door then pause doubting this can be the place until I spy a WANTED poster for George W. Bush stuck inside the window. We're on target.

The neighbours must love that, I say.

Don't be worrying about the neighbours, replies Dorothy. Go and get Jean.

As I approach the door I read the legend under the mug shot, indicting Bush for 'Acts of Terrorism' which recalls an analysis I have read somewhere recently of the ill-advised and misnamed war. Several moments elapse before I realise that I am thinking of Richard's op ed. The shock of Paddy's collapse has driven me so far past the pale of my life that I have become an outsider looking in at it. Much as I am now looking through the rippled glass panes in the door of this strange house while the doorbell's chimes die away but summon no footfall. Has Jean left or was she having me on? I ring a second time, holding my finger on the bell so that the chimes multiply and jangle which brings heavy feet thudding towards me until the door is opened by a very tall, very black youth, dreadlocks coiled on his head and shoulders thick as a ship's cable.

I'm looking for Jean, I venture. A friend of Pól's?

The young man nods enigmatically then turning and walking back through the hall shouts up the stairs, Jean. It's your granny, in a Dublin accent you could cut with a knife.

Her *ondt*, actually, I say to his receding locks.

Sorry about that, says he flapping his hands but without a backward glance. And I'm the grasshopper.

Touché, I murmur.

Jean comes down the stairs, muddy tears streaming down her cheeks which in turn are turning red. She has become a child dismayed by pain.

Now suddenly I can be calm again. I reach out to hold her but she pulls away, hugging herself instead.

We'll go to Cork straightaway. You'll see your Dad in a couple of hours. Dorothy will bring us home.

Looking at once lost and angry she glances past me to the car and leaving the door swinging brushes past me down the path and lets herself into the back of Dorothy's car. I pull the door shut and follow her.

Chapter Seven

With Paddy only semi-conscious Nóirín, Jean and I are thrown together, wringing our hands and our hankies. Squeezed together, to be precise, around the bed, granted a moment of privacy by the intensive care nurse who pulled a set of short curtains around us to improvise a cubicle. I quail at the sight of the figure on the bed, dwarfed by a humming cheeping bank of machines. Nóirín smiles wanly at us until Jean falls sobbing into her arms making her cry too. I hang back, unsure where or how to look. After a couple of minutes Nóirín detaches herself from Jean's embrace and steps aside to allow me approach the head of the bed. The figure lying there, chest bared to accommodate the sensors attached to the heart monitor, is no longer my brother. He is a changeling, neither fully alive nor fully dead, and, disturbingly, in that suspended condition he has taken on a look of Father. I pull back in fear of this transitional creature.

Is he—? I ask, half-turned towards Nóirín, half-afraid to lose sight altogether of the figure in the bed lest it dematerialise or shift shape further.

Nóirín puts a finger to her lip as her head sways slowly and, touching my sleeve, she draws me out of the cubicle. I follow her from the ward to the corridor.

You mustn't speak about him in the room, she admonishes me. He can hear you.

Yes, of course, sorry, I mumble, chastened. I just got a fright.

We all did, she grimaces.

What happened?

He was in his office, writing an article. I brought him a mug of tea and a couple of minutes later I heard a crash, she pauses to swallow a sob. When I went in he was slumped over the desk. The mug had fallen on the floor.

Fresh tears start in her eyes.

No warning? He hadn't complained of feeling unwell?

Not a word, she spreads her hands helplessly. I don't understand it.

It's strange, especially when he was so careful of himself.

She twitches her head and narrows her eyes at me a moment, sifting my tone for sarcasm.

I sigh, too anxious to parry her suspicion but wondering if he had mentioned his early morning telephone call to me.

Who's treating him? I ask.

Barry O'Sullivan. He trained under Paddy, and in America. He's very skilled. Oh Lena, she breaks suddenly, I'm so scared. What if . . .? I mean I don't know what to do. Should I call the kids and tell them to come home immediately?

I put my arm around her while she gives way to her grief. I could never come to love this woman but her present distress cuts through all my reasons for disliking her. She rests her head on my shoulder and I see with a tick of sympathy the furrow of white where the brown dye in her hair has grown out.

Let's ask O'Sullivan, I suggest.

The murmur of voices followed by snatches of banter and the thin sound of a radio playing drift down the corridor. Nóirín detaches abruptly and straightens up as if to impress her boss. She swivels around and I'm not sure whether she's embarrassed at having been seen to give way to tears or at allowing herself be supported, if not exactly comforted, by me.

A well-built man in surgical scrubs approaches and she briskly pats her face with a balled-up tissue.

Everything all right, Nóirín? The surgeon asks on reaching us.

Fine, thanks, Barry, she gulps and rams the tissue up her sleeve. This is Paddy's sister, Lena.

Yes, he nods, his grey eyes giving me a cursory look before returning solicitously to Nóirín's tired face. I was just coming to check on him. He hasn't had any excitement or agitation has he? His glance darts towards me again.

I only just got here, I say defensively. My niece is with him now.

And twice as likely as I to agitate him, I think, if she repeats her earlier hysterics. I wonder what my sister-in-law has told O'Sullivan about me or does he always mistrust blood relatives who often come bearing ancient grudges and seeking reconciliations to clear their own consciences, or, convinced that they know better than any spouse or life partner, who, after all, did not share the patient's early and formative years, what he or she needs, start advising the doctor, or those who are simply undone by the prospect of losing a loved one who is intrinsic to their identity and childhood memories. Blood is more volatile and apt to boil than any other bodily fluid.

Good, he says. I'll take a look at him now. He opens the door to the intensive care unit and ushers us through closing it softly behind us.

Nóirín and I stand at the foot of the bed as O'Sullivan confers with the nurse in the station. When he returns to the cubicle Nóirín beckons Jean to her side, taking her arm and gripping it tightly. The girl turns her face, swollen and angry with crying, to her mother and is about to say something when Nóirín glares meaningfully at her and raises her finger to her lips, as she did to me. Jean looks across her mother's chest towards me, fear standing in her eyes. I try to arrange my features in a reassuring smile.

All this time O'Sullivan has been watching the monitor, arms folded, one hand raised to grip his chin in a pensive attitude. It seems to me that we three are holding our collective breath as he does so and that a word from him could change each and all of our lives. At last he turns to us with a grave but not, I think, fatalistic expression. He gestures to Nóirín to follow him and as I make to join her raises his palm to halt me then swings away and, cupping her elbow, squires her to the door of the room.

Humiliated by this dismissal, I remain standing at the foot of the bed, head bowed, staring at a thin pale blue waffle blanket. Ugly as it is, for its dingy holy Mary colour, it is an easier object to be looking at than my brother's altered face. Amplified by the anxious silence, the intermittent sounds of the room strike my ear with surreal force: Jean's repeated sniffling despite the package of tissues I have given her, the constant drone of machines punctuated by an occasional beep or ping, the squeak of rubber-soled shoes on the polished floor, the rustle of curtains being drawn, the gust of voices when the door opens, all merging to underpin the impromptu moans and whimpers of pain or hoarse cries for help from the patients around us. I shudder and my stomach cramps with fear. This is the ante-chamber to death. The machines will determine who takes the ferry and who will be wheeled to a workaday ward downstairs before being discharged to resume the scurry of life beyond these sterile walls.

I am improbably relieved to see Nóirín return before I sink any further into the mire of despond. The shock and this unnatural place have shaken my emotional bearings. She gestures to me and Jean to follow her out of the room. On the corridor again she tells us that the surgeon is satisfied with Paddy's progress and that, if I don't mind, she and Jean will go downstairs for a cup of coffee while I sit with Paddy.

Barry says you're not to speak to him, just sit with him.

Very well, I respond, not bothering to take offence at their distrust of me.

With that, Nóirín leads us back to the bedside. Jean seems to have lost any volition and slouches dully behind her mother who caresses her husband's limp hand and whispers, We'll be back shortly, Love. Lena will keep you company.

The muscles around his mouth flicker registering something, comprehension, discomfort or possibly acquiescence and, momentarily, my brother returns. I remove my coat and try to get comfortable in the chair beside the bed as Nóirín and Jean back out of the cubicle.

Overcome now by the collision of today's events, culminating in Paddy's collapse, the rush to the airport, then to the hospital, and the heat in this room, I'm tempted to stretch myself out beside him for a nap. The impulse is checked, however, by the arrival of a nurse in the cubicle. At least I think that's what she is although the blue pyjamas still confuse me. What ever happened to the authoritative creak of starched white uniforms? These girls look like mechanics. She checks his pulse, the drip and the urine bag before leaning over him to say quite loudly in his ear, You're doing rightly, Mr. O'Neill. His eyes flash open, testing the sincerity of her reassurance.

There you are, she confirms. You'll be grand soon.

His expression changes to one of childish trust and his eyes close.

The girl leaves and my vigil begins.

Seated here, watching my brother in effigy, I am reminded of the women who sat through the night with corpses down the country, stern and upright in their black dresses, hands planted on their knees or telling beads, their whispered prayers vibrating on the air. I had seen them attend at Mammo's coffin and my nineteen-year-old self had looked away from them, frightened by their stubborn faith, which seemed to reproach my youthful vanity, and by their look, which seemed to pass right through me, to the moment of my own death. To allay my own unease I later persuaded myself that they were credulous folk, not diviners of souls. But confronted now, again, by mortality, my memory instinctively casts about for a prayer such as those I once offered by rote and without reflection.

Sacred Heart of Jesus I place my trust in Thee, I murmur.

How well Mammo knew that we all reach for the comfort of old nostrums and supplications when we are powerless over circumstances. Her 'little prayer' was one of the first we learnt. She instructed us to say it every day and whenever we were in difficulty. During our summers in Kerry Paddy and I recited it, with the family rosary, every evening after supper. Once home, however, where there was no nightly rosary, I forgot about it. But not Paddy. He asked me once if I remembered it and I said yes but that I didn't say it.

I do, he told me with innocent fervour. Mammo said we should say it every day and then we'll be safe.

I know, I said. But I don't believe that.

That's a sin, he said. Something terrible might happen to you.

He looked so genuinely frightened that I relented and told him I did say it sometimes, just not every day.

Good. Relieved, he went back to sharpening his pencil as a way to defer doing his arithmetic homework.

Maybe that's why the 'little prayer' has resurfaced now, reflex of childhood and a time when we could be happy together. Away from the Parents for two months, we were made much of by our grandparents and put our rivalries aside enjoying the liberty we had to play with the local children, running wild 'like little heathens', as Mammo said.

The last time I said it was when Mossie died. Then too I kept vigil beside a hospital bed. He lay with tubes replacing his bodily functions, his features whittled by disease to those of a bird, his pallor waxen, his mind drifting in and out of

consciousness. My prayers then were despairing pleas so inter-
spersed with promises to atone for past lapses, offers of big
donations to our parish church, and resolutions to attend mass
regularly that I thought Jesus must surely stride into the room
and with one touch restore my dying husband.

Instead, Mossie, in his last moments of lucidity, turned to
me with a calm look to say, I'm going to God.

No, I cried and lurched forward to embrace him, as if I could
tussle with God for possession of him.

He nodded once, shutting his eyes. His breathing slowed,
labouring, as his lungs closed down with a final stuttering
exhalation. I seized his face, calling to him, searching his eyes
for a glimmer of expression but he had gone away. I held his
empty body until the heart, understanding that there was no
longer anyone there and no more oxygen to fill the pump, ran
down and the flesh began to cool. I released the body and,
stunned, sat waiting for him to return until someone came,
shut his eyes, folded his hands and drew me away. I protested.
Or a voice very like mine protested, saying he'll be back, he
won't leave me and our child. But behind that frightened commotion was the implacable awareness that he was dead and I
was alone.

For a time afterwards I clung to Mammo's little prayer as if
it were a line that might keep me afloat in the wild sea of grief
but it could not turn back the waves of sadness that overwhelmed me in my first year of mourning and so I let it go,
relinquishing belief in a personal God.

Although Mammo was devout, the author of religious pam-
phlets and translator of Pascal's *Pensées* into Irish, and Father's
brother, Denis, was a priest, working in San Diego, religion
played only a perfunctory role in our early lives. Rather like a
bodily function, praying was regarded as a private activity, not
a subject for general discussion. We dutifully attended Sunday
mass (in the thruppenny side aisle seats because Father balked

at paying sixpence for the ones in the main aisle), went through the rites of holy communion and confirmation, and learned at school that faith was our duty and our heritage, memorising the Catechism in the same way as we did our six times tables or reams of portry. What is this life if full of care indeed. In my first year at university I traipsed to Lough Derg with Dorothy and a few others, all of us imagining that a weekend of self-mortification, weak tea and black bread, would ensure success in our exams, and back again the following year, ostensibly in thanksgiving, but with a request for the next round of exams slipped in as a postscript. More of a jape than a pilgrimage.

Now Paddy is trying to impose the principle of self-mortification on the rest of us without the religious dimension. And look where it's landed him.

Poor Jean, in her distress at her father's illness, imagined that she might have been the cause of it. Our flight had been delayed by an hour, due, in the stock phrase, to the late arrival of the incoming aircraft, code for a cock-up at Cork Airport. I had chosen to fly because I felt too distracted and jumpy to drive and thought, wrongly as it turned out, that it might be faster than the train. Muiris, who was in London for the week-end, had offered to fly directly to Cork and meet us there but I had told him to wait until I saw Paddy, advice I began to regret as we dangled in the limbo of the departure gate. Jean and I had eschewed the traditional Irish pre-boarding meal of a pint of stout and opted for American style coffee and muffins instead. It was amazing to observe the effect of sugar on the child. She went from being morose and weepy to wanly smiling and even conversational.

Do you think Dad might have had his heart attack because I said he shouldn't get Republican support for his campaign?

Her first full sentence since Dorothy and I had collected her rendered me almost speechless with astonishment. I stared at her face which was blurred and grubby with tears, runny mascara and a frosting of muffin crumbs, attempting to tease some sense out of her words but none emerged.

I'm sure you didn't cause his heart attack, dear, I soothed. But what's this about his cosying up to the Shinners in pursuit of his campaign?

Oh I don't mean *those* Republicans. The Americans.

Hang on, I thought he was running for President of Ireland, not the US.

He *is* running for President here, she said earnestly through a mouthful of muffin, At least he wants to, so he was planning to go to America to meet some Republican Senator who might push Lacey to nominate him.

I tried to decide which part of that story was the most ludicrous, the idea that Paddy thought he could get an introduction to an American Senator or that the Senator would be arsed putting pressure on the Taoiseach to choose a presidential candidate.

What made him think he could succeed in that mission?

Lacey wants to help the undocumented Irish and she wants more American investment, so she's making a big thing of letting the air force planes land in Shannon, she heaved a big sob, I said it was wrong to let war planes come in here because of our neutrality.

The girl was revealing the colours that lay under all that black, and they were more interesting than I had given her credit for, What's in it for the American Senator?

He wants to run for president there in the next election.

And he'll need *Paddy's* support? I had to laugh although Jean took it amiss. Maybe she just doesn't have much sense of humour.

He could get the Irish vote. That's where the undocumented come in. And Lacey wants their families back here to vote for her. Win-win, she shrugged. Except for the people who get bombed in Iraq.

I didn't think your father was a political schemer.

He says you have to be if you work in a hospital.

I can see that but this is a bigger game, with all due respect to him. Besides, the President here is the puppet of the Government, not the other way around.

He wants to be an honest broker.

Briefly infected by the unsavoury whiff of international intrigue I began to wonder was my brother a pawn in some bigger CIA plot. Where did he find these Republicans?

They're doctors. He met them at a conference a few years ago. One of them is on the board of the hospital where Nora works. He and Mum were going to stay with her in a couple of weeks. I suppose she'll come home now too. And Pat and Mike.

The way the girl brightened at this prospect made me realise how lonely she has been since her siblings took off. She has probably also felt herself too much the focus of her parents' attention and concern.

I don't know. It depends how bad he is.

At that she dissolved in tears again.

You mustn't blame yourself, child. This could have happened at any time. He's in the best place now. How easily the platitudes trot out when there's really nothing to be said. They'll give him great care in the hospital, I add, borrowing Claire's optimism.

She allowed the tears to roll down her cheeks, refusing to accept my word. The beep of a message landing in her phone distracted her. After honking into a paper napkin, she read the message and an instant later her thumbs were pecking rapidly at the keypad, composing her response.

I glanced up at the TV and found myself face to face with our leader. The state of her is an unfortunate reflection of the state of the nation. A vulgar lump of a woman with a raucous laugh who calls the men around her boys. Rumour has it that she wields a foul tongue in private but she has the last laugh because on her watch the march of a nation has become a stroll in a glitzy suburban shopping centre. The idea of my brother grovelling to this ignoramus may be dispiriting but the idea of his co-opting some bellicose Republican to his cause is downright spine-chilling. With a bit of luck his heart attack might put paid to his presidential notions, and to his lectures on the nation's eating habits. If he pulls through he will have to lead a quiet life, as befits a man his age, and leave the rest of us in peace.

A murmur from the bed draws me forward and, defying O'Sullivan's injunction, I ask Paddy if he needs anything.

His eyes pop open, Mammy?

No, I shake my head, hoping he doesn't see my horror at the confusion. It's me, Lena.

I thought . . . he works his mouth as if it is parched.

Do you want some water?

He nods assent.

I lift the beaker from the locker and place the straw between his lips.

Gripping it, he begins to suck, his eyes wary.

A sob swells in me, I'm so sorry, Paddy, I splutter, so sorry. Distracted by my tears I forget to watch him until he taps my arm and I see that the straw has slipped from his mouth. Oh shit, sorry. Again, I grin foolishly. Do you want more?

No, he whispers, thanks.

I study the pale face in the bed but it confuses me. Brother, father, grandfather, which are you? I can't understand how Paddy's looks, once said to favour the Bradys, Mother's maternal family, the 'aristocratic' side, according to her, have acquired the shape of Father's and those of Mammo before him. Have those bones been hiding there the length of his sixty-five years waiting for this moment to reveal themselves? I imagine that gene promoting itself, replicating those con-tours, planes and sockets over and over, sketches towards the perfect unborn, a willed striving out past flesh and blood. Looking down at the prominent veins and swollen knuckles of my hands, already stiffening with the arthritis I have inherited from Mother, I wonder whose bones will manifest themselves when I am whittled down at the last. Of whom am I yet another rough draft? Whose unfinished business is mine?

Will Paddy return to himself after this dislocation? Or will he be changed forever? He changed once before. Even Mother felt she had lost him when he married Nóirín. She wore black to the wedding and looked sombre throughout. Apart from the odd evening when he would visit Mother on his way home from a meeting in Dublin we have scarcely since then seen Paddy without Nóirín scowling at his shoulder. I dismissed her as a possessive so and so. Mother called her a pushy nurse who had married up. Having wooed him away from a nice girl he had been knocking about with, she wasn't going to let him go. She wouldn't trust him. Mother had seen those nurse-wives among Father's colleagues, and the others who tried to lure the men away from their wives. When I asked her if she ever worried that Father would be seduced she looked affronted at the suggestion and said certainly not, that she had enough self-respect to trust him.

When Paddy married Nóirín he got a new dose of religiosity and lost his sense of humour, or at least became subdued and no longer the winsome, funny boy and entertaining young man he had once been. From the moment Mother returned from the Stella Maris maternity home, accompanied by a nurse carrying the swaddled infant, Paddy won the hearts of all who saw him, and I was sidelined. It must have been a year later I stood one day at the threshold of our nursery while Mother and the nanny, who had replaced the nurse, bathed him in a large pink enamel bath, admiring his teeny rosy toes, laughing when he made spluttery noises with his mouth, soaping and rinsing him gently all over. As I watched, a murderous envy bulged in me and on its impulse I rushed into the room like a bull, hurling my weight at the bath, toppling it off its stand and sending water sloshing over the nanny who jumped backward with a yelp. Mother screamed as she clutched Paddy's slippery body to her. Catching the signals of their fright and distress, he uttered a piercing wail. I began to cry then, angry and confused.

You little brat! Mother rounded on me when the initial crisis had subsided. What were you thinking of? You could have killed your baby brother. Do you hear me?

I didn't mean to, I blubbered not knowing what else to say.

Paddy's wails continued to rip the air.

Go to bed, Mother ordered. I'll deal with you in the morning.

I'm sorry, I hiccupped pleadingly and reached my hand towards my infant brother.

Don't you touch him, Mother screamed, eyes flashing with the rage of a tigress as she clasped him tighter and wrenched her body away from me. Go to bed, wicked child.

Thus I was excluded as he grew up, two pairs of resentful eyes flashing in my direction when I happened on him and Mother playing board games or doing jigsaw puzzles. I was even held responsible for the time Paddy hilariously disgraced Mother in front of her friends. A 'perk' of his favoured position was to accompany her on Saturday mornings for coffee with her friends in Switzers' basement. There, bought off with chocolate éclairs, he was made to sit demurely while the ladies nattered until the day when, rebelling against this constraint, he launched a volley of choice curses and swearwords that turned the air blue and jolted the ladies into horrified silence. Outraged, Mother hauled him away and told him that as a punishment he would never join her for morning coffee again. Well played, Paddy. I, however, was castigated for teaching him to curse but my small hoard of swearwords paled beside the range and hue of the expletives he had mastered.

He was popular with the young country girls, vetted and recommended by Mammo, who came to mind us as children. Usually from big families they played with us as they might have done with their little brothers and sisters. We, in turn, enjoyed their good-humoured laughing ways and with them we were carefree and rambunctious as puppies.

Will you bring me to the dance next Saturday? He asked one cockily.

Go on with ye, she grinned and chucked him under the chin. Ye'll have to wait a few years before ye'll be let in there. Ye'll be a smash hit with the girls when ye do go but.

She was right and Paddy didn't even have to go to the dancehalls to prove it. Not long after we had graduated from the nursery and begun to dine with our parents, whom we now addressed as Mother and Father, Paddy turned his attention to the maids. Agnes, a bright, lively girl, was not afraid of Mother. She knew how to be respectful without being subservient or sullen. Hers was one of those quick faces that looks ready to find the laughter in any situation. Whenever she and Paddy encountered one another on the landing or in the hall the air around them rippled with anticipation. Muffled giggles escaped through partially closed doors and around corners. I would catch sight of Agnes sometimes clipping a strand of her unruly hair back into place or straightening her uniform. Paddy developed a new interest in the vegetable garden, promptly offering to gather lettuce, raspberries or artichokes as Mother required. To my surprise Mother either did not notice this flirtation or chose to ignore it, notwithstanding the help she had had to give some of the maids whose dancing partners presumed too far. When I met Agnes many years later, running her husband's family butcher shop in Cahirciveen, she smiled at being reminded of Paddy's partiality to her and said yes, we had a good time. I never told him about the encounter, feeling sure he would be annoyed at the recollection of his dalliance with her and particularly with me for reviving the memory in her.

There were many things we never spoke about and now it may be too late. Chief among them were the rows that regularly poisoned the air of our home, a torment we lacked the words to frame. They erupted at night when Mother had drunk more than her usual quantity of brandy and seized on some inopportune comment of Father's to inveigh against him as the architect of all her frustrations. At first he would try to appease or silence her but eventually his temper got the better of him and they set to with the cruel spite of two intelligent, articulate people trapped in a cage of their own making.

I'm sick of you, Medicine Man, was one of her regular jibes. Go away.

I might just do that one day. Like your feckless father.

Leave him out of it, Mother snarled. Remember who made you. Without me you'd still be driving up boríns to treat tubercular mountainy men. Getting paid in prayers and poitín, like your father.

Better than dying in a gutter in the Bowery. You live on delusions bred of fantasy.

Hark at him, the aristocrat manqué! I want a divorce.

Don't be absurd.

I could have been playing in the concert halls of the world. But you lured me back to here with your talk of revolution. All over now.

One night when I was about thirteen and Paddy ten, as I lay in bed unable to block out the bitter argument going on beneath me, I heard a footfall and whimpering outside my door. Coming out to the landing I found Paddy creeping towards the stairs. He carried an old cardboard case, and was coaxing Bran to follow.

Where are you going? I hissed.

We're running away, he sobbed. But Bran doesn't want to come.

Wait, I stayed him with my hand on his arm.

That's not my Mammy, he wailed, shaking my hand off. I'm going away. I'm going to get the boat to Liverpool.

Don't be mad, Paddy, I said, worried now by his determined tone. You don't know anyone there. You've nowhere to go.

I hate them, he blubbered. They frighten me. I want my Mammy back.

I know, I know, I said. So do I. It'll be all over in the morning. Come in here. I took his hand and drew him towards my bedroom.

Head drooping he eventually allowed himself be led away. Bran followed us. Setting the old suitcase on the floor I put Paddy into my bed and knelt beside him stroking his head until he cried himself to sleep. After a few more salvos downstairs the shouting stopped when Father, in a last shot, said he had to go to work in the morning to earn the money to keep Mother in her stylish clothes and beautiful home, slammed the drawing room door and stumped up the stairs. For a time afterwards I heard Mother tinker at the piano and the sound of crying rise through the floorboards then I too lay on the bed, bundling the eiderdown over me for warmth, one arm curved protectively over Paddy asleep now and snoring lightly. With a sigh Bran sprang up and settled at our feet. The following morning, as usual, a brittle calm prevailed in the house, forestalling any reference to the previous night. The echoes of the row replayed themselves over and over in my head until I could not concentrate on school work or anything else. Paddy's reaction was to redouble his antics and pranks, demanding Mother's attention, as if by making her laugh he could see off the demon who terrified us on those awful nights. Although silenced by the unspoken taboo on mention of these rows,

Paddy and I flinched in unison if the Parents let fly a sharp exchange, our eyes meeting for a second, mutually haunted by dread of another outburst.

Once, in the nineties, when divorce legislation was the topic of the hour, and remembering those rows, I asked Mother would she ever have divorced Father.

She bridled at the suggestion. Certainly not. People nowadays have it too easy. Divorcing and setting up with new wives and husbands. On and on like changing dance partners. Where does it end?

Was there never a time you wanted to change partners?

I would not have allowed myself entertain such a thought, she said, her sniffy tone belying her words. What good would it have done? I saw the women who had left or been left. Objects of pity and gossip. Besides, I would have missed your father. And he me.

Indeed, when he died she had sat in her accustomed chair weeping and repeating, What will I do? What will I do? while Nóirín and I stood on either side of her like ministering angels. I stroked her back saying nothing, knowing all too well that words in such a situation are meaningless. Besides, Nóirín's attempts at consolation were jamming the airwaves.

Paddy kept that old cardboard suitcase, covered with stickers from hotels in Paris, Strasbourg, Turin, Venice, Madrid, Lisbon, Galway and Wexford, under his bed for years. At the outbreak of another row I would go to his room to prevent him taking the case, filled with games and chocolate bars, and trying to flee. We would sit together or try to play a game of cards until the storm blew over. The impulse to protect one another may have finally cost us that bond. Or would we have fallen away from one another naturally? I only know that after he stepped in to save me a rift opened between us, leaving him embarrassed and resentful on one side and me petrified and paranoid on the other.

It was a bad business, Paddy, I say aloud, without premeditation. I never . . . I mean . . . I didn't. I'm sorry.

The faintest of flickers disturbs his features. He can hear me.

A tap on my shoulder startles me back and I glance around
the cubicle. Nóirín and Jean have returned from the coffee
shop.

Why don't you take a break now, Lena? says Nóirín.

I nod, still disorientated by the vividness of my memories
and rise slowly to leave the room. But before I do, I reach for
Paddy's hand and clasp it, feeling an answering clasp from his.

Chapter Eight

What's this? Groundhog Day? Am I snagged in a loop of eternal recurrence or stuck on a hurdy-gurdy making its second go-round? Maybe the past forty-eight hours were a bad dream brought on by indigestion (Claire might have had a point about the cheese) or, in all likelihood, God is having a good laugh at my expense because here I am again, in the early evening dark, under pours of rain, thwarted in my attempt to park outside my own house by Bernie Murphy-Benz's sleek machine. Lo and behold, as if to prove me right, there to greet me in the lane are Feargal Murphy-B, and his lopsided friend, mooching again under the self same company-issue golf brolly.

Apologies, Lena, Feargal opens my door and hoists the brolly like a flag to mark my return while his friend retreats for cover to the back gate, where he hunches glumly. We didn't expect you home so soon, he escorts me around the car to the boot from which he removes my carry-on bag. How's Paddy?

Out of the woods, thanks, I begin to pick my way between the puddles to the end of the lane.

Phil, can you bring the torch? Feargal calls over his shoulder.

His friend detaches himself from the doorway and falls into step on my other side, so that for an instant I feel as though I have been arrested.

When Feargal introduces us Phil smiles slowly and shakes my hand. At least I think it's a smile but it's hard to be sure in this light.

We meet at last, says he.

Yes, say I ritually although I don't recall having expressed any desire to meet him or hearing that he longed to meet me. Ill or well met now, we plod down the lane, following the unsteady track laid by the beam of his torch.

I gather you're Muiris Carmody's mother, says my new acquaintance, whose accent has a peculiar pinched quality. I imagine his lips pursing as if he is extruding the words like prisms and prunes.

Yes. Why do you ask?

He was a few years behind me in college. Or maybe I should rephrase that, he gives a half-laugh that might even be a snigger, I was a few years above him.

I glance at Feargal wondering where he found this uppity arsehole but I can't read his response in the shadows.

'Above', I echo his verbal pinch, So, did you look down on him or he up to you? I am too tired to make an effort with this designing fellow.

Nothing like that, another half-snigger, we were in different camps. He's Rococo. I'm Mieisian. He pauses as we turn into the avenue and under the glow of the street lamp fixes me with a donnish look over the top of his glasses, begging me to ask him what he means.

You don't say. Well, I'm weary and hungry.

I think Bernie mentioned our little scheme to you, says Feargal, sensing my irritation.

Indeed and it sounds like quite an ambitious project.

Well it's only at the conceptual stage, cautions Phil, there's a lot more work to do. I'll bring over some drawings to show you the outline.

Not tonight if you please. I have rather a lot to deal with at the moment.

We wouldn't dream of it, says Feargal, We understand completely. Any time in the next couple of weeks will do.

Yes but we need to start the work after Easter, Phil prompts him, when the weather is fine.

Feargal unlatches my gate, ushers me through and accompanies me up the steps to the front door, while crooked Phil proceeds parallel to us along the Murphy-Benz's path.

I hope Phil didn't upset you, Feargal mutters while I look for my key. He's just very keen, once he gets the bit between his teeth.

No doubt, say I, suppressing my doubts for the moment. I'll let you know when I make a decision. I open the door and half-stumble across the threshold, so eager am I to be inside and pull up the drawbridge. I turn to take my bag from Feargal and, seeing his hangdog expression, am almost moved to give him a tip. Instead I say, there are a lot of ramifications to this idea. I'm not sure it's right for you, me or the terrace.

Phil will do a good job. He knows his stuff.

And the planning officer, according to Bernie.

Yes. A valuable asset, Feargal smiles approvingly.

Has he designed anything I might know?

His firm did some of the redevelopment down in the Docklands. Mixed use buildings, offices, apartments and retail. He's good at marrying the old and the new. Excellent finish too, Feargal flows happily into salespeak.

A smart businessman, Feargal started out working as a mechanic in a garage near the North Strand, bought it when the boss retired, built it up, sold it, and so on, through another garage and second-hand car dealership, all the way up to the Mercedes agency. Now it seems he's on the lookout for a new and bigger deal.

I need to sleep on all of this, I temporise. What I really want is to soak for half an hour in a hot bath, sipping a glass of wine then fall into bed, conk out and forget crooked Phil, the Murphy-Benzes, their loony plan and the whole darn sleeve of care.

Feargal nods. Sure. I'll send Bernie around with Tanta.

Thanks, I say, covering my reflexive wince with a too-wide smile. I don't feel able for Bernie Murphy-B and her brisk chatter right now, but I do want Tanta's company, to ruffle the stillness of the house.

In my bedroom the red light of the answering machine winks insistently. There are seven new messages. I press play and, while the tape runs, start to peel off my travel-worn clothes.

Hello. Hello. Lena? Ned, here. Breaking news. Midnight meetings most strange. Our friends. You know of whom. Transatlantic calls. Argy bargy. Don't want to say too much on the tellyphone. Discretion you know. When you—

Not just now, Ned. I press stop. It feels creepy, even vaguely indecent, to undress to the sound of his breathy voice, albeit coming from a machine. Whatever ails him can wait till the morning. I strip down to my underwear, shuddering with cold and exhaustion.

Last night was the first I had ever spent in Paddy and Nóirín's home and sleep evaded me there till dawn. On previous duty visits to Cork I had stayed in a hotel, to spare Nóirín the 'trouble'. As soon as Nóirín's car pulled into the drive the front door opened, as if by remote control. Before I could marvel at her gadgetry, however, a woman's shape appeared in the wedge of light from the hall. A kindly neighbour I presumed, until, as I approached the door, I found myself facing a replica of my sister-in-law. I glanced from one to the other wondering had Nóirín cloned herself.

You remember my sister Eileen, said Nóirín, evidently registering my confusion.

Ah, yes, of course, I shook the twin's hand. When we moved into the full light I saw that she was slightly better preserved and dressed than her sister. Where Nóirín is grey and wispy Eileen is peroxide and neat but had I met her alone on the street I would have greeted her as Nóirín. I remembered the confusion she had caused at the wedding when, although she was in bridesmaidenly apricot, a colour that did nothing for her, people congratulated her as if she were the bride.

You must all be worn out, Eileen ushered us into the sitting room where a small fire burned in the grate. The kettle is boiled. I'll wet the tea. Her Cork lilt was compromised by a dour Brummie cadence.

Jean slouched up the stairs.

Would you rather a coffee, Jean? Eileen called after her.

No thanks, the girl mumbled and continued climbing.

Leave her be, Nóirín nodded. She's very upset.

Well you and Lena will have a cuppa and a sandwich I'm sure, Eileen breezed.

I'd prefer a glass of brandy if you have it, said I.

Eileen glanced at Nóirín, who responded with a fleeting moue. Eileen left the room and returned a few minutes later with a tea tray. When she set it down on the coffee table I spied a brandy snifter barely stained with amber liquid.

Are you stuck for brandy? I asked. Because if you are I'll go out and get some.

After another ocular exchange Eileen turned on her heel and exited. This time when she returned she planted the bottle in front of me and made to remove the glass that was more than half empty. I stayed her hand. I'll keep the glass, if you don't mind.

With something close to a harrumph she released her grip on the glass. I placed it on the table beside the bottle and poured a good measure for myself. Would anyone care to join me? I held the bottle aloft, magnanimous in my relief at getting hold of it.

Tea is all I need, said Nóirín wearily.

And I, said Eileen smugly.

Looking at her now I saw that the smugness and primness were part of the shell she had created to preserve her dignity.

She had worked in England and had married a widower, some years older than her who already had several grown-up children. When he died seven years ago his children inherited the house and promptly evicted her. At the time Paddy consulted me for advice but there was little I could do beyond contacting an English solicitor, who persuaded the stepchildren to give her a small ex gratia payment. Paddy and Nóirín had taken her in until she found work as a book keeper in a hotel by the railway station and took a small flat in the same vicinity.

We sat in silence for a time until I began to wonder whether the two women were communicating telepathically. That was no reason for me to stay mute, all the more reason for me to speak up, so I remarked, If Paddy pulls out of this I hope he'll call off his presidential campaign.

Why should he? Eileen turned sharply to me.

Too much stress and exhaustion would be bad for him I should imagine.

He won't give up, said Nóirín. He's put a lot of work into the campaign already. He knows he can't count on your support but there are plenty of others he can count on. She underlined that jibe with a curt nod.

I don't doubt it.

He'll make a fine Ucktoron, Eileen squared her shoulders as if standing to attention.

You are incredible Lena, do you know that? Nóirín whipped around to face me. There's your brother lying in a hospital bed after a myocardial infarction and all you can worry about is yourself.

I never mentioned me.

You only care about what your fancy friends in Dublin think. That's why Paddy left the place. To get away from the cocktail party circuit and gossip.

Even Eileen looked shocked at this attack.

And there I was thinking he came to Cork for work and stayed for love, I parried. He was quite the star of the cocktail party circuit in his heyday. In fact I met an old pal of his recently, Tim Gallagher, still lamenting his departure to the deep south. They were in school and college together. And I met Tim's new young missis who is madly pregnant.

There you are. That's what I mean. Tittle tattle. That's your life, Lena.

Is that really what you think, Nóirín, or are you just jealous?

I think it's time for bed now, said Eileen, standing up. We've all had a long day.

Some of us have, said Nóirín, but she . . . she, pointing at me, she didn't even cry when she saw Paddy. It might suit her if he dies. Then she won't have to divide their mother's estate.

Only that tears were running down her cheeks at this stage I might have laughed. You're being preposterous Nóirín, I said, but I'll put it down to shock.

He was dead. Do you know that? His heart stopped beating for a few seconds. I saw him.

Her words had the force of blows. She was standing over me now. Did you hear me? He was dead! Dead. Do you understand?

I tilted my head to look up into her face. Fear and rage contended in her small grey-blue eyes.

I'm sorry, I said. I didn't know. I don't want my brother to die. Whatever you might think.

Eileen moved in to hold her sister. Two matching pairs of eyes looked down reproachfully on me.

You're right, it's time for bed, I poured another drop of brandy into the glass and stood, Good night. I hope you both get some sleep. Taking the glass with me I went to the door, paused and glanced back to ask which bedroom I should use. The two women stood entwined, Nóirín weeping and leaning into Eileen, who tenderly swept damp strands of her sister's hair from her temple. I glanced quickly away. These united sisters had no need of me. I was alone.

Lena, Eileen called in a low voice.

I hesitated and waited for her to speak without looking around.

I made up a bed in the boys' room. First right at the top of the stairs.

Thank you, I nodded, still with my back to her. Once in the hall I paused to steady myself, took another swig of brandy, picked up my overnight bag and climbed the stairs.

Seated on my own bed now, I am midway through peeling off my tights when the doorbell goes. Bernie didn't waste any time bringing Tanta around. I hope he hasn't blotted his copybook or anything else while he was visiting. I finish removing the tights, drag on my dressing gown and go down to answer the door. Enter Bernie avec picnic basket, followed by Orla, her nine-year old daughter, carrying Tanta, and Malachi, her seven-year old son, bearing the dog's cushion and bowl. The dog casts me an indignant look, prompted, I suspect, by the big pink ribbon tied around his neck.

Thank you dear, I say, taking him in my arms from which he immediately struggles to be free. He looks very smart in his bow.

We gave him a bath, says Orla, he was a bit stinky.

After we took him for a walk on the beach, Bernie nudges her daughter.

No, Mum, Orla shakes her head.

Malachi looks gravely at her, a sweet little boy still in awe of his bossy big sister.

Hard to credit that there was once a time when Paddy had the same admiration for me. What a difference sixty years makes. No doubt some day Malachi too will cease to admire his sister.

Yes, Orla, Bernie is saying emphatically, and he rolled in the sand.

But Mum you said—

Thank you, Orla, Bernie widens her eyes meaningfully at the little girl then turns to me with an apologetic smile, Sorry, Lena. You must be exhausted. Feargal says Paddy is comfortable now.

He looked better this morning, more alert. The medicos agree that he'll make a full recovery if he takes it easy.

How's Nóirín? She must have had an awful shock, Bernie gives a little shudder, placing herself for a moment in Nóirín's brogues.

Bearing up. The nurse's training helps.

Good, she relaxes and, proffers the basket. I brought you some roasted tomato and basil soup, multiseed brown bread and liver pâté, just to save you cooking tonight.

You're too good, thank you, I take the basket and suddenly, tapped by that act of kindness, the troubling emotions of the past two days overwhelm me to the point that I want to hug my kindly little neighbour. Beneath all the flim-flam and glamour Bernie has the heart of a countrywoman, although she wasn't long about kicking the muck of Offaly off her heels.

Not at all, she shakes the golden bell, I was cooking for us anyway. Oh and I popped in a half bottle of burgundy too, for the digestion, she laughs.

You're a brick.

Don't bother washing the boxes. I'll get them tomorrow and I'll bring over Phil's plans. I'm sure you'll like them.

Aha! That pill was well and truly sugared.

We'll see, say I, with a mental reservation to be out all day. Thank you for the hamper, and for minding Tanta, I add, looking at the children.

Perhaps because he has heard his name, the dog comes bounding up from the kitchen, his pink bow in flitters.

Oh Tanta, you naughty puppy, exclaims Orla, have you eaten your ribbon?

Enchanted with himself, Tanta hurtles around the hall before making a lunge at his cushion, which Malachi still clutches.

Sit! I command but he ignores me and continues his skite, showing off now that he has our attention.

Malachi moves closer to his mother, who strokes his curly head, emboldening the little boy to say, I'll just put Tanta's cushion and bowl here. He lays the items carefully side by side on the floor then, stepping back, tells me, You have to keep it filled with fresh water.

That's right, I smile, Thank you for reminding me. I'll do it straightaway.

Okay, kids, let's leave Lena and Tanta to have their dinner in peace. Say good bye.

Bye-bye Tanter, the children's call brings the dog racing towards them, tail wagging in anticipation of treats.

Sit! I try again and this time the dog obeys and plumps down, ready to receive a cautious pat on the head from each of the children. I think he wants to go home with you, say I.

He can visit another time, says Bernie, a shade too quickly. Good night, Lena. She touches my arm and they are gone, into the rainy night, Orla holding Malachi's hand as they descend the steps.

Although the children were here only a few minutes the house feels colder and darker without them. It is an effect I have noticed before, when they have come to help decorate the Christmas tree or hunt for Easter eggs in the garden. When they are gone the quality of the silence in these empty rooms changes to the hollow note of absence. I face the shut door behind which only half an hour ago I was happy to retreat from Feargal, Phil and the rain but which now seems to divide me from life, so much so that I imagine opening it and calling Bernie and the children back. Restraining that impulse, I hook up the security chain and, force of habit, glance into the letter-box where I spy an envelope. Junk mail I presume. If it's more publicity for crocOgold I shall write to the leprechaun, threatening to injunct him and his agents against entering my property with their cheap flyers full of empty promises.

Retrieving the envelope, I see that it has already been opened and hastily sellotaped shut again. A scrawled note on the front: Lena. This came to us by mistake. Enjoy the dinner! Moira K. P.S. What do you think of the Murphies plan? Ill pop in for a chat someday. The devil take the wily Kielys. Just the price of them to open my post. Hoping for money or gossip. They're as rich as Croesus but wouldn't spend Christmas, bought their house for a song from Mrs. Crawford, a Protestant lady whose father had been in the Indian Civil Service and whose husband had fought in the Boer War. Her son died at Ypres in 1915 and her daughter had schizophrenia and spent most of her life in an institution. After the Major died, Mother would invite Mrs. Crawford to join us for Sunday lunch and called in to see her now and again until the old lady went a bit dotty and refused to answer the door, shouting through the letter box at her to go away. The poor woman ended her days in one room of the house, peeing into a bucket and sharing her food with the mice. That's when the Kielys turned up, and succeeded in cajoling her to sell, with the promise that she could live out her days there, surrounded by her parents' tarnished Benares brass and her husband's and son's war medals. When they eventually moved in they did some basic renovations, converting each floor to a flat, letting the garden and ground floor ones and occupying the top floor themselves. They also jerry-built a mews at the back which, while it may set a planning precedent for mine, is certainly not a model for it.

I glance at the envelope again. And the hell with the Murphy-Bs too. A hedge instead of a fence to make good neighbours: even if I say no, the plan goes ahead, on the Kielys' side but if they and I both want in, the project expands and it's moolah all round, including a handsome fee for Phil the Pill. The rub for me is that if I object they in turn will object to my plans, of which as yet they are ignorant. Checkmate.

Ah, no they don't. This is one provocation too many. I clench my hands, crumpling the envelope feeling an old, long-dormant, defiance steal over me. Under its influence muscles brace, belly tightens and mind hardens around my refusal. Emphatically NO. They've picked the wrong lady to push around. At my feet Tanta whines, catching the scent of my defiance. Yep, boy, I say, we've got a fight on our hands. I rip open the envelope and pull out an invitation card embellished with the starry circle of the EU and a stylised harp, plus a gratuitous greasy thumbprint, courtesy of Moira Kiely I'll warrant, requesting the pleasure of the company of Madeleine Carmody & Partner at a dinner given by the Association of European Lawyers. I'd almost forgotten the two-day conference on migrant workers' rights at which I am to chair a session. The mention of dinner brings me back to my empty stomach. Did Bernie mention wine? I drop the letter onto the seat and stoop to inspect the hamper. Sure enough, there's a half bottle of Nuits St. Georges nestled between the boxes of food, its cork part-drawn for my convenience. Let's go, Tanta, I call and, lofting the picnic basket in the crook of my arm, descend to the kitchen.

An hour later, restored by Bernie's fine fare, I climb the stairs to tour the house and check that all is in order before retiring. Although, as Muiris pointed out, and Paddy is apt to forget, I own this house, it has never felt like mine. Indeed, I am surprised to find myself still here. First stop on my tour of inspection is the office. Once Father's bolthole and now mine, it still feels like a headmaster's study. Even yet I feel the stern gaze of Polyphemus, the grotesque old model of the eye, which since my earliest memories had kept watch from the top of a bookcase, seeming to endorse Father's reproofs when I was in trouble at school or my exam results disappointed him.

There is a slightly musty chill here tonight but seeing the red light on the answer machine beckon I sit at the desk and press play.

Hello? Lena? Sorry. Ned. Again. I seem to have run out of time to speak so to speak. Must be more succinct. Yes. Certain goings-on afoot. Give me a tinkle when convenient. Pip pip.

Hi Lena, Dorothy speaks in a low voice, just wondering how Paddy is. Give me a call when you get back.

Lena? Lena? Ned here. Sincere apologies for disturbing you again. I just heard about Paddy on the Nine O'Clock News. Most distressing indeed for you and all the family. I hope he's recovering. We might speak about the other matters. In due course, of course. Semi-semi-urgent.

Lena, hi. Thanks for helping yesterday. I'd never have managed on my own. I'm so sorry about Paddy. It's very upsetting for you all. I'm sending lots of positive thoughts your way and out to the universe. Ring me when you feel like talking. Lots of love.

Claire and her voodoo. Still, can't do any harm I suppose.

Hullo there. Thought you might be home by now. Hope Paddy's pulling through. Take care of yourself too. Talk soon.

Since resuming contact a month ago Richard and I have maintained a cautious electronic to and fro, each of us taking the measure of the tension in the other between the desire for intimacy and the need for independence. Underpinning my wariness is a matrix of romance, apprehension, mixed memories and curiosity. While we speak with the ease of old friends I am unable to put the questions that now trammel my mind. They belong to a different species of communication, one where we have learnt to trust one another again, inching step by step along the high wire, not glancing down, not fearing the answer, not flinching at the truth. Tall order.

Upstairs I run the bath and while I wait for it to fill cross the landing to check on the bedrooms, with Tanta, ever inquisitive, scampering ahead of me. Moonlight pools coldly on the pale green bedspread in the Parents' old room. I close the curtains for no good reason other than to create a little bustle of movement and human warmth. After Mother's death I removed the commode, the walking frame, medicine bottles and other paraphernalia associated with her illness but I continue to put flowers or, at this time of year, a sprig of berries, in the vase on her dressing table. A wisp of life, or a homage to appease her spirit.

From there I move to Paddy's old room. Holy God! A nervy tingle runs like a horde of ants from my scalp all the way down my legs. The place has been burgled. I blink fast in the hope that my eyes are deceiving me. I even attempt a little prayer but get stuck trying to think of the patron saint of tidiness. Only Jude, the go-to man in hopeless cases comes to mind. No go. The chaos remains. The duvet trails from the bed and one pillow has been tossed in a corner. There is a dark heap on the floor that for one icy moment I imagine is a body. Tanta launches himself onto it with a growl, sending garments left and right before settling down to chew what might be a tee-shirt. A mug lying on its side on the floor has leaked a coffee stain onto the carpet. One of Mother's best Waterford crystal wine glasses stands perilously close to the edge of the bedside locker. The Parents' dressing gowns are tangled in the duvet. When the initial shock subsides I remember that Jean now occupies this room and, it would appear, her young man is making himself at home here too.

Telling Tanta to drop the tee-shirt I stoop to pick up the fallen mug. As I do my eye lights on a flash of bright orange under the bed. Tanta follows my look, dives under the bed and starts to worry at the object. I am about to call him off when the sound of the bathwater breaks on my ears. Still holding the

mug, I run to find high tide lapping the rim of the bath. I have
to release some of the water, which is now tepid because the
tank is empty, before I can step in. Immersed, I recline, loosen-
ing my limbs in the water as if putting down a burden, and
wait for the steam to purge the irritants from my head. I sink
further into the water as far as my chin. The steam condenses
on the walls blurring the turquoise paint. Slowly the colour
changes, rusting to orange. I snap bolt upright splashing water
all around and crying Guan-fucking-tanamo! Once out of the
bath I drag a towel around my dripping body and run to Jean's
bedroom. There indeed it is, spreadeagled on the floor where
Tanta, having dragged it out, abandoned it: a US prison-issue
jumpsuit. Revulsion and panic churn in me. The very sight of
the ugly costume feels like an intrusion in my home. My reflex
is to call the guards but there is nothing else amiss and they
wouldn't be able to answer the questions I have such as am
I harbouring an escaped prisoner or what kind of cuckoo do I
have in my nest. Pól the peacemaker is behind it, I'll warrant.
Maybe the dope thinks it would be a clever outfit for a fancy
dress party. I'll put paid to that. Down on hands and knees I
look under the bed where once Paddy kept his running-away
suitcase, to see if there are any more offensive objects there.
Nothing but dust and a balled-up sock. I roll the hideous
garment up and, glancing around at the soot black bundle of
Jean's clothes on the floor wonder why she wants to erase
herself so utterly. I am tempted to dump them with the jumpsuit but instead find myself picking them up, one by one,
folding each item and placing it in a drawer. Finally I carry the
Parents' dressing gowns back to their room and return them to
the hooks behind the door. I remove the glass and set it with
the mug on the table outside the door where I will see them
in the morning as I go downstairs. I perform these little tasks
without thinking but once back in my own room I pause for a
moment feeling displaced. I miss the girl who once lived here.

She is gone and the one who stands here now is lonelier than she would dare to admit. The chill she feels is not just the cold air on her humid flesh but the shades of lost ones. They have brushed against Paddy. Another layer of darkness encroaches.

I sit on the bed and pick up Mossie's photo. Most of all I miss him, just his presence, his calm reasoning tone when I got carried away, his caress, his laugh, his competence and enthusiasm for new things. We had our points of divergence too but most of the time we managed to accommodate for them. Like Mother on Father's death, I was overwhelmed by a sense of helplessness when he left me. Now sometimes I pray to him in the belief, or hope, that he is watching over me. He always did say he had to pray for the two of us. He adhered more devoutly to his faith and its forms than I did, taking it seriously enough to be a daily communicant. I respected his spiritual constancy but I never envied it. The emphasis on sin oppressed me and the simpering passivity of the Mother of God, vaunted as a model to young women was more infuriating than admirable not least when I considered the uncharitable snootiness of the nuns who educated me. Lest I give scandal, however, especially when Muiris was a child, I obliged Mossie by going to mass on a Sunday. I had even agreed to being churched a medieval practice that we had expected Vatican II would do away with, along with the raising of the ban on contraception and permission for priests to marry. Instead we got the mass in English and the priest facing towards us rather than away. Small beer. Mother too had insisted that I submit to the humiliating ritual notwithstanding that she disdained it as much as I did. Her view was that it cost nothing to go through with it, metaphorically holding my nose or crossing my fingers behind my back, and that it was not worth having a row over. I could not tell her that the only reason I acquiesced was that Mossie abstained from having sex with me until I had been 'purified' after childbirth. He was resolute in the face of my objection that it was arrant nonsense knowing that desire would get the better of me, which it did. In the same way he had known four years beforehand that I would come to love him, although on first acquaintance I found him brash and overbearing.

Often my adversary in court, he fought with determination, as if the cases mattered personally to him, which perhaps they did because he was a sole practitioner, a blow-in, presuming to get business in a small, vicious closed circle. It was after one such case in the Circuit Court, a workman's compensation claim where my team was for the plaintiff, that he persuaded me to like him better. Our side had lost because Mossie's private investigator had seen our client go up a ladder to fix a leaky gutter on his house. I was livid, with Mossie and with our client for being such an idiot. To compound my frustration after the day's hearing when I came out of court I found that the front tyre on my bicycle was flat. I was searching in my brief case for the puncture repair kit when Mossie, passing by, remarked, Not your lucky day, is it?

No, I snapped and continued to hunt for the kit. I could sense him standing nearby, watching my irritated scrabble in the bag, which, making me self conscious, redoubled my annoyance.

You should have won, he said.

What? I swung around.

You had a good case.

Until you destroyed it.

Not all our fault, he raised his eyebrows, waiting for me to acknowledge the facts.

Very well, yes, our man was stupid to go up the ladder. We believed what he said about his pain.

I'm sure he is in pain.

If he is he's not going to get much relief from it now.

Tell you what, he said in a change of key, why don't you come uptown and help me buy a birthday gift for my niece?

What? It crossed my mind to wonder had he been drinking.

I don't think you're going to find that repair kit and it'll be dark soon. You could leave the bike here for the night and in the morning I'll come in early and fix the puncture for you.

Is that by way of an apology for winning the case? If it is I'm not interested in being patronised. You can't win them all. That's the way things go.

Not really, he smiled, But it's been a long and frustrating day and that's another let down for you, he pointed to the flat tyre. It won't look so bad in the morning.

I glanced around the grey yard where dusk was gathering with the smell of sooty smoke from the nearby tenements. Pigeons, and gulls blown in from the river, pecked for food between the paving stones while our colleagues in their dark suits and overcoats started up their cars, mounted their bicycles or walked in twos and threes towards the quays, going homeward with banter and cheery calls of good night. I had a picture of myself still there, alone, struggling angrily with the tyre when the street lamps came on and the watchman prepared to lock the gates, and sighed with defeat.

Fair enough, you win, I smiled reluctantly. Again. How old is your niece?

Four. Let's go quickly before the shops shut. I know a good place on Dame Street.

As we walked he told me about his niece, his sister's daughter, who lived in Canada.

I need to get her something I can post. If I send my sister money for her she'll just buy clothes.

What about puppets? Or fuzzy felt? Books?

You see, I knew it was a good idea to bring you with me, he smiled and cupping my elbow guided me into a long narrow shop which jangled and clanged with the racket of mechanical and clockwork toys.

By the time we emerged from the shop, carrying a brown paper package of gifts, I knew it wouldn't be long before he invited me out on a date and that from there we would become a couple. I felt completely at ease in his company and, as he drove me home, I had a flash forward of us seated just so in ten years' time. The more I thought about him the more I acknowledged that my initial dislike of him had come from envying his easy self-confidence, forgivably mistaken for arrogance but which, as I came to know him better, I discovered was the certainty of an unwavering moral compass. One that I could do with now to guide me through the quagmire of demands from my brother and my neighbours, not to mention the lovebirds in my nest.

Chapter Nine

Isn't this exactly the kind of place you'd expect Mary Lacey to like? Dorothy casts a disdainful eye around the Dish and Spoon.

Yes, I follow her look. There is something uncomfortably familiar about the ugly hodgepodge of the décor. Its vulgarity goes with her personality, I add.

Sorry girls, Claire heaves a sigh as she re-joins us, I didn't have time to put on my make-up before I left home. The loos here are very confusing – all mirrors so you don't know whether you're coming or going.

The Lacey effect, Dorothy and I laugh together.

Is she here? Claire swivels around.

No. Lena and I were just saying the place is like her.

It's not *that* bad, Claire frowns.

It would be better if we got some service.

Where's your niece's friend?

I don't know. I have chosen the restaurant precisely to see Pól in action and because he assures me it's excellent, kissing his fingertips and shutting his eyes, in a breezy parody of a soi-disant connoisseur. It also happens, he says, to be our Chieftainess' favourite hostelry. He said he'd be on tonight.

Two minutes later Pól appears, looking surprisingly handsome in a pristine white shirt and black trousers, his long red hair tied back in a plait.

144

Hi Lena, he greets me affably. He distributes menus while I introduce him to the Bagettes, with whom he shakes hands, before giving me the wine list, muttering, Mary Lacey likes Chilean wine.

Chateau Pinochet, no doubt. We'd hate to deprive her.

I'll leave you for a minute to choose your dinner, he bows as he withdraws.

He seems a nice lad, says Dorothy. Well brought up.

He's a bit full of himself, I say, I just wish he'd cut his hair.

Just be glad he's not your son.

He might as well be, I carp, he seems to be living in my house. But I can't tell Paddy that because he disapproves of him. Apparently he calls him a conceited idler, and blames him for egging Jean on to egg the Minister for Education.

I hope it was free range, Claire laughs at her own foibles. Still, that's hardly a hanging crime.

True, I think he's harmless but I feel like I'm harbouring a criminal. He's a good cook, though. I'll give him that.

That's useful, says Dorothy.

Does he get ideas here? Claire looks dubious.

Not really, he's into slow food.

As in slow to cook or slow to eat?

Slow to cook and late to eat, I laugh. When he's the chef I'm not allowed to so much as peel a carrot.

Afraid you'll do it too fast, says Dorothy.

Probably. It's a ritual with him whereas Lady Jean can barely open a tin of beans.

A month into Jean's tenure I have come to accept that Pól is part of the package, as is his sister, Siobhán. To my surprise Jean had returned from Paddy's bedside three days after me, saying that Siobhán had managed to swing an interview for her at the online investment company where she works. My nose had twitched at that news and I had to stifle the groan that threatened to escape from me when she named it. CrocOgold seems to be the only game in town. Now she is busily writing the leprechaun's press releases while Siobhán manages the website. Geraghty has the smarts to get them young, pay them pennies and dangle the promise of big dividends on their shares when the company hits the billion euro mark. Any day now, he says. Not wanting to scupper Jean's first job I have kept my misgivings to myself. Besides a couple of moles in the crock might be useful. Siobhán, who often gives Jean a lift to the industrial estate where Geraghty has his money factory, is a chatty little article. Although running a youth hostel hadn't been in my plans, the kids' comings and goings reanimate the house which, without my noticing, had slipped from being a home to at least six people with frequent guests, callers and parties, into the chilly torpor of disuse.

Oh dear, this is a bit like being in an Indian restaurant, says Claire, gnomically.

Do you mean the décor? I turn my attention again to the eye-straining mix of garish flowered and striped wallpapers. Where have I seen that combination before?

I mean I can't see anything that I would want to eat. Maybe I'll ask for a boiled egg.

Don't be ridiculous, Dorothy exclaims. Have the pasta.

I'm off wheat at the moment.

What's wrong with wheat?

I read an article saying it's bad for you.

The sooner you give up reading all the trashy magazines in Dr. Smith's waiting room the better.

This was in *The Irish Times*.

It must be gospel so, say I.

At least have an omelette, says Dorothy restraining her exasperation.

Yes an omelette and salad would be nice.

Having taken our order and reassured Claire that all the eggs in the kitchen were laid by happy hens of independent means, Pól departs only to return in jig time with our Sancerre and fizzy water. Left arm folded behind his back, he pours me a taster of the wine.

That's nice, I say, welcoming the cool snap of the grape.

Herself has just arrived, he says, sotto voce.

I glance around, sensing the ripple caused by her entry and see that the restaurant has filled up with a lively crowd, some hoping no doubt to touch the hem of our leader, or better still, touch her for a favour, and afterwards boast of having her ear.

Who are all the men with her? asks Claire.

Her husband, a friend of theirs who runs her constituency office, and Father MacMahon, her brother-in-law, to say grace.

Where's her toy boy? I ask.

He usually comes in later, with a few others to make it look like he's only here by chance.

She must take us for fools.

It's worse than that, says Claire, Someone is getting hurt by their carry on.

That's right, Dorothy nods, Her husband and her kids, one of whom I think is handicapped. What about Geraghty? Does he have a wife and children?

A wife and three savages under the age of nine, says Pól and retreats to the kitchen.

Probably acting out, says Claire.

Lacey's children have my sympathy too, say I.

The rise of our leader from modest origins in County Leitrim is a paradigm of political advancement in our native land. Having inherited her father's seat on the county council, which was a reward for his prowess as a dual player in Gaelic games, she took over his agricultural contracting business and worked day and night to become a fixer extraordinaire using his contacts on the cumann, the county board and his old colleagues in cross-border trade, and within two years was elected Cathaoirleach. From there it was only a hop, skip and a few

well-nourished votes to the Seanad. Next stop the Dáil by way
of adroit vote management in her two-county constituency,
where the party needed a woman on the ticket. She bided her
time on the backbenches for eight years and as soon as peace
and reconciliation were in the air jumped on the BMW band-
wagon screaming for infrastructural investment in her area to
facilitate foreign direct investment in industry and stem the
'massive flux of emigration'. When she backed the right man
as leader of the party and Taoiseach she was rewarded with
the tourism portfolio and used it to channel a sizeable sum
into the lakes of Leitrim, promoting them as a holiday destination and encouraging developers of hotels and holiday homes
to sink uncertain foundations in the water-logged soil, some
of which belonged to her relatives, while European structural
funds were ploughed into a super highway across the county.
Her turn to be Taoiseach came at just the moment when our
economic fortunes started to look up, thanks to the EU money
that the Government's poor-mouthing, coupled with forelock-
tugging to our German and French masters, attracted, and to
the tax incentives with which it wooed the Americans. The
woman's guile and opportunism were unsurpassed and soon
she was the envy of her European peers whose countries by
contrast were mired in the evils of unemployment, rising costs
and security problems. Unlike some of her predecessors, Mary
Lacey has no aristocratic pretensions but prides herself on her
homely, plain-speaking approach. She knows better, too, than
to overplay the feminist card and can flip from flirt to bully in
the wink of an eye. Now, however, it seems she's getting too
big for her mucker's boots. The idea of putting a guttersnipe
like Liam Geraghty in the park makes me turn royalist to my
foundations.

Your niece's beau is very branché, Dorothy smiles.

His sister and now my niece are working for Geraghty.

For crocOgold 'riches untold'? Claire chants the tiresome jingle. Eamon was looking at his site last week. He was quite impressed.

Since Eamon's return three weeks ago Claire has been exhausted, rising early in the morning to set him up for the day before she goes out to work, rushing back at lunchtime to feed him, putting him to bed at night and lying awake till the small hours while he leaves the TV blaring because he says it helps him sleep, making the crocOgold jingle her lullaby.

He'd be better off putting his money under his mattress.

He just likes to follow these things. It's an interest for him.

To be sure, say I, but don't let him persuade you to put your savings into that leaky crock.

Claire colours slightly and says a little too vehemently, There's no way I would do that.

I hope not, says Dorothy shooting me a look that confirms she too has spotted our friend's fib.

Pól reappears to clear our starter plates.

What's herself ordering? Dorothy asks.

The usual I suppose, steak and kidney pie.

Nursery food, say I, She looks like a big overfed child.

It's all those growth hormones in the beef, says Claire.

She's beef to the heel anyway. I cross my own heels under my chair feeling suddenly self-conscious as I recall how when I visited Agnes Fitzgerald she remarked after the fond reminiscence of her good times with Paddy, that I looked grand and well-nourished on the food Mother had fed us and told me to tell my brother that the 'butchers of Ireland', whose organisation she heads, are not happy with him for telling people to eat less meat. We won't stand for it, she said. You can tell him that from me. I never delivered the message. She must have been relieved by news of his heart attack. For sure she didn't feel sorry for him.

Or the drink, Dorothy glances over at the table, Oh, and look who's coming now.

Claire looks around and I half twist in my seat to get a view. Liam Geraghty has entered the restaurant, flanked by two men, both a good deal taller than him, the bearded one I take to be his henchman, Myles' half-brother-in-law. The other lanky, drooping fellow I recognise, with some perturbation, is Phil Lannigan, the Murphy-Benz's architect pal.

True to her word Bernie had breezed in one evening with his plans and, as she put it, 'walked' me through them, inviting me to picture the double height atrium, the Mediterranean court-yard, grianán, non-denominational reflection room, and niches for art, 'not holy statues', all of which was fine and dandy but I had to ask where was the kitchen. Gosh, Lena, you're right! She had exclaimed, then, with a pretty shake of her golden bell, told me she thought he was planning to put it in the basement. I said I'd wait to see the final plans before committing myself.

Excuse me ladies, Pól reappears with a colleague to serve our main courses, tops up our wine glasses and melts away.

I wonder what she sees in him, says Claire putting on her glasses for a better look at Geraghty, He doesn't exactly have the bearing of a president.

She doesn't have much bearing herself, except what's on display in her cleavage, say I. She'll probably tout him as an example of the new young vibrant happening Ireland Inc., in-stead of a twenty-first century version of the gombeen man, which he is.

Between Jean and Siobhán I have begun to piece together a picture of the activities at crocOgold. They tell me Geraghty is out of the office much of the time, at meetings and shuttling between Dublin, London, Boston, Panama and Singapore, al-though he phones in every day, regardless of the time zone, making strategy suggestions based on conversations he's had with strangers at 30,000 feet, closing with his catchphrase,

'Boom, Boom, Boom'. He leaves the day to day running of the place to a preening fellow who avoids any direct contact with the staff unless they happen to be young, good-looking and male. The result is a somewhat anarchic and chaotic office with a talented youthful crew who work hard only to be berated by Geraghty when he returns for a day, telling them that they should be drumming up more business, poaching customers from their rivals and getting existing clients to invest more. To round off their stories the girls make a rapid pummelling movement with their fists, like a boxing kangaroo, in imitation of the gesture that accompanies his motivational booms.

I look away now from the table where Lacey is laughing at something Geraghty has said. I'd hate for them to think we were taking so much notice of them.

In a way it's a pity Paddy had to bow out, says Dorothy. He'd have been a better candidate than Geraghty.

Don't forget Didi, says Claire, I'd give her my vote.

Another day, another presidential candidate. Today's aspirant is Didi Doherty from Donegal, radio show hostess, agony aunt to the nation, mother of five, cancer survivor, holder of a masters degree in biomechanical engineering and author of a semi-fictional family memoir, according to breakfast TV. The race is turning into a circus, although Didi might not be the worst of the candidates, better than Paddy or little grinning Liam Geraghty.

True, I concur. I might even give her my number one, if I don't throw my own stylish cloche in the ring now that Paddy's on the ropes.

Would you really consider it Lena? Claire looks at me with an air of revelation. I think you'd be great, wouldn't she, Dor?

Dorothy cocks her head at me. Yes, come to think of it, you'd have all the credentials: poise, political family, lawyer.

And she's a woman.

Last time I looked, say I.

It's important Lena, insists Claire warmly. Women in this country have been put upon and putting up for decades, centuries. Her face settles in a dogmatic pout.

And set upon, I add softly placing my knife and fork together on my plate, having suddenly lost my appetite.

I feel rather than see my friends' puzzlement at this interjection. I fake a reassuring smile and say, I'm flattered but I don't think it's me somehow.

No, says Dorothy. I couldn't see you agreeing not to speak your mind. Everything you said would have to be vetted by the government.

That's a pity, Claire looks wounded. You'd be so perfect and I was looking forward to our First Fridays in the Aras.

You're getting carried away, I raise my hands. I haven't the slightest intention of putting myself forward. I like my privacy and my freedom. There's an end to it.

That's a shame, Claire looks cast down, taking my refusal personally. You'd be so much better than Didi or Geraghty.

Didi doesn't stand much of a chance, say I, against the Fianna Fáil machine.

Unless Fine Gael or Labour ran someone to split the transfers, Dorothy suggests.

Or unless Geraghty cocks up, I speculate, He has his fingers in a lot of pies and one of them could get burnt. Now, if you'll excuse me, I'm going to see the hall of mirrors.

Don't get lost, Claire laughs.

Only when I stand up do I realise that the restaurant has filled and the decibel level risen to the threshold of hysteria. Look at us, the diners seem to say, playing with our shiny new money. I ease and edge my way between the chairs, inhaling the odours of expensive perfumes, food and fruit of the vine. The last days of Rome come to mind.

For all the dim confusion of its décor the Ladies provides some respite from that madness. When I close the door of the

stall I see myself crouched over the bowl: a most unflattering
sight. I glance away and with a deep sigh let the floodgates
open. I piss like a horse, a stream redolent of the asparagus
that accompanied my starter. There's no escaping the animal
in us, no matter how hard we try. Whoever conceived those
mirrored doors has a keen eye for satire. An answering stream
resounds from a neighbouring cubicle. I rearrange my clothes,
flush and exit. Now the challenge is to find the washbasin.
My own image, refracted through a seeming myriad layers of
glass, distracts me from my quest. Looking down, however, I
make out a steel trough under a long mirror. No taps, handles
or pedals offering themselves I reach my hands vaguely under
the rim of the glass waiting for a miracle to happen, which it
does after several adjustments of my position up, down and
sideways. Having found the right angle I don't dare to shift in
search of soap. There is the sound of flushing from behind followed by high heels ticking on the tiled floor. A glance in the
mirror yields the features of our nation's leader kaleidoscoped
around me. A thousand Mary Laceys nod in turn at my reflection and send a polite impersonal smile ricocheting around the
space like a surrealist's nightmare. I force a smile in response
then straighten to look for a hand dryer, assuming a towel
would be too old-fashioned and ordinary for this setting.

It's over there, says Lacey in her grave Leitrim accent.

I follow the direction of her hydra-headed nod and see two
holes in the wall which I take to be dryers.

Thanks, say I advancing towards them.

As I wipe my hands she joins me at the dryers. Then, in a
move that surprises me more than it does her, I hold out my
slightly damp hand saying, Lena Carmody.

Mary Lacey, says she.

I think you know my brother, Paddy O'Neill.

Ah, yes, indeed. How is he? I heard he had a heart attack,
she responds without missing a beat.

That's how she got to be Taoiseach, I think, the good memory for people's names, the personal touch and the fake empathy.

He's fine now, I say, but he gave us all a fright.

I'm sure, she nods with condescension, I hope he takes his own advice and rests. He's not young after all.

Touché.

Oh Paddy's not one for lazing around.

Well I'm sure you'll see to it that he takes a break. With those words, coloured more by severity than sympathy, she turns to leave.

I follow her because I can't see the exit. When we reach what I take to be the door I find a handle and hold it open for her.

Thank you, she bows, Nice to meet you. Remember me to Paddy.

Yes, I will, I grovel and step after her into the maelstrom.

As soon as she has turned towards her table, where, to my surprise, the men rise at her approach, a wave of nausea passes through me at my own sycophancy. How could I have been so craven, so obsequious? Could it be true after all that the ghastly woman has charisma or was I befuddled by the mirrors?

You look as if you've seen a ghost, says Claire when I return to the table.

No. Just acres of Mary Laceys. Recalling the encounter now, another image slides across my mind's eye: myself and Old Brennan reflected in the mirror above the console in the office hallway.

When Pól arrives to clear away our plates and distribute the dessert menus I ask him who did the interior décor.

I've no idea, he replies, I'll ask the manager.

No sooner has he departed than Phil Lannigan appears in his place, Good evening, Lena, he greets me.

Good evening, I reply in curt acknowledgement, hoping that he will depart as swiftly as he arrived. Seeing the manager approach I beam welcomingly at him but thick-skinned Phil chooses to ignore the cold shoulder and looms closer, confidingly, cutting off the manager's access to me, I was passing and overheard you asking the waiter who did the interior design.

Idle curiosity, I try to brush him off.

Eimear Ní Neachtáin, he stretches the name sarcastically, and rolls his eyes, Graduate of the vaudeville school of design.

Thank you, I smile thinly and pick up the dessert menu.

Of course, I should have recognised the signature excess but ever since meeting the Mouse I have been trying to square the overblown interiors with the prim persona and have come to the conclusion that she is having a good long laugh, or at the very least a titter, at her credulous clients. Having got her name a few weeks ago from Myles, on the pretext that I liked the new office décor, I had rung to make an appointment with her, saying that I wanted to make over my house. She arrived punctually for what she called a 'pre-con', no fee unless she got the job. Pace Ned, she is a Town Mouse. In contrast to her taste in decoration her personal style was understated. She made the most of her low build and plain features by wearing a well-tailored navy trousers suit paired with a crisp white blouse and string of pearls, all supported by a pair of sleek black shoes with three-inch heels. The only flourish, if you could call it that, was a pair of large sparkly glasses acting as a hairband that pulled her hair back so tightly it stretched the flesh on her forehead till her eyebrows were hoisted in an expression of perpetual astonishment. She declined tea, coffee, water or wine, and proceeded at a smart clip on her narrow heels to the drawing room where, halting at the centre of the room, she made a 360 degree turn, her eyes darting into each corner in a way that compelled me to notice the yellowing of the wallpaper and paintwork, the fading of the once sumptuous velvet curtains, discoloured by years of coal fires and tobacco smoke and the threadbare Turkey carpet. Placing her brief case on a chair she moved around the room mentally stripping away the outmoded elegance of my home.

So you're a friend of Rosemary and Myles? I ventured.

Yes, she replied, stepping back and tilting her head to appraise the piano. Did you ever think of painting it white?

The piano? Are you joking? That's a Bechstein.

A pity, she says, still with her back to me. It's very big and dark looking.

It's a baby grand. It belonged to my mother. I like to play it sometimes.

Uh huh.

Her preliminary design arrived by email a week later and featured purple and silver flowers and stripes with dashes of lime green to sear the eyes. She also attached an invoice for expenses, transport and time, which smacked of sharp practice. So much for the complimentary 'pre-con'. I replied saying I would think about it, wrote a cheque for her 'expenses' and promptly deleted the file.

Now I wish I could press the delete button on lugubrious Phil as, leaning in again, he says, Bernie told me she showed you the plans.

Yes, I keep my eyes fixed on the list of sweet treats.

About the kitchen, he begins.

Without taking my eyes from the menu I say slowly, Mr. Lannigan, I do not wish to discuss your drawings here. As I told Bernie, I will consider them when they are complete.

But they are, that's what I'm trying to tell you, he half-whines.

Very well, then there is nothing more to be said.

The kitchen is in an annexe.

As in the seat of the pants school of design? I suggest, Now if you don't mind I would like to order dessert.

I wouldn't recommend that for you, he remarks and spinning on his heel stalks away.

What a rude fellow, Dorothy exclaims.

My neighbour's architect friend, I explain.

I'm surprised, says Claire, Because Bernie's so sweet.

Mmmmm, is the only response I can make. Just to spite that creep I'm going to have the trio of chocolate délices.

Me too, says Dorothy.

I think I'll join you, Claire smiles guiltily, It'll probably keep me awake all night but I'll be awake anyway with Eamon's telly going.

You should just pull the plug on that, say I.

Glaring at me Dorothy says, So it's a trio of trios so.

Make that a quartet, a male voice resounds above us.

Looking up I see Ken standing behind Dorothy and winking mischievously at me.

Dorothy twitches around impatiently, What are you doing here?

I was on my way home from the meeting when I realised I'd forgotten my house keys. So here I am, Ken grins but there is flicker of hurt in his expression as he affects a lost puppy look, hoping to tease Dorothy out of her pique.

While she lifts up her handbag and rummages in it for her keys Pól comes over to offer Ken a chair and a menu.

I've decided, thank you, he says, seating himself, Lena knows my order. I'll take a glass of red wine too please.

Dorothy ostentatiously drops the keys back into her bag, her features working to maintain their frosty expression.

I have always liked Ken for his easy, friendly manner and his natural generosity. He bristles with an energetic optimism that covers a certain restlessness, hence his arrival here tonight, avoiding the return to an empty house from his St. Vincent de Paul meeting. Since retiring he has redoubled the charitable work he has been doing for nigh on fifty years. Mossie had been in his VdeP chapter where he developed a close friendship with him. When Mossie fell ill Ken rounded up some solicitor colleagues to come into the office and take over his live briefs. They saw the cases through and handed me the fees in toto.

Now, he raises his glass to toast us, and having sipped his wine turns to me. So, Lena, we'll be expecting invitations to shindigs in the Park.

Don't look at me, I protest, There's the fellow you need to talk to, by all accounts. I nod in the direction of Liam Geraghty's table.

My money is on Paddy.

He's not running, Dorothy frowns, Have you forgotten he had a heart attack?

Ah-ah, Ken wags his head, I've just heard on the news that he's put that behind him and is looking forward to the presidential race.

What? My spoonful of délice drops from my hand to clatter onto the plate.

Good, cheers Claire, After all he's best placed to know if he's able for it and we were only saying he'd be a more suitable candidate than the other two.

And Ms Lacey says he's too old and should put his feet up, I remind her.

That's to protect her toyboy, says Dorothy.

True, but she has a point, I grimace. He's bonkers.

I agree with Claire, Ken weighs in, He'd be a serious contender. In fact, he adds, I'll campaign for him.

I shake my head in disbelief, I never imagined I'd end up in the same boat as Mary Lacey.

There's still time to jump ship, Ken laughs, After all, it's mainly a ceremonial role and Paddy would carry it off much better than the other two. He leans forward eagerly to look straight into my eyes, Why exactly don't you want him to run, Lena?

His frank expression disarms me and I hesitate. It's a fair question. When Father retired there had been a suggestion that he might be an agreed candidate for the presidency. He was quite chuffed by the idea but Mother vetoed it. What would I do up there? She said, not unreasonably, We'd be prisoners.

It's a great honour, said Father, wounded by her failure to acknowledge the respect for him that the proposal entailed, We would be ambassadors for our country. You might enjoy the travelling.

Not when I couldn't walk down the street on my own.

Dining with kings and queens. Being applauded wherever you go.

Mother narrowed her eyes at him, Are you feeling all right? Have you fallen into your second childhood?

No. But I think it would ill behove us to refuse such a request, if it was felt to be in the best interests of the country. The President is a conduit too for negotiations on trade or diplomatic affairs. It's not all an exchange of nullities.

Granted, but Mrs. President is a nullity.

You could be a patroness of charity, Father glowed at the noble prospect.

I already do charitable work, said Mother with asperity, I'm afraid I must be too prosaic to share your vision. But if you insist, by all means accept the job. I'll stay here.

You used to be idealistic too, Father tried once more, You shared my hopes for this country. Now we have a chance to serve it again in a way we can be proud of. To show its pride.

If only that were true, Mother's expression softened to that of a parent forced to tell her child that Santa Claus doesn't exist, Can't you see the Government just wants a compromise candidate to save itself the bother and expense of an election? It wants someone uncontentious and loyal.

When did you become so cynical?

At the same time as you became disillusioned. The dream was traded off piecemeal and we did nothing to stop it, Mother sighed.

Life is better now all the same, said Father, At least we control our own destiny. Farmers own their land. We have standing among other nations and the freedom to negotiate good terms in the market with them. And our children were not born into a subject race.

Granted but there's a new breed in power today and they're not a crowd I would want to be beholden to for anything. Cometh the whiff of profit and prestige, cometh the opportunists. I'm as sorry about it as you are. Just don't ask me to kowtow to them. Maybe it was too much to hope we could be pure and uncorrupted.

Defeated, Father shrank into his chair and picked up his book.

Now Paddy has a dose of the delusions and it's embarrassing to see him make an eejit of himself, drawing the ire of the butchers, the brewers and vintners not to mention the sports organisations who don't like his campaign to end drink sponsorship of sport.

Maybe I don't want to see him humiliated, I say. I think it's not so much that I don't want him to be President, although I'd rather he wasn't but the hubris that makes him assume he has the sort of statesmanlike standing that would fit him for the role. And Nóirín would be an embarrassment.

There's nothing very statesman or woman like about the other two either, Ken argues with justification. What if he won?

I'd have to eat my chapeau, give Nóirín some advice on how to dress, send Jean and her pals to the park and suggest that he appoint me and you to the Council of State.

Perfect, Ken claps his hands, You see, it wouldn't be all bad.

Chapter Ten

Unaccustomed to walking before sunrise, Tanta pulls ahead then pauses to glance anxiously over his shoulder at me.

It's okay, I reassure him, I know what I'm doing. Sort of.

Taking me dubiously at my word the dog turns away and presses his nose to the ground, sweeping for a scent on the promenade.

Sleep had evaded me on my return from dinner at the Dish and Spoon. None of the usual devices had sent me off, not counting backwards from a hundred, counting sheep or my blessings, not listening to the BBC World Service, with its reports of corruption, rebellion and civil war in distant lands, the Brits' lament for their lost empire, and certainly not the local offering of blather and monotonous popular music, interrupted by insidious crocOgold jingles. Ken was right, as I heard in a hiatus when shifting the dial, Paddy is back in the race. Big eejit. That information drove me out of the bed. The newsreader quoted him as saying that the experience of his recent illness had given him a renewed sense of the 'value of human life, family and friends' and 'compassion', qualities he would bring to his role if the people saw fit to do him the honour of electing him president. Pshaw I say, leaning strongly on the 'P' that stands for several things, including poppycock. Stealing Didi's Ur-mother lines might seem like a smart move but it's Geraghty's slippery connivance he needs to outsmart.

I should come out more often at this hour. The quiet is soothing, coloured only by the indolent sound of the full tide, the swift clatter of the first DART and the occasional car going by. Tanta and I are alone in this world where the air is tense as a held breath, waiting for light to break over the sea. We walk as far as the Joyce Tower at Scotsman's Bay where we see the first of the morning dippers park up and stroll to the Forty Foot. As if drawn by a magnet, certainly without a plan, I find I am following them to the changing shelter where, commanding Tanta to sit and wait, I strip and, not glancing left or right at my fellow bathers, descend the slippery steps and push off into the cold water. I hear Tanta whine behind me and one of the men soothe him as I strike out in a crawl through the gap in the rocks that enclose the swimming hole then roll onto my back and float, looking up at the sky that has brightened from grey to indigo giving myself over to the water, allowing it to bear me up epi oinopa ponton wishing it was wine, and away from the land the tide on the turn and yes I have read that scandalous book yes the water so shocking cold it slows the blood in my veins yes without understanding much but relishing defiance of the censor the old blue cover wrapped in brown paper bought off a barrow on Henry Street for 3s/6d forbidden nightblue fruit blue for the sea too on the way to buy the royal blue taffeta that set off the officer's scarlet like the fireworks shimmering in the water under the not quite risen sun but the photo is black and white almost sepia now colour of lost time fadó fadó the sea oh the sea long may it stay between England and me. May it scour my head or shrive my soul out here.

The noise and ripple of splashing near at hand shakes me from my drift.

Hallo, hallo, calls a male voice, Ahoy there!

I pop upright and begin to tread water, looking around for the source of the voice. A man with a head shiny as a seal's, his face defined by a dark moustache and goatee is gaping at me with some concern.

I'm just waking up, I splutter.

Good. He draws away a little from me respectful of our nudity and sets himself upright to tread water too, You looked as if you were asleep and might wake up in Wales.

Wouldn't that have been a nice surprise for them over there? Aphrodite of the foam but what would Richard say if he heard I had swum naked to his shore while he was away crusading?

I'm sure, Sealman said, but it's cold standing around here. I think it's time to swim in.

To prove the point his lips have cyanosed and, perhaps because I see him turn blue, I am suddenly taken with the shivers myself. Yes, I say, kicking my legs up behind me and facing inland. The shore, visible now in the first light seems very far away and as I begin to swim I fear I may not be strong enough to overcome the current which is dragging against me. I glance at my companion who, seeing the panic in my eyes, says, Swim towards the rocks to the left—they're closer and that will correct for the tide.

Okay, thanks, I breathe and pressing my face to the water begin to swim, hauling my arms high and long, kicking hard, refusing to think of the distance to be covered. After a short time my limbs begin to turn to lead and I feel as if an invisible hand has a hold of me, rendering all my effortful swimming futile but I push myself to keep going one stroke at a time, impelled in part by the urgency of avoiding a lifesaving manoeuvre that would bring our naked flesh into contact, although at this point mine is so cold I could have open heart surgery without an anaesthetic. When at length we reach the swimming hole I notice that the retreating tide has exposed some of the concrete steps which are treacherously covered with seaweed and in my exhaustion am at a loss to know how

I will ever get out of the water. Standing above the steps I see a second, slightly older, man gripping Tanta's collar with one hand as the dog yaps in distress, and in the other a lifebelt which he offers to throw down to me. My gallant swimming companion, however, has swum ahead of me and is slithering up onto the steps where, when he finds a footing, he clings to the rail and tenders his free hand. I clasp it and my body slackens with relief and exhaustion. He winces at the unexpected weight and we balance for an instant on an invisible fulcrum, me limp and ineffectual, he straining every ligament to keep me from sinking. I see the pain in his eyes but am hypnotised by a prompting to let go and fall, spiralling all the way down to the bottom of the sea, to sleep and not to dream or wake, not ever, not in Wales or anywhere else. When I am on the point of slipping back a rough hand presses my buttocks, shoving me up so forcefully that I fly out of the water like a bar of lemon soap squeezed between wet hands.

Thanks, I laugh with embarrassment as the men around me applaud.

The one holding Tanta releases him and the dog comes rushing to my side, jumping up and licking my wet and salty legs.

Good boy, good boy, I say fondling his eager little head.

Here, you better dry yourself quickly. The man hands me a towel, glancing circumspectly away from my flesh, exposed in all its sagging glory.

Yes, I say through my chattering teeth and look around.

Sealman is towelling himself and the third, presumably the one who whooshed me out of the water, shakes his head saying, You gave us a fright there.

I know, I'm sorry. I got carried away.

Handing the towel back to its owner I am struck by the unconventionality of our situation, three men, strangers to me, and I, standing around chatting as if we were at a cocktail party, but all stark naked at dawn of a morning in February. Come back Jimmy Joyce, I think, tipping a wink to the Martello tower, here's a sight for your weak eyes: Circe and the Lotos Eaters all naked in the scrotumtightening nipplepinching paralysing mortal cold. The vision fades and I hastily pull on my clothes, trying to chafe some circulation back into my limbs.

This'll warm you, Sealman, now dressed in jeans and a down jacket, offers me a thermos cup of black coffee, which, I realise as I inhale the steam, is spiked with whisky.

A gift from the gods, I smile gratefully.

You shouldn't go swimming on your own at this hour, admonishes the older man who had held Tanta.

I know. I hadn't really intended to, I say. It just looked tempting.

Best cure for a hangover anyway, he probes.

Maybe, I shrug as if I wouldn't know. It's the first time I've swum here. My father and my brother were regulars back in the day when it was for 'forty foot gentlemen only'.

Well, me and Cyril are here every morning at this hour, if you fancy coming back. Only don't pull a stunt like that one again, he smiles.

Don't worry, say I, handing back the empty cup, I'll bring my own towel and a flask next time. Thank you, thank you all, I bow gratefully to my rescuers and, beckoning Tanta, leave the bathing place to set off for home.

On reaching our terrace I spy a light in Miser Kiely's window, and himself silhouetted there. Probably up all night counting his money, by candlelight because he wouldn't want to be using up the electricity. I swivel my head away to the right, taking in the bend of the bay where the city simmers already in its sickly yellow haze of pollution, dominated by the stacks of the Pigeon House, their warning lights flashing like fool's gold. I'm hoping Seán Kiely doesn't spot me and come down to get free legal advice on some trouble with a tenant. At one time he had me plagued with his petty quarrels and dreams of big awards. That all stopped when Mossie appeared in my life. If he was with me he would say in a genial but firm tone that we were relaxing for the weekend and would be more than happy to give him legal advice any time between 9 a.m. and 6 p.m., Monday to Friday. Just phone the office and make an appointment, like a good man. No surprise, no appointment was ever made. Of late, however, Seán has begun to take advantage of my solitary state, starting with feigned concern about Mother, and latterly about me, before sidling into worries about his properties, and from there to hints about my house and whether it's too big for me now. He has even offered to do running repairs for me, an excuse to sneak a look inside and fantasise about what he could coin from the place if he got his grubby hands on it.

If only Mossie were with me now. He'd have enjoyed the morning swim although he'd have preferred I wore my swim-suit. In the summer we frequently came down to Seapoint for an early dip. The tingling sensation of the cold, salt water stirred an appetite for sex which we had with urgent haste when we got home before putting on our sober work suits and selves. Its charge stayed with us all day, however, and when we met on the stairs or in one another's office it wavered in the air between us kindling a covert knowing look and smile, as if we were conducting an affair.

The sea was Mossie's element. To my surprise our first date was not an invitation to dinner but to go sailing with him. On the water he was a different person, relishing the salty air and the challenge of harnessing the wind to scud through the waves. I had only sailed a couple of times before that outing, when friends of our grandparents took Paddy and me out in Waterville. I fumbled with the sheet trying to remember the little bit I had been taught about playing the wind but soon Mossie took it from my hand played it till the jib was nicely filled and cleated it. When he called, Ready about, lee-oh, I glanced around mystified but before I could ask what was happening he had pushed my head down roaring at me to switch sides before the boom swung across.

Sorry, he grinned when we were seated on the opposite transom, I think I need to give you some lessons.

Yes or make me walk the plank, I laughed.

I wouldn't do that, he placed his hand on my knee in a reflex then swiftly pulled it back saying, Excuse me, and returned to helming.

I don't mind, I said.

He turned to look at me again, tilting his head, Are you sure?

Yes.

It was the same look, a mix of smiling appraisal and respect that he gave me eighteen months later when he proposed. That sunny August Saturday we bowled happily along the coast, trailing his new boat, chatting lightly about work and about Kennedy's chances of being elected president until I noticed dark clouds rolling in over the sea. This would be our maiden voyage in the new boat and, although she was an Enterprise like her predecessor, I shuddered apprehensively.

Nervous? Mossie asked.

A little, I nodded and lit us two cigarettes.

Thanks, Mossie took his and inhaled deeply, We'll be fine. She's a sturdy vessel. Trim and fit in all her parts. Besides, she has a very competent skipper and a beautiful crew.

If you say so, I conceded through the veil of cigarette smoke.

At the sailing club in Wicklow we set to rigging the boat and ourselves, checking the wind, studying the course, joking with our competitors, then launched into the choppy water, spray breaking over the bow and lapping the gunwales to splash our faces and waterproofs like the small hands of a child drawing us out to play. Mossie quivered with competitive intent, the same gutsy determination that he showed in court and settlement negotiations, indicating the boats we needed to watch for, *Queen of the Bay* and *Mollipop*. At the starting buoy we jostled to get inside the wind, the air loud with curses and the flapping of sails as craft wheeled about, trying to keep close to the line. When the starter hooted all cursing and clamour ceased, sails bellied and tautened, harnessing the wind to drive us forward. We pulled ahead but *Queen of the Bay* caught up and took our wind shrivelling our sails.

We'll catch him on the run, Mossie said tersely and adjusted our angle till the sails filled again. Get the spinnaker ready.

We gybed close to the buoy and the minute we came around I let the jib out and watched it belly, trapping the wind. *Mollipop* flagged in our wake. On the beat our concentration intensified as the wind picked up and white horses danced on the waves destabilising the boat. We began to reef in the sails. A sound of rushing water to port caught Mossie's attention and he jerked his head around in time to see *Mollipop* coming up on us again.

Watch out, he hissed urgently, Loosen the jib again. That bastard is going to spill his wind.

Sure enough, *Mollipop* came level with us and tipped her wind into our sails. Our boat heeled sharply with the impact and before she could right herself a sharp gust of wind pushed her further over and within moments we were both in the water and the boat had turned turtle.

Lena, Lena, Mossie called out. Stay with the boat.

I'm here, I called.

Are you all right? He swam up beside me, worry creasing his face.

Wet but fine, I said, one hand gripping the gunwale.

Wait there, he ordered and disappeared underwater.

The waves jostled about us as if trying to separate me from the boat. The chill of the water numbed my hand till I couldn't tell whether my grip had held or slipped. I continued to tread the water pushing against its weight like going uphill on a bike in high gear.

A few minutes later Mossie surfaced holding one of the sheets and began to scramble onto the upturned keel. Reaching over he hauled me up beside him.

Sorry about this, he sighed. We'll wait for the rescue launch. You can go in to shore and we'll right the boat.

I tucked my arm into his and he patted my hand saying, It'll be fine.

I know. It doesn't matter.

We huddled side by side in silence, marooned on the turtle back of our upturned hull, watching the launch approach from the jetty, while the rest of the boats continued to round the next buoy. When the rain that had been threatening all afternoon suddenly broke upon us we laughed together and turning to face one another kissed while the rain ran over us and drummed on the keel of the boat, sealing us within its lush noise. I love you, Mossie said, his mouth still touching mine. I raised my hand to his cheek and returned his words.

Much later, that evening when the regatta supper was over and someone had put on dance music, Mossie and I stepped outside for air. The rain had passed and the long sunset of high summer lay on the sea like balm.

I've been meaning to ask you, he said after we had strolled for a few minutes, hands lightly clasped, would you mind if I called her *Lady Lena*?

Who?

Herself, he jerked his thumb over his shoulder in the direction of the boat.

I'd have to think about that. Are there any duties attached?

No. Apart from marrying the skipper.

I see, I paused before adding, very well then.

Really? He halted to face me. Do you mean you'd be willing to spend the rest of your days with me? Even after the soaking you got this afternoon?

Yes, really, I smiled. I'm not afraid of water.

We kissed then, slowly, deliberately, as if rolling the words wife, husband, marriage around on our tongues finding a new shape for our feelings, our bodies moulded together, the waves softly clapping against the harbour wall, wanting to hold that momentary sensation forever. Solemn and glad with our new promise we turned to walk back towards the clubhouse where someone had started a conga. The growing line of dancers snaked out onto the pier, the music following them through the open door, its drumbeat and their squeals and cheers rebounding off the water. Far behind those exuberant calls I heard other voices that I had struggled to keep at bay. Rough, dark voices grazing my ear. I flinched to push them away and tightened my grip on Mossie.

Is there something the matter? He murmured.

Not a thing, I quickly shook my head. Come on, I skipped ahead of him, let's join the conga.

Waiting to cross the road I see an unusual sight. Siobhán's little car is idling outside the house, parallel to mine, engine running and hazard lights blinking. I am about to wave at her when, glancing up to the front door, I see Pól and Jean emerge, each swinging a bulging refuse sack. I watch as, on reaching the car, they open the boot, cram the sacks inside, close it and walk around to the passenger side to sit in, Jean in front, Pól in the back. Siobhán pulls away immediately in the direction of town, hazard lights still blinking. What can they be up to? Certainly not going to work at this hour on a Saturday morning.

Still mulling over this episode I cross the road and am about to open the front gate when an even stranger sight arrests me. So strange in fact that I am convinced I am hallucinating. Was there more than whiskey in that coffee? I take a deep breath to steady myself. Never ever again will I come out this early in the morning. Never. The hallucinatory figure approaches, taking definite if mighty peculiar shape. Here comes Moira Kiely, rounding the corner in saggy candy pink track-suit bottoms and a shabby pink anorak, half-jogging half-shuffling. The hideous headscarf, which she has been wearing since circa 1965, has slipped down to flop on her shoulders. She is red-faced and her eyes look as if they will start right out of her head.

Lena, she pants on seeing me, the very one. She halts shakily, her hands still held in fists at waist height, her breathing ragged.

What's the matter Moira? I crane forward ready to catch her if she topples.

Even Tanta is concerned, whining and jumping up against the pink legs.

Fine, she gasps. Fine. *Gasp.* She stoops, pressing her hands to her thighs and trying to catch her breath.

Will I get Seán? I ask.

No, she gulps. No. I'll get my breath. Raising her hands to clutch my arm as a prop she drags herself upright again. At this proximity I can feel the heat radiating off her face. I ran around the block, she gasps. I'm training for the mini-*gasp*-marathon.

Good for you, I say while thinking, not really. Look at where the jogging landed Paddy.

Yes-*gasp*-to raise money. There had to be a money angle if Moira Kiely was to put on her running shoes. For the parish-*gasp*-community-*gasp*-hall. Father Horgan says it needs a new-*huff*-roof and-*puff*-windows.

Father Horgan, who has been parish priest here for the past twenty-seven years, is in need of a new roof himself. The last time I spoke to him was at Mother's funeral where he reprised his eulogy for Father, with whom he had enjoyed theological sallies outside the church on a Sunday morning, including references to Mammo's religious tracts, recreating the confusion between herself and her mother-in-law that had dogged Mother in life. After his own mother died he had been a regular guest in our house, calling late in the evening for supper with the Parents, yet in the eulogy Mother remained only a footnote, described as Father's helpmeet [*sic*], and the woman behind the man, certainly not a version of her that anyone in the church that day recognised.

Very commendable, I say waiting for the request that will come as surely as the swallows in summer.

Would you like to-*puff*-sponsor me?

I don't have any money on me right now, Moira. Another day.

I think I should sponsor an ambulance if she's this pooped from doing a circuit of the block. It must be the hint of spring in the air that has us all out and about this morning doing unlikely things. Amn't I after nearly swimming the channel?

There's plenty of time yet. The race isn't until-*puff-puff*-June. I'll call in one evening.

Do that, I smile without sincerity and lift the latch on the gate.

Before you go, she plucks at my arm again, Did you get my note?

You mean the message you scribbled on the envelope addressed to me, which you had opened?

Yes, sorry about that. The postman mixed us up.

An incomprehensible confusion in my view although I don't tell her that, What's the problem, Moira?

Seán looked at some of Phil whatshisname's work in town the other day. He says it's good as long as he doesn't get too fancy. You know Bernie, she likes the bit of glamour, she rolls her eyes like an exasperated mother.

I can't say I'm averse to it myself.

Oh but you're very stylish, Lena. Old school stylish.

Old school stylish. The gall of the woman. I'd have her know I was a Pond's girl in my day, 'leading the way to natural loveliness' as the ad in *Social and Personal* put it. Now I feel like the last redoubt of class and taste.

They're quite mothren, the pest continues.

That must be why there's no kitchen. All the old folk will have to eat takeaway.

Oh Lena, her hand flies to her mouth to cover her snaggledy teeth when she laughs, you're so comical. Bernie thinks so too.

Does she now? My glance darts to the Murphy-Benzes' windows hoping Bernie can't see us talking because if she does she'll surely come out and there'll be no getting away from here or from the masterplan.

But seriously, Lena. There is a kitchen in the latest version. Ask Bernie to show it to you. But Seán says we'll have to make him sharpen his pencil, Euro signs flash like a halo over her head.

You mean pare him down?

She nods vigorously. He's a bit pricey. I know Bernie is talking to Liam Geraghty about it but all the same—

That's the first I've heard of his involvement.

Well she is, her eyes, which have resumed their normal beadiness, widen with affirmation. That will help with the cost.

Maybe, I demur.

Anyway Father Horgan thinks it's a good idea.

What's he got to do with it?

They're casting the net very wide now. Next thing you know they'll be looking for EU structural funds.

Well it's in the parish. I thought it only right to tell him.

It's not on parish land. Besides it's supposed to be non-denominational.

I know, she gives a dismissive shake of her head. But that only means we'll take in a few Prods if we're stuck with vacancies.

That's wasn't quite how I understood it.

Well Father said he'd help in any way he could.

Very decent I'm sure.

I'm not saying he'd give any money but you never know.

Ah God! I could laugh till I crack. So that's what has Moira Kiely kitted out in her charity shop joggers. Any cash left over from the community hall will go into the project. To secure that funding Seán will be down at the presbytery advising the priest to sharpen his pencil on the community hall and offering to do the devil and all himself. Even being up this early I couldn't get ahead of the wily Kielys.

That's all very interesting, Moira, I say with finality. But I really must be going. Good luck. I open the gate and enter my domain while Moira waves and resumes her shuffling jog, puff-panting with the effort.

As I insert the key in the front door I hear the phone ringing inside the house. I step into the office to pick up.

Yes, Ned.

Lena, I'm glad I caught you. The early bird and all that. Ha!

Very wise, I say, wishing I hadn't been caught. My hips creak as I sit, no longer used to so much exercise.

It's about our friend. Not looking good so to speak.

That's not news, I feel myself droop, waiting to hear the worst.

He was in here very late last night.

On his own?

Yes. Solus. I came down letting on I'd heard a noise and wanted to investigate. He told me not to worry, he had an important file to read. Said he couldn't sleep.

The insomnia is catching.

Was he making phone calls?

Yes. Yes. That's it. I went down to the kitchen to make him a cup of coffee but left his door ajar, Ned says with pride.

Quite the Hercule Poirot, I laugh.

I thought the same myself, he giggles. Anyway, I heard a bit of a conversation, well, an argument really. The miles gloriosus was very angry, saying he needed receipts, papers to prove the transaction. Not just 'airy promises'. The other side must have bounced him back to the leprechaun because our man says 'to hell with him' and 'he's sent me out to bat alone'. When I brought in the coffee, black with two sugars, the way he likes it, he was sitting staring into the receiver.

My mind leaps ahead through all the legal, financial and personal implications of Myles's reckless folly, and returns to my sheer incredulity at his lack of judgement, not to mention taste in allowing himself be seduced by the mousy Ms Ní Neachtáin and blackmailed by the conniving Mr. Geraghty.

I fear he's in deeper than we thought, I say. Any idea where the other person was? I'm guessing the call wasn't local.

Boston. That's one of the last things our glorious soldier said, if he didn't get the documents he'd go to Boston and personally break the other fellow's balls. I think that's when he hung up. It's a disgrace. And Mossie's name still on the door. Still on the door, Brennan's voice rises in his agitation.

Yes, it is extremely disappointing, I say, reining in my anger in order to abate his. I can only assume he's having some kind of mid-life crisis or got himself into debt.

Exactly, says Ned. Whatever it is he's up to his oxters in it. When I gave him the coffee he looked that sick I asked him again was he all right, hoping he might like to talk, man to man so to speak. But he just says 'I'll be game ball, Ned. Thanks, thanks.' First time he ever called me by my first name.

About time he called you by your proper name. No sign of the Mouse while all this was going on?

Not a squeak.

I thought not. Thanks for filling me in, Ned. I'll think it over and see what I can do.

Yes, do that. Let me know if I can help. Pip pip.

I return the phone to its station and sigh. There's something rotten in this State and its name is Geraghty. I shut my eyes as a shudder runs through my limbs, aftershock of my cold dip. The sea O the. Should have let go of Sealman's hand in the Forty Foot. I'd be full fathom five, now, food for the fishies, all care dissolved. Geraghty may not be the problem, maybe he's a symptom. Leprechaunitis. National hysteria has created a new idol, all glitter but no gold and I'm either a fool, a hostage to his fortunes, or a voice in the wilderness, the Cassandra no one wants to hear.

Chapter Eleven

The exterior of Phil the Finagler's flabby drawings for the Murphy-Benz's nursing home, 'Iteration 3', to use his parlance, is a tall, dark, ugly block with one corner lopped off the top. Minus the other corner it would look like a coffin. Phil's idea of a joke? Were he here I'm sure he would tell me it's a statement but quite of what I'm not sure. It looks like he's giving us the finger. He won't be sharpening his pencil, if I have my way, pace Seán Kiely, but taking out his eraser. Trouble is, Bernie's very persuasive and Phil has friends in high places. He has relocated the belatedly added kitchen, this time to the floor above the dining room. He'll need a dumb waiter or several speaking ones to ferry the food to the residents. The building takes up most of the putative site, the footprint as they call it nowadays, leaving very little space for parking. It's surely not in Feargal's interests to be forcing people to use public transport. Missing the essentials is obviously lanky Phil's fingerprint. What can Bernie and Feargal be thinking of? Do they really want their elegant home, and the terrace of which it is part, to be overshadowed by this post-post-post-mothren excrescence? As I stare at the screen something begins to stir or ripple along the base of my mind, too inchoate for a thought, too irksome to be disregarded but while I wait for it to surface and solidify my mobile phone beeps to announce a new message. Muiris' name lights up and I read: Hi! 4go ur prncpls 2day & by I.T. C biz supp. p.10. Tlk l8tr. M xox. Once upon a time my son knew how to spell. Now there's no need to but it takes me a few minutes to decode the msg.

Okay Tanta, I say, it looks like we're going out again.

In the hall I take his lead off the stand which sets him jumping and yapping like a wind-up toy.

Rrrrrrinnnnggggg. Botheration. Rrrrrriiinnnnggggggg. The doorbloodybell. Whisht, whisht I hiss under my breath while Tanta segues from hopping and yapping to pointing and barking, almost tripping me up with his flailing lead. Dear God, don't let it be Bernie come to enthuse about Phil's folly. I tiptoe to the door, waving my hand at the dog to get him to pipe down and move back. A peek through the spyhole shows a woman in a pink track suit, her face half-hidden by large sunglasses, her head twitching anxiously this way and that. Surely not Moira Kiely come for her money already? I crack the door open, holding Tanta back with one foot. The vigorous woman before me fills her expensive tracksuit with more substantial curves than Moira could ever rise to.

Yes? I say curtly.

Oh, hello Lena, she says but even when she removes her dark glasses she remains a stranger to me. Lena? She smiles uncertainly.

I shake my head, still at a loss for a name.

It's Rosemary, she prompts, Rosemary Mulvaney. Myles' wife. Her voice teeters on the last word.

Of course, say I, fitting the face to my memory of Mrs. Myles whom I have met only a handful of times and they not today or yesterday or even the day before. I'm sorry, I smile, I was just going out. Come in. I step back, holding the door wide to admit her.

Well . . . if you're sure it's . . . She glances warily at Tanta before crossing the threshold so I pick him up, cradling him under my arm where he wriggles in protest.

I'll put him downstairs, I say. You go ahead to the drawing room, I gesture with my free arm to the open door at the end of the hall.

Would you like a cup of coffee? I ask before descending the stairs.

No thanks. I have a bottle of water here. Her elbow flaps to indicate the bag hitched over her shoulder and whose handle she grips so tightly that her knuckles are white.

Rosemary is a games teacher in a girls' school, which explains the tracksuit. I assume she is returning from a hockey match or practice. Her first elevens regularly win the Leinster Cup and some of her past pupils have gone on to play for Ireland. She's the one who actually pursues the sports while her husband juggles the metaphors and the remote control for the telly.

When I return to the drawing room, bearing my mug of coffee and a glass of water for her I find my visitor standing with her back to the bay window, as if defending goal.

What can I do for you? I ask in a breezy tone intended to dispel the glum expression on her face, although I suspect I know what caused it. I place the glass on the table beside the couch.

I'm not sure, she studies me for a moment, waiting for me to shoot.

Is there anything the matter with Myles? I oblige, to draw her out.

I don't know, her lower lip trembles. I was hoping you might be able to tell me.

Well if I can help you I will. Please, sit down.

She drops onto the couch, allowing her body to sag gratefully for a moment before pulling herself upright, hands pressed together in her lap to brace her spine, and shutting her eyes as she composes herself.

I take my place in Mother's old armchair and wait for her to speak, although I don't really want to hear what she has to say, fearing that it will draw me into a lie.

After a deep breath she begins, I'm worried about him. He seems distracted, preoccupied. He works very late, he's not sleeping, he even goes back to the office at night and sometimes at the weekend. When I ask him what's wrong he says he has a big case on and that it will all be over in a few weeks. Then we'll go on a holiday. Just the two of us, somewhere fancy. At this her composure dissolves and the tears which have been gathering break free. I don't need to go somewhere fancy, she gives a desperate little snort, I just want him back the way he was. I think he's having a breakdown. Or else he's in some kind of trouble.

You poor dear, I murmur, and wait.

The only sounds in the room are Rosemary's sobs and sniffles and the tick of the clock on the mantelpiece paying out the short moments of my patience. I'm sorry, she gulps and wipes her eyes and cheeks with a crumpled tissue, sorry to disturb you. I just don't know where to turn, she blows her nose and directs a pleading look at me. Is he involved in a big case? I know you've retired but Myles says you're still kind of involved in the office. After this speech she pulls a plastic bottle from her bag and takes a long slug of water.

That I'm looking over his shoulder? Is that what he says?

She nods, shamefaced.

He exaggerates. I kept track of some of the files I handed to him because I felt I owed it to those clients. But I honestly have no idea what he's working on at the moment.

Are you sure? She directs an oddly suspicious look at me.

Absolutely, I block the look and wait for her to tackle.

She sniffles again, I mean, if it's not work what is it? Her voice rises on a note of hysteria. My friends think he might be having an affair with someone in the office.

With *me*? I laugh but seeing her expression change I apologise. I don't mean to offend you but I am almost old enough to be his mother.

I know, she mumbles. She slumps again, looking defeated. I didn't really think it was you but might there be someone else there who . . . ?

I couldn't possibly speculate on that, I reply, consoling myself with the thought that I have no concrete evidence of her husband's affair with the Mouse. I'm afraid you'll just have to ask Myles.

He'll fob me off, the way he has already. She shakes her head vehemently and taking a swig of water for courage blurts, I followed him one night.

That was risky, I say, surprised to discover that Old Brennan and I are not the only amateur detectives in town.

I wanted to see if he really was going to the office, she continues. And he did. I saw the lights come on in the hall and then in the window of his office so I went home.

There you are, I shake my head. Nothing to see. He was working. I don't recommend working so late but these days there is a lot more pressure than when I was in practice. People expect everything to be done immediately. I make a feint at levity, it's the age of instant communication without information.

Maybe, she pulls a face, but I wasn't convinced so I drove around for a while and went back.

Determined lady, I think. Did anyone turn up? I ask.

I saw shadows against the window and a few minutes later a very strange looking woman came out. Her face twists with distaste, not really a woman, if you know what I mean.

A transvestite?

She nods slowly, eyes wide with alarm, I just can't believe . . . I mean, Myles isn't . . . wouldn't . . . she shudders with revulsion. I mean, it's disgusting, isn't it?

I flash her a sympathetic smile but I'm thinking damn Brennan and his 'ladies' of the night. He left out that bit of his story to me about the mysterious midnight meetings. I understand how you feel my dear but I don't think you need to worry on that score. I suspect that person was visiting the tenant in the top floor flat.

Oh, her mouth falls open slackly as this new possibility sinks in, I forgot about him.

Ned is lonely, I say to placate her.

He must be very lonely, she says, regaining some of her games mistressy command. I didn't think you'd allow that sort of thing.

It's Ned's home, I shrug. I can't stop him entertaining his friends. I trust him, I add, thinking he's straighter than her husband.

But isn't the late night work fishy all the same?

As I say, it's unusual but the only person who can answer your questions is Myles. Seeing her mouth wobble again, I ask her, Have you thought of suggesting that he see a counsellor? If he's stressed or anxious about something he might need professional help.

The tick of the clock marks the silence between us. I glance at it while I await her response. Half past one. Time to blow the final whistle.

I did, she responds eventually, but he was having none of it. Said it would be a waste of money and time. I can't get through to him, she splutters with exasperation, the ball rolling just out of her reach.

That's difficult for you. I draw myself out of the chair, and say firmly, I'm sorry I can't offer you more help.

Taking the hint, she rises too. Thank you for listening, she sighs, wearily.

You'll just have to wait and hope that Myles sorts out the problem, whatever it is. Then you can discuss your holiday plans.

I hope he sorts it out soon because I can't take much more of this. Once again she dissolves in tears, this time cupping her face in her hands and pressing them to my shoulder. I curve my arm around her strong back and pat it distractedly as I ponder how to get Myles on side without humiliating his wife, and me. Holding her steady while she releases her pent-up tears I look past her head toward the window, my glance coming to rest on the garden. A magpie flashes by and perches in the bare apple tree. Conditioned by Mother's superstitious nature, I watch for a second one to break the bad luck. Orla and Malachi's voices rise from their garden, followed by the thud of a football. I am about to return my attention to Rosemary when a movement on the wall catches my eye. Not a magpie. The Kiely's cat? No, it's longer and lankier and slithers over the wall between the Murphy-B's garden and mine, coming to land on two feet.

Bastard! I breathe, craning forward.

He isn't, you know, Rosemary snuffles against my shoulder then, pulling away from me, continues, He's normally a wonderful husband and father. That's the problem.

I'm sorry, my dear, I say, I didn't mean Myles. I was speaking about the person who is trespassing in my garden. I'm afraid I'll have to ask you to leave now. I step closer to the window and see the creep strolling around, proprietarily, camera in hand.

Of course, yes, she gapes with fright. But shouldn't you call the guards?

I'm tempted to but I know who he is.

Are you sure? Her own worries temporarily forgotten she joins me at the window. Why is he taking all those photos?

He thinks he's an artiste, I say. I need to go down and put manners on him. Don't worry. I can handle this. He's a friend of my neighbours.

I'll let myself out. Thank you very much, she seizes my hand. You've been very kind and understanding. I'll try talking to Myles again. Maybe this will all blow over.

I hope so. I'll drop into the office one day during the week and see if I can discover what's going on.

I don't want to make trouble for you, she pauses in the doorway looking apologetic.

No trouble, I need to see the accountant anyway. I watch her pink form move ahead of me through the dusky hall, the garish, girlish colour a brazen camouflage for her troubled heart. Hard as it must have been for her to demean herself by coming here, it will be a thousand times worse if the things I suspect Myles of turn out to be true, and if I cannot save him from himself. A wave of anger rises in me at his crass and selfish behaviour.

Another wave follows fast, this time directed at the intruder in my garden. As I descend the stairs to the kitchen I feel a momentary regret that Mother gave away Father's rifle when he died. Tanta flies across the lawn, in full cry, making straight for the rowan tree that marks the spot where we buried Bran. There, while Tanta cocks his leg against the trunk, I see, with disbelief, an answering arc of piss rain down on the other side of the tree. Steam rises from the urine in the cold air where Phil Lannigan stands, legs akimbo, fluther in hand.

Piss off, he snaps aptly at Tanta, who has begun to bark, and stealing my line.

Hey! What the hell do you think you're doing in my garden? I call.

Oh, hi, Lena, he says, packing his goods away in haste. Natural fertiliser, he gives me his crooked smile.

Apart from that offensive behaviour, I say. I didn't give you permission to enter my garden.

I wanted to get some shots of the whole site, he explains, caressing the camera slung around his neck, There was no need to disturb you.

Asking my permission would have been a courtesy, not a disturbance, I say, and using the bathroom would have been merely civilised.

There's no need to be so Protestant, he purses his lips in mock disapproval.

I ignore that sally and walk past him to the back gate which I unlock. Go now, I say.

One minute, Phil begins.

Absolutely not, I say. Out. Or I'll call the guards. I remove my mobile phone from my pocket.

Whump! the thud of the football against the wall, followed by a squeal from Orla sets Tanta off again, this time because he'd like to join the game.

Hi Tanter, Orla calls. The dog yaps and stands on his hind legs against the wall, tail wagging hopefully.

With a pained smile Phil slouches towards me, talking all the way, We really need to get the planning permission sorted before Easter so that we can start work in May.

For the second time today I am being treated with the condescending indulgence accorded to an old bean whose mind is unravelling.

I say nothing but remain holding the handle on the gate, reluctant to open it too soon lest Tanta bolt.

Your greenhouse will have to go, Phil is saying as he nears me. Which would be doing you a favour really because the frame is rotting and there's not much growing in there.

I start to punch the emergency number on my phone.

Phil raises his hands and smartens his pace. Okay, okay, he says. I'm leaving. But I'll have to come back.

Losing interest in the kids' ball, Tanta resumes barking at Phil, prancing along beside him as if challenging him to a fight.

Good boy, Tanta, say I.

Phil glances down at the dog, his upper lip curling with distaste. The Hound of the Basketcase, he sneers.

Clenching my jaw and my free hand with the effort to contain the seethe of my rage, I open the gate decisively. The jangle of shattering glass brings us both up short. Snapping my head around I see that Malachi's football has demolished two panes of the greenhouse roof. On the instant, Tanta, equally startled, dashes through the gate, which I continue to hold open, and down the lane.

Quick, I shout, catch him.

Phil breaks into a loping run, hands clasping the camera to his abdomen, and gives chase.

I follow him, calling the dog.

At the junction of the lane and the avenue that leads to the main road Tanta pauses to pee and Phil half-stumbles, half-lunges to seize his collar, at which Tanta, protesting, turns and snaps at him. Fuckit, says Phil, snatching his hand away and releasing the collar.

Now it's my turn to lunge. I seize Tanta's hindquarters and scoop up the wiry little creature who twists and flails against me. Thanks, I pant.

Phil is straightening himself and examining his hand, which, I am relieved to see, is not bleeding, although he winces histrionically as he flexes his fingers. Next he examines his camera.

Are you hurt? I ask.

Yes, fine, he says brusquely and, turning away from me, rounds the corner.

Tightening my grip on Tanta, I carry him back to the door in the wall, which, just to thwart me, has swung shut. Canting my left hip to balance Tanta there, I reach my right hand into my trousers' pocket for the key. Not there. I shift my stance, transferring Tanta onto my right hip, over his vigorous objections, and fumble in my left pocket. Not there. I push the gate. Not a budge. I must have left the key in the lock. Hell, I exclaim, feeling the air go out of my tyres and a sudden chill ripple through me. I'll have to go round to Bernie who has a spare key for my front door. I begin to walk down the lane, Tanta now weighing heavy on my arms.

As I pass the Murphy-B's garden I hear Orla scold her brother, Look what you've done now. You bold boy.

It was a accident, the little boy wails.

Mum'll *kill* you, his sister crows, confident that his trouble will cast her virtue into high relief. Just when she's trying to keep Leener sweet.

Thank you little Miss Napper Tandy.

And then *Leener'll* kill you, Orla piles it on while she has the advantage.

She can't kill me twice, Malachi says stoutly, showing more wit than I'd have given him credit for.

That's right, Malachi, I call.

Say you're sorry, Orla hisses, determined not to let him off the hook even if I have.

Sorry Leener, the blithe sing-song in his tone reveals that he no longer cares about his sister's scolding.

That's okay, Mal, I reply, you did me a favour really because I'll be knocking down the greenhouse anyway.

Bernie opens her door almost the moment I ring the bell, as if she's been standing behind it awaiting me.

Come in Lena, she says immediately. I'm so sorry. I don't know how many times I've told Malachi not to kick his—

I hold up my hand and say, Don't worry about it. I just need the key to the front door please. I locked myself out going after Tanta.

Of course, come in. I was making a quick coffee for Phil. I'll be running back to the shop when Feargal gets in.

Really, I won't stay, thanks.

Oh come on, she says, making to shut the door so that I have to go one way or the other. With the click of the snib I'm trapped.

As usual it takes me a few moments to get my bearings in the Murphy-B's house. Although configured on the same pattern as mine, the glacial minimalism of its décor gives me the impression that I am on a film set. There are none of the clashing colours and patterns favoured by the Mouse here. All is whiteness, the floors a chequer board of black and white tiles, the only colour provided by a large abstract painting in a wash of forest hues.

She leads me across the hall and down to her kitchen which has been modernised and extended with a sunroom-playroom running the width of the house. Phil sits on a stool at the long granite-topped island massaging his injured hand, his eyes fixed dully on the television screen that hangs at the far side of the room. Bernie keeps the box on day and night even with the sound muted. A game-show is in progress involving coloured balls, questions which run across the bottom of the screen to give the viewers a vicarious stake in the competition, gullible participants dazzled by the short-lived glamour, a male presenter, grinning like a Cheshire cat, his female scorekeeper and electronic gadgets for the winners. Phil, for all his pretensions, is riveted.

Put Tanta down, Bernie says. He can go out in the garden.

When she opens the sliding door the dog races to join the kids who are now bouncing up and down on their trampoline.

She calls to Malachi who climbs slowly down to earth and approaches the house with his head hanging.

Now, what do you have to say to Lena? She asks when he reaches us.

I put my hand on her arm in a bid to stop the child's humiliation and say, Leave it, Bernie. Malachi has apologised already.

She casts a sceptical look at me and the child starts to mumble.

Chin up, Malachi, Bernie persists. Look at Lena when you are speaking to her please.

Drawing himself upright, the little boy stares at my waist and parrots, I'msorryIbrokeyourgreenhouseLeenerandill-payforitwithmyownpocketmoneyeventhoughimsaving-foranewgameonplaystation.

Thank you Malachi, say I. I accept your apology. You're very kind to offer to pay for the glass but I wouldn't dream of taking your pocket money. Besides, as I told you, I'm going to knock the greenhouse down so you can smash another window if you like.

Can I really? His expression changes to one of delight and he looks up at his mother, seeking permission for a wholesale demolition job.

No, you certainly may not, Bernie scolds. Lena's just being nice. She turns to me to add, Orla told me about the incident. I'm dreadfully sorry.

Please don't worry about it, I say. I think Tanta wants to join you on the trampoline.

The child scampers off and reaching Tanta picks him up and flings him onto the trampoline, sparking another lecture from Orla who says the bouncing will make the dog puke, a prospect that inspires Malachi to redouble his jumping.

I turn around and move towards the counter where Bernie has poured me a mug of coffee.

I heard that, Phil twists his head but not his eyes away from the telly momentarily.

I shake mine, not sure what he's talking about.

Why are you knocking down the greenhouse? He returns his attention to the screen.

Because, as you observed, I don't grow anything there.

Frankly, I don't believe you.

I'll have to go shortly, Bernie intervenes. But maybe as you're here, Lena, we could get Phil to walk us through his plans.

Good idea, he swings around fully now, back to the screen. Sociologically fascinating, he says jerking his thumb over his shoulder. Consumerism is the new sex.

Not in my experience, I say.

Oh really, he gives me the professorial over-the-top-of-the-glasses look with eyebrows raised and a pucker of his lips that I think he imagines to be seductive.

The plans, Bernie reminds him.

The plans are not the problem, I sigh. It's the concept that bothers me.

But we've specced it all, her eyes light up like Tanta's antici-pating a treat. It's a win-win all round.

I don't think it fits the area. My eye snags on the screen above us as the ubiquitous rainbow appears with its brimming crock of gold. I met Moira Kiely this morning, I say, turning to Bernie.

Yes, she and Seán are very keen, she insists. That's good for all of us.

She mentioned that you're talking to Liam Geraghty about it.

I was going to tell you that. It would be a sweet little deal for him. Different from his other projects, she darts a glance at Phil who nods, and I remember the feeling that impinged on me this morning, without forming a thought or words. That's it: the two men were dining together last night in the Dish and Spoon. In cahoots, of course.

Doesn't your niece work for him? Bernie continues.

She's just started there. At a very low level, I brush off the implied request. The interweaving of small town connections is beginning to strangle me. If Bernie brings Geraghty into the project, Myles could wind up illegally investing clients' money in a nursing home to be built in my back garden. Poor Rosemary, along with many others, would never believe I knew nothing about that.

I'm sorry, I say, at last. I'm simply not persuaded of its merits on any level.

Maybe you need a little more time, Lena, Bernie cajoles.

Are you sure? Phil drawls. Or is that what Muiris said?

I don't need Muiris to feed me lines, I say.

It's none of Muiris' business, says Bernie sharply. Then, fearing she has offended me, follows up with, I mean, it's not his style of project.

No but even if it was I wouldn't be interested.

I think you don't understand the overarching paradigm shift behind the plan, Phil continues pedantically. It's ahead of its time.

The profit motive is hardly a novelty.

Look, Bernie cries, reaching for the remote. Isn't that Jean and her pals?

Christ almighty, I exclaim, looking at the screen. So that's where they were off to this morning.

Isn't it a bit early for an Orange parade? drawls Phil.

Chapter Twelve

Obeying the amber light at Frascati I draw the car to a halt. While it idles I take a moment to compose myself and wonder how I come to be giving Phil o' the Piss, his belongings and condescending smirk a lift to town. Bernie had been right. Jean, Pól and Siobhán had appeared on the TV, all three grotesque in orange prison jumpsuits like the one I had dumped, placards aloft, outside the American embassy. A cordon of gardaí in riot gear surrounded the perimeter fence of the embassy and faced the chanting protesters.

Stupid kids! I exclaimed then wheeled about to face my hostess. I'm sorry, I'll have to go. I need to get Jean out of there before there's any trouble. Paddy'll have another heart attack if he sees that. And he'll blame me.

Of course, said Bernie. She opened a drawer and rummaged for a minute before producing my latchkey.

I slid open the door to the garden and called Tanta who was having too good a time to respond to me.

At Bernie's instruction Orla caught the dog and carried him to me, chiding his resistance with a mother superior air, then handed the squirming bundle of fur and determination into my arms.

Bye bye, Tanter, she said. You be a good boy.

At the hall door I came face to face with Phil, zipped into his anorak, laptop bag dangling from one hand, camera from the other, the weight of his ego depressing his shoulders.

If you're going towards town maybe you could give me a lift some of the way, he suggested. My car is in for repairs.

I'm going to Ballsbridge, said I.

That'll be fine, he grinned, happy to have got part of his way.

I'm leaving now, I snapped, too anxious to get going to have an argument with the lanky lout.

When he was buckled into the passenger seat he told me that he lived in Kimmage, adding miserably, but I suppose I can walk from the Bridge of Balls.

Yes, said I. That or get a taxi. Although something tells me he's too tight to pay for a cab.

About the plans, he persists now in a confiding wheedle, you know, between us, Bernie and Feargal don't really understand them. They're business people: good for the money but not the aesthetics. Not like—

That's enough, I say and, swinging the car into the bay of a bus stop, I pull up.

What's the matter? My impertinent passenger swivels his head imagining there's a problem on the road.

You, I say. You're the matter. I don't know what I was thinking of agreeing to give you a lift. Out.

But I can't walk from here, he whines.

Try crawling. That would suit you.

His mouth falls open, aghast.

Hurry up. There's a bus coming.

Sure enough the bus comes blaring up behind us and in my rear view mirror I can see that the driver is swearing roundly at me.

Phil gives me a filthy look then winces histrionically as he hauls his bags and gangling limbs out of the passenger seat. Once on the pavement he slams the door so forcefully that the car shudders. I signal right and nudge my way back into the stream of traffic. With schadenfreudian satisfaction I see Phil the traitor put out his hand to halt the bus which promptly engages gear and lurches away from the stop. I give the bus driver a thumbs up in the mirror. At the same moment heavy drops of rain commence to spatter the windscreen. Good enough for the creature.

Having parked on Clyde Road I hasten to the embassy and the scene of the protest aired on TV. In addition to the gardaí posted against the perimeter fence there is a circle of them on the road, which has been closed off with steel barriers. More barriers confine the orange-suited crowd to the footpath. A man standing on an impromptu dais shouts into a microphone, his words garbled by vehemence and volume. Off to the side the TV crews huddle together, smoking and clasping paper cups of coffee, the cameras shrouded in plastic hoods. I scan the crowd for Jean and her friends, standing on tippy toes to see past the gardaí.

Excuse me, I say, craning to look over one of the blue shoulders.

The garda turns to face me and for a moment I stare nonplussed at her delicate tapered eyes, which widen wonderingly.

You'll need to stand back, Missus, she says surprising me further with her Donegal accent. There's another lot on the way and there's going to be trouble.

Very well, I step back.

Hi Lena! Pól waves from the crowd. He nudges Jean and points to me.

She glances around fearfully and I seize the moment to beckon her over. She frowns and, saying something to Pól, rejoins the monotonous round the protesters are tracing.

Jean! I call in the sharp note I used on Tanta, with the same effect.

Startled, the garda in front of me snaps around again. Do you know them? She asks.

Yes. That's my niece.

Well if I was you Missis I'd get her out of here. This is going to turn nasty.

That's what I'm trying to do but she's ignoring me.

Is she the one with the short hair?

I shake my head. That's her friend. She's the one that looks like a panda.

The garda's features tauten for a moment with the suspicion that I'm taking the proverbial.

There, I point and elaborate, the one with the black hair and the white face. Beside the lad with the orange pony tail—to match the suit. I beam chummily to get her on side again.

Do you want me to fetch her for you?

Can you do that? I mean without making trouble for yourself.

I can try. So saying she opens the barrier, steps inside and has a word with one of her colleagues.

When Jean comes around again she calls to her by name which I can see gives the girl a fright. She hesitates and the garda says, Your aunty wants you.

Careful not to lay a hand on the girl she and her colleague nevertheless block her path back to the protest leaving Jean no option but to approach the barricade.

Is it Dad again? She stops a couple of feet from me, as if afraid that I am going to snatch her away. A good instinct because that's exactly what I want to do.

Yes and no, I hedge.

The garda opens the barrier again and points Jean through the gap.

Thank you, I say to her. To Jean I say, Come on, the car's over here. You can leave that ridiculous sign there.

It's not ridiculous, she raises it again so that the slogan screams at me: END rENDition STOPovers at Shannon.

Pól made it.

Brilliant, I say with asperity. But it's not travelling in my car. The same goes for the suit.

I'm not coming in the car. She confronts me with a defiant pout. If there's nothing wrong with Dad I'm going back to the protest.

There might be when he sees you and your pals on the TV news.

Are we on the news? Her expression brightens despite herself.

How do you think I knew you were here?

She shrugs. I didn't think about it.

There seem to be a lot of things you didn't think about missy. Now, either you come with me or—

A volley of shouts and the sound of many running feet break out behind us. Horror possesses Jean's features as she looks past me to the protest. Catching her fear I seize her arm and swing around to follow the direction of her look. A new band of protesters has arrived at the embassy, older, bigger and gruffer than Jean's lot. Some yell insults at the gardaí while others try to pull the barricade aside to join the first group. The gardaí in riot gear close in on them, batons aloft.

Pól, Jean cries, trying to shake off my grip.

You can't help him, I say. You'll only get hurt yourself. Leave it to the gardaí.

Police and ambulance sirens chase each other in the distance.

They're pigs, she screams trying to pull free of me. It's a peaceful protest.

It was until that bunch arrived. Can't you see? They're hijacking it.

The journalists have dropped their coffee cups and fags to crouch and weave between the rioters and the police, cameras and microphones nosing in for a good angle. A black maria pulls up in the middle of the road and disgorges more riot police. Moments later an ambulance appears. The siren dies as the paramedics jump out and open the back of the van. Hefting a stretcher and medical kit they move towards the mob which parts then closes around them. The chants and insults ratchet up as the garda reinforcements fan out around the crowd.

Pól! Pól! Jean's cry rises shrilly.

I grip both of the girl's arms as much to calm as to restrain her. It's okay, I say. I don't think it's him.

It is, it is. I know it is, she sobs and struggles to get free.

Sure enough when the paramedics emerge from the crowd bearing the stretcher I spy a red tail dangling from one end.

I told you, I told you. Seething hysterically, Jean wrenches free but the ambulance is already pulling away, the whop of its siren resuming.

Come on, I say, trying with a level tone to counteract her agitation. We'll follow it.

Okay, she gives in and hastens away with me.

Stale, muggy air clogged with moans and curses envelopes us as we enter A and E. Here, in the waiting area, people sit on or sprawl across the rows of hard plastic seats while others lean against the wall or slump on the floor, all malcontent, sick and despondent. On high a pair of TV presenters beam with smug obliviousness, their blather drowned out by the moans and cries of the wretched below, the wham-wham-wham of re-peated kicks to a vending machine delivered by a man who has paid for a drink but received nothing in return, and the loud complaints of a woman who has waited nine hours with her sick daughter, a girl about Jean's age, lying curled on the floor, a balled-up anorak for a pillow, a scarf for a blanket. Nearby sits an old man, elbows on his knees, hands intertwined, head bowed as he calls help help me please someone please help me help help

Jean turns to me, eyes agape with childish dread. Where is he?

Let's ask at reception.

Triage, the harried receptionist tells us.

Can we see him? Jean presses forward.

You can try, the woman says. Knock on that door.

Some minutes after we have knocked the door cracks open and a nurse squinnies out. We ask for Pól and with a suspicious dart of her eyes from right to left she admits us, shutting the door behind us immediately lest the waiting horde should storm the gap. Within is a scene of clinical concentration punctuated by the beeping of machines and the noise of copious vomiting, a sound that makes my stomach turn over. I inhale deeply, conscious of the need to remain composed for the girl's sake.

This way, says the nurse briskly.

We find Pól reclining on a bed, a large dressing on his forehead and a splint on one of his fingers. He manages a rueful grin when he sees us.

What happened? Jean bends over him and touches his face.

I'm not sure. I think someone pushed me from behind. Or was pushed into me. I fell. I think someone stood on my hand. It happened very fast. I banged my head. His eyes roll upwards to indicate the dressing. Then I must have blacked out for a couple of minutes because next thing I was on the stretcher. My ribs hurt. It's hard to breathe and to laugh. They think I may have broken one when I fell but they say there's nothing they can do about it.

Was it the cops?

How quickly the urge to blame someone fills the place where a moment earlier fear had held sway.

No. Not them. Some of those others who came along.

But who *were* those randomers?

He shrugs, Shinners maybe.

No maybe about it, I can't help saying and, now that I have spoken, follow up by asking, Are they keeping you in here for the night?

Yes. They say they have to hold me for observation because I blacked out.

With a new note of panic in her voice, Jean says, I'll stay with you.

They won't allow you to, I tell her, then say to Pól, I'll collect you tomorrow. Just call us when they discharge you.

Thanks, Lena, he gives me the thumbs up.

When Jean emerges from the cubicle tears are streaming down her face.

He'll be fine, I say. It's just a precaution.

It's all horrible, she sobs. Horrible. I don't want to leave him here.

I know, I soothe, but there's nothing you can do for him.

With bowed head she trails behind me through the waiting room and out across the hospital campus to the car park. Rain is falling but its chilly drops are almost a relief after the unnerving atmosphere of the emergency department. Evening closes in as we drive home along the seafront. Too worn out to talk, we sink into our separate silences. Jean keeps her head averted from me, facing out to the darkling sea and I sense that she is still crying. I long to comfort her but know enough to respect the distance she has set between us.

The house feels cold and hollow when we return. No sooner are we in the door than Jean makes to run up to her room.

Wait, I call her.

She halts but keeps her back to me.

I think we both need a drink.

That does the trick. She loses the slouch as she returns to the hall.

First, I say, take off that ugly garment. You make me feel like a jailer. Second, you can let Tanta out while I fix the drinks.

Fix being the key word. A small dose of gin for her and a double for me.

When I switch on the light in the sitting room I pause for a moment, flashed back under its weak glare to Rosemary's morning visit. I pick up her half-empty water glass and crumpled tissue from the side table. Can it really have been only today that I was so intruded on? Tanta yaps as he races across the garden, ready either to rout any more unwelcome visitors or play with the heaven-sent football but I am as disorientated as if I had just returned from a long journey. Not even the familiar routine of pouring a drink can allay my unease.

Ah no. It can't be true. A peremptory blast on the doorbell. Déja entendu. I'll blast whoever's on the other side of the door.

The moment I slide back the cover on the spyhole I hear Moira Kiely's voice call, Don't worry, Lena. It's only me. She waves a sheet of paper in front of the glass as if it is a white flag.

I open the door a crack and snap, What is it?

I brought the sponsorship form, she enthuses, thrusting the paper at me.

She has shed the pink tracksuit in favour of her habitual frayed coat and the scarf is knotted under her chin now.

Good, I try to smile, but unfortunately I don't have a pen on me. Maybe you could come back tomorrow.

I have one, she whips a biro from her pocket, I can fill it in for you.

I don't have any cash on me, I try again to deflect her.

Don't worry, she waves the pen and paper, you can give it to me later. Making a play of folding the page and pressing it against the wall in an effort to force me to let her in, which I ignore, she begins to write, then, without taking her eyes off the page, asks, Did I see you on the telly?

I've no idea what you saw on the telly, I sigh. I've only just got home. I'd rather do this another day, if you don't mind. My niece . . .

I saw her too, she turns and pokes her narrow face at me, and the lad with all the hair.

Well God bless your eyesight, Moira, I say, and goodnight. I've had a long day.

Yes, goodnight, she rolls up her sponsorship sheet. I've put you down for €50.

Only when I have shut the door does the import of her final words sink in. Fifty effing notes! The conniving bitch! I open the door again to call her back but she is already half way down the road. Putting all that marathon training to good use. I haven't the energy to chase her now but the most she'll get from me the next time I see her is a flea in her ear.

I take a bracing swig of the gin I had just poured myself and replenish the glass before descending to the kitchen where Jean is seated at the table, busily thumbing a message on her phone.

I'm not going to lecture you, I say, placing her drink in front of her. Because I think you saw today the risks involved in any protest.

It was okay until those others came along, she grumbles continuing to text.

Maybe but that's my point. That crowd will always muscle in on a demonstration, looking for new recruits and publicity. They wait to see what way the wind is blowing before getting involved.

We still have a right to make our point. She puts down the phone and jutting her chin at me says, Grandpa fought for what he believed and it didn't do him any harm. He's the family hero.

Ah . . . well . . . I pause to consider this curve ball, as Myles would likely call it, then busy myself with rummaging in a cupboard for peanuts or crackers to accentuate the tang of the gin. You can't compare the two things. He certainly wouldn't if he were here, I resume when I sit down. He was objecting to the presence of a colonial power within his own country, not the activities of other countries outside Ireland. He would say now we have a forum for legitimate objections.

It's a new form of colonialism, she retorts. We can't pretend that we're not implicated.

I have never seen the girl so animated and, while I want to counsel her against getting drawn into more foolishness, I can't help warming to the fervour that makes her eyes spark. I have a fleeting recollection of Mossie bringing food and beer to the students who occupied the buildings in Hume Street scheduled for demolition because he admired their spirit. Nevertheless, I think he would have shared my apprehension about today's antics.

You have to be careful not to be used and drawn into the firing line, I say at last.

But a protest doesn't mean anything if you're not taking a risk. Grandpa had to risk his life didn't he?

In a war yes, yes, he did. Two wars. For the right to self-government.

Well that's no use if you let other governments walk all over you.

I wouldn't describe it that way. Now we have a our own parliament, we can use that to voice our views. There has to be compromise in everything. Negotiation. We can't isolate ourselves. They tried that and it didn't work.

But this is a sell-out, not a compromise.

Tell that to the people who are employed by American companies here. Your own boss I think has business interests over there.

She frowns at me. That's different. And anyway he's a douche-bag.

Oh God, my head is spinning with this girl and her arguments. My own are sounding feeble. I've lost the knack. Lost myself it feels like. The truth is she's challenging my complacency. And Father looms near, keeping stumm as ever about what he did and saw.

On the pretext of calling Tanta in I get up to catch my breath. I stand at the open door waiting for him to burst from the shrubbery and run across the damp grass. The lamp in the back lane snaps on, making a shadow play of the garden. A little rush of dizziness takes me, blurring my mind, and the rough hands maul me again, the voice coarsened with rage and lust snarling in my ear traitor hoor traitorhoor traitor traitoor. I wait a moment gripping the door for reassurance, wanting to shut out the evil shades and am relieved when the dog hurtles past leaving a trail of muddy prints on the kitchen tiles. I close and bolt the door.

Dad said Grandpa went on hunger strike in prison, Jean continues when I return to the table. He stood up for his ideals.

Paddy is worse, filling her head with this stuff. Next thing she'll be on hunger strike. I take it all back about her being overweight.

Yes, I reply, but that was part of a civil war here. The war in Iraq is not our war.

See, she spreads her hands and flashes me a triumphant smile, you agree with me. That's why we shouldn't let the American military flights stop here. We're taking a side and it's the wrong side.

I don't disagree but I don't want you to get hurt. There are other ways to object.

Like what? Write a letter to the paper? She scoffs. Dad's always saying he's going to write a letter to the editor. Then Mum reminds him that they publish his articles so he gives up that idea until the next time.

It's a joy to see the girl laugh. The white make-up seems to crack open like a shell liberating the bright young woman within. Suddenly I envy her this energy and freedom to be herself, to laugh at her father and take on a cause. How naive and self-obsessed I was at her age. Maybe instead of scolding her I should get out there with a banner too. But I draw the line at the orange suit.

That wasn't quite what I had in mind, say I. You could write an article yourself.

With that flippant suggestion I recall Richard's article criticising his government's lack of forward planning. When I expressed my surprise to him at a member of Her Majesty's forces sticking his neck out like that he had corrected me by saying, *Former* member. I'm retired. My concern is for the troops in there. But the chaps in Whitehall don't care about them. Still mourning their lost colonies. Were he here he might agree with Jean's point about a new form of colonialism but my mission is to keep her out of trouble.

And there it is: I have expressed the impulse that I had been trying subconsciously to hold back, the maternal wings are shaking themselves out to enfold and protect her and—oh lordie, who'd have thunk it?—they might even open to embrace the opinionated Pól. The sight of him so pale and brave in the hospital bed, coupled with the risk that he might have suffered a serious head injury, gave me a jolt. Running through this mothering impulse is the vestige of an old ache that surges occasionally in the lightless hours between night and day, banishing sleep. No grace or physic came to fill the gap left by our inability to have more children or to ease that grief. Mossie took comfort in the mantra that it was God's will and said that he was happy with our lovely son. Each of us in our way tried to protect the other from the sadness we felt, his soothed by prayer, mine by a hovering sense that I had been somehow damaged and that Muiris was a miracle. Now, against my expectations, this lumpen girl has crept in and pitched camp in that empty spot.

With that sudden access of maternal care I raise a more immediate concern. Have you eaten? I ask. Because I've just realised that I've had nothing all day, not since I abandoned Bernie's carrot and pecan cake at lunchtime to rescue you.

I didn't need rescuing, she retorts.

Well Pól did. And that could have been you.

I suppose so.

She affects nonchalance but I see the flit of fear in her eyes.

By way of a peace offering I say, How about a cheese sandwich?

Yes, that would be good, she nods vigorously. I'm starving.

That's a term your Grandpa would not have approved of, say I. He'd have said you may be hungry but you certainly are not starving.

Well then I'm very very hungry, she emphasises.

I move around the kitchen taking out the sandwich fixings, glad of the occupation which helps defray the tension between us.

Maybe you should go into politics, I suggest, as I smooth the mayonnaise over the bread.

I'd only do that if the system changed, she says with a mildly condescending smile. There's no point joining a broken and corrupt system. It's out of date. All tied up with big business. We need a new model. This protest is only a baby step. People have to see how our lives and our governments are controlled by a handful of super-wealthy individuals and multinational corporations. We think we're free but we're not. Not really.

I look up and wave the knife at her, Please listen to me, Jean. This could get nastier next time out.

We won't let that happen, she boasts. I bet Grandpa would've agreed that we have to preserve our independence and identity.

Yes but having established those rights we're open to make deals with other similarly independent and self-confident countries, say I. After all, it's his party that's in power now.

This Grandpa she talks about is a pure stranger to the child who was only two when he died. She bawled so loudly at his funeral that she had to be taken out of the church. Thus, perhaps, began her career of protest because she chose the moment when Paddy was about to embark on the eulogy. Her Grandpa is a graven image, vibrant as his hero Napoleon, not the aloof, exacting man whose air of perpetual disappointment in us made it nigh impossible to love him.

Hang on! I exclaim, I've something to show you. I finish cutting the crusts off the sandwiches, arrange them on a plate and hand it to her. Take these into the breakfast room and light the stove, I'll be back in two ticks.

In the office I remove a small key from the top drawer of my desk and with it open the cupboard where I store confidential papers. From the back of the lowest shelf I remove a box labelled 'Muiris' and place it on the desk. I sift the school reports, copy books and drawings that I have kept since Muiris' childhood, his first wobbly images of Mammy and Daddy, his name on a card, the S reversed, letters from Irish college, pining for his dog, Rusty, and requesting more tuck, until I find a cassette tape and under it a folder with the title 'History Project: Interview with my Grandfather, Patrick J. O'Neill, 20 October 1982'.

In the breakfast room I hand the folder to Jean then crouch before my dusty old boom box and insert the cassette. Taking my seat at the table I start in on a sambo while a youthful Muiris introduces his grandfather. Moments later, Father's voice establishes itself in the room, through some throat clearing and fidgeting before the microphone, unsure of his position and its capacity. Or vice versa. Muiris reassures him that it's on and recording.

Very well, Father says. I hope you're right.

It's fine Grandpa.

Good, good. Then, let us begin.

Yes, maybe you could start with your parents, your child-hood? Muiris' voice quavers a little anxiously now that he has been given control.

Ah, the long view, I see, Father sighs. I can let you read my research on your O'Neill ancestry.

Jean looks at me in astonishment and whispers, Is that really Grandpa?

I nod, somewhat astonished myself at how natural it is to hear the familiar tones again, and how, eliding the gap of twenty-two years, his presence impinges on the room so that I glance around in search of his face.

He sounds like you, says Jean.

Me? How so? I pull a face at this bizarre suggestion.

I don't mean his voice but the way he says things. It's like the way you'd say things.

That's a pretty strange thing to say, I must say.

But he has an Englishy accent.

The Jesuits, I explain.

Thank you. Muiris tries to divert Father from his four cen-tury long excursus, obsession of his declining years. But you don't need to go all that far back. Just if you could tell me about your parents and maybe your grandparents.

I have never listened to the tape before although I did read Muiris' account of his grandfather. At the time I was struck by how forthcoming Father had been with him, given how reticent he had been when we asked about his activities, dismissing them with the phrase, 'it was all a long time ago'. Now I wonder was he protecting people or was it still too fresh and painful in his memory, which, in a curiously ambiguous phrase, he boasted was 'like a vice'. I glance at Jean who listens intently to the tape, mechanically chewing her sandwich as she leans forward, almost holding her breath. In this encounter across the generations I am irrelevant and, if the girl is right, I am merely the vessel into which my parents have been poured and presumably their parents and so on all the way back, maybe even to the Great O'Neill. It is a disconcerting if instructive glimpse of myself as improvisation, a ball teetering briefly on the jet of a fountain, sustained for an instant only to subside. Nearby, Jean rises as I descend. Tilting my head in the direction of the sound I try to listen with her ears as Father describes his parents and their families, his father's father who had established the medical practice that Daddo had inherited and which Father's sister, Mai, later took over. His mother's father had been a prosperous farmer and draper in Killarney, active member of the Parliamentary Party, a Redmondite, who once ran for election but lost by a mere 125 votes. He never knew his paternal grandmother who had died before he was born. His maternal grandmother, a schoolteacher from Dingle, had instilled a love of the Irish language in him and that was why he had joined the Gaelic League when he came to university in Dublin.

Did you speak Irish at home?

Occasionally, with Mammy. She translated some English and French religious texts into Irish. I liked to help her with those.

How come you didn't speak Irish with my Mum and uncle Paddy? Muiris is moving off point I fear.

Ah, that's a good question. I can see Father's slightly wistful expression as he says this. Your grandmother attended a convent boarding school in England where she learnt French and Spanish, not Irish. I did try to teach her in the early days of our marriage [This is news to me.] but I regret to say she wasn't sufficiently interested. I had brought her back, you see, from teaching music in England. I said she should put her talents to use here.

I wish we didn't have to learn it at school. Muiris can't help himself.

Jean laughs and motions a clapping gesture to support this sentiment.

You must learn your language, Father upbraids him. It's a badge of our identity, part of how we define ourselves. Without it you can't access your history, your heritage. I think your father understood that even if your mother doesn't. [Ha! I might if it had been better taught and I had been encouraged to learn it.]

And then you joined Sinn Féin is that right?

Yes. I wasn't going to be conscripted into the British Army thank you very much. Then, after the 1918 election, you see, we were all elated and optimistic. We had our own assembly, the Dáil, and the message went out to the world that we were now an independent nation. There was a hope, you see, that, like other small states, we might be recognised at the peace conference and from there it would be only a short step to managing our own affairs. You have to understand, you see, that being occupied by another country is like always having an unwelcome stranger in your house, one who makes the rules. No matter what private corner of the house you are in you can feel his presence, he's breathing there in the corner, waiting to catch you out, to take the food from your hand or the chair from under you. In the end sadly that hope was dashed.

Did you run for election?

Good lord no. I was only nineteen. I helped with the campaign, putting up posters, licking envelopes. Canvassing, attending meetings, that sort of thing. Dog's body work. We were the foot soldiers if you like. You, now, you could join the Ogra, you could—

Maybe when I go to college, Grandpa. I've too much homework now.

Don't work too hard, Father says lightly. [Not a line he ever took with me.]

You said you were a foot soldier, does that mean you joined the IRA?

I joined the Volunteers, Father is quick to correct him.

But it was the same thing.

Later. And don't run away with the notion that it's also the same as the mob in the North now. It was the legitimate Irish Republican Army. Part of the shadow administration we set up.

So you fought in the war of independence? And in the civil war?

There is a long silence before Father resumes slowly, I did what was necessary. It's not glamorous. I saw what happened after 1916. I was about the same age you are now. When we had our parliament I thought we could proceed that way but there were others, you see, unfortunately, who were spoiling for a fight. Once that began it would have been cowardly not to engage.

Where were you then? In Dublin or in Kerry?

Another long silence. In the background a fog horn blows. A match is struck. I can see Father cup his hands around the bowl of his pipe, and suck the stem to get it lit. Another match rasps, more sucking followed by a racking cough.

I did what I was told. I went home. I was in a flying column, he says at last.

What did you do, ambushes, arms raids?

Yes. It wasn't work I relished, believe me. You couldn't understand what the times were like, the sheer terror people lived in. Women and children were terrorised. Lorries full of soldiers, wearing trench helmets, driving through the towns, soldiers raiding houses, the Black and Tans, commandeering whiskey, cigarettes, clothing, anything they took a fancy to, firing off shots, turning houses over, sometimes even burning them. They stopped and searched men on the street, rounded people up, subjected them to brutal treatment. Brutal. Brutal humiliation. That was nearly the worst, stripping men, throwing them into the river or the lake and making them walk home naked, beating them on a whim, accusing them of being Volunteers or members of Sinn Féin, even when they knew well they weren't. They had no respect for anyone. You could hardly walk down the street without being taunted, insulted or searched.

Did they do that to you?

Agh, it was a long time ago. He reprises the old line tetchily. Don't you have enough material now?

I'd like a little more but I can turn off the recording for a while if you want a break. I probably need to turn over the cassette anyway.

The tape runs on blankly. I reach across, stop it and turn it over.

Where were we? Father asks.

I had asked you if the Tans or the soldiers ever treated you badly, the way you described?

Had you? More coughing and pipe cleaning, dottle being knocked into the fireplace. Yes. Yes. You had. That's right. Indeed. Ah, yes. Yes. They did. They did lift me. Once. I went to a dance you see. A couple of fellows grabbed me as I was coming home, accused me of being at an illegal meeting. I told them I had been dancing and I never knew that was illegal. They said there was a curfew—this was the invention of the local officer in charge—I said I could dance well enough in the dark. Then one of them dealt me a blow with the butt of his revolver. Here. [So that's how he got the short scar that bisected his right eyebrow. He told us that as a child he had tripped on a rug and fallen against the corner of a wardrobe.] Nearly put my eye out.

Is that why you became an ophthalmic surgeon?

No. I don't think so. I mean I never thought of that. But it might have been there somewhere in the background I suppose. Needless to say that made me more determined, you see, to drive these people out of our country.

What did you do then?

Worked harder of course. Ranged wider around the area. We were in bad need of arms. The fighting, the things that were done, that we did . . . I hope you never ever have to do them. His voice sinks away. It's never easy no matter how much anger you have or how much you hate. Or how much you dream. All terrible. It doesn't get easier and it never leaves you be. Don't let anyone tell you different.

Do you think the violence was necessary?

Yes. I'm sorry to say I do. Not on its own. But the British never responded to anything but violence. Years of debating and negotiation for a home rule Bill and they betrayed us. They lacked the imagination to see the consequences of their actions and policies. Of course we were using the electoral system too. We elected councillors, set up our own administration, courts and so on. They didn't like that. It was easier for their bowsies to deal with the physical stuff. You see, ever since the seventeenth century the Irish had the reputation for reckless bravery. Our infinite capacity for excess. Ha, yes. They made use of that in their colonies but they forgot about it when they came to keeping *us* under their thumb.

Were you never caught?

I was. Oh yes. I was. Father becomes more animated, his reticence overtaken by a sense of angry pride. They wouldn't let me be, their orange spies following me, hoping I'd lead them to more of us. I went on the run. Well I couldn't let them go on raiding my parents' home, wrecking the place. Mammy was in fear every minute of the day mostly for my younger brother and sister. My older brother, Denis, was away in Maynooth training for the priesthood. I was doing guard duty at a court hearing. An informer tipped the local officer off. They took us away in the back of their lorry, all of us, even the litigants, and a couple of women, witnesses, soldiers surrounding us with bayonets fixed. I can still see the contempt on their faces. A few of us were held out in a field enclosed with barbed wire for two days until the so-called authorities were ready to question us. We pleaded with them to let the women go, which they did after a few hours. They kept me locked up for three weeks, beat me, turned a hose on me, starved me, threatened to shoot me if I didn't betray my comrades. Barbarians. Pagans. Another long silence. More coughing. I think that's enough isn't it?

Em, yes. Maybe another day we can talk about the civil war.

Awful, awful. There is a catch now in Father's voice. Worse. That's enough. I'm tired.

Thank you.

Jean sits in silence as the tape hisses to its end.

That's brilliant, she says. Can I play it for Pól some time?

I suppose so. I'm beginning to have a better understanding of Pól's line of study, especially as he's fond of quizzing me about legal procedure and brokering settlements between contending parties, specifically from my experience of dealing with unions and employers, because he's interested in conflict resolution. I tell him that he should just do law rather than a pick and mix of subjects without ever getting to first principles in any of them. But no, he says he needs to come at it from different angles, get an overview, see the big picture. He has big ideas, and it's possible I envy him the energy that drives his ambition.

It kinda felt like Grandpa was here in the room for a while, didn't it?

Yes, yes it did, I say, surprised to find that I miss the sound of his voice now that the tape has run its course. Although I never heard him speak like that.

When a strange woman at his funeral described Father as a 'honey man' I wondered for a moment had she come to the wrong obsequies. But no, she went on to explain that she often met him on the seafront, when each was walking their dog, and they would stop to chat, an easy, uncomplicated exchange of pleasantries. He had included her in the circle of women to whom he liked to present a nosegay of his cherished pink lily-of-the-valley, a harmlessly chivalrous gesture that, irrationally, never ceased to irk Mother. I had seen the man the stranger knew only in flashes, most often when he and Mother joined us at the end of our summer holidays with our grandparents' in Kerry.

Once back on his native soil, Father shed some of the formality that marked his Dublin persona. He was happy to linger on the pier jawing, usually in Irish, with the fishermen, or playing pitch and toss on the road with men who had been his schoolmates and later his comrades in the struggle for independence. He spoke to them with more vigour and emphasis than he ever did to us, as if by speaking in the tongue that he loved, and that he had successfully campaigned to have taught at his private boarding school, he drank from a stream of perennial youth. Inspired by that holiday rejuvenation, he taught us to swim, took us cycling and fishing but most of all on those holidays he enjoyed spending afternoons helping his mother with her translation of Pascal. At night he and Mother played bridge with the local bank manager and the priest. It came to me in later life that the man we saw on those holidays chafed inside the three piece suit and starched collar of the esteemed hospital consultant. Mother it was who had suggested, shortly after their marriage, that they move to Dublin where he could train in a specialty, arguing that there would not be enough work in his father's practise to support two households. This no doubt was true, and it was also true that she could not have borne to live in a small rural town. While Father enjoyed the status and comforts his career brought him, there was a restlessness in him which he channelled into his genealogical research, boring us all at dinner with stories of likely ancestors he had exhumed, a history professor manqué. There, in part at least, was the frustration that erupted from time to time in the ugly rows with Mother. He and she had become the misaligned projections of one another's ideals but now and then, notwithstanding the intemperate and vitriolic words they exchanged, a tender understanding gleamed between them, like a coin on the bed of a stream, its lustre mostly obscured by the water's fluctuations and burden of debris.

The girl pushes her plate of half-eaten food away and leafs through the folder containing Muiris' project, illustrated with copies of documents and photographs. There is a sketch too that he made of his grandfather which, although done in charcoal, is animated by a glint of nobility.

Did he do another tape about the civil war like Muiris asked him to do?

I don't think so. I think Mother filled in that part of the story for him. He joined the anti-treaty side, and was jailed by the Free State government, people who had been his comrades. They had learnt their methods from the Brits and then doubled the punishments—another example I suppose of what Father called our capacity for excess. The conditions were vile. That's why they went on hunger strike.

How long did he starve?

Seventeen or eighteen days I think. He always had digestive problems after that.

So he did achieve something in the end. Didn't he?

I'm not denying it. I'm only saying it was very different from what you and your friends were—

To my relief, and probably Jean's, my phone rings. Muiris, I mouth at her as her phone also hops at the same moment.

Hi Mum, are you all right? Uh oh, my son only calls me Mum when he's worried.

I'm fine, Love, why?

I saw you on the news. At the American embassy. What were you doing there?

The scuffles looked nasty.

They were. I get up and walk into the kitchen, to eliminate the distraction of Jean answering the same questions from Paddy.

Jean and her pals were there, I explain. I went to pull her out of it.

Jesus! Stupid kids. Did you get them?

I got her but not Pól. He was injured in the mêlée. They're keeping him in hospital overnight, for observation.

Send her back to Cork, Mum, before she causes you any more trouble.

I'll see. By the way we've just been listening to the tape of your interview with Grandpa.

I can't believe you still have that.

It's very good. You got him to open up. Maybe you should give it the National Archives.

I don't think it's that good, he laughs. He wanted me to destroy it afterwards. Said he had talked too much and maybe his memory was flawed.

That's odd considering he used to brag about his good memory.

I think he was pleased when I showed him the project. You know what's weird though, I asked him would he do it again and for the longest time he said nothing then he said it never went away and he started to say something about you then he just stopped.

What about me? A rill of dread slithers down my spine.

I don't know, he said something happened and he felt guilty. I asked you once, don't you remember? But you—hang on, I have to answer the door.

The sound of the Nine O'Clock News streams into the space left by Muiris' departure, its tone and rhythm unvarying, no matter the story. On and on, and now I hear Father's voice telling Muiris it never went away. Never. How did he know? Who told him? That harsh voice, let her taste an Irishman for a change. Never far away.

The sound of Muiris greeting his caller shakes me back to the present.

Sorry Mum, he says, Cormac has come to pick me up. We're heading out for the night.

Go on so. Have fun. Thanks for calling.

Wait—did you get the paper?

Damn. No.

I'll drop it in tomorrow morning.

Thanks, enjoy the party.

I will now that I know you're okay. Good night, he says softly.

Good night, I say to my sweet adorable son, still a child in my heart.

I hang up but remain looking at the screen on the phone where an image forms of myself and Father seated in the back of a car, me arrayed for the altar, my veil made of Mammo's Carrickmacross lace. Turning to me, Father says, Is there anything you want to ask me and I reply no, my anticipation of the day and the night ahead briefly compromised by the old childish feeling that I have failed a test. I try to dislodge it by reminding myself I am now moving out of Father's orbit and into a new life. Good, he says, pats my hand and to my surprise adds, You look lovely. Was that it, Father, I address the phantom shape, the question I should have asked? What was it you could not tell me outright? You were right, the rage the hurt the pain never diminish.

Back in the breakfast room I find Jean still seated, her head drooping over the table, defeated.

That was your father, I take it, I say gently.

She nods without looking up.

He'll get over it.

She turns a tear and mascara-stained face towards me. I just want to make a difference, she wails. Why can't I be respected? I'm not a child.

I know, my dear. We'll talk about it when Pól gets back.

Do you think they'll let him out tomorrow? Anxiety strains her expression and her lower lip trembles.

Yes, they'll need the bed, I give her a rueful smile.

Good, she nods. Taking up the sandwich plate she stands.

Leave that, I say and with both hands brush the streeling hair off her face. Go to bed. I kiss her lightly on the forehead.

She trails wearily from the room and on the instant my phone rings. I don't need to look at the screen to know it's Paddy.

How could you let my daughter get involved in that mob? He barks without preamble. You should be ashamed of yourself. Disgraceful. Incitement. That's against the law you know.

I incited no one, I say calmly.

You were there, egging her on. I saw you waving.

Beckoning not egging, I say. I was trying to get her away from the protest.

I nibble a sandwich while Paddy rants.

She could have been arrested or worse. I sent her to you for safekeeping, not to be sending her out to wave banners and cause public disorder.

Safekeeping! The bread stops my gob before I can expostulate. I swallow hastily, which sets up a choking cough.

Don't think you can put me off by pretending to choke, says my brother, the doctor.

I wasn't pretending, I splutter, eventually. That's the first I heard of Jean being here for safekeeping. That's a new line. Why not admit that you sent her here to keep an eye on me and your 'birthright'?

I don't know what you're talking about. She needed to get a job, I . . . we . . . wanted to be sure she would be safe in Dublin. To keep her away from that MacCartaigh fellow and his sister, she's worse.

Ah, now I see, say I. She's an adult, Paddy. I can't police her every move.

Well I wish you would! He sounds defeated. Have you any idea of the damage this will do?

To whom or what?

To us. To Ireland. And to me.

So that's what's eating you.

I mean it. Protesting against the government of the most powerful country in the world. Scandalous. Biting the hand that feeds us.

It's time we learnt to feed ourselves. I glance at the remnants of our snack, modern equivalent of peasant food. Besides, between you and me, I think they had a point.

Well you're wrong and they're wrong.

Their methods may have been naive, as I told Jean, but locking people up without a fair trial is an abuse of human rights.

You can't really mean that. These people have to be taught a lesson.

We could all learn some lessons. I'm tempted to tell Paddy about the tape we just listened to but that might be incendiary just now.

Look, Lena, I don't care what you think just don't go filling Jean's head with this claptrap. She's too impressionable. We're worried about her.

I understand that but you should have been straight with me about that before sending her up here.

Nóirín . . . I mean we . . . we were afraid you mightn't take her.

You might have been right. Anyway she's here now and I got her out of there before she came to any harm, I placate him and decide against telling him about Pol's injury. Maybe she's learnt her lesson.

I sincerely hope so, he tries to regain his upper hand. I suppose I should thank you.

Yes I think you should.

Very well. Take it as said. Goodnight.

Poor Paddy. He turns his anguish into anger and winds up gnawing his own innards.

While I was speaking to Paddy two text messages had landed in my mobile phone. The first is from Bernie: Hi Lena! Saw u on nws!! WELL DONE!!!!! Ta 4 tkng Phil hom. A V GOOD deed. X-wife got the car bcos of kids!!! F gng to fnd 2hnd whls 4 him. Hope u got chnce 2 cht re plns. Have a luvly evng! Tlk soon, XO.

Well, well. The surprise is that the creep had a wife at all, not that he didn't keep her.

The second text is from Richard: Hello there, let me know if it suits you to chat tonight. Standing by, R.

At last, someone who has not seen me on the news! The message has the effect of a window flung open on a stuffy room. Richard's foreign but familiar tones will distract me from the proliferating complications of my life.

Hi, he picks up the instant I call. So what's new?

I sigh deeply. You wouldn't believe me if I told you.

Try me.

I synopsise my traumatic day as best I can. Now I'm jaded, I say.

I'm not surprised, he laughs. The business with the kids is a bit worrying. Tell them to step back.

I've tried but Jean is stubborn. Thinks her Grandpa would approve, so I dug out an old interview Muiris did with him for a school project. It was weird to hear Father's voice again.

Ah, interesting, says Richard in a thoughtful tone. Did it cover the . . . deal with . . . I mean . . . his whole life?

No, only his early activities. The war of independence. Why?

Oh nothing. Just wondering. That's all. Yes. Interesting, he murmurs then, covering this lapse, says cheerfully, Well my day was a doddle compared to yours. Sat through one of our interminable monthly meetings between the Israelis and the Lebanese. Lots of coffee breaks to facilitate talks en marge, and a glass of whiskey afterwards to decompress.

That sounds very civilised. I could do with a mediator here.

I'd be delighted to oblige but it's a slow process, twenty-six years here and counting.

Those poor people. Pól might take up where you leave off some day.

Good luck to him, Richard laughs. I can brief him when I visit.

Yes, well I haven't let the kids in on that yet. It's stupid but I feel kind of awkward about saying it. Afraid they'll laugh at me I suppose. And well, I'd rather Paddy didn't know.

They won't, Richard laughs. As for Paddy, it's none of his business.

No, no, I say quickly. No. It's not.

We'll have a good time, he adds, and to hell with him.

Chapter Thirteen

Myles stands when I come into the room and reaches across the desk to shake my hand. My old office has been given the Mouse treatment, in shades of green and pink. It's brighter but it looks more like a suburban wine bar than a solicitor's workplace.

Formalities done, he gestures to one of the two overstuffed chairs set before the desk and waits for me to sit before resettling himself in his large leather swivel chair.

Shoot, he spreads his hands, in full control.

Suddenly feeling, as he might say, caught on the back foot, I get back on my feet saying, Let's go for a walk.

A *walk?* He swivels his chair towards the window behind him, It's pi— It's pouring rain.

Good for the complexion, say I, You look as if you could do with some fresh air. That's an understatement. There is a sickly yellow tinge to the skin around Myles' eyes and his cheeks are pale and puffy, his expression taut with strain.

But I don't . . . I mean it's . . .

Indulge me please, Myles. I speak firmly now. He may resent my recourse to a superior tone but unfortunately for him, as a board member I have leverage over him. I would prefer to have our chat away from the office.

It's not bugged, you know, he gives a desperate little laugh.

I know, I smile, hoping Brennan isn't lying with his ear to an upturned glass on the floor above. Please, I retie my scarf and button up my coat purposefully.

I had taken the precaution of making an appointment to see Myles, to ensure that he did not rush off on the pretext of having a consultation or court hearing to attend. It's Thursday and I have come in part to deliver on my promise of last Saturday to Rosemary, in part because of yet another mission report from Agent Ned. According to Brennan's breathless account, matters had taken a nasty turn on Saturday night. Myles had turned up at the office and started making phone calls that involved a lot of shouting and swearing. Then the Mouse appeared and shortly afterwards Geraghty's sidekick. More shouting and swearing followed by a loud crash and a shriek. Concealed on the landing above, Brennan saw the Mouse scurry out of the office and down to the kitchen, wailing. Next there's a ferocious ringing of the doorbell and banging on the front door. The Mouse peeps out of the kitchen but retreats when she hears a woman's voice calling Myles through the letter-box. When Myles eventually answers the door he's holding a bloodstained handkerchief to his nose. Enter Rosemary – there's the perversity of people for you: they seek advice in order to ignore it – who has hysterics at the sight of the blood. The wounded soldier fobs her off claiming it's a nosebleed. She gets another shock when the henchman-half-brother-in-law comes down the stairs to greet her, genial as soap and, saying he can't keep the wife waiting, you know what your sister is like, ha ha, and skips out. Deceived for the second time that day in her hunt for her husband's mistress, Rosemary shepherds Myles out a few minutes later.

Brennan waited to see what the Mouse would do and was rewarded by the sight of her peeping again from the kitchen then slipping like a shadow through the hall, lit only by the glow of the streetlamp behind the fanlight, to creep up the stairs to the office where she made a quick call and, having retrieved her coat and bag, scurried back down, cracked open the front door, glanced from left to right then vanished.

Very well, if you insist, Myles rises slowly and reaches for the mobile phone on his desk.

You can leave that here. Now that I have gained the upper hand I intend to play it. I draw my own phone from my bag and place it beside his, Snap!

But what if . . .?

That's the point. No interruptions. Just a private talk between you and me.

I don't understand. He shakes his head, We could go and have coffee if you want to get away from the office.

A walk would be bracing.

Once outside the front door he punches open a large umbrella which dwarfs my collapsible one. As we move down the steps I make out the logo stamped in gold on its dark green skin. Are you investing with the leprechaun? I ask.

What? He snaps around to face me.

The brolly. I point upwards, crocOgold.

No. No, he protests too hastily. A client must have left it behind. I don't know where it came from.

Good, say I, because I wouldn't believe those slogans. Around the rim of the umbrella run the phrases 'bullion from heaven . . . follow the rainbow to crocOgold . . . singing in the rain and shine . . .'.

Myles scans the inside of the brolly, I never looked at them. And I can't read them from here.

Just as well.

We proceed in silence to Stephen's Green, passing Wolfe Tone, still caught out by the foul weather, poor sod, and after him the Famine group, Ireland's via crucis, to enter the aisle of bare dripping trees bordering the park.

I meant it when I said you need fresh air, Myles, I begin as we skirt two pigeons squabbling over a half-eaten hamburger, You don't look well. Is everything all right, at work, at home? Rosemary, the kids?

All well, thanks. You know yourself, work is always busy.

Yes but maybe you drive yourself too hard. You should take a holiday, go away with Rosemary for a while.

He halts suddenly and raps out, What? Gardening leave? Is that what this is all about? The corner of his mouth twitches horribly. You can't do that.

I'm not *doing* anything, Myles. I'm only saying you look tired, you need a rest.

Huh, he relents then adds, I'll think about it. Pulling up the collar of his raincoat he resumes walking.

I can't say I ever actually liked Myles. When Mossie realised he was dying he at first tried to persuade me to sell the practice and go to work for someone else but I refused saying I wanted to keep the business in case Muiris might decide to follow us into the law. Then, knowing that some of his clients and the bank manager would doubt my capacity to run the business, he said we would need to bring another man into the firm. He poached Myles from one of our biggest rivals because, like him, he was an expert in contract and, Mossie said, he knew when to fight a case or settle, and he had never seen him run one without merit. He could be abrasive but the clients respected his ability.

Now I wonder was it an error of judgement on my part to hand over the running of the office to him. I'm guessing that the power has given him a sense of omnipotence and invincibility which made the hole and corner business with the Mouse seem thrilling at its outset but here he is, bowed by the weight of debts and empty promises. We continue in a silence broken only by the drumming of rain on our brollies beneath which Myles' mutiny rises like steam.

I was thinking, I venture after a few more minutes of this mute resentment, since you updated the look of the office—

Yes. How did you get on with her? He snatches the opportunity to change the subject, Eimear . . . I mean the designer?

Fine. She had some interesting suggestions.

Good. She'll do a smart job, he boasts, great attention to detail.

No doubt, say I, closing off the digression. But that's not what I want to talk about. As I was saying, maybe it's time to streamline the processes in the office too. Get in a management consultant to go through the place. Make one of the others, Jim or Louise, a partner and take on a new person. After all, we never fully replaced me.

Not necessary. He hastens his stride as if to escape my inconvenient ideas, Jim wouldn't be able for the extra pressure and Louise's pregnant so she'll be off on eternity leave soon.

That's not a bar to promotion, I match my stride to his. Meanwhile, I'd like the consultant to run through the figures. I'm sure there are ways to tighten things up on the administration side, new systems and so on.

Everything is game ball, Lena. There's nothing for you to worry about. He speaks firmly and deliberately, with a touch of condescension. You're the one should be taking a holiday. Go on a cruise, enjoy your retirement.

I'm surprised at you Myles. A few years ago you'd have been the one pushing a new gameplan.

I'm not against a new gameplan, as you call it, but why fix it if it ain't broke? His voice rises on the last words then, seeing an opening, he adds, As we're on the topic there's the question of the flat. I'm worried about Brennan.

I'll bet you are, think I but I say, Why? He sounded chipper enough the last time I spoke to him.

Well, you know how he is. He's not . . . you know . . .

I pause and turn to face Myles, watching him work his expression of impatience round to one of dutiful concern, No. I don't know.

He's getting a bit doddery, he continues lamely, he could fall down the stairs or something when the building is empty.

I see. He'll appreciate your interest in his welfare.

You don't have to tell him I said anything, he flusters. It's just . . . I thought I should mention it.

Yes. Thank you, I resume walking. To get back to—

A jingling sound that I initially take to be loose change in Myles' pocket persists and repeats becoming the ringtone of a mobile phone. Myles doesn't have spare change.

I thought you left that behind, I say.

I have two, he confesses, opening his coat and reaching into the breast pocket of his suit. He pulls out the second phone and squints at the name of the caller.

Don't answer.

I . . . I have to, he halts and cuts me the look of a hunted man.

Leave it, and tell me what's going on.

Nothing, he all but shouts, his face reddening. The phone stops ringing and, frustrated, he returns it to his coat pocket.

I take a step back and glance around hoping there's no one we know in the vicinity. A blind man, led by his patient dog, overtakes us. He is certain to have heard every word, maybe even imagines it's a lover's quarrel and so, eyes front, passes by.

Nothing is wrong, Myles seethes, I don't know why you're doing this, dragging me around in the rain, telling me to take time out and talking about restructuring the office. Unless you're trying to get rid of me. You'll have to try harder if that's what you want. Flecks of spittle gather at the corners of his mouth. Now, if you don't mind, I'm returning to the office where I have work to do. Squaring his shoulders he starts resolutely towards the nearest gate.

I'm not going to get into a slanging match with you here, Myles. I catch up with him at the fountain of the three Fates, its dark water ruffled by the breeze, revealing glints of the wishful coins tossed into its basin, And I'm not trying to get rid of you but I'm concerned about you and the office.

A sudden sharp gust of wind catches his crocOgold brolly and he struggles to keep it right way up. I watch his hapless dance before the dispassionate goddesses, who, in the blur of rain, take on the features of the Mouse, Rosemary and me. I know which one is spinning Myles a line, leading somehow to Geraghty although I can't quite tie them up.

The article in last Saturday's paper that Muiris wanted me to read was headed 'Irish Consortium Builds Luxury Hotel in the Pacific'. The accompanying photo showed a tall, wedge-shaped black building, towering like a temple of doom above a sandy beach, over the caption: 'Artist's impression of greenGold resort on Cape Darien'. I carried it into the office and opened up Pisspot Phil's plans for the Murphy-B's retirement home. Spot the difference, I murmured, glancing from one image to the other. The buildings were identical, the Cape Darien one a scaled-up version of the Seapoint one. The resort, according to the paper, is designed by Philip Lannigan 'whose signature can be seen in the new Dublin skyline keystone buildings in the ducklands. He also has a skin in the project.' Phil's 'signature' it would appear is the half-coffin effect. Is the nursing home a mock-up, or mockery, of the fool's greenGold? Do the Murphy-Benzes have skin, or even a stake, in the hotel too? And does the hotel have a kitchen and a car park?

It was no surprise to find that greenGold is spawn of the ubiquitous leprechaun who has suckered a bunch of investors into buying land on an 'unspoilt' (undeveloped) Pacific island to be promoted as a new holiday destination and stopover for cruise ships, an alternative to the overpriced Caribbean and oversold Costa del Sol. ('Weary of the Caribbean?/Cape

Darien is the place to be at ease in.' 'Costa del Sol losta its appeal?/Cape Darien is the real deal.' I did ask Jean who comes up with this drivel but she said no one's allowed to criticise the 'creatives'.) News of this scheme confirmed the queasy feeling I had on seeing Lannigan with Geraghty in the Dish and Spoon. Far from paradise, however, the article informed us that the isle is full of discontent because the building work is eighteen months behind schedule and some of the investors are getting twitchy. A spokesman for greenGold is quoted as saying: 'The company are in negotiations with a new contraductor at this pint in time and except construction to recommend in the very future going forward.' I think I know who'll be footing that bill.

Rosemary came to see me on Saturday, I say now.

She *what*? Myles gives a final tug at the umbrella which snaps shut leaving him exposed to the downpour. His eyes flash with anger.

Here, I raise my transparent brolly, We can share mine.

Very well, he mutters, grudgingly moving into its limited shelter, What did she say? She had no right.

Only that you seemed to be under a lot of pressure. That she hardly sees you. She wanted to know what was happening at work to cause you so much stress.

I'm sorry she disturbed you, he relaxes a fraction, no doubt because I didn't mention his lady friend. I tell her she worries too much. The kids are at an awkward age. Teenagers, you know, he tries for a dismissive note, I'll have a chat with her. Confident that he has scotched my inquiries, he strikes out with the furled and useless umbrella, as if it were a cane adding swagger to his gait.

I'm glad to hear that, I say, but I'll be hiring a management consultant anyway to look at our processes and see whether we can streamline them and make savings. Call it a spring clean.

Waste of time and money, he snaps, Most of those guys are chancers, with their PowerPoint slides and their Harvard Business School spreadsheets and their high—

The phone goes off again and before I can say anything he has pulled away from me, whipped it out of his breastpocket and ducked into Leeson Lane where he huddles against the wall for privacy.

Ten to one that's the phone he uses to communicate with the Mouse and she's not happy about last Saturday's shenanigans. He's a sap and it'll be a long way from Cape Darien he winds up if he doesn't get the money back pronto. I move on a few paces and mount the first two steps of the nearest building to avoid being splashed when buses lumber by. I smile at the students hurrying into their college, laughing as they curse the rain.

Sorry, Myles mutters as he rejoins me, looking haggard and bedraggled. The cockiness he displayed when we left the park has drained away. His hair is plastered in streaks to his skull and his glasses have fogged up. Let's get back. I'm drenched.

I don't speak again until we are close to the office and then it's to say, The consultant I have in mind is not a chancer. He's the son of some old friends of mine. He's a good man and I advise you to cooperate with him.

Myles glowers at me but I press on.

He may say everything is fine and there's no need to 'fix it' as you say. Or he may have some practical suggestions. Just keep an open mind.

It's not necessary I'm telling you.

Well let's be sure about that. The more you resist, Myles, the more I'm going to think you have something to hide.

That's ridiculous and it's offensive. He swings away and starts up the steps. As I follow him he glances suspiciously over his shoulder at me.

I left my phone on your desk, I explain. Remember? With yours. Had I known about the second one I'd have advised you to leave that too.

Give me a break, Lena, he sighs. I forgot about it.

Back in his office I make one last attempt to get him to come clean, I still think you need to take some time off. Why don't you go on a cruise?

What are you talking about? He snaps like a cornered dog. I mean . . . No. Rosemary wouldn't like that. He struggles to master himself. We'll take a weekend somewhere down the country.

Good. Mind yourself, I smile, picking up the phone and dropping it into my handbag.

A singularly unsatisfactory morning I conclude when I leave the building, having looked in on the others there and exchanged pleasantries with them. As ever, they smiled politely, tolerating me. I could see my irrelevance in their eyes, mixed with a certain wariness, as they scrambled to find something to say. On reaching the pavement I glance up at Brennan's window. No sign. Probably out delivering documents.

I hasten towards the car feeling damp to the bone. On reaching it I pull my keys from my bag but hang on – what's this? Key in hand I pause and stare at the front wheels, trapped in the yellow jaws of a clamp. Please no, I want to scream. I step closer and pointlessly check the registration plate then look from my watch to the receipt on my windscreen. Twenty minutes past the expiry time. Twenty bloody minutes. Outrage boils in me to the point that, like a three year old, I want to kick the clamp.

Bummer, says a man walking by.

Couldn't have put it better myself, I reply, somewhat mollified by the stranger's commiseration.

I reach for my phone to call the clamping gaugers and, pulling it out of my bag, hear an unfamiliar ring tone. I turn it over in my palm and see the screen light up to display the name Donal Sheehy. No one I know.

I press the answer button but say nothing. Mr. Sheehy begins to speak, fast and angry, Myles, Myles, you bastard, are you listening to me?

I grunt but he's not waiting for a response.

Release that money today or I swear to Christ you'll be sorry, he seethes. I'm sick of your games. It's my money. I gave it to you in trust. If it isn't paid over by close of business today I'm reporting you to the Law Society. Do you hear me?

Breath held, I press the red button, which I'm guessing Myles has been doing for some time. In the few minutes it takes me to walk back to the office Sheehy calls twice more but I let the calls ring out.

On the next call my own name lights up and I answer the call.

Lena, it's Myles.

Yes, I know. I'm on my way back. I look up and spot him standing inside the opened door.

My car is clamped, I say when I reach him.

That's bad luck. I should have warned you they've got more vigilant in recent months. He ushers me into the building and hands me my phone. Take the money out of petty cash if you need it.

You might want that for Mr. Sheehy, say I, returning his phone.

What?

I answered his call on a reflex, I fib, he sounded angry.

Don't mind him, he flusters awkwardly. He's a hothead. I'll call him later. I'm rushing to a consultation now. With that he spins on his heels and starts up the stairs.

On reaching my trapped car I call the clampers who tell me they'll be here in fifteen minutes. Sure thing. I get in and switch on the engine to generate heat. From the radio an indolent male falsetto babbles over a ukelele 'colours of the rainbow so pretty in the sky' not another crocOgold ad surely? 'hear babies cry' catching them young if so 'troubles melt like lemon drops' I wish 'dream that you dare' rain on the windscreen melts the red brick terrace 'oh oh oh oh oh' no rainbow above the chimney tops no oh no no slow slow slowly condensation fogs the windows and I am lapped in weary confusion, bearings lost.

An hour later, released from the clamps I reverse out of the parking space, pointing the car in the direction of Leeson Street then turn left onto the bridge. The rain is teeming now and I set the wipers to fast, their frantic motion fanning my aggravation with Myles. Approaching Upper Leeson Street I am forced to slow to a crawl behind a tail of cars. A timely traffic report explains that a bus has broken down on Morehampton Road and is blocking the left lane. I indicate right and divert into Appian Way, following my old route home through Ranelagh whose flatland dinginess has been upgraded to bourgeois hip, the launderettes and greasy spoons replaced by Botox clinics, pricey bistros and foreign language DVD rental shops. Every side street is lined with 'For Sale' signs, ladders over the rainbow that comes and goes.

After crossing the Dodder I swing on a nostalgic whim into Whitebeam Road intending to dip my wing at our old house but find myself disorientated. I am looking for the beech tree that animated our front garden with the drama of its seasonal changes, greener than all the rest in spring and summer, more brazen in autumn and steelier in winter. On my second pass up the road I realise that the tree has been felled and the front garden cobbled and gravelled to accommodate three cars. I pull up opposite the house, confident despite the presence of the cars that there is no one at home. If anyone were to ask me what I'm doing staring at a house I sold four years ago I could not give a rational answer except to say that in some wishful, irrational part of myself I'm hoping to see Mossie open the front door and hail me with his reassuring smile, then take me by the hand and lead me up the stairs to the bedroom to lie again where we lay so many times admiring and delighting in one another's flesh, tasting one another's salty milky secretions, our entangled limbs sleeved with sweat, until for a moment consciousness withdrew and we rested breathless against the warm steady flank of life.

Shorn of the tree the house today looks naked and cold, no longer the haven where Mossie, Muiris and I were content even if our dream of a band of children to follow, of school shoes, polished by him to a high shine, lined up in the hall, of Sunday afternoon picnic sails with a merry crew, was thwarted by the hysterectomy I underwent two years after Muiris' birth. When Muiris started school I returned to work in the office, glad to occupy my mind with other people's problems rather than submerge it in the repetitive and thankless tedium of domestic activity. For the next five years our life moved in an ordinary, unexceptionable, blameless rhythm, that I know now was the pattern of happiness, only to be disrupted by the rogue cells that rampaged through Mossie's body, devouring him cell by cell till only a husk remained, a shrivelled parody of his hale, handsome, reliable, optimistic self. All lost now.

No trace of our life hovers there. I will not come this way again. I hear the saw grinding through the branches of the glorious beech and their fall to earth, see the stump burnt to prevent it reclaiming its space in the harsh gravel, leaving the roots to ramify through the soil, urgently seeking water and a soft place to send up shoots until, exhausted, they contract and wither in the dark. No exit. No way back. No hereafter.

Chapter Fourteen

The crowd waiting in the arrivals hall is so dense that unless I push forward I might not see Richard, or he me. The apron of white space between the glass doors and the barriers restraining the greeters has the look of a stage and some of the travellers coming through take advantage of this to jump up and down, waving and cheering at their waiting friends and families, flourishing cheap straw hats or football scarves. A hen party emerges with all but the bride-to-be wearing red devil's horns. She sports a halo and strap-on wings. The holiday mood is so infectious that the occasional business commuters look like party poopers. I'm beginning to feel I should be wearing a funny hat or carrying a flag to welcome Richard.

Suddenly there he is, at the glass doors, his head just visible between the red horns of three she-devils. Or at least I think it's him. Panic freezes me for a moment at the sight of the paunchy, limping man with stubbly white hair who halts, leaning on his stick and turning his head slowly to comb the crowd. Capsized for a moment by the discrepancy between my girlish memory and the man before me I hesitate to wave. I see his head swivel in search of me, a note of disappointment beginning to twitch on the ruddy cheeks, a tic I remember. I right myself, straighten up, inhale, and prepare to take the measure of this ordinary stranger. He is shorter and broader than the man of my memory, wears a waxed Barbour driving coat over a tweed jacket and check shirt and, god bless him, a paisley cravat. An off-duty soldier is as easy to spot as a priest on holiday. I wave and, catching sight of me, his expression lifts in a familiar wry grin. I worm my way between the press of mothers and fathers and aunties and grannies and wives and husbands and children and babies and lovers and buddies and chauffeurs with their sign boards, to the opening in the barrier. There I hesitate momentarily unsure how to greet my guest, whether with a handshake, a hug or a kiss.

Hullo, he presents his hand to be shaken and leans forward to kiss my cheek.

Welcome back, I say.

He smiles around at the hubbub. Am I in the right country?

Sometimes I ask myself the same question.

Let's get out of this madness, he prompts as a new wave of travellers emerges from the baggage area and the crowd of greeters surges around us.

Good thinking, I turn to lead the way to the car park.

Outside, I am about to step off the footpath when a taxi speeds through, all but slicing off my toes. Gobshite, I spit, springing back onto the path.

With a whoop of laughter Richard reaches to steady me, saying, I'd forgotten how much you swore.

He gave me a fright, I retort.

You don't say. Here, take my arm, Richard crooks his elbow towards me. I glance up from the proffered elbow to meet his smile and, accepting his invitation, link his arm, closing the circle of time past and present to step forward in a reprise of our first encounter.

I turn the key in the ignition and reach to move the gear shift from park to drive but the lever snags on the handle of Richard's stick.

Apologising, he moves the stick to his other side.

War wound? I ask.

Believe it or not, no. He caresses his knee. I was cleaning a gutter and the ladder slipped. Broke my femur. It didn't set properly.

That's awful, I wince. I suppose you were lucky you didn't crack your skull.

Yes but I didn't quite see it that way at the time. I do remember thinking as I fell this shouldn't be happening. Then I tried to drag myself around to the front of the house to call for help but I blacked out with the pain.

But how did you . . . I mean you were a soldier.

It was only ten years ago and by then I wasn't really on active duty. I had a desk job.

You used to say you'd hate that. You'd rather be dead was what you said.

How well you remember! That's the sort of stupid bragging a young man would do. I didn't relish the job and I retired two years later but I'm glad I'm still here. There was a moment when I was lying on the ground staring at the sky that I thought I might be dead. My greatest fear used to be that I'd be left for dead on the battlefield with a bullet through my head or chest, unable to move, waiting for God or the ferryman. Instead, Bronwen found me when she came home from work and called an ambulance. Much more prosaic.

Yes I can imagine, I say quickly, discomfited by Bronwen's suddenly appearing between us.

I focus on merging with the line of traffic bearing towards the M50 and, eventually, swing down onto the southbound motorway, which is flanked by the featureless red brick backs of warehouses, the occasional apartment block, their balconies crammed with bicycles, buckets, mops, and racks of limp laundry, and a half-built shopping centre with multiplex cinema, the frayed edges of our modern megalopolis.

Have we run out of talk already? I venture as that bleak desolation begins to infiltrate the car.

Good lord, I hope not.

That's a relief, I laugh. So how was your flight?

Short and noisy. I was seated beside the bride-to-be, already half cut. She thought it was 'way romantic' that I was coming to visit my girlfriend of more than forty years ago. Said she couldn't even imagine such a long time. I told her I couldn't either. Her bridesmaid, who was sitting beside her, said she never again wanted to see the shit who dumped her a year ago, even if she lived to be a hundred. I pointed out I wasn't quite that old. Then I bought them a drink and had one myself.

You were well entertained so, I say.

It passed the time.

It doesn't feel like forty-five years.

The flight was only an hour.

Ha. Well sometimes all the years seem only that long. Or maybe what I mean is they aren't that long when you've lived them.

Maybe we don't have that much to show for them.

Surviving, I say, keeping going, that's enough. Raising our children. You have grandchildren.

True. He shifts in his seat and I feel, not without embarrassment, his attention full on me. You look well, Lee, he says after a few moments, reverting to the familiar name he had given me.

Thank you, I flush.

I take the offramp at the junction and, navigating the tangle of roads that wind between

the construction sites for tomorrow's high-rise suburbs, emerge from under the Luas bridge, new trams for old, past the entrance to Leopardstown race course where we had the odd flutter in our youth, cross the dual carriageway and, with the reassurance of a homecoming, descend the quiet avenues of Victorian and Edwardian houses, nested in mature gardens, all the way to the seafront.

Not again, I exclaim as I make to draw up in front of the house.

What is it? Richard asks.

Some so-and-so has swiped my parking space.

This time I can't blame Bernie because it's not her natty little Merc in the spot but an old and somewhat dusty Volvo.

Cheeky, he says. Surely it's residents' parking only.

No. But I use traffic cones to reserve my spot.

Ah, he nods gravely. So we shall have to acquire some more.

First thing tomorrow, say I, gratified to have an ally. Meanwhile I'll have to park the jalopy in the lane.

To my relief today there is no sign of Feargal, who must be at work, or of Phil, probably at home nursing his sore paw. On opening the car door I hear Tanta yapping at the back gate which surprises me because I had left him shut into the kitchen. It's not Felicia's day and it's unlikely that Jean has come home from Geraghty's sweatshop in the middle of the afternoon. Maybe Pól, back from college, let the dog out.

It's okay, Tanta, I call, it's only me.

And me, Richard chimes in, prompting a renewed frenzy of barking.

When we return to the front of the house, I notice that the offending car has a Cork registration and a Padre Pio sticker on the windscreen. A thud of foreboding starts in my gut and quickly ratchets up to a drum roll when, on opening the front door, I see a pair of strange coats on the hall stand and hear voices with a disturbingly familiar lilt rise from the direction of the kitchen. Tanta continues to yap in the distance.

Wait in there, I point Richard towards the drawing room.

He halts and looks at me quizzically, Is there a problem?

Intruders.

Seriously? He glances about, his expression suddenly sharp and tense.

Don't worry, I can handle it. You go on in there and pour us a pair of drinks. I'll only be a minute.

Fertile as it is my imagination could not have conjured the horror I find in the kitchen. For a moment I fancy it's my turn to have a heart attack as the blood rampages in my chest and ears.

Paddy and Nóirín are seated at the table with a pot of tea and a plate of biscuits between them, as if this were their home and I the guest. Tanta barks outside the back door.

What the blazes do you think you're doing? I ask.

Taking tea, says Paddy.

I mean *here*. In my house. As you well know.

I have meetings in town and Nóirín thought it would be nice to see Jean.

Why didn't you tell me you were coming? I glance from one to the other.

It was a last minute decision. We told Jean. We'll use Mother and Father's room.

I shake my head in denial and disbelief. If only I could go out and come in again to find the house undisturbed.

That doesn't suit me.

It's only for a couple of nights. We'll be no trouble.

I don't think you understand me. This is my home and I didn't invite you.

As soon as I open the back door Tanta rushes in, barking as he scampers up the stairs to the hall and into the drawing room where the barking increases. He's found Richard.

That dog needs more exercise.

Leave the dog out of it, Paddy. You're in no position to lecture anyone, man or beast, on diet and exercise. The urge to give him a clip in the ear aches in my hand. Now, I think it's time you and Nóirín left and checked into a hotel.

Calm down, Lena, he patronises. I have a right to stay in my childhood home for as long as it exists. You could at least have told us about your plans.

What plans?

Don't take me for a fool, Lena. I knew you were up to something.

I don't know what you're talking about.

I don't want to see the house destroyed and I'd like to have some of our parents' effects. As mementos.

Or as assets to fund your campaign?

You seem to forget that your brother is recovering from a heart attack, Nóirín chips in with wifely smarm. He can't take too much stress.

Then he shouldn't have come here unannounced. Apart from anything else, it's damn bad manners.

Look, Lena, we need to discuss this. Nóirín sits at the end of the table between us, Henry Kissinger in a floral skirt. We met your neighbour and she told us about the nursing home scheme.

Which neighbour would that be? I ask, although I have a hunch it was Moira Kiely with her dratted sponsorship card.

That ghastly Kiely woman, says Paddy.

At least we agree on something, say I, ignoring Nóirín. I hope you told her she's too old to be running around looking like a demented rabbit.

Certainly not, he bursts. But I did tell her you'd need my permission before anything happened to the house.

Really? I begin in anger but as a faint light breaks on the otherwise treacherous horizon I give way to a smile. That's very interesting. What did she say?

Some blather about me being a doctor and of course I'd see the merit in it all. And she asked me to sponsor her.

Which you did, I assume.

What do you take me for? Of course I didn't.

Good.

A footfall on the stairs recalls Richard's presence. I look out and see that he is half way down to the kitchen, taking the stairs sideways on account of the gimpy leg. When he sees me he pauses, raising his eyebrows. I flap my hands and whisper, Wait upstairs. I'll be there in a minute.

I meant it when I said it doesn't suit me for you to stay here, I continue on returning to the kitchen. I have another house guest. You'll have to go.

We'll be out most of the time, Nóirín insists. You'll hardly know we're here.

Leave it, Nóirín, Paddy gestures to her. We know when we're not wanted. His face lengthens with the aggrieved expression of one who is neither understood nor appreciated. Mother and Father would never have wanted this, he declares and makes to rise from the chair but, before he is fully upright, totters and drops back onto the seat.

Nóirín is instantly at his side undoing his tie and opening his collar. Now you've upset him, she snaps at me.

Dread sinks through me as I watch her minister to him.

He waves his hand and rasps that he'll be grand in a minute.

Nóirín stirs a spoonful of sugar into his tea and offers him the cup to sip. He obliges but pulls his head back wincing at the taste of the sugar.

Phone the Royal Marine, he says to her at last, casting a disdainful look at me.

I face it down, as the mean thought sneaks in that this is a performance for my benefit, Paddy the comedy man of the R&R, recovering his instinct for hamming up his role. Calling his bluff I say, Good idea and leave the room.

I find Richard in the drawing room, left hand leaning on his stick, his good leg occupied with kicking a tattered old ball of Tanta's which the dog scurries to retrieve and, growling, refuses to drop at Richard's command.

Stubborn little bugger, isn't he?

An apt description of my brother.

The intruders?

I nod, Welcome to the war zone.

Just as well I'm always armed. Although he grins as he says this, something tells me it's not a joke.

That's reassuring, I say doubtfully.

Actually, as a matter of fact, it is.

Tanta suddenly releases the ball and in a swift reaction Richard drives it under Father's armchair. Diversionary tactic, he says and, turning to the table behind him, raises a glass and hands it to me. You look as if you need this, he smiles and, raising another for himself, says, Cheers.

I echo the toast, meeting his smile as the glasses chime. Apologies for abandoning you.

Don't worry, I'm used to fending for myself.

The front door slams.

They're gone, thanks be, say I. Now we can relax.

Good, he sinks into Father's chair and Tanta, who has been scraping and growling under it for the past few minutes, emerges bearing the ball, embarrassingly covered in dust. I wonder briefly was Bronwen a houseproud wife.

Facing one another suddenly, like the long married couple we might have become, a new shyness overtakes us. Are we strangers, old friends, nostalgic lovers or lovers to be?

The last time I had seen Richard we had been kissing one another with ever quickening desire on the Hill of Howth. Our embraces became urgent and exploratory as, reaching his hand inside the cup of my bra, he fondled my breast. Desire flickered up from my groin, and when I opened my eyes his face filled the sky, the sun behind him gilding his dark hair. Moving my hands under his shirt my fingers traced arabesques over his back till with a soft moan he sank his head to my breast and began eagerly sucking the nipple. His other hand moved down under my skirt. His touch on my pubis sensitised every atom of my flesh till from the soles of my feet to the tips of my fingers my body yearned towards his, seeking climax. My legs gripped his waist and my hand reached down to clasp his erection which nudged blindly inside his trousers needing release.

A brisk rustle in the bushes on the slope above us was followed by an embarrassed giggle and the vulgar call, Have yiz no homes to go to? punctured our exquisite moment.

Swiftly, as if stung, Richard rolled off me, sat up and yanked my blouse over my exposed breast. Get dressed, he ordered, looking this way and that in search of the brats who had disturbed us. Someone might see you. And then your father would have me shot. Or do it himself.

He fished a pack of cigarettes out of his pocket, shook two free, lit them both and handed one to me.

It's only the tinkers, I said recalling a small encampment we had passed at the foot of the hill.

I don't care. I'll tan their little tinker hides if I get hold of them, he scowled.

The first pull on the cigarette routed the last tremors of desire and left me in a hyped-up jangle. Exhaling forcefully through my nostrils, I said, Father doesn't have a gun any more. Mother made him hand it in to the police when I was born.

Hmmm. I wouldn't be so sure about that. I'm not taking any chances.

You must have a gun too. I charged him.

Of course. He brushed a strand of hair from my cheek and tucked it behind my ear. We need to keep our wits and arms about us these days at the rate your lot are raiding our barracks.

Not 'my lot', I fired back, my haste covering, I hoped, for an uneasy and surprising feeling of disloyalty. That's in the North.

That's what I'd call hairsplitting. The flying columns are taking off from this side of the border.

Well they don't have my support. Or even Father's, I ventured. He says it's the throes of a dying beast and that in all likelihood the new Government will introduce internment. When Richard's eyes widened at this information I thought maybe I had gone a step too far. It's all to preserve good relations with your lot, I added hastily.

I know, he smiled grimly, your Mr. de Valera is a cunning pragmatist. He lumped us with the problem child of Northern Ireland.

That's not quite how it happened, I snapped, disliking the way the conversation had turned and the part I reactively, atavistically, played in it. Let's go, I stubbed out the cigarette, and taking my hairbrush from my bag began vehemently pulling it through my hair.

Evening sweeps rain clouds across the sky, darkening the windows. In the intimacy created by this dimming of the light we both make to speak at once.

I waited—

I wondered—

We fall silent again.

As if the ether could not bear its weight our skype and telephone talk has avoided the question that leans in close now, compelling attention.

In his face I see reflected my own hesitation at opening the door to the past.

After you, he waves his hand to usher me through.

It was all such a long time ago, I sigh and pause, the hinges of my tongue jammed by an unexpected ambivalence towards this man. I had sometimes imagined that were I to see him again in person for even an hour or two together I could put to him the questions that had plucked at the corners of my mind over the decades since last we met. That, I fancied, would rout the brutes whose foul breath and words stalked my sleep and startled me, over and over, maybe as I rounded a bend in the road, lifted a stray hair from my sleeve or plumped a cushion on a chair, investing those banal, unremarkable actions with terror. Now, on the threshold of that memory, I balk, repelled by the evildoers who haunt me yet. I stare into foetid darkness and I am afraid.

I can't—can't see clearly, I begin without knowing how I will continue. I mean it's so long ago, so far in the past.

The past is here and now, says Richard, moving his head around to take in the room till his eyes come back to rest on me.

Maybe I just wish it would go away. I glance down at Tanta's manky ball covered with the dust of months or even years. Symbolically apt.

It's like this, I begin again, trying for a pragmatic tone. I never understood why or even really what happened. It was the timing you see. That's what undid me. I mean losing you, yes, that was crushing. That was painful. That possessed me, filled me with anguish. But coming so soon—so immediately. Just when I wrote to you. Do you see what I mean? After a while I convinced myself, oh way down deep inside, that I had always known we could never be together. That the sense of being doomed accentuated the passion. And then the horrible— I halt, wondering at myself. I don't know what I'm saying. I spread then clasp my hands. Or who spoke. I stare dully at Richard. Sorry, I say.

He glances down and with his stick nudges the dusty old ball towards Tanta who has lost interest in it. And I don't know what to say, he says. I certainly didn't want to end our friendship. I liked being with you. I felt . . . I was . . . compelled. I was devastated you know. He looks up at me, his tongue tied, eyes imploring me to understand his reticence.

No I didn't know, I enunciate with a hint of frost. You didn't say that in your letter. And while the Parents weren't happy about our friendship they never forbade me outright to see you.

I had tried to limit the Parents' meetings with Richard, telling him to stop at the end of the road when he brought me home, and inviting him to the house only when I knew they would not be there, until, wise to me, Mother insisted that I bring him home for afternoon tea. There passed an awkward two hours during which she quizzed him about his family while Father grilled him about his regiment and tours of duty, and whether he spoke any Welsh. Unaccustomed to such scrutiny, and to having to juggle two lines of conversation at once, Richard stammered polite but perfunctory replies, disappointing Father by his ignorance of his native tongue.

The next afternoon, when I returned from saying farewell to Richard, for another indefinite separation, Mother called me into the drawing room. She was seated at her escritoire in the corner, addressing invitations to the annual charity auction she organised. With her reading glasses on she looked officious but seeing the tracks of tears on my cheeks she began softly, acknowledging that these goodbyes were hard on me.

I snuffled and rubbed my nose raw with an already very wet handkerchief.

Love can be painful, she said.

This wasn't helping. I made to leave the room.

Wait, Mother said. I need to speak to you. Sit down.

I plumped down sullenly onto the couch.

She turned round fully in her chair and removed her glasses to look at me as she told me that Father was worried about my love affair with Richard because it was distracting me from my studies. I said I would get back to them now that he was gone.

I can see he has touched your heart, she continued, but we're concerned that he's not serious about you.

Of course he is, anger flashed in me. What makes you think that?

He doesn't write very often, much less visit.

Then why is Father complaining about him distracting me?

Because you are on edge all the time. You're preoccupied, thinking about him, maybe worrying about him, waiting for letters that don't come. Or not very frequently.

No I'm not. I brazened on, covering my discomfiture at what I knew to be the truth and my surprise that it had been noticed. Raising the stakes I said, I expect we'll get married.

Mother's expression was sceptical as she asked, Has he mentioned marriage to you?

Not in so . . . well . . . I mean . . . I just know we will. I made a mental note to study the art of lying on the hop.

Is that what you want? To be a soldier's wife?

What's wrong with that? I mean he's not an *English* soldier.

He's British but that's beside the point. You'd be very lonely when he's away. Especially living in a new place without family or friends.

I'll make friends.

That may be harder than you imagine. At the very least you need to finish your degree before you do anything else.

I won't need it. I don't care about that. I just want to be with him.

I understand that but the degree will only take two more years. If he really loves you he'll wait.

What about me? I don't want to wait. My voice rose and, springing up from the couch I shouted, You and Father don't understand the first thing about love.

Au contraire, Mother replied and replacing her glasses bent again over her invitations.

Resentment of her perverse skill at uncovering the doubts that I had been struggling to suppress overtook me and I flounced out of the room.

Richard smiles. They probably knew that if they forbade you to see me that would increase my stock and you would take pride in defying them.

And wouldn't I have been right?

Oh at the time it would have seemed dramatic and passionate, star-crossed lovers and all that but in the long run it probably would have caused more heartache than happiness. It would have ended badly.

I can't help giving a short bitter laugh as I say, Instead of how beautifully it did end?

You're deliberately misunderstanding me, he bridles. I'm saying it would have put great pressure on us, on our relationship. We might have torn one another apart. I can't say more than that I hated to break with you. But I—he spreads his hands helplessly—I felt I had no alternative. As you said in your letter we should have met in another place and time.

That was a bit novelettish, I wince.

True, but you had a point.

I reach to switch on the table lamp beside me. The light glints off the nail polish I applied last night in a mood of almost girlish anticipation. I need to recover something of that mood now. A picture flashes across my mind of the hen party that accompanied Richard to the arrivals hall, squawking with excitement and alcohol. The girls looked not much older but more savvy than I had been when we coorted.

He leans forward into the pool of light. Don't you see? You say my letter was cold but it had to be. I couldn't offer you any hope, or allow you to think I had regrets, although I did. It had to be final. Then I got your letter. Not very warm either, in fact. He nods for emphasis. Our letters must have crossed somewhere on the Irish Sea. I thought of replying but I didn't want to cause you any more trouble.

Trouble? I twitch my head.

He nods slowly. It wasn't really a coincidence that we happened to write at approximately the same time was it?

I don't know what you mean. I stiffen defensively.

His eyes hold mine for an instant till I lower my head and mumble, You knew?

Yes. He reaches forward and takes my hands.

I swore Paddy to secrecy, I fume.

He must have been afraid too.

But then how did you—

Your father told old Foxy Fenwick, the ambassador. They were friends as I recall.

I nod, He and Mother played bridge with the Fenwicks.

Your father obviously asked him to pass the word along the line to my CO.

I stare across the hearth to where he sits but see Father there, in his usual chair, his face stern as he tells his friend of my humiliation, and I flush with outrage and shame at his clandestine meddling. Was there a glint of satisfaction in his eye at having found specific cause to drive Richard away, notwithstanding his innocence of what was done to me?

He had no right—

He had every right, Richard retorts. In the circumstances.

But it wasn't you. You didn't do it, my voice rises, then, shuddering as the ugly faces of my attackers and their coarse words return, I sink my face into my hands overwhelmed again by terror.

When Richard prises my hands from my eyes I see he is almost genuflecting on the floor in front of me, his bad leg sticking out to one side. Sorry, I sniffle. I can't talk about it. I can't let them come back. They come back you know. I can't keep them away all the time.

I understand, he says softly, dropping back to a sit on the floor. But you're safe now.

He kisses the palms of my hands, first one, then the other, tentatively, delicately.

Taking one of his hands in mine I rise from the chair, draw him to his feet and lead him out of the room.

In moments we are naked. The cheval glass, hoarding the last silvery light of dusk, casts a gleam over our pale flesh, and look, here she comes, shimmering up from its depths, that girl, hectic with the first rush of lust, shedding her clothes to wonder at her own beauty, sure of herself now, reaching to kiss and touch here and here and here, and this and this—

Chapter Fifteen

Before opening my eyes I stretch my hand across the bed, expecting to touch warm flesh but find nothing. Did I dream it all? The airport, the return here, the earnest talk, the almost sex? Looking around I see the far corner of the duvet rolled back. Reality so, and Richard is up. I hear the splash of the shower, hardly one of the kids at this hour. Out of habit I switch on the radio for the morning headlines.

Sources close to the Taoiseach say three candidates are seeking the party's nomination for the presidential election. It is believed that the eminent heart surgeon, Mr. Patrick O'Neill, is one. He will be a guest on tonight's Late Late Show.

I switch it off again. So that's what brings Paddy to Dublin. The big eejit. Ah well, being taken for a ride comes before a fall. Funny all the same that they didn't tell me. Probably afraid I'd finagle a way into the studio audience. No fear. The two hours of egotistical eejitry would be the death of me. Besides I've better things to be doing this evening.

On our return from dinner last night I paused for a moment in the hall, antennae scanning the air for further disturbance. We had walked back from Monkstown and the dew that had begun to fall, mingling with the salty tang of a sea mist, spangled our hair and coats. Erotic anticipation flickered between us. Richard brushed his hand over my buttocks and I brushed my lips to his cheek.

You go on up, I'll have to let the dog out, I murmured apologetically.

Don't be long.

As I descended the stairs to the kitchen the racket of the TV rose to meet me and my elation flatlined. The kitchen was empty but I found the kids curled up on the sofa in the breakfast room, transfixed by the screen, beer bottles with wedges of lime poking out of them in hand, and Tanta asleep between them.

Good evening, said I. At the sound of my voice Tanta perked up for a moment, looked at me, then, with a grunt, resettled into the nest he had made for himself.

Jean, by contrast, sat bolt upright and whipped around to greet me.

Pól aimed the remote at the screen, paused the picture, and waved.

I acknowledged him with a nod saying, I thought you'd be working tonight.

Got a reprieve, he smiles. I'll be on tomorrow and Saturday.

Ever since the demonstration he has been spending more time here than in his own house, on the grounds that he is recuperating. I'm beginning to think I should be charging him rent. The only reason I don't is that I'd prefer to have him, and therefore Jean, under my eye than for her to be camping across the city with a bunch of smart alec peaceniks.

Well Miss, I turned to her again. What have you to say for yourself?

She winced. I'm so sorry Lena. I didn't think—

It's time you started to think. What possessed you to let your parents in here without asking me first?

I . . . oooh . . . I meant to tell you, she shrank into herself in a futile attempt to disappear. I really did. I just kinda forgot— She broke off, gaping in horror over my left shoulder as Tanta emitted a low growl, without budging from his place.

Pól, assuming a manly air, frowned and half-rose from his seat.

Aren't you going to introduce us? Said Richard from behind me.

Yes of course, I flustered swinging around and resting my hand on his arm. I . . . yes . . . em . . . This is Stephen Baxter, a friend, a legal friend, visiting from Britain.

We had agreed on this sobriquet over dinner to protect him while Paddy is around.

He stepped forward to shake their hands.

Pól's eyes slid from Richard to me and a small smile creased his features.

I just came down to get a glass of water, Richard explained.

Fine, said I. Help yourself.

What are you watching? He glanced from the screen to the kids.

Jean was beaming, imagining, wrongly, that she was off the hook. *Saving Private Ryan*, she said.

Good film, said Richard. Made here too wasn't it?

Yes, Jean nodded enthusiastically. Pól needs to watch it for his course.

Ah, so it's work? Richard grinned at Pól.

Sort of, Pól shrugged. I'm giving a seminar paper next week: Pornography or Propaganda? Psychological Effects of Shifting Paradigms in the Cinematographic Presentation of Warfare and International Conflict Resolution.

Quite so. Richard all but yawned. Best of luck. He swung around and, tipping me a bemused nod, returned to the kitchen.

So, Jean, I resumed, spoiling for a little conflict myself. I'm waiting for your answer.

I'm sorry. I just . . . oooh . . . oooh . . . She winced and cringed and shook her hand in the air as if it had been stung. It was all kinda sudden you know.

Well I don't know anything. Not even how they got in here let alone got the notion they could waltz in without asking me.

She started to wind a strand of hair around her finger. I don't either. I mean I didn't *ask* them. I guess Dad still has keys or something.

The curse of Snow White and the Seven Dwarfs on him. I never thought I'd have to change the locks.

She tugged the strand of hair so hard that it made my eyes water.

They gave me a hell of a fright, apart from anything else, I explained. Did you see them this evening?

Yes, I had dinner in the hotel with them. Dad was in a foul mood.

He'll get over it. Now, I'm going to bed. You can let the dog out before you go up.

Yes, of course, yes. Jean nodded vigorously. I'm sorry, Lena. I really am.

It's done now, I sighed. We'll let it go this time. Goodnight.

I was about to leave the room when Pól said, Wait.

What is it now? I sighed.

A strange woman came to the door while you were all out.

What kind of a strange woman? A new rankle of irritation rose in me. Was she wearing a pink tracksuit?

Yeah, she was. How did you know?

And was she looking for money?

No. He appeared puzzled. She was looking for her husband.

Rosemary?

She said his name was Myles. She seemed to think I must know him. I said I never heard of him. Then she asked who I was and when I said a friend of the family she looked disappointed and that was it, he shrugged. She just left.

I heaved a deep sigh. Very well, thank you.

As I climbed the stairs I began to wonder was Rosemary Mulvaney a bit cracked. I couldn't even conceive of the idea that Myles and his sporting metaphors would be waiting for me in the sack. He'll be getting a yellow card from me in the morning.

It was a relief to find Richard warming the bed for me. We lay in the darkness and slowly, silently explored and kissed one another, the urgency of remembered desire outrunning capacity.

I'm sorry, he whispered, taking my hand as we lay side by side.

Don't worry, I replied, we don't have to rush these things.

You've no idea how many times—

Ssssshhhh. Don't torture yourself. There'll be time enough.

I must have dozed off because when I open my eyes I see him standing naked in the centre of the room, his skin still red with heat from the shower, and scented with my orange blossom shower gel.

Hello, say I.

Oh, there you are, he replies, turning to face me, his freshly-washed cock standing to attention.

I smile and, pushing back the duvet, crawl to the foot of the bed from where I lean forward and take it in my mouth.

Afterwards I say, That's given me an appetite.

Me too, says he, kissing his way down the length of my torso till he buries his face in my groin. I shut my eyes and give myself over to exquisite pleasure.

When we are replete with sex and hungry for food I say, There's the makings of a fry in the fridge, if you want to get started on that while I have a shower.

He opens one eye and looks at me. Is that an order?

Yep. Chop-chop.

I suppose I'd better get dressed first.

Good idea, I wouldn't want us to shock the kids.

When he has left the room I make haste to wash and dress too. I am about to leave the bedroom when the phone rings.

Brennan. I answer it on the off chance that he knows what brought Rosemary here in the dead of night.

Lena? Is that you? He half-whispers.

Yes, Ned. What's up?

He's gone. Vanished. Disparu. AWOL.

Who? Myles?

The very one. Didn't turn up here yesterday. Missed a consultation and a High Court hearing. The phone was hopping. He wasn't at home. No one had the foggiest where he was. And there's no sign this morning either. Not a good sign I'd say.

No. I sink onto the bed. Something's up. Rosemary came here last night while I was out.

The girls below have been talking to her. But they're talking to the wrong one if you ask me. They'd need to set a trap for the Mouse so to speak.

She's already set one for him. Now I'm beginning to wonder is he trying to wriggle out of it.

Oho. You could be right. He hasn't been himself these past few weeks. Hasn't been bringing in the usual Friday box of fresh cookies. I was rather partial to the chocolate chip ones myself. The girls thought maybe he was on a diet.

Or he was economising. I think Rosemary should be calling the guards.

You don't think . . . The shrill pitch of hysteria rises in Brennan's voice. I have touched his own vulnerability. I mean he wouldn't . . . would he?

No. I'm sure he wouldn't do anything foolish, I try to placate him. He's probably gone to check out his investment.

Ha! Good luck to him so, he cackles. Maybe he's eloped with herself.

God, I hope not, I say. I'll call Rosemary later. For now, however today's appointments need to be cancelled. I'll call his PA, Carol isn't it?

Yes, yes. She's the one. They're all in a swither down there.

I'm sure they are but there's nothing more we can do for now. Thanks Ned. Keep me posted. I end the call and, clutching the phone, shut my eyes to absorb this latest trouble. Poor Rosemary. She must be frantic. But how to tell her that it's her brother-in-law and her friend she needs to talk to, not me?

As I descend the stairs to the kitchen I hear a low murmur of conversation. It ceases when I enter and from the breakfast room four pairs of expectant eyes glance in my direction. Correction, five pairs: Tanta has followed me and wants his food. I feel like Moses come down from the mount without the tablets. Jean, wearing Mother's robe again, looks in sore need of some tablets. No sign of Pól. Paddy is cloaked in inscrutable solemnity, Nóirín simpers and Richard beams all around as if he couldn't have asked for better breakfast companions.

He alone has the manners to stand up when I come to the table. Good morning, Lena, he says, pulling out the empty chair for me, I trust you slept well.

Yes, thank you. Have you got everything you need?

Nóirín has not put out a cup for me but she has taken the large silver teapot from the sideboard in the dining room and is filling Richard's cup from it.

I'm being very well cared for by Mrs. O'Neill, as you can see, he grins.

Call me Nóirín, she titters, Mrs. O'Neill makes me sound so starchy.

For one ghastly moment I feel like throwing up all over the table.

Then you must call me Stephen, he says shooting a look at me.

Good job too because in my bewilderment at the scene before me I had forgotten his alias.

Following this look Paddy says, Mr. Campbell was telling us he's here for a law conference.

It's Baxter, dear, Nóirín corrects him, and turning to Richard, says with a girlish laugh, Getting his soups mixed up.

He's not the first, Richard assures her.

What are *you* doing here? I ask my brother and his wife when at last I can speak.

Jean's taken the day off work. We came to collect her but she needed to have her breakfast first.

I bet she did. I retreat to the kitchen to make coffee and bang my head against the wall. No wonder Paddy's looking so sour. The spectacle of his wife flirting with a British lawyer would be bitter as gall to him. In need of air I open the back door and release Tanta who rushes into the garden barking like crazy. The noise has the happy effect of drowning out Nóirín's wittering. So much for my dream of a good fry up swimming with egg yolk. I'll have to make do with soggy Cheerios and toast.

Jean, I call as sweetly as I can, could you come here for a moment please?

The girl appears, moving slowly, and stands hangdog in front of me.

Get them out of here, I hiss at her.

Oh Jesus, Lena, I'm sorry, she raises her paler than usual face, her eyes brimming with contrition. I'll just get ready and then we'll go, I swear, she clasps her hands at her waist.

Then go. I grit my teeth. And take some Aspirin while you're at it. You look dreadful.

Yes, thanks Lena. She makes to leave.

Hang on, I halt her. Where's Pól?

She swings her eyes towards the ceiling.

Tell him to get going too, I mouth at her.

Nodding assent she withdraws.

I snatch up the coffee pot and a mug and march back to the breakfast room.

. . . but first Lena's going to bring me for a spin, show me some of the sights, Richard is trying gamely to lighten the mood.

Good, Paddy says, then, looking perplexed, adds, I can't help feeling I've met you somewhere before.

Jean's gone up to get dressed, I cut in.

She looks a bit peaky, Nóirín says, levelling her eyes at me. She must be working very hard.

I'm damned if I know what she's driving at, unless she thinks I've made the child an indentured labourer. Chance'd be a fine thing. I'm too soft, that's my trouble.

Geraghty seems to expect them to work long hours, I say. I'm not sure he pays very well. He tells them they're learning on the job.

Yes but where have I seen you before? Paddy is like a dog with a bone.

I don't know, Richard replies coolly, maybe you're thinking of someone who looks like me.

Nóirín, the born-again schoolgirl, chips in, I think maybe I've seen you on TV.

I doubt it, Richard raises his eyebrows at me, I rarely watch it, let alone appear on it.

Oh well, maybe you just look as if you should be on TV, Nóirín gushes. I have to confess I'm addicted to Coronation Street.

That's not a sin, Richard absolves her. I'm an Archers fan, in fact actually.

I don't know how you can put up with those ghastly accents, Paddy barks.

This is getting out of hand.

I thought you ladies were anxious to be off early to the shops today, I turn to Nóirín. I'm tempted to add that she'll surely need to buy something stylish to wear for her TV debut tonight.

Yes, when Jean comes down we'll get the DART into town. There's no rush, this is a little holiday for me, Herself replies in a tone that tells me to back off.

I think of Richard's gun and wonder where on his person he keeps it. The tabloids would love the story:

BREAKFAST BLAST; BLOOD ON THE CROSSAINTS; CHEERIO TO PRESIDENTIAL HOPELESS.

No one can arouse such murderous intent as one's family. Blowing the smoke off my fantasy gun I smile and say archly to Richard, the weather bids fair for our spin.

Yes. Speaking of which, he pushes back his chair and stands, I'm going to step outside for a smoke.

I'll join you, Nóirín springs up, plucking her handbag from the floor, I'm gasping.

When they have gone I pour myself another cup of coffee. It's going to be a long day. I prop my elbows on the table and inhale the rising steam which forms a welcome scrim over everything in front of me, particularly the sight of my lover and my sister-in-law in the garden. I have never seen the woman so animated. Paddy averts himself from the sight.

Tell me, I ask him, what exactly is this presidential campaign all about?

I love my country, he pauses for applause. I also feel it's completing Father's legacy.

Jesus, Paddy. You're delusional. Father's dead. We're living his legacy. No completion needed.

The indignant look he gives me falters a moment before he goes on the attack, Why are you always so negative? So resentful?

I shake my head. I'm not negative just realistic.

Jean's return silences him. She's a paler shade of white now, thanks to the ghostly make-up and the contrast with the black weeds.

The sound of the doorbell pierces the cold silence in the house.

Answer that please, I say to her. And if it's Moira Kiely tell her I'm out.

I have as good a right as anyone else—

I'm only half listening to Paddy because my ear is tuned to the voices in the hall which fill me with alarm. What brings Claire here at this hour of the morning? No doubt she's in some kind of crisis but I'm not in a position to deal with her difficulties now. Ignoring Paddy I rise and tiptoe to the door the better to hear what's happening upstairs. Oh no, Jean is letting Claire into the house. Any moment she'll be in the kitchen blowing Richard's cover and Paddy's fuses at the same time. I climb the stairs as fast as my creaking bones will carry me, recalling that at one point in our youth Claire had a soft spot for Paddy and he had briefly coorted her. The sight that greets me in the hall drives the innocent memories from my mind, leaving it temporarily and uncharacteristically blank. Jean stands holding the door open as Claire backs in, lifting a Zimmer frame from the wrong side over the lintel. Slowly the figure attached to the other side of the frame appears: Eamon. At least I assume it is he. Once a burly, ebullient man whose face had the sheen of the bon viveur, capped with trim fair hair, he is now shrivelled and grey. Instead of the broad pinstripe suits he favoured in his youth, he wears a tatty ski anorak over a faded blue cardigan and a pair of loose corduroy trousers. Jean shuts the door and retreats to the kitchen.

Good morning, Claire sing-songs. We were just going for a walk along the seafront and thought we'd drag you out as well for some fresh air.

I know Claire too well to be taken in by her breezy manner. Dragging Eamon and his frame up the steps and through the front door is excessive if all she wants is to ask me out for a walk. She's obviously desperate for someone to share her burden.

That's a lovely thought, I say, but I'm rather busy this morning. Maybe one day next week we can have lunch and a walk.

Eamon's head, which has been dipping towards the floor, snaps up to look at me and for a minute I glimpse the playboy beneath the wrinkles and the wispy hair. You're looking well Lena, he says, more than can be said for me.

Don't be fooled by the dim light here, I reject his attempt at flattery.

Claire pipes up, We can sit here and wait for you, can't we Eamon?

Yes of course, he nods, whether intentionally or not, I can't be sure. But I need to take a leak first.

Holy Mother of God! I'll never get them out of the house.

The loo is just down here, Claire glances at me over her husband's hooped back and mouths, Sorry about this.

I manage a rictus which I hope passes for a smile.

As they start to shuffle towards the loo Tanta darts up the stairs in a torrent of yapping and begins to dance around Eamon's feet.

Tanta! Stop! I command the dog but he continues his capers until Eamon aims a kick at him from under the Zimmer frame. This has no effect on Tanta but it destabilises the frame which flies into the air. Eamon, still clinging to it, topples backwards, dragging Claire down on her knees beside him, resulting in a knotty muddle of limbs and aluminium. Tanta redoubles his barking at the sight of this new monster. I stand transfixed while my mental calculator estimates how much Claire will claim in damages against me. Then I stoop to help her disentangle herself.

You really have to be more careful Darling, she scolds Eamon. Come on Lena, between us we can get him up.

No, wait, I say and going to the top of the stairs call Jean who appears at the double, eager to ingratiate herself with me. Go out to the garden and fetch Rich—Mr. Baxter and ask him to come in and help us, please, I tell her.

Eamon rocks from side to side muttering, Help me up dammit.

Yes, Darling, Claire crouches beside him. Lena has sent for reinforcements.

While we wait I draw Claire aside, stepping into the office, to explain my predicament and Richard's assumed name.

She laughs merrily at the story, saying, It's better than a play.

Well it's rapidly turning into a farce, say I. Just remember the name Stephen Baxter.

It's nicer than Dickie Davies.

Really, Claire can be exasperating. It's Richard but you can forget that for the moment.

I'll try, she says, which does not reassure me.

To my relief Nóirín doesn't come trotting on Richard's heels.

Instead, Claire beams and claps her hands at the sight of him.

I press my finger to my lips imploring her silence, then explain to Richard, who is smiling back at her, what has happened. So, we need your help getting Eamon off the floor, I conclude, although now that I know the old sod is alive I think a kick would be in order.

Very well, Richard studies the tangle on the floor as if it's a conundrum. Finally, directing me to pick up the Zimmer frame and place it in front of Eamon, he lowers himself gingerly to the ground and, laying the stick down, attempts to roll him on to his front.

Don't be pushing me around, Eamon snarls.

He's trying to help you, Darling, Claire soothes.

I don't need his help. Eamon scrabbles his heels uselessly then flops back.

Come on old chap, Richard tries to cajole him. Just roll with the push.

I will not, Eamon reddens with frustration. We stopped taking orders from your sort a long time ago.

Claire crouches again and with Richard's help rolls Eamon on to his front where he manages to get up on his knees and grasp the frame which I am holding.

Richard meanwhile hauls himself up, and rests on his stick.

How do you do? He smiles and offers his hand to Eamon now that they are both upright.

Claire is dusting Eamon down.

Bloody terrible thank you. Eamon tries to straighten himself defiantly.

Would you mind escorting Eamon to the bathroom? I ask Richard. Then we can go down for a cup of tea.

Now that Claire is here I figure I might as well dilute Nóirín and Paddy. Besides, Eamon probably needs fortification after his fall. I know I do.

When the men emerge from the toilet Claire guides her husband to the top of the stairs, takes the walking frame from him and hands it to me, then moves his right hand to the banister and, holding his left arm, helps him descend. I take my metaphorical hat off to her for her saintly patience with that bollocks.

Richard and I wait as they descend with painstaking slowness. For a moment I want to seize his hand and run away but instead I touch it and whisper, Sorry about that. Thanks.

Between ourselves, he mutters, I don't think he's as doddery as he makes out.

That doesn't surprise me.

Maybe Claire enjoys being a nurse.

I hate to concede the truth of this but she does seem to like the caring role.

In the breakfast room, Paddy has half-risen to greet Claire, who is airkissing him while Nóirín fusses over Eamon, directing him to sit in a comfortable chair and tugging at his anorak as she does so.

This party has grown like Topsy, she exclaims.

Where's Topsy? Eamon's head swings around.

It's just a phrase, says Nóirín.

It's hardly a party, says Jean.

I'll have a Bloody Mary, says Eamon, dropping into the chair.

Oh it's far too early in the day for that, Nóirín fakes a laugh. A cup of tea would do you all the good in the world.

Nonsense woman. I don't have much time left and I intend to make the most of it. He glances at Jean. Topsy, get me a Bloody Mary with a slice of lemon and bring a bottle of Tabasco sauce. There's a good girl.

Nóirín shakes her head at Jean who turns to me.

He's right, I say, it's not going to make much difference to him now. In fact I might join him.

Atta girl, Lena, Eamon pipes up. You always were a sport. We could have had a right time together, if it weren't for her grey eminence over there.

Thank you, Eamon, I say in as final a tone as I can muster. I'll get the drinks.

I'll do it, Richard offers.

That's very kind, Stephen, I say with emphasis, but I can't let my guests do all the work.

Not a problem. I feel quite at home.

Jean will help you carry the drinks down, I smile over at the girl who looks like she wants to go back to bed.

She obliges, dragging herself up from her seat.

I'll refresh the tea, Nóirín adopts a martyred tone, peeved at being displaced I bet.

Topsy, where's my Bloody Mary? Eamon calls.

Coming right up, Richard calls back as he and Jean leave the room.

The child's name is Jean, I say, beginning to feel like a garda on point duty, making a balls of it too, just like the gardaí.

Claire and Paddy are nattering like long-lost friends, he appearing charmed by her attention, she being rather more effusive than is strictly necessary in the situation. When she has finished complimenting him on his recovery from his heart attack I hear her drop the fatal word, 'President'. In response he embarks on a rigmarole about how he is going to smarten up the office, suggesting that the president is a cultural leader who complements the work of the political leaders. He will fill the Aras with singers and poets and musicians.

Don't forget, he says, our first president was a poet and translator, An Craoibhín Aoibhinn.

But you're not a poet Paddy, I interrupt what I now understand is a long rehearsal for his TV appearance tonight.

I can be a patron. Were the Medicis poets?

No. They were the Pope's bankers. You might be in danger of over-reaching yourself, if you follow their example, or at least of over-stretching the presidential budget.

I think it sounds wonderful, Claire claps her hands. It's like the Kennedys' Camelot.

Look what happened to them, I say.

At that moment queenly plump Nóirín Bouvier O'Neill re-appears bearing aloft the silver teapot and a chipped mug.

Remind me, Claire, where did we last meet? She asks, as she fills the mug.

I'm not sure, Claire frowns.

I think it must have been at Mossie's funeral. That's right. I was expecting Nora.

Poor Mossie, Claire droops sorrowfully for a moment.

A fine man, Eamon pipes up. Good sailor too. He liked the cut of Lena's jib. Isn't that right?

Yes, well, he's gone to a better place now, Nóirín looks pityingly at me.

The great regatta in the sky, I quip to show her that I do not pity myself.

I'll be setting sail there myself any day now.

Don't say that, Darling, Claire flinches.

This'll put wind in your sails, Richard announces, without apparent irony, as he and Jean enter the room. She's carrying a tray on which sit three glasses of Bloody Mary and a bottle of Tabasco.

Richard lifts one glass off and hands it to me. I seize it gratefully.

He places a second glass and the bottle of Tabasco in front of Eamon whose eyes light up at the sight, reserving the third glass for himself.

I didn't think Eamon should drink alone.

Absolutely not, I agree.

Here, Topsy, Eamon waves the Tabasco bottle at Jean, pour some of this into the glass, like a good girl, until I say 'when'.

Jean is her name, says Claire.

I can tell by the hunger in Jean's eyes as she approaches the table and takes the bottle from Eamon's hand that she longs to have a drink too. Poor kid.

When, Eamon calls. Now hand me the glass.

It's hard to tell whose hand is the shakier when Jean picks up the glass but as soon as Eamon has a hold of it and takes a sip his shake miraculously calms. I think of what Richard said in the hall and glance at Claire, wondering whether she's aware that she's being gulled. She seems deliberately to have turned away from the sight of her husband drinking and is comparing notes with Nóirín about their offspring.

Paddy has shut his eyes and begun to drum his fingers on the table humming softly, as if to absent himself from the debauchery around him. I hope to God he's not planning to sing on the Late Late. After a couple of seconds of this he breaks off and, turning to Richard, says, do you have any interest in music Mr. Campbell?

Call me Stephen, Richard begins.

Baxter, dear, says Nóirín in a tetchy reflex.

Are you sure that's your name? Eamon pipes up, Because you remind me of someone. But he wasn't a Stephen. Let me see, wavy . . . gravy . . . navy . . .

I obviously have a very common face, says Richard. Nóirín thinks she knows me from Coronation Street.

Maybe Eamon could be your court poet, Paddy, I laugh desperately.

Paddy's head flicks from one of us to the other, Funny you should say that, Eamon. I was just saying to Mr. Campbell that I thought I had seen him somewhere.

Baxter! Nóirín raps out.

It wasn't at Mossie's funeral, I say.

No, no, no, Paddy shakes his head.

It's on the tip of my tongue . . . Eamon persists, What rhymes with navy Topsy?

She's Jean, Darling.

Nóirín might have been right. It probably is too early in the day for Eamon to be drinking. I scan the room, anxious for distraction but can find nothing to draw him away from this dangerous path. I think of motioning to Jean to knock over his glass or spill the Tabasco or do a handstand, anything to create a diversion, but the child has retreated to the armchair and is curled up half asleep. She surprises me, however, by rousing herself to say 'Ravey' and going back to sleep.

I want to scream. A shrill sound suddenly echoes through the house snapping everyone to attention and I fancy it is coming from my mouth until Tanta bounds up the stairs in full cry. If only I could do the same. Instead, I reach over and poke Jean. Will you answer it please, like a good girl, and say

I'm not at home, even if it's the Pope himself? Especially if it's the Pope.

Did you hear the one about the Pope?

We don't want to hear that one, Darling, says Claire firmly.

Oh why not? Say I, anxious to deflect her idiot husband from speculating about Richard's name.

Where's Topsy? I'll tell her later.

It's Jean, I say, and she's gone to answer the door.

She could make me another Bloody Mary while she's at it. He slugs the last of his drink.

An anxious expression flits across Claire's face and she says, rising, Maybe we should be going for our walk.

Before she can extract Eamon, however, Jean returns with Pól, with his jacket on, rubbing his hands as if he has just come in from the cold, instead of simply rolling out of the bed and down the stairs. Cute as pet foxes these kids.

Hi Paddy, hi Nóirín, the boy smiles all round.

Paddy suffers the informality and inclines his head to say, Good morning, Pól.

Ah, Pól, Nóirín manages a neighbourly smile. I met your mum in the supermarket last week.

Hello Pól, I say to validate the pretence. How are you?

Hi Lena, he deadpans like a seasoned ham, I hope I'm not intruding. Nothing would do him of course but to join the circus.

Hi Claire, he continues his lap of the table. Claire resumes her seat, pleased to be remembered.

Eamon beams around, We've the makings of a good party now, Topsy.

It's Jean, I remind him, again.

Be a sweetie and topsy up my glass, then I'll tell you girls the one about the Pope.

I can see he has taken Pól of the flame-red locks for a girl but no-one bothers to disabuse him.

Jean goes to take the glass from him but Richard gets up to say he'll do the honours. I aim a warning look at him as he takes Eamon's glass.

I hear you're working in a nice restaurant, Nóirín focuses her smile on Pól.

Yes. It's Mary Lacey's favourite. She and her husband come in every week.

Paddy glances my way, vindicated by the image of our Taoiseach's marital harmony.

Anyway, Topsy, Eamon continues, the Pope was in bed one morning—

We're not talking about the Pope now, Darling, Claire strives for an airy tone. We're talking about Pól.

Pól who?

Pól MacCártaigh, the boy says.

Oh, oh, I see. Eamon blusters as he shifts his paradigm. Anything to Tony McCarthy?

No.

A pity that. Great man for the horses. Isn't that right Paddy?

It is. He gave me a few good tips in his day.

Dead now, I suppose.

Sadly, yes.

No harm, mutters Nóirín and for once I'm in agreement with her.

So he rang the bell for the nun to fetch him the po'.

Richard returns with Eamon's drink and doses it with Tabasco before handing it to him.

Are you a man for the horses, Mr. Campbell? Paddy asks.

BAXTER!

I like to watch but I'm too mean to bet, says Richard.

Are you sure you're not Scottish?

Quite sure.

So the nun said 'A blow Your Holiness?'—

Darling, I think it's time we went for our walk, Claire stands up.

Walk? Who said anything about a walk?

I did. Now let me help you out of the chair.

Am I actually screaming now or is that the frigging door-bell again? This time I'll answer it. Any excuse to escape the bedlam in my breakfast room. Tanta has already flown up to the hall but has stopped barking. When I arrive he stands snuffling under the door, his tail wagging. It's not Moira Kiely or Rosemary Mulvaney anyway.

The sight of Muiris framed in the doorway is a balm to my pent-up nerves.

Oh boy, am I glad to see you, I say, letting him in.

Is something the matter? Concern furrows his face.

I touch his cheek and smile, Nothing mortal. Only a clat-ter of mismatched and uninvited guests, including Paddy and Nóirín.

Great, his expression softens. I'll run down and say hello. I just came round to put up the planning application.

Thanks. It may be best to say nothing about that for the moment. We'll deal with it when they leave. If they leave. I hook my arm in his. Come on. You might bring sanity to the proceedings.

Muiris gives an exasperated snort when, I outline the events of the past twenty-four hours, including Richard's alias. Ma, he says, Sometimes I think you like to create chaos.

Moi? I'm just too bloody tolerant.

Why can't you be upfront with Paddy and Nóirín? There's nothing wrong with having Richard here.

I can't explain it all now, I sigh. There's a lot of history there. Paddy didn't care for Richard, any more than the Parents did.

You talk as if it was yesterday, Muiris remonstrates. I mean this all happened before I was born. I'm sure Paddy couldn't care less any more.

I'm afraid he does, say I.

Then he's ridiculous too. I give up. Let's go down, he says. I can't stay long.

Nóirín's face softens at the sight of my son. Paddy, too, gives him an affectionate smile. They've been fond of Muiris since he was a child and joined their summer holidays in Schull where he sailed and swam with their kids till I thought he'd grow fins. A kindness I am grateful for because they were happy times for him and helped to fill the long school holidays after Mossie's death, and my holidays were limited to August.

I'm glad you're looking so well, Paddy, he says now.

Thanks to all Nóirín's good care.

Is that Mossie? Eamon interrupts.

No, Darling, it's Muiris, his son.

I'm seeing a lot of familiar faces this morning. Maybe I'm in heaven already.

Some chance I want to say.

Don't be silly, Claire chides, then, turning to Muiris, says, But you do grow more like your father every time I see you.

I'll take that as a compliment, Muiris smiles his father's smile, stirring my heart.

I introduce him to 'Stephen' giving his arm a quick admonitory squeeze.

How do you do? Richard shakes his hand and glances approvingly at me.

I'll make you a coffee, I say, when Muiris seats himself next to Nóirín.

I was just telling Topsy here the one about the Pope—Eamon proceeds.

I think you finished that one, Claire rises again. We'll be on our way.

Richard goes to help Eamon out of the chair but the old codger flashes him a look of protest, I don't want to go for a bloody walk. I want Jean to give me another Bloody Mary. That one was like holy water.

I'll give you one later, Claire says.

You got my name right, Jean smiles.

Of course I did, Eamon braces his shoulders in a gesture of pride. Your name now, he eases around to face Richard, is annoying me. It's here somewhere, he points to his head.

Stephen Baxter, says Richard.

No, no, no.

Yes, I say firmly. Hadn't you better get going now if you're going to walk? It looks like rain.

He's told you his name, Darling.

Darling? No, wait, I've got it. Something . . . gravy, wavy . . . . Bingo! Davies, Eamon laughs. You see, I haven't lost all my marbles. Dickie Davies. Davy Dicks. Gravy Dick.

Richard shakes his head, You must be confusing me with someone else.

No I'm not, Eamon jabs at his lapel. I remember you. Lena's beau. But you let her down all the same.

You're right Eamon, Paddy stands, glowering thunderously. I smelt a rat from the moment I saw this so-called Mr. Campbell. You, sir, have a nerve coming into this house after what happened.

BAX—Nóirín begins but thinks better of it.

I invited him, I say.

You're worse. Paddy's face is flushed and swollen. After what he did to you. Have you no pride?

He wasn't the culprit. You know that. Vindicated, I glance at Muiris who shakes his head slowly, incredulous.

It was his shagging fault. He rounds on Richard, I suppose you think you can come in here with your lies and stories as if nothing had happened.

Paddy love, settle down, Nóirín pats his arm.

A cad and a cheat, Eamon weighs in, likely wishing he could take a slug at Richard.

Ignoring this invective Richard replies evenly to Paddy's charge. As you say, it was a long time ago. Lena invited me. I didn't intend to cause her any embarrassment. Then or now. He looks at me, Do you want me to leave, Love?

'Love!' Paddy bursts. You have the nerve to call my sister 'Love' after what you did to her. To us. His wattles are puce and saliva bubbles at the corners of his mouth, You should be ashamed of yourself.

Don't go, I say to Richard. It's time for you and Nóirín to go, Paddy. I've tolerated this intrusion long enough.

Lena, take it easy, Muiris intervenes uselessly.

What do you say I did that you find so offensive? Richard is getting riled now.

You seduced my sister when you knew there could be no possibility of a marriage between you. And . . . and . . . the . . . you know. Paddy stops suddenly.

Richard's jaw has tightened. Something has passed between them that I am not apprised of. I glance quizzically at him but his response is a twitch of his head.

A rotter, Eamon is on a roll.

Pól looks from one to the other of us, trying to put the pieces together. Here's more grist for his essay.

Jean also follows the argument but hers is a look of baf-flement.

I might have married Lena, if your father hadn't been against it.

What did you expect? Paddy blusters. This was a new nation finding its feet. We didn't need your sort coming in and taking away our girls.

'A nation once again', Eamon croaks, shutting his eyes for sentimental effect.

Oh shut up, Eamon, I say. This was never a nation, just a bunch of feuding chieftains.

An outraged silence unites the motley group for a moment. It's true, I add, still wondering about what Richard has just said.

That's a disgraceful slander on our father and his cohorts.

There was too much blood shed chasing a dream and I wonder was it necessary, say I.

Richard's eyes swing from Paddy to me and back again.

Where's my Bloody Mary?

We really have to go now, Darling. Claire moves again to get Eamon up and out of the house, but he brushes her away.

Muiris casting a sympathetic look at me, intervenes. It's all in the past, Paddy. Whatever happened it was a long time ago. Mum is entitled to invite whoever she wants to stay.

Muiris is right, I add. You can spare us the rhetoric. I wasn't as naïve as you imagine. Besides, I seduced Richard, not the other way around.

Don't be silly. You may think you did but he was a man after all.

Meaning what exactly?

He should have known better than to exploit your advances.

Aren't you being a bit Victorian? says Richard.

Certainly not. Paddy drops back into his chair, gasping like a landed fish.

Nóirín cuts me a fierce look, Now see what you've done. Paddy's not a well man.

Muiris rests a placatory hand on my arm.

But I'm not stopping now. I know, I say. All the more reason he should have stayed at home and left me in peace. He seems to forget that I'm sixty-eight not sixteen.

That depends, says the Pope—

That's enough, Claire tries to haul Eamon out of the chair. We're leaving. Pól, could you help us please? At last Claire has found her mettle.

Pól steps around the table and hauls Eamon to his feet at which the old codger, gesturing widely with his arm, chants, 'Sayonara, is it too soon to say goodbye?'

No, say I, standing up to see them out. Any excuse to flee this maelstrom.

'Neath the blossom tree'.

I'm really sorry, Claire whispers when we reach the hall. I should have—

Oh forget it. I just hope Paddy doesn't take another heart attack out of it.

'Sayonara . . .'

Maybe you and Richard should go out for a while, she suggests.

Yes and not come back, I snort.

Goodbye, she pecks me on the cheek.

Bye. I'll call you about the next First Friday.

Don't let the bastards get to you, Lena. Eamon stretches up to be kissed.

I wouldn't dream of it, I say and shut the door on the bastard.

Two down and two to go.

Chapter Sixteen

In the kitchen I find the youngsters, for a wonder, stacking the dishwasher.

Eyes starting from her head, Jean hisses, What was *that*, Lena? I've never seen Dad so angry.

He's a spoilt pup. It's time for you to take them away before any more damage is done.

In the breakfast room the pup is still resting against the chair back, his head tilted to the ceiling, eyes shut. Nóirín is at his side stroking his paw. Through the window I see Richard in the garden, lighting a cigarette.

Muiris tenders Paddy a glass of water.

Is he all right? I ask Nóirín.

I think he will be. He needs to rest.

Here, we'll move him to the armchair, Muiris puts down the glass and springs forward to help Paddy, plumping the cushion for his back then shoots an anxious look at me.

I nod and touch his arm reassuringly. I'll take Tanta outside for a minute, a bit of air would do me good.

I join Richard on the garden bench. Seating myself, I hold out my hand in a reflex, fingers forked to take his cigarette. I inhale deeply as of old but my lungs aren't what they used to be and I fall to coughing. Richard pats my back then lets his hand rest there.

I seem to cause you nothing but bother, he says quietly. Would you rather I left?

Absolutely not! I straighten up. Paddy can't dictate how I lead my life.

You let him send Tops—sorry, Jean, to live with you.

Temporarily, theoretically. He reminded me that . . . about . . . I turn away slightly and face down the garden to the door that leads to the back lane, That night. I suppose I'm unfair to him.

Richard gives a quick laugh. I think you two can't help trying to always get one over on the other. It's in your DNA.

Maybe. Which makes his presidential nonsense the ultimate oneupmanship.

Possibly but I daresay Nóirín is behind that.

Oneupwomanship so. I try another pull on the cigarette and this one goes down a bit more easily, lightening my head. Was that true? I turn to him. What you said in there.

He nods slowly, Yes.

The bit about Father, I mean.

Taking a fresh cigarette from the pack he pauses to light it and is about to speak when his look fixes on the breakfast room window. Driving smoke from his nostrils he says, I think you have another visitor.

Following his line of sight I make out a golden bell swinging in the centre of the room. Do my family, friends and neighbours have nothing better to do today than aggravate me?

Just be glad it's not Moira Kiely, I sigh, standing up. Dropping the cigarette, I grind it vehemently into the path. I hope to the Lord Harry Bernie's not talking up her plans. I'd better get in there before she does. Otherwise we'll have to resuscitate Paddy.

Richard tops his cigarette, returns it to the pack then, using his stick, rakes the accumulated butts of the morning to his feet and leans down to pick them up.

Tanta snuffles at them in the hope of food.

I scurry on down the path.

Inside, Bernie is going full tilt with Paddy and Nóirín while Muiris pours the tea. Happily, the topic appears to be health, specifically Bernie's concerns about Feargal's heartburn.

Hi Lena, she chirrups, I just popped in to deliver your invitation to Feargal's surprise fortieth birthday party.

Seeing Richard, she halts and her eyes switch to full beam. Now I know what brought her in. She offers her hand, today crowned with garnet nails. Hello, I'm Bernie, Lena's next door neighbour.

With a slight bow Richard takes her hand. How do you do, I'm Ste—Richard, an old friend of Lena's.

Confused, she directs her attention to me, eyebrows soaring.

When is the hooley? I rush to forestall any questions that might set Paddy off again.

He, however, half shuts his eyes, refusing to acknowledge Richard's presence.

Saturday week, she replies and, glancing around the table, adds, You're all welcome.

Thank you, we'd love to come, I take Richard's arm lightly, to let her see the score. Unfortunately, Paddy and Nóirín will be back in Cork.

We could come up that weekend, Nóirín parries my dismissal with a smirk.

That would be great, thanks, Muiris leaps in before I can fire back. Is it okay if I bring someone?

Yes, of course, Bernie awards him a sunny smile, curiosity piqued.

Nothing to my own curiosity. I shoot him a look of surprise but he brushes it away with a defensive nod, rejecting my maternal interest.

After a series of bitter rows and the eventual bust up with his last boyf eighteen months ago, he was heartsick for a long time, retreating into himself, rejecting my attempts to console or counsel him. I recognised and understood his despondency and his need to be left alone but my worry for him preyed on my heart and stole my sleep. Even when I say nothing he intuits my concern and he feels suffocated. This cool aside about his new squeeze is either a ploy to give me the good news without having to suffer my pleasure for him, and the inevitable volley of questions, or it's a decoy to draw me off Nóirín.

I was just going to tell Paddy about our—Bernie opens a second front.

It's lucky you called, I rush to head her away from the minefield. You're the very person Nóirín needs. I turn to my sister-in-law whose eyes narrow with suspicion. You see, I continue, Paddy and Nóirín are appearing on the Late Late tonight and Nóirín needs something smart and—how to put it? 'televisual'—for the occasion. Isn't that right Nóirín?

What? Nóirín's face creases with doubt. I yes no but—

Who told you that? Paddy snaps, rousing himself from his funk to challenge me.

It's all over the airwaves, I beam. I was going to call and see if we could get tickets.

Preposterous, he puffs. You know you hate the programme. If you want to see it you can watch it at home, with a G and T in your hand.

Good point. But it might be an interesting cultural experience for Richard. If we tell them who we are they might send the roving mike our way.

Over my dead body! Paddy shouts, his temper burnishing his waxy pallor.

I might sit that one out, Richard looks almost as upset as Paddy at the prospect of his face being relayed into the nation's homes.

I forbid you to go, Paddy declares and I watch as he turns into Father. Do you hear me? I forbid you in the strongest terms.

Nóirín starts stroking his hand again to soothe him while giving me another of her bitter looks.

I could bring you to the shop now, Nóirín. Bernie backs me up, keen to reduce the temperature and make a sale, I got lovely new stock in from Spain during the week.

Dazzled for a moment Nóirín clasps her hands before swiftly recovering her parsimony, You're very kind but I was thinking of going to Clerys.

Clerys isn't what it used to be, Bernie plays her. It's all designer concessions these days.

Really? Nóirín pales at that thought. Well, maybe, in that case . . . she glances half fearfully, half imploringly at Paddy.

Meanwhile, Bernie's professional eye is appraising her. I have a very smart coat dress that would look well on you.

Under this scrutiny I see the frump straighten and brighten until, also touched by the glamour Bernie has thrown, I smile her way and say in unaccustomed sisterhood, Go on girl, that dress has your name on it.

Yes, go, Paddy motions limply with his hand in what I take as an acknowledgement that I know how to dress. I'll be all right here.

Hooked now, Nóirín directs a worried look at me.

Richard touches my hand, more to reassure her than me, and says, We're going for that spin aren't we?

Of course we are. I nod to Nóirín, Away you two go.

Muiris, seeing his aunt's dilemma, says, I'll sit a while with Paddy.

That would be wonderful. Relief smooths Nóirín's taut expression and she beetles out of the room saying, I'll just get Jean.

Leave her be, I call after her, fearing any delay.

Yes, we should go, Bernie adds with another wave of her wand, I'm late as it is.

And now we are four, each of us locked in our particular mutinous silences.

After a few minutes Richard takes up his cup and moves into the kitchen. Muiris follows him. I hear the kettle being filled and the murmur of conversation. There must be more oxygen there than here.

I remain seated, bamboozled in the aftermath of the morning's siege, nerves braced for another incursion. And lo, here it comes: a knell plumbs the silent house. I tense before identifying the source as the grandfather clock in the hall . . . two . . . three . . . echoes overlap . . . four . . . sound out the present . . . five . . . sift the minutes . . . six . . . tot the hours . . . seven . . . toll the years . . . eight . . . rue time lost . . . nine . . . bear forward . . . ten . . . eleven . . . past tomorrow . . . twelve. In our student days Paddy and I would remove the weights before going out, to prevent the chimes alerting the Parents to the hour of our return. Changed times now. I look over at my brother who sleeps, as if bewitched, oblivious of the time being paid out while his cheeks fill and sink steadily with his breath, swell and subside, until one day the clock will stop, then where will we be? Emptying out, sinking.

Would that I could sleep now. I move to the couch, stretch out and close my eyes. Dear God. The inside of my head is aswarm, images, snatches of conversation, fragments of memory spring from every crevice, competing for attention, leaping away before I can catch hold of them. My eyes open only to focus on the cracks in the ceiling. I shut them tight. But I can't keep out the old dread. Now, stirred by Paddy's charge against Richard, it works its familiar way through me, its chill slicks my back, grips my stomach, ices my hands.

Two men wait in the shadows, utterly still, preparing their gallous deed for Ireland.

In all these years, I have never spoken of that night with Paddy.

Did you tell Father? I ask him now.

No response. Only his breath, swelling, subsiding, swelling, imperturbable.

Paddy, I raise the volume. Paddy.

What? What is it?

It's nothing, I neither change my position nor open my eyes. Here he comes on his bike. Did you tell Father about that night?

What night?

In the lane. The men.

Jesus Christ, Lena, I had to tell him. Those thugs would have come back for us.

What did you say?

Faint afar the doorbell rings, followed on cue by my Pavlovian poodle. I refuse to answer this one. Let Muiris or one of the kids go. It might be Nóirín, although that would be a quick turnaround.

Friends you know.

Who? Of who?

Someone touches my shoulder.

That girl. You know the one. With the—

Mum, wake up, Mum.

Uh oh. My eyes pop open and find my son's face grave with worry, What is it, Lovey? I sit up and swing my legs to the floor.

It's the guards. They're at the door. They need to talk to you.

The guards? What about?

Before Muiris can answer, Paddy continues, Not them. Friends I tell you—ask that fellow. He knows.

What? About the guards? I'm on my feet now but unsteady as I oscillate between two time zones.

Those so and so's.

Shush. You better not say too much about them while they're in the house.

I move towards the kitchen where Richard sits, talking to Pól.

From the breakfast room Paddy's querulous voice runs on as if I'm still there . . . the girl . . . astigmatism . . . upset . . . Father was going to . . .

I glance around at Muiris who has followed me, distress contorting his expression and say, Check on Paddy. I can handle this lot.

Are you sure? What's up?

I've no idea. Unless they're going to charge me with theft of a traffic cone.

Seriously?

No. Go on back to your ailing uncle. I'll be down in five minutes.

There are two gardaí in the hall, one a young man, squatting as he beckons Tanta to him but failing in this because the dog is on guard and standing his ground. Attaboy. The other, a woman, patrols the space between the front door and the stairs. The youth, a mere stripling, stands when I appear, and removes his cap. The woman halts mid-stride, her cap remaining firmly anchored to an elaborate chignon and, stepping forward, introduces herself as Detective Inspector Nolan and her companion as Garda Doyle.

Having dispatched Tanta down the stairs, I lead my visitors into the drawing room and invite them to sit down. The lad takes out a notebook and biro and glances apprehensively from his boss to me.

How can I help you? I ask her.

By telling us anything you know about Myles Mulvaney and where he might be.

I shake my head. I'm afraid I know nothing of his whereabouts. Why do you ask?

Mrs. Mulvaney came to us this morning. He hasn't been seen for two days. Was he in any kind of trouble?

Not that he told me but I had told him I was concerned about the office—

The telephone cuts me short. I glance at the display: Ned. Of course. Anxious to prevent his leaving a breathless and possibly incriminatory voice message, I turn to the detective and say, I need to answer this. I'll only be a minute.

She nods.

Lena, Lena, I'm glad I caught you, Ned rushes in as soon as I pick up.

I'm sorry, I say stiffly, I have visitors. Now isn't a good time to talk.

Aha, La Belle Nolan I'll be bound.

Yes, I'll phone you back this evening.

Very well, tread carefully, so to speak. I said nothing. Pip, pip.

I replace the receiver in its base.

We interviewed Mr. Brennan earlier, says herself, sharp as a knife. It's a miracle she doesn't cut herself.

I see, well I doubt I can add much to what he said. As you probably know I'm retired.

You said you were worried about money.

That's an old trick, I smile.

I beg your pardon? She bridles defensively.

The lad pauses in his note-taking to slide his eyes from her to me.

Jumping the gun to try to catch me out.

She shakes her head. Not a budge out of the chignon and cap. They must be fixed with nails.

I said I had concerns about the office.

Garda Doyle resumes scribbling.

Concerns of what nature?

I was disturbed to learn that Liam Geraghty had been taken on as a client. I believe that he, or one of his employees, is connected to Mrs. Mulvaney.

Aha, now I've started a ripple in La Belle Nolan's professional impassivity.

Her sidekick adjusts his grip on the biro, the better, I presume, to speed it.

What exactly was your concern in relation to Mr. Geraghty?

The more he promotes his schemes the less I believe in them and him.

So it's just an opinion, she pushes. Or do you have information that leads you to this conclusion?

Yes, it's an opinion rooted in what my late husband would have called a gut feeling. Oh Mossie help me now. I've got one foot in the quagmire.

I see, she bestows a false smile on me.

She must have gone to poker school, this one. But I can see through her bluff. She's hoping that by making me think that she thinks that I'm dotty I'll jump to my own defence with a cogent explanation of my distrust of Liam Geraghty.

It comes from long experience of dealing with all manner of people in difficult situations, much as you do, I elucidate and return the condescension. And I don't care for his associates. Now, if that's all . . . Having got the upper hand I rise to signal the end of the interview, I'll see you out.

She hesitates then rises too. If you think of anything important you can call me at this number, she draws a card from her pocket and hands it to me.

The lad snaps an elastic band around his notebook and, replacing it in his breast pocket, stands.

As I cross the room to lead them out I glance down at the garden. Suddenly a pair of sparring magpies tumbles from the rowan tree, flapping like a chequered flag. The disturbance raises an image of vulgar Phil pissing against the tree's trunk, endeavouring to mark his territory.

You could try Cape Darien, I muse, coming away from the window.

The lad quickly fumbles to unbutton his pocket and remove his notebook and pen again, then, poised to write, he casts a pleading look at me.

Cape Darien, I repeat, C-A-P-E – new word – D-A-R-I-E-N.

D.I. Nolan ponders this suggestion a moment before asking What's the connection there?

It's the Lep—Geraghty's latest investment project, according to the papers. He may have got Myles involved.

She takes this in cautiously then says, Thank you, I'll follow that up.

I can't guarantee you'll find anything but it's worth a shot.

Any lead is helpful, she says reaching out her hand to shake mine. We'll be in touch again.

Good, I hope it does help. I take her hand and look into her hazel eyes. Nothing there. The mask is impenetrable, re-inforced with the steeliness of an ambitious woman in a pro-fession designed by and for men.

I escort the gardaí into the hall and find Muiris there help-ing Paddy into his overcoat. At the sight of us they pause, Muiris still looking worried, Paddy straightening to say, Good afternoon, Guard.

La Nolan bows and returns his greeting. Garda Doyle, in her wake, gives a quick little smile.

Everything in order, Sergeant? Paddy addresses the young man.

Yes, thank you, herself responds.

I skirt the momentary stand-off to open the door. Good bye, I say and good luck.

When they have gone I sag onto the hall seat leaning my head back until I regain my composure.

Mum, Mum . . . ? Muiris leaves Paddy to his coat and approaches me.

I'm fine, I say, straightening up. Just fine.

But what did they want?

I raise my hand to silence him. I'll tell you another time. Nothing to do with me. It's connected with the office.

That's a relief, he smiles, relaxing. I'm bringing Paddy back to the hotel. He needs to lie down.

Good, say I.

Paddy finishes buttoning his coat, steps forward and nods curtly at me.

I'll be watching tonight, I tell him. Break a leg, as they say.

You'd probably like that, he huffs.

Oh for God's sake, Paddy. I'm not that heartless.

Yes, well, goodbye.

Take my arm. Muiris, eager to escape this familial ding-dong, directs his uncle.

The phone is ringing again, an intrusion to be welcomed now.

I'd better get that, I say. Bye-bye.

Expecting that it is Ned impatient to hear about my interview with La Belle Nolan I go into the office but Dorothy's name lights up on the screen. I make to answer the call then stay my hand, and drop into the chair behind the desk, lacking the resilience for a dose of the 'I told you so's'.

Not that either of us could ever have anticipated the calamitous breakfast scene. Dorothy had, however, taken the opportunity during a recent meals-on-wheels round to try to get me to see her version of sense.

Tell me, she had begun, what you're really hoping for from Richard's visit. I mean he's really a stranger.

I'm not sure—

For heaven's sake, Lena, she cut my lie short. I know you better than that.

I'm hoping to understand what happened. I feel like a door was slammed in my face. One minute he was telling me how

much he loved me and missed me when we were apart, the
next he dropped me with no explanation. I just want to know
what went on behind that door.

It's fairly obvious what happened, she insists. There was
someone else or he was a bolter. Which ever it was, what he
did was hurtful and mean. Why can't you talk about that on
the phone? Dorothy's exasperation rose.

I squirmed under her objections and tried to deflect them.
It just isn't the sort of thing you can talk about on the phone. I
want to talk to him face to face. And he wants to see me again.

So what? You don't know one another, not really. He walked
into your life, then walked out of it without warning and now
you're saying that's okay. What's to stop him doing it again?

I wouldn't let him. We've both been married to wonderful
people, at least he says Bronwen was 'a marvel'. We're looking
for different things now. There's a kind of reassurance in our
shared past. Even when I saw his photo in the paper and again
online, his smile looked the same as it did back then, the way
his eyes creased up almost to slits. It was a happy smile.

So you're wondering how he can be happy without you?
She shook her head at me.

No but I wouldn't mind feeling the light of that smile on
my face.

That's not enough, Darlin'.

It's a start. What's the worst that can happen?

He can hurt you all over again. And you don't need that at
this stage in your life.

I've grown a tough hide by now and I'll make him leave if I
think he's toying with me.

There's a soft underbelly to the toughest hide. Why even
take that chance? You can't simply pick up where you left off,
or where he broke off. It's too hasty, impulsive. She gave me
a sympathetic look, then, catching herself, laughed. Oh God,

listen to me. I could be talking to my kids. And they're well past listening to me.

Exactly, I smiled. I appreciate your concern but I'm not quite ready to abdicate from living. I'd like to have someone to go on holiday with, to make plans with, to have dinner with.

Yes of course you would and you should have someone special, but it doesn't *have* to be *him*. I think you're trying to fix the past and that can't be done.

I know that, I said, dismissing the truth of her words. Imagine if it had been you and Ken.

He would never have treated me the way Richard treated you, and if he had I don't think I'd forgive him.

Forgiveness, I muse. That's the thing, I'm not sure forgiveness is needed. It wasn't all Richard's fault, I began, then retreated from the shadow threatening to close off the weak midday sun.

As the car pulled up outside the next client's house I put my hand on the door handle and said, I'll do this one. I got out, took the meal from the boot and brought it to the elderly woman who always sat at her window waiting for us. After a short exchange of pleasantries I returned to the car. Suddenly Mother's voice was at my ear like the buzzing of a wasp, Lena, Lena, Lena, when will you stop chasing rainbows? You have to accept you can't regain your youth.

Now, as Dorothy begins to speak into the answering machine, I hear Richard call my name.

Hi Lena, hope you're . . .

Here, I reply to Richard, In the office.

. . . this morning. Claire told me about it. Would you and Richard like to come over here for a bowl of pasta tonight? Nothing fancy, just ourselves. Around eight.

Tanta precedes Richard into the room and comes to sit at my feet, where he whines and gives me a reproachful look. I know, I bend to fondle his head, frail as a bird's beneath his woolly hair. You didn't get breakfast. And neither did I. This day is a mess.

With a grunt of agreement, the dog curls up on my foot, ready to move the moment I do.

I'm glad I found you, Richard says on reaching us. I was afraid you'd been arrested. And Muiris was sure of it.

Poor boy. Ever since Mossie died he's been afraid of losing me too.

Understandable. He moves to the centre of the room and sweeps it with his glance as if taking his bearings. This feels different, he concludes.

What does? I look around not sure what he's seeing.

He stands for a moment, eyes fixed on Father's old roll-top desk, now home to my laptop, briskly shakes his head and says, Yes? What?

You said something was different. I wondered what you meant. That's all.

I meant . . . he pivots on his stick and, coming to a halt, points to the top of the bookcase. It's gone. That thing. The giant eye.

Polyphemus. He was the first thing to go. Ugly-looking yoke. I dumped a lot of stuff. Father was a hoarder of miscellanea. A biographer's dream, had anyone wanted to write about him.

Surely there were some items of interest.

Nary a one. Unless you count copies of speeches he gave at medical dinners and conferences, articles for history journals, newspaper cuttings and the family tree he built in an effort to verify his claim to be the true heir to the Great O'Neill.

I take it he wasn't.

No, some fellow in Spain got there first but Father decided they were cousins and they became quite friendly. It was an amiable fiction on both sides I think. I just wish he'd been less delusional and more practical. A quick shudder runs through me as I recall the long evenings spent in this room, with only the ticking radiator for company, surrounded by files, railing against Father in my head as I opened every file, jotter, scrapbook and envelope, frustration mounting at the absence of any evidence that he had provided for Mother. For an intelligent man, I continue, he had a blind spot about money. Hang on, I snap back to the present. When were you ever in this room?

Ah, well, Richard gives a bitter smile and props himself against the bookcase. That day your mother invited me to afternoon tea.

How? When? I was with you all afternoon.

Not all, he shakes his head slowly. Not when you were upstairs getting ready to come out for the evening with me. Your father brought me in here to talk. That's when he told me to leave the field.

I plant my elbows on the desk and sit forward in wonderment. Did I hear that right? He *asked* you to break with me?

He didn't *ask*, Richard corrects me. He told me, very clearly, to 'behave honourably' and step down. Said it was too soon for such a friendship, you were too young, that you needed to get your exams. But I knew what he was really driving at.

It takes a few moments for this disclosure to fully register in my cerebral cortex and when it does I am capsized. Is it possible that I was the dupe of my father and a man I once imagined I would love forever? Could this fellow, whom I have welcomed into my house, and into my bed, be a stranger to me after all? If so, it's fifteen love to Dorothy. To even up the score, however, I begin to seem a stranger to myself.

Why didn't you tell me this at the time? I ask evenly.

He looks up, shamefaced, as he should be. Your Father asked me not to, he claims. Told me to simply retire from the scene. That you were volatile and vulnerable.

Anger forms a cold hard fist inside me. And you accepted that without protest?

No. What do you take me for?

I don't know what to take you for right now.

I told him I loved you, that in time I would like to marry you. That I could make you happy. But he was adamant. Wouldn't listen to me. Said he knew you better than I did. That he needed to protect you from yourself.

My anger turns to resentment. I scramble to right myself. Are you saying he tried to make out that I was unstable, to put you off?

I don't think that's fair. He seemed genuinely worried about you. I said I'd look after you but he didn't seem to believe me, or he didn't want to believe me. Then he stared at the big eye for a few seconds and said he was sure I wouldn't be so fool-hardy as to defy him. I understood him.

He was threatening you.

Yes. I knew he was serious. He had the means to carry out the threat. Or at least to try.

Now it's my turn to glance up to where the old Cyclops once sat. Possessed of a new, sharp clarity, I say, If you had told me all that back then, everything would have been different.

In my mind's eye that dark night in the lane unpicks itself and another story streams into its space, not the lived life the apocryphal drowning woman sees but the one that might have been.

I didn't want to spoil what I knew would be our last night together. He gives a rueful smile. You were so vital, so beautiful. I wanted to hold you in my memory like that. I'm sorry. He bows his head.

That was selfish and mean. You deceived me. I remain stony, refusing to take this man's trespasses against me lightly.

He rubs his hand over his face and his expression wobbles. Maybe so, he says, but defying your father wouldn't have served any purpose. He was determined to protect you. How would it have helped if I had told you what he said?

I'd have travelled with you the next day. We could have married in Britain.

He laughs and I see that old smile bunching up his cheeks and closing his eyes, then, growing serious again he turns his eyes on me and concedes, Yes, yes, I believe you actually would have done that. You were more impulsive than me. But that's just it. I knew you wouldn't have accepted your father's edict and might have done something rash. And he would have come after us or after me. To kill me.

Don't be daft, I say. He had put all that behind him.

Richard's head sways slowly and says in a level tone, No he hadn't and yes he would have done that. Or as a minimum arranged for it to be done.

That's paranoid.

I'm afraid it's not, he insists. Apart from which, it would have been utterly impractical at that point. I had no home to give you. I was due to return to Germany. You'd have been alone.

You had a family, parents, brothers. Wouldn't they have welcomed me? I retort.

Richard directs his attention to his feet.

I let a pensive silence settle for a while then say, They didn't know about me. Is that it?

He looks up, raises his arms and lets them fall in a gesture of defeat. I didn't . . . I mean . . . there were . . . Look, he sighs, I don't know any more. It's too late for all this. Is this why you asked me to come here?

I look down at the old scratched desk and its accoutrements, souvenirs and home made gifts, keepsakes of affection and memory and, glowing among these, a photograph of Mossie and a ten-year-old Muiris, hands on the tiller of the *Lady Lena II*, soft hair tousled by the sea breeze, faces brimming with joy in the warmth of their closeness, the exhilaration of the sail, a moment of pure happiness captured on the fly. A wash of love courses through me and I know I do not regret the lived life.

In part, maybe, I return to Richard. I might never have contacted you only I saw your picture in the paper. It brought back memories and the old questions began to nag me again. I knew nothing of your circumstances, I just wanted to close the file if you like. I didn't really expect us to hit it off so well. Once we did I thought sure what did we have to lose.

No. He shakes his head vigorously. I don't really believe that.

What do you mean? It wouldn't have occurred to me otherwise.

Maybe not but when it did I think you imagined I could help you exorcise the other memory—

Don't be absurd, I protest, perhaps a little too loudly. That would be using you.

He raises his hand to placate me. I'm not saying that was the only reason. Let's be honest: we both knew there was a spark, that we might be friends and lovers again but now that I'm here I feel like a scapegoat for the past. And that's not right or fair. I can't change what was done to you. I wish I could wipe your memory clean of that night but I can't. That's asking too much of me. He sits back in the chair, one hand on the crook of his stick moving it away from him and back with a metronomic rhythm. I'm only a simple chap after all, he concludes. Don't expect me to work miracles.

Propping my elbow on the desk I rest my forehead in my hands and massage my temples with my middle fingers. Pain grips my skull. I recall the night I happened on the newspaper photo but it is Tim Gallagher's jovial face that swims into view as he apologises for his maladroit remarks. Maybe you're right, I allow. But the two events are so bound up with one another that I need to disentangle them.

In that case you're talking to the wrong person.

But it was on account of you, I insist. You were part of the hurt. The lie.

You weren't the only one lied to, he shakes his head. You deceived me somewhat too.

What do you mean? I bristle.

Your letter made no mention of that incident. Yet that was why you wrote, wasn't it?

I nod, caught by the turning tide. I thought of writing about it but the words wouldn't come. I couldn't form them. The shame was too overwhelming, too paralysing. And I hadn't heard from you since you left. I felt abandoned. My eyes rove the room in search of rescue. To repeat your question, I return to him, What difference would it have made? As it turned out you had already written your final letter.

True. I had put it off because I couldn't bring myself to do it. But then I heard about . . . was told . . . what was done to you. I was filled with a blind fury. You've got to believe that I wanted to come to you immediately. The CO forbade me to leave the base. I hit him and he hit me back, pinned me to the wall and said he could have me drummed out for insubordination. I apologised and then he said that if I left without permission I would be regarded as a deserter. What could I do?

You could have told the truth in the letter.

I wish I could. Remember all our mail was censored. The CO warned me not to mention the incident in the letter. Be a bastard, he said. Tell the girl you don't want to see her again. A clean break. He illustrates this with a horizontal cutting gesture. I wasn't given a choice.

Because if I knew that you knew . . .

Precisely. In the back of my mind I thought some day I'd make it up to you. Then I got sense and realised that would only hurt you more. In the event it would hardly have changed the outcome, would it? So you see, each of us was trapped, in our different ways, and constrained to lie.

I've always hated lies.

Sometimes silence can be the worst lie. Even when it's well intended. You should talk to Paddy. He knows things that might help you – I won't say forget the horror but answer some of the questions that haunt you.

He couldn't know . . . I pause. Unless . . . unless . . . When I asked him just now why he told Father he started muttering about friends and some girl but then he told me to ask you.

Me? He gives an indignant snort. The bastard. It's for him to tell you what happened.

I'm beginning to feel I'm caught in the middle of a conspiracy, I push back my chair and stand. Tanta springs up and scampers out to the hall. My head is throbbing, I say. I need some air.

It's not a conspiracy. I had no part in any of this, says Richard firmly. Although I may have been the catalyst. This concerns your family, your people. He glances again to Polyphemus' perch and shudders. You know I can't help feeling that the eye is still staring down at me.

I follow his glance and say, I get that feeling sometimes too. Let's go.

Chapter Seventeen

In the hall I pull on my coat, hat and gloves and stoop to attach Tanta's lead. The dog circles my feet in giddy excitement.

I'm going to take him for a walk along the seafront, I tell Richard, who is making for the stairs.

Fine, he says. I think I'll rest a while.

Good idea. It's been a busy morning.

You could say that, he tilts his head, gives a little wave, then turns to climb the stairs.

I watch his halting progress for a moment thinking this may well be the last I see of him, as, once upon a time of innocence and intensity, my eyes had followed the red flash of his dress uniform past the Martello tower until it disappeared from view. That night I yearned towards him, impatient to see him again. Now, I see that I was taken for a fool, mocked by a protective circle which extended even to my lover. I hover between revulsion at my own gullibility and rage that I should have been so patronised. I'm not sure whether I want him to stay or leave but I'll give him time to pack his bag and call a cab if that's what he's minded to do.

Okay, Tanta, let's go, I address the dog who is now whining and pawing my leg. Before I can unlatch the door, however, it opens into my hand. Tanta backs away but his tail is wagging. Friend so, not foe.

Felicia. Of course. In all the commotion I had forgotten that it is her day. The young woman enters, wreathed in the chill of the March air.

Hi, come in, I greet her.

Hello Lena, she smiles at me but instantly leans over to stroke Tanta's head as he pirouettes on his hind legs for her. Good boy, good boy, she laughs.

You look cold, I say. Make yourself a coffee. I'm just taking him out. We've had a lot of visitors this morning.

That's nice, she says.

Not really, I pull a face. You don't need to do my room today.

Is there anything—At the sound of a footfall on the landing she glances up, eyes widening as they track Richard from the bedroom to the bathroom. She gives me a wary smile.

An old friend of mine, I reassure her.

Ah, yes, she nods, restraining a grin.

I'll see you later. I move to open the door again and flee this mild embarrassment.

But Felicia stays me, her hand on my sleeve, and half-whispers, Can I talk to you for a minute, Lena? Darting an apprehensive look up the stairs, she adds, In private?

Of course, I usher her into the office. Tanta follows, glued to her heels.

What's up? I ask, and shut the door behind me.

She looks down and twists her hands together, It is . . . I mean . . . I don't know how . . . I am sorry but . . .

Are you in difficulty? I ask. Sit down, take your time.

Seated behind the desk again, watching the nervous young woman before me I reassume the detached listening mode of my solicitor self, waiting for the client to open up.

You see . . . Bernie . . . she . . . she didn't pay me for six weeks. Felicia's expression runs from fear to despair.

What? I had recommended Felicia to Bernie about two years ago and, until now, the arrangement has been very satisfactory,

Felicia doing three hours' cleaning next door twice a week before coming into my house, occasionally babysitting and helping out in the shop at busy sale times or if Bernie is away. Getting better cast-offs there too.

What did she say?

Every week no cash and she will pay me next week. Felicia spreads her empty hands, But next week no cash.

I don't understand that when she runs a shop.

I'm sorry, Lena. I don't know too. Tears well in her eyes. It's what she says. But I must pay the rent or my landlord will put me out.

Yes, yes, I know, you must. Don't worry, I believe you. I'm just mystified. I unlock the top drawer in the desk and take out my cheque book. How much does she owe you?

Seven hundred twenty euro. I am very sorry. I will pay you back.

I hand her a cheque for €1,000 in case Bernie doesn't come up with the money soon.

Thank you, Lena. Thank you. She clutches the cheque and her face relaxes.

You're welcome. Don't be stuck, I say. I hope she does start paying you again soon, for your sake and for hers. If she doesn't it means there's something serious wrong. Just let me know what's happening. Don't worry, I'm sure it's only temporary.

Thank you. Me also, I hope she can pay me again. I like her so much and the children. Before she always pays me. No problem. Please don't tell her I ask you.

No. I won't say anything. I shut and lock the drawer and rise to leave when a new question forms in my mind. Wait a minute, I sit down again. How long did you say it is since she paid you?

Two months. I have used all my saving for the rent.

Since January in other words?

Yes, that's right.

I cast my mind back to find the moment when Bernie had begun to soften me up for the presentation of her nursing home scheme and, as I do, I see again the miserly glint in Moira Kiely's eyes, bright as a neon rainbow.

I understand, say I, more to myself than to Felicia.

She leans forward, believing I have hit upon a solution whereas I have only stumbled on the problem.

Apologies, I assume an air of confidence that belies my gut feeling. I'm delaying you. It's probably a slack time of year for them both. Maybe in a couple of weeks it will be better.

Oh my God, I pray that it will be okay soon.

We'll work something out. Now go on and make your coffee. I'll have to drag Tanta out now because he'd probably prefer to stay here with you, I smile to hide my concern.

When she has left the office I pick up the phone.

As I anticipated, Ned stumbles over himself in his eagerness to report his news. I let on to know nothing, he insists. Told her detectiveness I'm only the caretaker and message boy, like a courier. No involvement in the business side of things. She was quick though, asked me would I ever be carrying envelopes to or from Mr. Liam Geraghty or crocOgold or greenGold. I allowed myself a little ponder then concluded that no I wouldn't. Also asked me if I knew a fellow by the name of Philip Lannigan. Said I never heard of him.

Interesting, say I. I wonder what she has on Geraghty. Funny that she's jumping to tie Myles in with him. She knows more than she's letting on.

She's a fine woman but. I told the two of them to drop in any time. I wouldn't mind seeing her in civvies, tresses unbound. And the dear boy – Puss sat beside him purring. Good phenomenones as they say.

I hope she doesn't have cause to drop in here again, I say. And I hope to goodness Myles hasn't done anything stupid.

That's what the Mouse said.

The Mouse? When? My ears prick up.

This morning. After the Garda Sugar and Candy left. Oh I've had a busy day I can tell you.

Nothing to mine, I sigh. But go on, what did she have to say? So he's on his own wherever he is.

Well, she's going nowhere, Brennan scoffs. Except looking for him. Less than an hour after La Belle Dame en Bleu and her squire leave and I'm on my way out to deliver some documents and go to the bank the Mouse tumbles in through the door, all trína chéile, asking have I seen him, and where is he, and she needs to talk to him urgently. I tell her to calm herself and catch her breath but then she starts in about being away in Boston, only back last night and Myles not answering his phone or his email for two days. Nothing for it but to bring her up to my sanctum sanctorum and give her a dose of whiskey to soothe her nerves, so to speak. I didn't want her upsetting the others downstairs and blathering out of turn in front of them. When she gets a hold of the drink she relaxes and starts to tell me she knows nothing of Myles' whereabouts and turns on the waterworks because she hopes he hasn't done anything foolish. And it's all her fault. And she thought it would all work out in the end. And she didn't mean any harm. And so on and so forth. Knocked back the whiskey in one slam and held the glass out for more. I complied.

Did she happen to say what 'it' is? Or do I need to ask?

No need at all. The drink made her garrulous. After the second slug off she went at a gallop so to speak telling me all how she and Geraghty go back a long way. Started out on a magazine, him in accounts, herself flogging advertising space. Then he left to set up on his own, and a couple of years later, the magazine folds, she uses the redundancy package to do a course in interior folderol and la di da. And here's the juicy bit: who do you think lends her the money to start her business?

Geraghty?

The very one.

Was there a histoire there? Of the heart?

She says no, but I wouldn't take any notice of that. It might not have been the heart if you take my meaning. I'll tell you what I think: he uses her to recruit clients.

I absorb this proposal. It makes sense, except for Rosemary. What about Mrs. Myles? I thought she introduced them.

Don't forget the half-brother-in-law. Hints can be dropped here and there with a little salt on the tail of the mouse so to snare him. 'Poor Mouse is hungry. Poor Mouse is struggling to make ends meet. Poor Mouse needs a leg up and a dig out.' Rosemary might take pity and tell Myles he needs to do a makeover in the office now that he's top dog and all the rest of it.

I tap an arpeggio with my fingers on the desk while Ned marshals his facts and speculations to build a tolerably credible case. As a theory it works, I say. Only it doesn't bring us any closer to finding Myles.

Not unless he smelt something bigger and nastier than a mouse and went to check on the investment.

I suggested to Garda Nolan that she look in Cape Darien.

Ooohhh. That's a long way off. Hot I'd say, he drifts, his tone turning dreamy. Yes. Hot. She'd need the sunscreen.

I'd rather not dwell on La Belle Dame undercover in her bikini, I say. I imagine she'll contact local police.

Naughty, Brennan laughs. She certainly needn't bother going all that way herself because she won't find anything except a pyramid of sand. It's a sorry state of affairs, Myles bringing the office into disrepute. I thought more of him, even if he did want to evict me. Hah! A certain gentleman of our acquaintance must be rolling in his grave.

Very likely. Thanks Ned. Keep me posted and I'll do likewise.

To be sure. Pip pip.

I replace the receiver and slump. My head swims. The Cyclops rises through the blur. He saw all. The blind spot. Ah yes, if Father were here today he'd surely be putting his money in crocOgold.

Come on, Tanta, I say. Let's get out before anyone else lands in on top of us.

I cross the road and the railway bridge and descend to the shore. The tide is out and the exposed seaweed on the rocks exhales a pungent reek. Shells and pebbles crunch under my feet. I give myself over to the nippy breeze, the distant sweep of wave on sand and the silver light, willing them to scour me of the exasperation brought on by the morning's callers and their clatter of ailments, appendages, confusions, blue jokes, off-key songs, curiosity, apologies and misguided confidence that they know what is best for me. There are days when I want to walk right out of my own head. For now striding by the sea will have to suffice.

Just as the water, tired of fumbling with the shells and pebbles on the shore, retreats into itself, irritation deepens to the pain reopened by the disclosure of Richard's knowing silence. There I was, one minute bathing in nostalgic affection, the next I am chained to a rock with remorse eating my liver. Yes, yes, I know all the arguments, I let myself in for it, brought it on myself, have only myself to blame, made my own bed. I can beat Matt Talbot's self-flagellation into a cocked hat but that won't banish the scarred young woman who cowers in my heart, terrified lest anyone see her shame and despise her for it. I pick up my pace, as if I can outstrip this retrospective self-castigation. One day I'll end up ripping out my own heart.

Half-way down the pier I run out of steam, as does Tanta who sits down, refusing to budge. Here, little chap, I give in. I carry him to a stanchion where, having set him on a patch of rough grass, I perch awkwardly, facing into the harbour. I'm turning into the Ancient Mariner, memory my albatross. But now the emphasis falls differently on the remembered scenes and words, their meanings freighted with all that was hidden from me because I could not speak of my own pain and taking their cue from me my family laid a poultice of silence on that wound. They thought they were protecting me but could not stop me gnawing my own entrails.

Mother's voice breaks on me, asking, What happened to you? She stood behind me, studying my bruised breasts and ribs in the mirror of the shop fitting room.

Nothing, I said and hastily covered the marks with my arms.

She withheld the brassière she had chosen, waiting for an honest reply.

I slipped in the bath, I fibbed.

I see now that she knew everything and that was why, shortly after her return from the Wexford festival, she suggested with expansive breeziness that we go into town and buy me some new clothes. After she had bought me a dress, a skirt, a blouse and a jacket she marched me to the lingerie department on the principle that the stylish woman dresses from the inside out. I accepted this attention with a bad grace. Even the lunch afterwards in Mitchell's dainty café, with its potted palms and ladies' string quartet, could not brighten my mood.

A little bit of gratitude wouldn't go astray, said Mother at last in justifiable pique.

Sorry, I mumbled. Thank you. I just don't feel very well. It's my time of the month.

She shook her head knowingly at me and asked, Are you sure there's nothing you want to tell me?

Yes, I said. Nothing.

Think about that, she continued. There are times I fear for you, she laid her hand on mine, the way you take things to heart. The trouble is you're also self-willed. You have to learn to bend a little, otherwise you're going to find life very difficult. Believe me, I do understand.

I repressed the impulse to cry, lowered my head and continued to pick at my food.

A seacat casts off from its terminal and, engine throttling loudly, executes a 360 degree turn, driving waves up the side of the pier which spatter me and Tanta. Flinching, the dog stands to shake himself but I relish the elemental tang of salt on my lips. The ferry clears the harbour, and picks up speed as it plies its route to Holyhead. I glance at the sky which is criss-crossed by wavering contrails and am pierced hit with a sudden regret at the thought that Richard may well be taking off too. Following Tanta's cue I stand and shudder briefly in the March breeze whipping in from the sea.

I resume walking, my eyes still tracking the ferry towards the horizon and my mind turns to Myles. Has he boarded a boat or plane and vanished, or worse? I glance around, could he have done what some do in this place . . . ? Surely not, surely not. I face the lighthouse at the pier's end knowing that behind it the base of the mole shelves away into the water whose dark embroilments lure the sick at heart. I must not look that way. I halt and shut my eyes, resisting that vertiginous pull, then, with an effort, spin on my heel and quickly retrace my steps, speaking nonsense aloud to Tanta to keep myself present and alert. But guilt hounds me with questions, why didn't I keep a closer eye on him, why wasn't I more conciliatory, more thorough, more persistent, kinder, smarter, anything that might have pre-empted a desperate act. Neurosis broods in the void where information and facts should be. Someone must know something. I rummage in my pockets but my phone is not there.

Keep going, Tanta, I rally the dog. We've got to get home.

Tail up, snout forward, the dog complies and trots ahead of me, bent on returning to Felicia.

And there's another mystery: her story of Bernie's impecu-
niousness or belated stinginess. Coincidence or connection?
She and Myles chase one another through my hasty head and
both pursue Liam Geraghty, who in turn runs after the evanes-
cent rainbow's end. If Brennan is right my neighbour and my
colleague have been sold a mess of potage, or sand, and the
Mouse is the one La Belle Nolan needs to interview. Reason is
slowly replacing panic in my neurons and I begin to breathe
more easily. There are steps I can take. I know what I must
do next. It's true what Richard said, sometimes silence is the
worst lie.

A teenage girl, eyes red with crying, answers the door of
the big house in Cabinteely and wordlessly shows me into the
sitting room. On seeing me Rosemary startles and commences
to weep. She seems already to have assumed the worst and
cast herself in the role of the widow receiving callers, her snug
tracksuit replaced by navy trousers and a crumpled blouse.
One hand squeezes a tissue while the other clasps that of the
Mouse, who inclines her head, sans turban today, towards me.
I halt, dumbfounded by this tableau of improbable sisterhood.

This is a friend of mine, Rosemary says. Eimear Ní Neachtáin.

Yes, I recover myself and sit. We've met.

This is my first visit to Myles' new home and I am impressed
by its American scale. The spacious hall and reception rooms
display confidence, and to every bedroom, I bet my bottom
dollar, a bathroom. Although they moved in here only a year
ago, it's obvious that Myles and Rosemary did not consult the
Mouse about the décor. The sitting room is a formal combination of eggshell blue and daffodil yellow, relieved by a couple
of conventional landscapes and a large black and white studio
portrait of the family, mother, father and four children. For all
the digital retouching, however, there is a tightness in Rosemary's smile. A recent picture I'm guessing, made to reassure
themselves that all is well under this new roof.

Do you have any word? Rosemary sobs now. I went to your house last night. You must know something. Please help me.

I heard you called. That's why I'm here. But I'm afraid I have no information for you.

I'm so frightened. What if he—

Hush dear, we don't know anything yet. We can't let ourselves rush to the worst conclusions. (Hark at me! Only thirty minutes ago I was about to search for his remains at the back of the pier.) I came to see how you were doing and also to ask you a little more about your concerns. I know you've probably told the guards everything, I glance at Eimear as I say this, wishing she would absent herself but she remains, a study in empathy. I plan to go into the office, I continue, to have a look at his files and see if there's anything significant there. The guards will probably need to take his computer. Did he mention any worries to you?

Nothing, Rosemary pulled a face. He said nothing to me. He just seemed stressed but he said it was business and he didn't want to worry me about it.

Does the name Donal Sheehy mean anything to you? Still my eyes are on Eimear, whose mask slips just a tad.

No, no, no, Rosemary shakes her head. Nothing. She emits a long sigh and, letting go of the other woman's hand, leaves her seat and crosses the room. I don't know anything. You all think I know things that I don't know. I'm sick of the questions. I told you, she rounds on me. I told you there was something wrong but you just thought it was in my head.

No, Rosemary. I didn't. I spoke to Myles but he was evasive. I also said I would get a consultant to look through the books—

At this Eimear springs from the sofa from where she has been observing us, and, going to Rosemary, embraces her waist, Don't worry, she says. They'll find him.

Rosemary brushes her away. Yes, yes, of course you all say that but you don't know anything. It's all pretending. It's very hard to be in this position. She twists her body from left to right, like someone sinking in quicksand. The not knowing is the worst, she cries. I just want Myles back. The children need their father. We're sitting here in limbo and no-one is doing anything. Things run through your head, you can't sleep, can't eat, for thinking about him. Do you understand? She fixes me with a look of angry bewilderment.

I do, I say. I am truly sorry for you. I want to help. I'll go now. If you need anything, please call me.

Yes, thank you, her head droops. Where are the kids? She snaps up suddenly to look at Eimear.

I think they're in the kitchen, says herself in a monstrous little voice. I'll show Lena out and then I'll check on them.

No need, says Rosemary brusquely. I'll go in. She looks at her so-called friend, as if noticing her for the first time, and says, You can go too. I don't . . . I mean . . . I need to do something.

I'm happy to stay, says Eimear, a touch too firmly. I'll make us some tea.

Rosemary puts a hand to her head. No, please. I'd like to be alone with the children. I'll call you if I hear anything.

Well, if you're sure. The Mouse's crest has fallen and she darts an accusing look at me.

I'll let myself out, say I, retreating from this scene of duplicity and despair.

I have just unlocked the car when I hear the titupping of narrow heels and Eimear's voice, flung like a lasso to capture me, saying, She's addled, poor thing.

So I see. I sit into the car and make to pull the door shut but your one catches hold of it and leans in over me. I had a few other ideas for your place, she squeaks in a perfect non-sequitur. I could mail them to you.

Don't bother thank you. I've changed my mind. I give the door a little tug but she refuses to let go, determined no doubt to establish why exactly I had called to Rosemary.

That's a pity, says she. I was looking forward to the challenge. If you change it back again let me know.

Challenge, the cheek of her. Maybe she was hoping to lure me into crocOgold, in a bid to save it.

What was all that about? I jerk my head towards the Mulvaneys' house.

What do you mean? She straightens defensively. Rosemary's a friend of mine. We go back a long way.

I bet you do, I say. But you go further with Myles.

She goggles at me through the big sparkly glasses, then, after a fearful glance over her shoulder, seethes, I don't know what you mean.

I think you do. Brennan has told me of your late shifts in the office.

She vents the laugh of a harridan. That old codger. He's bonkers. Myles told me to take no notice of him.

Did he now? Why would he have said that?

Well . . . it was . . . you know . . . when I was dealing with the painters and decorators, she struggles to restore her self righteousness. Yes . . . because sometimes we were there at the weekend. He has some pretty strange friends I can tell you. We could turn his flat into a beautiful penthouse apartment. You'd make a fortune out of it.

I have no wish to become a landlord. And I assure you Ned is far from bonkers. What he does in his personal life is no business of mine, or yours. I simply rely on him to protect the office. He told me you were there this morning.

I . . . ah . . . well . . . She gabbles . . . I was in the area so I just popped in to see if Myles might be back. Yes, that was it. Then I came on out here, to be with poor Rosemary.

Indeed, I say. Goodbye, I give the door a good yank, which shakes her hand free and causes her to totter. I slam it shut and turn the key in the ignition.

It's not true, she shouts at me over the noise of the engine. It's a pack of lies.

She continues to spit abuse at me as I pull away through the estate – sorry, development – of about ten houses, some not yet finished, and out to the road. If Rosemary could see her 'friend' now she might get an insight into the true nature of their relationship.

Back at home, I am astonished to discover Richard is sitting in the breakfast room. His face is hidden by *The Guardian*. On returning from the walk I had merely let Tanta back into the house, grabbed my handbag from the hall stand and left again without seeing anyone and, in my eagerness to talk to Rosemary, had scarcely given him a thought. His bad leg is stretched before him, stockinged foot propped on a dining chair. He does not see me, nor, it seems, does he hear me, deafened by combat and the drone of the hoover overhead, accompanied by Tanta's high-pitched protest. I tiptoe into the kitchen, happy enough not to have to talk, and in need of food. An egg will do. I put the water to boil, set the timer to five and a half minutes and sit down to wait. Perhaps after all it is better that my mission to tell Rosemary the truth about her husband and her friend was aborted. She would likely not have believed me, especially when the Mouse is being so solicitous of her, and is herself apparently at a loss to know where Myles has gone. If silence can be a lie too much truth can sometimes be a liability. Now that she knows I'm on to her Ms Ní Neachtáin is sure to contact the leprechaun. God forbid that he'll be the next to appear on my doorstep. I need to quiz Jean a little further about him. Hang on, where did I put that card? I run up the stairs to the drawing room and meet Felicia at the door, dragging the hoover into the hall. She is plugged into her iPod so I smile and give her a little wave.

DI Nolan's card is on the table where I left it. I dial her number and wait a while for her to pick up. She apologises for being on another call and says she is following a definite line of inquiry. I tell her what I know about Ms Ní Neachtáin's work for Myles and suggest that she find out what connections she might have with Geraghty. She repeats the name aloud and I picture her sidekick scribbling it down as fast as his leaky biro will let him.

Thank you, Lena, says she, although I don't recall inviting her to use my first name. I'd be grateful for any further information you can give me.

I hang up with her parting words echoing in my head. Who has already given her information? Not Brennan, he's like the Sphinx. I review the meeting with Rosemary and glimpse again the twitch of the Mouse's nose when I mention Sheehy. Did he go further than the Law Society, as he had threatened to do? A million to a hayseed he's the informer/informant.

I dial Dorothy's number next and reach her voicemail where I leave a message accepting her invitation to supper, on condition that we can tune in to the brother on the Late Late.

An ugly smell assails me when I open the drawing room door. Buggeration. The blasted egg. I hurry downstairs to the kitchen which is filled with steam and a sulphurous stink. Through the mist I discern Richard at the stove.

Ah, there you are, he says. I'm afraid I didn't manage to defuse this in time.

Sure enough the egg has exploded and its fragments are scattered around the hob, the counter, the splashback and floor.

Perfect, I sigh and open the back door to let the steam out. That's all I needed.

I didn't know you were home, says he.

I hadn't expected to find you here, say I.

Yes, well, I stepped out to get a paper, he smiles awkwardly. Would you rather I wasn't here?

I don't know to be honest. I turn away from him and, taking a cloth from the draining board, begin to mop the water swilling over the stovetop.

He runs his hand down my spine and murmurs, I thought we had got past all that—

Feeling me tense under his touch he draws back.

All what? I ask, moving to the sink to wring out the cloth.

The things that happened a lifetime ago, he continues. I mean to say, we've come through other experiences. Worse things maybe. We're changed.

Not changed, just modified. Our former selves haven't vanished. They're still us. We're still them. I am assiduous in my mopping up.

Can't you stop that for a minute and look at me? He says with exasperation.

I half-turn to him, cloth still in hand.

I don't understand why you're so angry with me. He appraises me for a moment. I came here in good faith to renew our friendship. I didn't expect to be insulted.

I start to twist the cloth tightly in my hand. Water drips to the floor. Point taken, I say. I have no business accusing or abusing you. I had a feeling that we could get along nicely together again. I think maybe I rushed things. Maybe I wasn't ready for all this. It's possible you're right and deep down I was hoping to understand what happened back then. I wring the cloth so tight that it scorches my palms. I never really believed . . . or maybe didn't want to believe . . . that your feelings for me had changed so abruptly. I needed answers but what you've told me has set off a whole new chain of questions.

Paddy has the answers. Wincing, he grips the back of a chair. I told you I wanted to come back when I heard but I was persona non grata here.

You wouldn't have had to come to the house, I protest.

Richard is shaking his head. That's not what I meant. His eyes hold mine a moment coldly. I wasn't welcome in your country.

I look down at the tortured cloth and let it unfurl. What are you saying? Do you mean Father—

He used his influence.

No, I stepped back. That's going too far. Besides, you told me you did come back. You met Eamon, and talked about me.

That was many years later. No one would have cared by that time. There were more important matters in hand.

I take a moment to absorb this new disclosure. I don't like it, I say.

Neither did I.

I mean I don't like the hugger mugger behind my back. It gives me a creepy feeling to know that Father was conniving and controlling my life, my choices, as if I was a child or a simpleton.

If it's any help, says Richard, I understand. He was controlling my life too, as if I were a thug or a spy.

And if he hadn't done that where would we be now?

Very likely in the same place. It wasn't me or your Father or you that changed our course, it was the weak-minded bastards who attacked you, seeking a bit of perverse glory for themselves.

I suppose so, I turn away again and spread the cloth on the counter. Its pattern jumps and blurs before my eyes. The ground seems to be shifting under me, as if there is something there I can't see but it is influencing my life.

You need to talk to Paddy.

I will, I nod. Tmorrow. Go on back to your newspaper. I'll finish up here.

Can't you let your cleaning lady do it?

No, I can't leave a big mess for her. Besides it's best to do it now before all the egg dries in.

Very well, I'll get out of the way. As he moves past me he runs his hand lightly down my spine and drawing his lips close to my ear whispers, I'm sorry.

I tense under his touch resisting the erotic flicker it lights in me.

He limps back to the breakfast room.

For one who was once such a laissez faire suitor he has become a very persevering fellow. Moithered with loneliness I presume.

Reaching beneath the kitchen sink I take out a killer spray and attack the egg stains with it. Under the influence of the harsh chemicals they begin to dissolve and I wipe them clean. Taking the dustpan and brush from the broom cupboard I stoop to gather up the eggshell scattered like shrapnel on the floor. In the shadow of the kitchen table the fragments darken, blacken, and I am on the ground again arms pinioned pain is a blade sunk in my flesh panic stifles the rising tide of cries that need to be heard but there is no air no air only the stink of rotting leaves and the men's stale breath sickening me and their rough words lashing me traitor hoor traitor hoor traitor bitch suck this taste a true Irishman for a change then suddenly the boys are here rupturing the darkness bicycles flung to the ground shattering their little cargo of records and there is shouting scuffling kicking the thud of punches landed the crack of a forceful blow with a stone a howling swearing running feet and all the while my body abandoned filthy lost crawling away to curl into the darkness stay there scrabbled into the earth but the boys' hands are hauling me up, Paddy and Tim, pulling my clothes around me I struggle leave me leave me

Lena, Lena, what's happened? Says a light woman's voice above my head.

Leave me, I say.

Oh God, what is the matter?

I look up and into the face and anxious almond eyes. I put out my hand.

Her warm hand takes mine. Can you get up, Lena?

Felicia? I say.

Yes, yes. It's me. Let me help you. Did you faint?

I'm not sure. I glance down. My head swoons blackly for a moment. Dizzy, I say. I got dizzy. The shells, yes the shells, I start to scoop them in my hand. The scattered remnants of Paddy's records in the lane the next day. Broken music. We had come out to collect our bikes, still lying on the ground, the front wheel of Paddy's buckled. Rain fell mingling with the blood on the stones. I made to pick up the pieces of Paddy's treasured LPs. Leave it, he said. They're no use now. I'll replace them, I said. Yes, yes, but come on. We wheeled the bikes into the garden. I glanced back. There she lay, curled in a dark heap, the terrified girl burying herself in the shadows, her wound lodged deep in me.

They're broken, I say, looking at the scraps in my hand. Broken. Memories.

Tanta appears and sure that I am holding out the scraps for him begins to nose them.

No, I say. Dirty. Dirty. I drop the shells into the dustpan.

Looking up he begins to lick my face instead. I drop the dustpan and brush and hug his little body to me, soothed by its warmth.

I will clean all, says Felicia above me.

No, I shake my head. There's too much.

Yes. It's okay, Lena, she insists. I can do it.

I turn and smile wanly at her. Very well, I say. Thank you. I release Tanta who resumes poking at the shells and placing one hand on the seat of a chair start to pull myself up.

Felicia grips my waist. Sit, she says. You must sit. No more dizziness.

I'm fine, thanks, I say, sinking onto the chair. You're very kind. I tilt my head back and shut my eyes for a moment welcoming the play of light and warmth that falls through the window. Tanta springs into my lap sensing that something is amiss. I stroke his back rhythmically.

Where is your friend? Felicia asks. The gentleman.

Richard? I say, momentarily surprised to recall that he is here. In the breakfast room, I think.

She approaches the door to the other room and knocks although it is open.

Hullo! Calls his voice from within.

Mr. Richard, says Felicia. Will you come please? Lena is dizzy.

On my way. Paper rustles and I hear his uneven step approach.

What happened? He stands beside me, concern furrowing his brow.

The face I see is a new one, as if my vision has been rectified and the contours of the remembered face that had clouded the present one removed, leaving this man, who might be his father, before me, a decent old boy, taken all in all, a friend.

I'm not sure, say I. A touch of vertigo I think, when I bent down. All that talking.

Yes, he says. Take your time.

Felicia moves away and busies herself at the sink then brings me a glass of water which I sip gratefully as if it were a G and T.

Tanta leaps down and starts to poke at the egg shells again until Felicia shoos him away with the brush which she manoeuvres round my feet.

Time is the problem, I say to Richard.

It doesn't always heal, he concedes. Can you stand?

I think so but give me your hand.

He obliges and draws me upright.

When we are seated together on the couch in the breakfast room he says, I've something to show you.

He riffles the newspaper until, finding the relevant page, he folds it back and presents it to me.

Once more I am looking at the mock-up of Phil Lannigan's chipped oblong. Further down the page is a photo of Liam Geraghty.

They're calling him the Wizard of Oz, says Richard.

Ha! More like the straw man, say I.

They say he has property and projects all over the place but some of his clients are getting jittery. He didn't return the journalist's calls.

I'll bet he didn't. I skim the page. An anonymous investor speaks of delays in payments. Odds on that's Mr. Sheehy.

I put the paper down and tell Richard about my visit to Rosemary's house and how the Mouse was lying in wait for Myles' return.

Ah-ah, Richard purses his lips with a doubtful expression. I don't think she's waiting for him. She doesn't give a monkey's about him. It's this chap she wants, his finger stabs at the page.

Geraghty? But why go to Myles' house? She can contact him herself. Brennan says they know each other well.

What if he's disappeared too? You said she was in Boston. My guess is she was looking for him there. She didn't find him but she knows that Rosemary is connected to him, or to his bodyguard.

I let this idea settle for a moment and then I see it all. You mean he's double-crossing her and Myles, the whole bloody lot of them.

Exactly. He's probably been salting money away somewhere that's not in his portfolio and has gone to ground there. I'd say all your mouse found in Boston was a brass plate, if that. He leans forward to study the photo of the dream palace. Where is Cape Darien anyway? That name is very familiar.

No idea, say I. Somewhere near Panama, it says here.

I don't think that's right, he cups his hands behind his head and leans back, staring into the middle distance. There's something odd about it. Let's look it up on your computer.

Chapter Eighteen

I'm agog to see what magic Bernie has wrought on Nóirín. Subsiding into the soft cushions of Ken and Dorothy's armchair, a glass of burgundy in hand, I am glad of this respite after a day spent scurrying from one disaster to another, anxious as the little red hen.

Richard lowers himself into the chair beside mine. Now that I'm down I'm not sure I'll ever be able to get out of here, he pants.

Don't worry, says Ken. I have an eject button.

I catch the warning look that Dorothy flashes at her husband who has been on his best behaviour all evening despite his long-standing aversion to Richard.

Thanks mate.

Ken busies himself adjusting the TV screen to give us a better view of it.

The two men have arrived at a tolerant rapport after a fidgety start as they attempted to find a frequency on which to communicate. Like most of my male college friends, Ken had been leery of Richard first time around. His race and occupation told against him from the outset but, atavism aside, Ken had confided to Dorothy that he thought him a bit too fond of himself, a bit of a 'boyo'. He was outraged by the 'cavalier' way that Richard ended our relationship, calling it a scandalous insult to me, and a slap in the face to those friends, himself included, who had welcomed him into their group, even if they hadn't warmed to him. Dorothy told me at the time that she had never seen Ken so riled up or talking in such aggressive terms. This evening, however, she had primed him to act as if he were meeting Richard for the first time, for my sake, lest too much harking back ran the party aground.

While Ken cleared up after the meal, and Richard went outside for a smoke, I told Dorothy how surprised I was that he was still here.

I think you'd have a job getting rid of him now, she laughed.

Ken aims the remote at the screen which opens on the cheesy Late Late Show host, whose mother apparently never told him to take his hands out of his pockets when he was speaking to someone or, in this case, to the nation. Happily, the sound is mute while we wait for the star turn of the show.

Look, look, exclaims Dorothy after a few minutes. Here they are.

Ken turns up the volume as the audience applauds the appearance of the presidential hopeful and his bean chéile— Paddy will surely feel obliged to throw in the cúpla focail as a form of patriotic ingratiation.

Is that really her? Dorothy's eyes round at the sight of Nóirín.

I have to scooch forward and peer at the screen to confirm that the woman in the well-cut navy and white coat dress, set off by a cleverly knotted scarf of primary colours, is indeed my sister in law. Bernie obviously told her to get the hair done and the RTE make-up artist managed to erase her characteristic scowl. She is a creature transformed. Paddy, unfortunately, not.

Yes, say I. Who'd have thunk it possible?

The brother doesn't look too bad, considering, says Ken.

So-so, I concede. The make-up artist has given him a better colour than he had at breakfast.

He was mostly red with rage this morning, Richard laughs.

That was his own fault, I say.

Ken bounces Richard a knowing smile.

It was, I insist, but am distracted by a beep on my phone.

Dorothy's goes off a second later.

Claire, we laugh together.

Sure enough, the third Bagette has spotted the new Nóirín on air.

She looks like the Queen!!! Her text marvels.

She's only half her age, Dorothy says. Well, two-thirds anyway.

She'd love the comparison all the same, say I. She can't get enough of the palace gossip.

Ken flaps his hand at us. Sssshh, the two of you. Let's hear what Paddy's saying.

The host is leading him through the family background, the heart of Paddy's presidential notions.

Host: . . . and you have a sister, is that right?

Dorothy nods at me, and Ken gives me a thumb up.

But I am not well pleased. He can leave me out of it, I say.

Host: You lived in a troubled time. I mean Ireland in the 1950s was not a particularly happy place was it?

Paddy: I wouldn't go that far. Of course there was poverty after the Emergency, and many people had to make do with less than they have today. But there was entertainment too: cinemas, music hall, theatre, dances, races. We weren't all miserable all the time.

Host: In Dublin, maybe. But it was also the time of the so-called Border Campaign. Your father had been involved in the Anglo-Irish War and the Civil War. What was his position on that campaign?

Paddy: Well by then he was in the Senate and he would have spoken out against it. He wasn't happy about the existence of the border but he didn't want to see more war.

Host: It affected your family all the same, didn't it? There was an incident you were drawn into I think, involving your sister, a kidnap attempt was it?

I jerk bolt upright, spilling wine onto Dorothy's rug. My whole body trembles with dread.

I am aware of Dorothy turning a puzzled look on me but am too transfixed by the unfolding horror to respond.

Paddy: Well, ah . . . yes . . . but . . . well . . . I think these fellows thought they could get him to lean on Dev, you know, to recall the soldiers from the border. Luckily I came upon them in the lane. Behind our house you know. They got a fright you see and I . . .

Host: Did they seriously think that kidnapping your sister would bring Dev to heel?

Paddy: I don't know. Maybe they had just gone rogue.

Host: Like today's dissidents. But you managed to rout them.

Paddy: Something like that. Yes. Got a few cuts and bruises but they took off.

Host: You were only what? Sixteen? Fair play to you. Your father must have been proud of you. Maith an buachaill. [*Flash of the host's ironic smile.*] That deserves a medal, or at least a round of applause.

The audience dutifully claps and the camera pans the crowd coming to rest for a few moments on Jean who is frozen open-mouthed in shock. Beside her sits Pól, his face furrowed with incomprehension.

That's your niece and her friend isn't it? Dorothy asks. They seem as stunned as we are.

Eyes still starting from my head, I look around to see Dorothy staring at me, Ken at her and Richard at the ground.

Host: Did you know you were married to a hero, Nóirín?

Nóirín: No. Yes. Of course. He's a hero to lots of people. His patients.

Host: Yes, very well said. [*More applause*] On the lighter side of life, Paddy, I think you were an amateur singer or actor too—

Turn it off, Dorothy instructs Ken. We've heard enough for one night.

Ken zaps the screen and Paddy's face dwindles to a streak then vanishes altogether.

Are you all right? Dorothy touches my hand.

I recoil, wincing again at the pain of my arms being dragged behind my back, the sensation of pure disgust filling my gorge. I crouch over my knees and rock back and forth. A strangled high-pitched whine reaches my ears. I know it is coming from me but I cannot stop it. I draw the old pelt of darkness about myself once more and hug it tight.

Some time later, a hand comes to rest tentatively on my back. I become aware of soft movement and whispers around me.

Lena, Lena. Dorothy speaks close to my ear. You're safe. You're here with us. We're minding you. You don't have to say anything.

Our phones beep again.

My rocking slows down and the whine dies away. I feel defenceless as a child.

That's it, good girl, Dorothy soothes.

I raise my head from my hands and take in the three worried faces that watch me.

Sorry, I give a wobbly smile. I just . . . I gesture towards the screen. I wasn't expecting that.

I don't think any of us were, says Ken.

I can't believe . . . I mean—

You've had a shock, Ken continues. Take your time. If you want to talk we'll listen. If not, we'll call a taxi to take you and Richard home.

Richard nods and, leaning across to take my hand, squeezes it firmly.

I sigh wearily and cast my head back, shutting my eyes. Do you remember those letters, Dor?

Which ones were they? She asks cautiously.

The illiterate hate mail.

After a moment's pause she says, Yes, yes, I do. When we were in college. We thought it was someone in the class.

I shake my head. It was them.

Who? I don't understand. Her hand rubs my arm gently while she waits for my explanation.

It was September. Richard had left to re-join his regiment and I had been haunting the hall stand for two weeks expecting, or hoping for, a letter from him. Instead, one day I found an envelope that bore neither stamp nor address, only a name unevenly typed and briefly confusing because given in Irish. Puzzled, I turned the envelope over and back before opening it.

TRAITOR HOOR

The words leapt from the cheap blue paper, so stark and alien that for a moment I wondered were they too Irish. Even when their meaning had sunk in, I continued to read, despite my revulsion, impelled to understand what the writer or clumsy typist wanted of me.

DAUTER OF THE REPUBLIC, it began.

STOP BETRAYINYG YOUR COUNTRY.

STOP CONSERTING WITH THE EMENY.

THE SASANACH WILL DIE.

WERE WATCHING YOU.

ERIN ABU.

Between lectures that morning I showed the note to Dorothy who wrinkled her nose at it before telling me to ignore it, saying it was probably sent by some eejit who had set his cap at me and was jealous.

But who would do a thing like that? I glanced around the corridor where other students milled about in small convivial groups, a good-natured crowd. It wasn't sent. That's what's weird. There's no stamp.

What do you want to do with it? She looked perplexed. Bring it to the guards?

I looked at the flimsy page again. I don't know. I don't suppose there's much they can do about it.

Not really. They'll think it's some kind of a prank. The best thing is to forget about it and let the person see you don't care.

I tore the offensive note into tiny pieces and dropped it in the first bin we passed.

A few days later a second letter came and a third shortly after that, each repeating the threats of the first. Sickened by the violent message I grew nervous, glancing around whenever I left the house, taking fright at the sound of footsteps behind me in the dark evenings or at the sight of lone men on the street and at the bus stop. After I had shown her the third letter, Dorothy urged me to give them to Father but I hesitated, embarrassed by their crudity, which debased my feelings, and afraid that he would forbid me to contact or see Richard again. Meanwhile, he, whose reassurance I craved, remained frustratingly remote and silent. Why aren't you here I wanted to cry out to my absentee lover, and not those faceless ones with their foul threats. I tried several times to start a letter to him but, spelt out on paper, my fears seemed hysterical, especially compared with the risks he was exposed to every day.

Once, he had rounded on me when, with a querulous voice, I had told him that I feared for his safety, and told me I couldn't do that. It's just a job, he added. Worrying isn't going to change anything except make us miserable when we're together. He, in turn, imagined he had no cause to worry about my safety. Finally, however, I called his friend Harry at the embassy and asked him if he knew where Richard was or could he tell him to contact me. Harry said he'd try but he wasn't sure he'd be able to reach him. When I got no word from him I began to doubt Harry's sincerity, wanting to blame him rather than Richard.

You never did show them to your father, did you? Dorothy asks now.

I shake my head. I couldn't.

Are you sure it was the same ones tried to kidnap you?

Yes, they used the same words. Traitor, and the other word. The exact same. One of them had a Cork accent. It wasn't a kidnap attempt.

You mean they—?

Ken rises from his chair and, tactfully signalling to Richard, they leave the room, Ken pulling the door behind them. I hear him offer Richard a liqueur, a 'bit of sticky'.

Yes, yes, I nod vigorously, tears now running down my cheeks as I relive for her the pain and degradation of the attack. Paddy and Tim disturbed them, I conclude.

Dorothy is crying too. She blows her nose loudly. I can't believe you didn't tell me about it at the time.

I didn't know how to talk about it, say I. I felt so sick, so ashamed, so dirty, I didn't—

But it wasn't your—Dorothy breaks in.

I put my hand up. I know, it wasn't my fault. It's impossible to explain. I've spent a lot of time trying to get rid of that feeling yet it never quite goes away. All I can think is it's to do with the perversion of intimacy involved. A man can talk about being hit or mugged and be a bit of a hero if he hit back. It's different for a woman, even other women will see her as having somehow let herself down.

You surely don't think I would have—

I couldn't be sure. That's the point. I felt I had to hide it. And I thought if I didn't talk about it then it might go away. That I could bury it. Stupid mistake.

So you never told anyone? Not your Mother, or Mossie?

I nod. Only Mossie. Not Mother. But something Richard said yesterday makes me think Mother and Father knew. That makes me feel like a fool on top of everything else.

Listen to me, darlin', Dorothy takes my clammy hand in her warm one. You're not a fool. You know that. If it was the other way around and I was telling you that story what would you say to me?

Right as usual, I concede with a weak smile. I've had clients who've been bullied and harassed by bosses or managers. Some of them have had the same feeling. It took them a long time and a lot of courage to come to me.

There you go, says Dorothy. You know it objectively. Now you have to convince yourself. Maybe this is the first step. Paddy might have done you a service tonight.

What! Are you mad? I'm going to kill him tomorrow.

I don't think you need to go that far but yes wait to see how you feel tomorrow.

He's not getting away with this. President my arse. He can go to hell.

You'll need to talk to him. I know it's painful going back over it but it was a very long time ago. You can't let it go on preying on you. That's giving those men huge power over you still. They're assaulting you over and over again. Stop giving them oxygen, drive them out of your head.

Easy said but—I wave my hand to indicate futility, or is it failure?

The waterworks start again. Intellectually, I know Dorothy is right but the tears gather force, spewing up from a dark cave deep inside me, eternal, painful, familiar tears. I have carried this secret so long within me, fed it on nightmare and memory that it has swelled like a tumour, hard and real, which I have tried but failed to ignore. Instead I have protected it, covered it up to make sure no suspicion or trace of it escaped to besmirch me or make me an object of gossip.

I look up to find the two men standing above us, watching in silence. Guardian angels.

Sorry, I sniffle. I messed up your nice evening. And your rug, I look guiltily at Dorothy.

Don't be silly, she says. It's easy cleaned. Are you sure you feel better now?

Yes, I incline my head deeply. I'm fine. I stretch my hand out to Richard who, bracing himself on his stick, takes it and helps me up for the second time today.

Easy does it, Ken steps in to support my other arm as I stand uncertainly, a new-dropped foal.

At home Richard offers to let Tanta out, urging me to go to bed.

Thanks, I sigh. I don't think I've ever been so tired in my life.

I'm tempted to crawl up the stairs but, determined to pre-serve some dignity, haul myself up painstakingly, hand over hand on the banister. When I reach the top I pause to catch my breath.

What's the matter, Lena? Jean is standing before me, dressed for bed—I think—in an oversize tee-shirt, her pale legs bare.

I'm weary, that's all.

Did you see Dad on the telly? She asks, with a look of urgent horror.

I did, I reply.

But what was he talking about? Her head juts forward in search of an explanation. Without her make-up she appears younger and more vulnerable than I am accustomed to seeing her. There is even a childish sprinkle of freckles over her nose. A puffy redness on her cheeks and eye sockets tells me that she has been crying. And now, as if she had peeled a layer of herself away, I am looking again at Paddy's stricken face the night he tried to run away and hear his words 'That's not my mammy'. My heart is pierced and I reach out again to embrace my bereft little brother.

What is it, Lena? The girl's voice re-establishes her features over those of the confused child.

Nothing, I lie. Déja vu.

Richard is right, this house is full of ghosts.

Was it true, what Dad said? He wouldn't talk about it in the car on the way home. Mum was cross with him. She asked him what he was thinking of. He told her to stop it and he wouldn't say anything else. What happened? Were you really kidnapped?

I pause a moment to compose myself before answering.

Lena? She presses and I see that I must tell my story again. I take her hand and lead her back into her bedroom.

There I find Pól seated on the bed in a pair of tiger-striped boxers and a tee-shirt. He is hunched over his laptop as if he is about to plunge into its restless stream of data.

We thought we might find something about it on the internet, Jean explains.

You won't, say I, sitting on the end of the bed. Because it didn't happen.

What? Incredulity twists Jean's face. You mean Dad made all that up? No wonder Mum was pissed at him. Did you hear that Pól? She turns to the lad and touches his knee.

Slowly he emerges from his mesmerised state and, shaking himself, exactly as if he has just come out of the water, looks at her and then at me. Oh, hi, Lena, he says and quickly bundles the duvet up to conceal his shorts.

Lena says the kidnap never happened, Jean repeats for him. Dad was tripping or hallucinating, she laughs with relief.

Seriously? The boy runs his eye over the screen, for fear of missing some new scrap of news or tattle, before asking, So what did happen?

Nothing, says Jean brightly.

No, I'm afraid Pól is right, I begin. Something did happen but not the way your father described it.

The girl droops.

For the third time in two days I describe a crime I have spoken of only once in fifty years. This tale is possessing me. Like the Ancient Mariner I'm beginning to feel doomed to tell it over and over, but in this version I omit the degrading details of the assault and concentrate on Paddy's role, tailoring it to my audience, thus mitigating the father's lie to protect the child. Each word moves into place next to another like counters in a game that has a thousand and one permutations.

When I have finished I look at Jean, now scrunched up beside Pól who has put his laptop aside and hooped one arm around her shoulders. Real life trumps the virtual for a moment. Her young face flickers from disbelief to incomprehension. The impulse to cry plucks at her mouth and eyes. Pól strokes her shoulder.

That's shocking, she says. It's . . . it's dreadful. You must have been in bits. I don't know what I'd have done.

I can tell the girl is truly disturbed, her imagination supplying the fear and revulsion that I felt.

Yes, I was, I say. I was shaken for a long time afterwards.

How come Gran and Grandpa didn't know?

They were away when it happened. They came home a couple of days later. I told them I had a migraine.

Why didn't you and Paddy go to the cops? Pól asks.

Fair question and the answer is I'm not really sure, except that I didn't want the Parents to know. I was afraid they would be angry with me, blame me some way. I told Paddy not to tell them.

I'm glad Dad found you, Jean gives a lopsided grin. And his friend. But I don't understand why Dad lied about it on the telly. That's . . . that's random. I mean why not tell the truth?

Yeah, that's a weird one, Pól agrees.

I have no idea, I say. I intend to find out tomorrow.

Where does your man, Richard, come into it all? Pól persists. Paddy seemed to be blaming him for something.

That's another long story, I say. He had nothing got to do with the assault except that those shits thought I was a traitor for dating him.

Because he was a British soldier?

Aha! I narrow my eyes at him. How did you know?

I was curious after Eamon blew his cover, Pól shrugs. So I googled him.

Cheeky monkey, I can't help laughing. Everyone was suspicious of him. Those were the times that were in it. I'm sorry, I say pushing myself up from the bed, I'm going to have to go to bed before I nod off here. Standing I look at the young couple, so at ease together, unabashed by my presence in their bedroom and am caught by an afterthought. Did Paddy drive the *two* of you back here?

No, Pól says. I took the DART.

I see, say I and turn to Jean. You do know I'm supposed to be protecting you from him, don't you?

You're not going to tell Dad, she says with a note of panic. Are you?

No. I shake my head gently. I have other fish to fry with him. Goodnight.

Goodnight, the kids say in unison and for a moment I am tempted to kiss their foreheads like babes.

Out on the landing again I hesitate. A crack of light under my bedroom door tells me Richard is in there. I move towards it then pull back. Tonight I need to sleep alone, to be still and wait for the evil memories to fade. I turn and tiptoe to the door of the Parents' bedroom. Once inside I switch on a bedside light, shut the curtains and undress quickly. Wrapping Mother's robe around me I slide under the quilt. Even now the robe retains the scent of her favourite cologne. I shiver in part with the cold, in part with the exposure of the evening, of having been forced to reveal the offence and shame that had lain so long coiled at the base of my memory. I am raw as a creeping creature stripped of its shell.

I shut my eyes against the resurgent memory which threatens to overtake me again and brace my limbs to deflect it.

As the memory bears down on me with suffocating force I try to cry out but my throat is filled with sand. I wake suddenly and feel Mossie's presence enfold me. I reach for him but clasp only air. I switch on the bedside light, pick up and read my watch: 4 a.m., the hour when our side of the world hovers between day and night as I hover between past and present. Mossie alone had seen the legacy of those men's violence. In fright, at first, he had drawn back, then approached me with a tenderness that helped anneal my wound.

Are you happy? His hand held mine, his thumb softly rubbing my forefinger.

It was the third day of our honeymoon and, warmed by the lemony sunlight of early May, we were strolling through the noisy streets of Rome.

Of course, I responded, giving his hand a quick squeeze and gesturing widely with my free hand asked, How not, here, with you?

He raised his eyebrows, his expression challenging my defensive brittleness.

I dodged his look by turning my head towards the crazy blaring traffic. We had just come from Sunday mass in St. Peter's. Stepping out of the basilica I had whipped off the obligatory mantilla, stuffed it into my handbag and taken out my sunglasses, grateful for the wave of heat and swarming life after the oppressive tedium of the church. At the Confiteor I had stumbled, as always in recent years, at the triple knock on the breast accompanying the repeated mea culpa, mea culpa, mea maxima culpa. My shame but not my fault, not my fault, ran the counterpoint in my head. Most definitely not my fault. As if he could hear those words Mossie had turned to glance at me before returning eyes front to continue his prayers. His devotion was palpable. Watching his profile I observed that with his utter absorption his features softened and the corner of his mouth lifted a little. I envied the soothing grace he found in the ritual. Now, as we sauntered, we were to all appearances just another blithe young pair of lovers, the shadow of the nightmare that had shaken my sleep invisible. Yet I felt it stalk me, nudging me towards the kerb, an old trick it had of trying to goad or lure me to the edge of a railway platform, cliff or pier. Sensing my semi-stumble Mossie curved his arm around my waist and held me upright.

Careful, he said.

Yes, thanks. Stilettos, I offered as explanation.

That's the price of being the most elegant lady in town, he smiled.

I was raised never to sacrifice style for comfort.

Do you want to sit down for a few minutes?

No, no, I'm fine, I bluffed, imagining that somehow I could outwalk the shadow.

Are you really though? He pressed.

I nodded, despite knowing what he was really asking me, knowing that I must answer without knowing how.

You were screaming in your sleep last night. And there's the other . . . well . . . you understand.

His sombre face and polite reticence about the word sex made me sad for him and for us. During our courtship, even after our engagement, Mossie had controlled our intimacy, pulling back when our embraces became too 'intense', his word, in line with the church's teaching and out of respect, he explained, for me. When I suggested that we use contraception he balked saying that I was letting myself down and that he was prepared to wait till we were married. In those weeks and months of thwarted desire and hungry fantasy I had not anticipated that, when at last we had sanction to be naked in one another's presence, his eyes, fingers and tongue playing delightedly over my flesh as grinning boyishly he said that seeing me thus made him dizzy, me arching towards him, arms reaching, all of my body yearning to close with his, both of us unfettered and ardent, the approach of his erect penis would cause me to freeze in the sudden grip of fear and twist my face away.

What is it love? he whispered kneeling above me, Is it too soon? That time of the month?

No, I said, It's just. Maybe it's too fast. I need a little time to acquaint myself with all of you.

He bent to kiss my breasts and my belly and I tried to regain the lost excitement that only moments ago had sparked my every nerve-ending. He moved down to work his tongue over and between my labia, flickering over my clitoris and slowly a new beat pulsed through me but died again at the moment of entry and I pulled away curling my knees into my belly, foetal in the marriage bed. He rolled away and I heard or felt the accelerating movement of his hand along his penis and the gasp of climax. I sank inside myself, shamed by what I felt to be my failure. He said nothing more but went to the bathroom and on his return snuggled against my back kissing my spine and we slept. Slowly slowly the next afternoon we tried again but the fear lodged deep inside me repelled him. That night, after a few glasses of wine and a good dash of crème de menthe we had almost managed an unsatisfactory consummation but seeing the fear in my face he had pulled back and I had fled to the bathroom where doubled over on the floor I sobbed. He knocked on the door which I had locked and asked was I feeling ill. Yes, I lied, must be something I ate.

Now, on our third day together, he was waiting, justifiably, for me to explain my night terrors.

I had to wake you, do you remember? He prompted.

I remember, I said, recalling how the men in the lane had returned and I had screamed at them to go away. We paused to sit on the rim of a fountain whose merry splashing made an incongruous background to this painful talk. Closing my eyes I looked up, wanting to bury my face in the big lion's mane of the sun. And so, for the first time, I recounted the events of that horrific night in the lane. My voice was low and even, stripped of feeling, unfamiliar even to me and I realised too that for some reason I spoke without the personal pronoun as if it were a news bulleting about someone else, a girl I knew once but had not seen in a long time. She sat beside me, naive for all her wisecracking sophistication, and I wanted to shroud her from harm. When I had finished speaking I looked at Mossie but his face was dim and blurred. A sudden fear rippled through me that I might disgust him, that the respect he had felt for my pure state might be sullied and I seem soiled or despoiled.

Maybe I should have told you before. Before we . . . I fingered the bright gold wedding band that I had not yet grown accustomed to.

No. It was your business but I realised something must have happened to make you nervous. An expression of hatred curled his upper lip, I'd like to kill those men.

You'd never find them now. I gave a weak smile, trailing my fingers in the water that danced in the basin behind me.

He took out his cigarettes, offered me one, took one himself and lit both using four bendy cardboard matches in the process. Stupid things, he tossed the small black card embossed with the name of our hotel onto the ground with a vehemence that startled me.

I drew long and deep on the cigarette, and said, exhaling, I feel I've disappointed you. I'm sorry.

Don't say that.

It's not . . . It's not what it should be is it? I glanced up at him.

Nothing would ever erase the memory of the sad grave disillusionment in his eyes.

It's not what I anticipated on our honeymoon, I'll grant you that. He dragged on his cigarette and stood abruptly.

For a moment I was afraid again and started to blather that I would make it up to him somehow, that I loved him beyond all reason but he stopped me with an impatient gesture to stop me embarrassing myself.

His face tensed, jaw jutting. What upsets me, apart from the offence to you, is that those men weren't brought to justice. Who knows how many other girls they waylaid, damaged or worse?

I flinched at his tone of accusation and said, I didn't know how to speak about it. I too was 'damaged' as you say. Young. Scared. I felt they were always watching me after that the way they had been waiting in the lane that night. I didn't see them properly.

It's wrong, he said, It's all wrong. It's evil. He began to pace before me. And I'll tell you another thing that makes me angry, he jabbed the air with his cigarette for emphasis, winding himself up to a pitch of bitter anger. Their mantle of idealism. That was a slur on the men who died for our freedom. They were just gutties. Nobodies. Show them a real fight and they'd run away, the way they did from two gossoons. Children. That's all Paddy and his friend were.

I know but I suppose they achieved their aim.

No they didn't, he scoffed. A girl and two children. What did they think they would achieve apart from the perverse pleasure of raping you? What kind of an 'achievement' is that? His voice rose and passers-by began to stare at us.

I stood and went towards him placing my hand on his sleeve to restrain him.

He snatched his arm away as if I had stung him and turned his back to me. I walked around to face him.

You can't take this out on me, I said. I haven't changed. It wasn't my sin or my crime, it was theirs. All I want is for us to be happy. Surely it's better to know everything, to be open with one another. Maybe now we can start again, start better.

Wincing a little at my words, he stared obstinately at the ground. I apologise, he sighed and raised his head to look at me. You're right. I allowed myself get carried away. Forgive me. He took my hand and raised it to his lips. I love you, he said. And I respect you for telling me this. I know it wasn't easy. Come on, we'll go back to the hotel. We have another five days of holiday before us, Mrs. Carmody. Let's make the most of them.

Yes, let's. I caught his mood, finding a haven in his trust as an unaccustomed lightness billowed through me.

Chapter Nineteen

There are four missed calls and voice messages on my mobile, three from numbers I do not recognise. The fourth is from Muiris and I can guess what that's about. As for the others, my mind flies to Rosemary, the Mouse and DI Nolan, bearing news of Myles. Dread plumbs my stomach.

It is ten o'clock on Saturday morning and the house is completely silent. I have come downstairs after a fitful sleep, my mind wavering on the boundary between dream and memory. The doors to the bedrooms stood open when I passed but the rooms were empty and the steam from recent showers condensed in the bathroom. The only sound is the tick of the grandfather clock beside me. I have taken my phone from my handbag, which I had left on the hallstand overnight. Weak sunlight falls through the panels of coloured glass that flank the front door, shedding lozenges of yellow, red and blue on the worn carpet. When I was a child I had tried to scoop up the colours like jewels in my hands and couldn't understand why they vanished at my approach until, one day, Paddy crowed you're all colours Lena, you look very pretty, and, glancing down, I saw that indeed my dress was motley as a stained glass saint's. I drew him into the orbit of the light and we lay down to absorb the magic hues, fancying they would remain imprinted on us when we moved away. Stepping into the light now, and raising my arm, I see the motley colours transposed to my sleeve, fool that I am. The clock's mechanism whirrs deep inside its case as it works up to telling the hour. Even so the chime startles me, seeming to reverberate in the marrow of my bones. I leave off my childish game and descend to the kitchen, the stern repeated tone following me, diminuendo. Strangely, there is not a sign or yap of Tanta in the kitchen or breakfast room. I open the back door and call his name but there is no answering scurry of paws. I might have slept a hundred years and woken to find that all around me have moved on, abandoning me at a bend in time.

At least they left some coffee. I fill a mug from the pot and stick it in the microwave.

HiLena – AineNíLoingsighfromd*Examiner*anseo – please-callmebackonthisnumber.

I listen to the message a second time but can shake no sense out of it. I try the next one.

Hello Lena. This is Sarah Walshe from the *Sunday Independent*. I'd appreciate if you could give me a call when you have a chance.

Curiouser and curiouser. I try the third message.

Good morning Lena. Didi Doherty here. Can you ring me back please as soon as you get this message?

No, I whisper to the air, disconcerted by this succession of calls. I have never courted the press even when I was involved in high profile cases against big employers, knowing that whatever I said would be editorialised to fit another person's agenda so I'm not about to ingratiate myself with these hacks now. There'll be more comfort in talking to my lovely son.

Hi Mum, he picks up immediately. Is everything okay with you?

Yes, now that I'm speaking to you, I say. The house is deserted. I was beginning to wonder had everyone been taken up in the Rapture.

You mean Richard's not there?

No. Not even the dog.

That's a bit weird. Tanta's probably asleep in a patch of sunshine or on Gran's chair. Do you want me to come over?

No thanks. I'm fine. You were calling.

I heard that Paddy told some story last night, on the Late Late, about you being kidnapped. Did he lose the head or what?

You could say that. He made the whole thing up.

I thought I'd have heard about it, if it was true. But why make up such a story?

That's what I intend to find out this morning. I've got a string of messages from journalists. I can't imagine what they want with me.

It could be to do with Paddy's story, you know a profile of him and you: 'The Super Siblings'. Colour supplement stuff.

God, you're probably right, I say, dawn beginning to break slowly on my jaded mind. One of them was from the *Sindo*.

Perfect, Muiris laughs. Next thing you'll be on the cover of *Hello*.

Absolutely not.

Think of the glamour, he affects a camp giggle.

I'll leave that to Nóirín. Bernie did the fairy godmother on her. She looked very smart.

Really? I'm sorry I missed that. While Muiris is more benignly disposed towards his aunt than I he agrees with me about her lack of dress sense.

She's probably turned back into a pumpkin now.

Stop it, he protests but he can't help laughing.

If that's all you wanted I'll let you go, I say. Have you any plans for the day . . . with your new friend . . . ?

Good try Lena. I can see the smile on his face. Yes, Damian and I are going into town shortly for brunch.

Do I have to wait for Bernie's party to meet him?

No but I also need to meet Richard in less stressful circumstances.

Aha! Well if he's still here we can arrange that. Yesterday's shenanigans may have scared him off. I try to sound flippant although recollection of our tense conversation yesterday evening still rankles in me.

I hope he's not that weak or fickle, says Muiris. If he is you're better off without him.

That's a familiar line. Don't worry, I'm sure he'll turn up, I say, overriding my misgivings. Go on and enjoy your brunch.

Thanks. Good luck with Paddy, let me know what he says.

I will, goodbye.

I remove my steaming coffee mug from the microwave and set it on the table beside the phone. I consider calling Richard to establish his whereabouts but change my mind. Muiris has a point, if he's run away he's not worth chasing. I wish Tanta had a phone. He's the one I'm really worried about. After a few reviving swigs of coffee I go to the back door and call him again. Still no response. The air feels chilly and damp as, clasping the mug for warmth, I walk slowly down the path, looking to left and right, appealing to the dog and promising treats if he will come out from wherever he is hiding. He has never disappeared before.

Leener, Leener, Orla's voice soars over the wall. Tanter was kidnapped.

What? I ask, crossing the dew-laden grass to get closer to the wall. What do you mean 'kidnapped', Orla? Is he in there with you?

No. We saw him going down the road with a strange man.

A strange man? Did he have a walking stick?

Noooo. He was on a lead.

The man I mean.

Yeah, he was an old guy, Malachi joins in.

Whew, I say. He's a friend of mine. Thanks lads. I turn to go back inside but am halted by the sound of Feargal's voice calling me.

We saw Paddy on the Late Late, he says when I respond. Disturbing story he told.

Yes well, don't believe everything you hear on the box, I sigh, growing heartily sick of this affair.

Don't worry, Feargal scoffs. But I assume Paddy's a reliable source.

Not necessarily.

Very well, if you say so, he replies but I can hear the doubt in his voice. Bernie will be relieved. You know she's always been nervous about the back lane.

Yes, that's why she parks in my spot on the road. I try to make this sound jokey. For a moment I'm tempted to ask Feargal about Felicia's equally strange story, and Bernie's shortage of money but decide to wait until I see Bernie. There may be something going on that he doesn't know about.

Instead I say, I'm going back indoors, see you later.

Sure, says Feargal. We may have a chat later if you're around, about the em . . . the project. We seem to have . . . em . . . well to have hit a bit of a roadbump.

I count to ten silently.

Lena, are you still there?

I am but I think you know my view of this scheme, at least Bernie does. I start to trail back through the wet grass to the path.

Well maybe we could have a chat sometime. He is keeping pace with me on his side of the fence.

Not today, I say. I have a lot on my plate right now.

Sure, maybe during the week. Take care.

I have a notion that Feargal's 'roadbump' is a pyramid built of sand. If I'm right he gives more credence to what he sees on TV than he pretends, and there'll be no surprise birthday party.

As I open the back door I hear the phone ringing. I hurry in and snatch it up.

Yes, I pant.

Is this Lena O'Neill? A strange voice inquires.

Yes, this is she. Who wants her?

Hello, I'm Elaine Smith from *The Irish Times*.

Another one, I can't help saying.

Sorry?

I've had umpteen calls from journalists this morning.

Like who? She snaps. Did you speak to any of them? I bet that wagg—sorry—did you speak to Sarah Walshe?

No I didn't speak to any of them. What is this all about?

Good, she softens her tone. The reason I'm ringing is that I heard your brother, Patrick O'Neill, on the Late Late last night. He told a story involving you and you know it's a great—I mean it's a terrible story but I wanted to get your side of it. Would you be willing to give me an interview?

I would not, I say. The cheek of these people thinking they can make copy out of my degradation.

Would you think about it even? You say other people have been onto you. That shows how important the story is. For the women's perspective you know. I mean we don't get many insights into women's experience of the violence in the past. We need to balance the record.

Fair enough but my past is private and it'll stay that way.

That's a pity, she persists. I'd let you read the article before it went to print. You could make any changes you wanted.

In that case I might as well write it myself, I laugh. If I ever decide to go public that'll be the way I do it.

You'd be helping your brother's campaign, she tries another tack. Otherwise . . .

Blackmail now. Thank you and good day. I end the call.

No sooner have I put the phone down than it goes off again. Don't tell me that pushy one is ringing me back.

That was a definite negative, I say picking up. And if you call me again I'll report you to the gardaí.

I am the gardaí, says a woman's voice.

Ah, oh. Sorry, I fumble. I thought you were someone else.

This is Detective Inspector Nolan. We have received some news of Mr. Mulvaney.

Yes, good—at least I hope it's good.

It gives us reason to believe he's alive.

Relief fires through my synapses. That is good news. Do you have any idea where he is?

I'm afraid I can't disclose any information at the moment but we're following a definite line of inquiry. I just thought you would like to know. If you have any more thoughts on this situation I'd appreciate a call.

Yes, of course, that's very reassuring. Good work on your part. If I can think of anything useful I'll let you know.

By the way, did I see your brother, Mr. O'Neill, on the Late Late last night?

Aha! Now we're getting to the real reason for her call. Yes, say I, without concealing my exasperation.

Shocking story, she says. It must have been very frightening for you. Were they ever caught, those men?

I'd really rather not talk about it, Detective. Thank you for the information about Myles. I'll be in touch if I have anything to give you. Over and out. I hang up.

I curse the instrument in my hand and consider flushing it down the loo.

The silence in the house is eerie. Where is everyone? I glance down again at the phone. I'll go over to the hotel and confront Paddy before he retreats to his southern fastness. I'm bound to spot Richard and Tanta on the road as I go.

Les voilà, only a short distance down the road. Richard's back is to me, and he appears to be talking to someone. Tanta strains at his leash trying to drag him towards the park below the path. Richard, resisting, is canted to the right, his hand

leaning on his stick. When I draw up beside him I see that he
has been ambushed by Moira Kiely.

I switch on the hazard lights, open the front passenger
window and call out, Good morning.

Ah, there you are, Richard beams at me, glad of rescue
I'll bet.

Hello Lena, Moira pushes him aside to poke her head
through the window. They're rooned. Did you hear?

What? I lean closer to the window.

Completely rooned. It's all over the papers this morning.

I'm sorry Moira, I haven't seen the paper yet. I'm on my way
to an appointment.

Mr and Mrs Perfect there. She jerks her head towards our
terrace. So much for their big plans. Serves them right. Seán
had his doubts all along. He keeps his ear to the ground.

Like the worm that he is I think. You mean the nursing
home scheme? I ask.

Yes, yes, we knew it was iffy from the start.

But what about Father Horgan? I can't resist getting a rise
out of this double-eyed bee. I thought he was in favour of it
and you were on board with him.

Ah not a bit of it, she spits. Seán was telling him to not
to be jumping the gun or anything. And sure I was only doing
my bit for the community centre. I'll be round to collect your
donation, unless you have it handy there, she slides her eye
to my handbag on the floor. Mr. Richards here has given me a
fiver for it.

I peer past her to see Richard's face. He nods and rolls his
eyes skyward.

And he a Prod, I laugh. And a foreigner.

No matter, says Moira. It's all legal tender.

Indeed, say I. Now I really must be off. Do you want a lift,
Mr. Richards?

Yes please, he gasps.

You can put Tanta in the back.

Reluctantly Moira stands aside to let him open the door.

What a dreadful woman, Richard says, settling into the seat beside me.

Yes and the husband is worse. But what the hell was she blathering about?

Search me. I haven't had a chance to get the paper yet. Were you going somewhere? He rests his hand tentatively on my knee.

I'm hoping to catch Paddy before he leaves. I'd rather talk to him face to face.

Good idea. I can go to a pub and read the paper.

Sure. When I reach Dún Laoghaire I let Richard out. I'll give you a call when I'm finished, I say.

Best of luck, he smiles. It's going to be tricky.

I know. But I'd like to clear the air.

Paddy, Nóirín and Jean are seated at a window table in the hotel dining room, facing out to the bay. None of them sees me approach. Paddy starts when I greet them.

Lena, he says, standing up, fussing to pull over a chair and summon a waiter. What'll you have? He blusters.

The truth, say I, seating myself opposite Jean who gapes at me.

Have a cup of tea. Would you like some breakfast? A poached egg or a fry?

They're bad for my heart.

Not in moderation, he huffs.

I shake my head slowly. You know why I'm here, Paddy. Perhaps we need to discuss this somewhere else, alone. I look at Nóirín who is pointedly staring out the window.

To my utter surprise, she inclines her head towards me and says, I agree. You and Paddy need to talk. Come on Jean, we'll go up to the bedroom, I have to pack our bags.

Jean's eyes dart from one to the other of us before she says, Sure, Mum, and pushes back her chair.

Nóirín, say I, as she rises to leave. You looked great last night. That outfit really suited you.

Thank you, my sister in law scans my expression for a trace of sarcasm and finding none, smiles a little coyly as she adds, Your friend has a good eye, even if she is a bit pricey.

It was worth it, say I.

Nóirín turns to go then, pausing, pivots to face me and says, I was a bit surprised though that she wanted cash, for such a large sum.

Who? Bernie? I ask, credulity straining now.

Yes, she nods. I asked her what discount she'd give me for cash so she knocked €15 off the price and I went out to the ATM.

That was a good deal then for both of you, I smile approvingly. No flies on Nóirín. But I agree it's unusual. She must have needed it for change.

Nóirín gives me a sceptical look then beckons Jean, and mother and daughter leave the dining room.

Do you want to stay here, Paddy, or go for a walk on the pier?

He looks awkwardly about him before answering. Let's walk.

Together we leave the dining room, he pausing occasionally to acknowledge the greetings of people who saw him on the telly, polishing the presidential gravitas already.

While he goes to fetch his coat I go to the car and get Tanta. We are strolling to and fro outside the hotel entrance when my phone rings.

Yes, I say expecting it'll be Rosemary.

HiLenaAineNíLoinsighanseo.

Sorry, I didn't catch that.

My name is Aine Ní Loinsigh, she enunciates slowly, Corkily. I'm calling from d*Examiner*.

Are you another journalist?

Yes, yes from d*Examiner*. Depaper.

I'm sorry, I have nothing to say to you.

It's only that I saw your brother Paddy on deLateLate last night.

And here he comes. I glare at my brother as he descends the steps to join me. At least I think it's him, he's so muffled in his coat, scarf and hat that only his eyes are visible.

You and half the nation, I say to de journalist. But I have nothing to say. Thank you. Goodbye.

I hang up and wag the phone at Paddy, saying, This is only the beginning of the trouble you've caused me.

What do you mean?

Bloody journalists ringing all morning to get my side of your ridiculous story.

He begins to walk away.

I switch off the phone, return it to my bag and hasten to catch up with him. Tanta gets there first and jumps up to paw his leg, pom-pom tail wagging in expectation of a greeting.

Yes, yes, Tanta, I see you. Paddy yields and tickles behind the dog's ear, giving me a chance to come up beside him.

Are we going to talk or are you going to sulk? I ask him.

Releasing the dog he begins to descend the path towards the harbour. Talk I suppose, he mutters.

Good. What exactly was that all about last night?

Look I don't really expect you to understand, Lena, but it's a complicated business going on a show like that.

Oh bro, give me a break. I don't care what you say about yourself or your own family but you could have left me out of it. Besides it wasn't even true.

Yes it was, he looks around sharply.

It wasn't a kidnap attempt, it was an attempted rape. Luckily for me, you and Tim came along at the crucial moment. And I have always been grateful for that.

I know, I know. But I couldn't say that on a family show. Could I?

You didn't need to say anything about it.

They needed some drama, a story. Colour—

'Colour' ! Cop yourself on. That's obscene. An assault is not colour, it's violence and a crime.

I mean they wanted an anecdote that would catch people's attention. They say it's the modern form of storytelling. They do their research these people. They got wind of an incident somehow.

We reach the pier and Paddy pulls away from me, stretching his neck to see over the wall.

I know what happened, I say, coming up alongside him, lest the breeze whip the words from my mouth. You let something slip to them in the green room then retracted it but the host wasn't going to let it go so he sprang it on you on air. The trouble was you didn't have the guts to say no comment.

Head bowed now, he walks on, and I keep pace, waiting for him to respond.

After several minutes of morose silence he says, You're right. Yes. Look, I'm sorry, Lena. I didn't set out to involve you, it just happened that way. It's not easy when you're sitting there in front of an audience, under all those lights, the microphone in front of you. I'm sorry if it upset you, if it's caused you problems but you're well able to deal with the journos. He glances at me and I see contrition in his eyes.

I'd rather not have to deal with them, I say. Couldn't you see that overpaid cretin was making an eejit of you?

Nóirín wasn't happy about it either, Paddy shrugs. But you know, he adds with defensive vehemence, Seeing that bounder yesterday morning in our parents' house brought it all back to me. I don't know what possessed you to let him across the threshold not to mention . . . not to mention . . .

That's my affair, I say, ignoring the attempt to divert me into an argument about ownership of the house. It just happened that we found one another again and without premeditation we sort of picked up where we had left off. I got answers to questions that had plagued me for a long time, I need to put the pieces of my story together. The truth, I want the truth. Do you understand that? Each piece is very clear and very painful, like slivers of broken glass lodged in my flesh. They nag. They won't let me be. Do you understand? I repeat, raising my voice.

Keeping his head averted, as if he can't face me, he says eventually, Yes. I do. The memories visit me sometimes too. I try not to entertain them. At those times I pray, he glances quickly at me. I know you don't go in for that. But it does help. Do you remember Mammo's little prayer?

I do, I say. Mossie thought suggested praying too. But it makes me feel like a hypocrite. Praying without belief.

I don't know what more I can say. I'm sorry about last night. I won't repeat the story. It'll be forgotten in a week.

Yesterday, when I asked you what you told Father you started to talk about someone being a friend of someone else. We were interrupted. Richard says you know more about those men.

Does he now? Paddy snorts. He knows it all too. Why didn't he tell you?

He said it was our business, not his, that you should tell me.

He was the cause of the business.

No he wasn't. He was a pretext for two shits to indulge their grotesque fantasies.

We continue to walk in silence and, gaining the end of the pier, step through the gap in the wall to where the dark and oily sea assails the bulwark. For a few minutes we stand in silence watching the water maul the rocks and slide hissing away then return to the lee of the wall and the tame water inside the harbour. We face inland now, walking towards the Victorian seafront nestled against the rampart of indigo hills.

Those men were friends of one of the maids, Paddy begins. She typed up the letters.

What? I halt and look at him. Which maid? Not Agnes?

No, not her. He shakes his head emphatically. A dumpy little one with an astigmatism. Father was going to treat her, Consumpta or Concepta. He caught her using his typewriter one day. She had to come clean then.

So that's how they picked their time, I say as some of the little pieces come together. They knew the Parents were away.

Exactly. Those men were going to come back. That was in the letter Father found her typing.

Liquid ice pours through my veins. What did he do? Did he go to the gardaí?

He sacked her on the spot. Then he dealt with the men.

My head begins to swim. I'm sorry, I say. I feel a bit blurry, I need to sit down.

Paddy offers me his arm and we move to a bench.

I stare across the harbour to the west pier. I seem to see myself over there as I was yesterday, sitting on a stanchion, facing this way. A pure stranger. I am going around in circles, meeting myself, or versions of myself, in different places and times. Tanta jumps up onto the bench beside me and I put my arm around him welcoming the heat of his vitality. I try to picture the maid Paddy has described. What kind of a woman or girl sets another up to be raped? Gradually the sourpuss surfaces from the past. She never returned a smile or a greeting. I suppose she was jealous of me. Small blame to her for that but for what she did no mercy.

Consolata, yes, I say. She must have put those brutes up to it. But what do you mean Father dealt with them? I glance at Paddy.

What do you think? Paddy stares straight ahead. He has pulled his scarf down from his nose and mouth and I see that his face is pale and there is a unhealthy yellow tinge around his eyes.

He went to the gardaí.

No, no. He dealt with them himself.

You mean he—?

He felt he had no choice, my brother says.

A harsh cold clarity possesses me. Blood pounds in my ears. My breath comes in short ragged bursts. I am welded to this bench, fixed in this moment. This knowledge cannot be gainsaid. It cannot be erased. From now on and forever I must carry it with me, and it will weigh heavily on me.

I didn't know, I protest. I didn't know. Revulsion rises in me, yet I cannot look away from that ruthless side of Father, obverse of the genteel, courteous man so many saw. And you knew, I whisper.

Not till years later. He told me. He said I wasn't to tell you. But probably I should have. After he died at least. You had a right to be told.

I do. But I don't understand why he didn't go to the police.

That would have involved you and me – and Tim – giving evidence. He didn't want that. Also he blamed himself for what those fellows did to you.

Incredulous, I turn to Paddy. What do you mean?

He inhales deeply before looking me full in the face. He was sorry he didn't deal with that other . . . that bloody Brit . . . first.

My palpitating heart sucks the blood from my extremities but my brother does not flinch.

Excuse me, I don't feel well, I say and twisting sideways, spew the contents of my stomach onto the ground.

With a whine Tanta jumps off the bench.

Paddy lays a hand on my back. That's it, he says. Good girl, get it all out.

Sorry, I sit back and bump my head against the granite wall. I wish I could, I say. I can't believe he even contemplated doing that. I begin to cry. The tears spill down my face as I repeat, I can't believe it I can't believe it . . . can't believe reason deserting me.

Paddy hands me his handkerchief and I blow my nose and wipe my mouth.

After a few minutes he says gently, Let's go back.

Yes. I stand and wobble for a moment, every limb quaking. Paddy cups one hand under my elbow, taking Tanta's lead in his free hand, encourages me to walk. We make slow progress. I am too sick and sore to speak and Paddy has covered his face again so we say nothing. The pier is livening up, with young couples pushing buggies or carrying babies in knapsacks and slings, people walking their dogs, joggers, kids on skateboards and bikes, and a lone busker playing a squeezebox, badly, in the shelter beside the bandstand. How Paddy loved to stand gazing at the bandsmen in their red uniforms with their shiny buttons and even shinier instruments, his head rocking from side to side with the music. Mother would stand holding his hand until she wearied of the brassy sound and cajoled Paddy away with the promise of a treat when we got home.

As we near the hotel Paddy advises me to come in and have a cup of tea.

I shake my head, not wanting to face people in my dishevelled state.

Sit down there, he says, and I'll bring one out to you.

Thanks, I take Tanta's lead and sit on the garden chair he indicates. A mother and her son romp on the grass before me. For a moment their happiness in one another brushes me like a warm wing.

356 ~ AISLING MAGUIRE

Paddy returns with two cups of tea and sits beside me.

That's good, I say, sipping the drink that he has sweetened to revive me. About what you said, I resume, calmly now. I take it that Father got someone else to deal with those men.

No. He shakes his head. He did it himself.

But how? I mean what did he do?

Shot them.

A shadow falls over me and the world darkens. I thought Mother had made him hand his gun over to the police.

Well either he deceived her or he got another one.

Hard to imagine him getting away with that.

He got away with worse. I know he had one because I saw it once.

Resigned now to seeing my old certainties dissolve, I turn to Paddy and say, Go on.

Do you remember the day Father got into a rage because someone had moved Polyphemus?

I cast my mind back and a desultory Sunday afternoon in the drawing room materialises, rain streaming down the windows, the fire tetchily settling its hot coals in the grate, me trying to race through my piano practise, Mother, her eyes remaining focused on the Sunday crossword, occasionally upbraiding me, an-dan-te, Lena, slow and steady, Paddy on the floor, playing with his Meccano set, suddenly Father, who had gone to his office, was back, thundering, Who moved Polyphemus? Which of you was it? His eyes flashed as he looked from me to Paddy. I froze under his glare. Was it you? No, I shook my head, no. You? He rounded on Paddy who bowed his head miserably and, almost imperceptibly, nodded. Look at me, Father barked. Paddy reared his head, as if it had been pulled back by the hair. I saw the tremor of fear run through his body.

What's the matter, Patrick? Mother said. You're upsetting the child. Come here to me Paddy.

The steely glare that Father directed at her silenced her immediately. He's coming with me. He seized Paddy by the ear, the first and only time he laid a hand on either of us in anger, and, hauling him to his feet, marched him out of the room.

I remember feeling sorry for you then, I say. You wouldn't tell me afterwards what happened beyond that you were never to touch the Cyclops again.

That's where he kept the gun.

What do you mean? I look at him askance.

In the dummy. I got up on a chair one day and lifted old Polly down. All I wanted was to see how the inside of the eye was put together, like opening up the back of a watch. Instead of finding a diamond, or a web of nerves and blood vessels, I found a revolver.

That's unbelievable, I say. I wonder was it still there when I threw the thing out.

I doubt it. He would have got rid of it after doing away with those men.

I suppose so. What did you do when you found it?

I go the fright of my life. I put the eye together again and replaced it on the shelf. Wrong way around as it turned out. That's how Father knew. He ranted and raged at me and when he got all that out of his system he went very cold and stern and started saying 'You. Saw. Nothing.' Which was nearly more scary than the shouting. I thought he wanted me to say I saw a gun but when I did he banged his fist on the desk, You saw nothing. He made me say it over and over. By the end he had me nearly believing that I saw nothing. A crude form of brainwashing. He also stopped my pocket money for a month. I hated him from that day.

No wonder you wouldn't talk about it afterwards.

An image flashes up of Richard saying that Father was looking at the Cyclops when he threatened him.

I still find it hard to picture him going out and killing those men in cold blood then coming home to supper, or his bridge game, or going to work, as if nothing had happened. I feel as if I'm seeing double. I know Father was severe and forbidding but I this cold brutality is something else. It jars with his genteel, cultured veneer.

The two go hand in hand, says Paddy. When you think of it, most of his friends had fought and killed too and yet they were charming people to meet. Richard the same, although I never found him charming. These people would say they act to preserve the good and the beautiful, Paddy flutters his hand in the air. Father was protecting you, and me. Maybe we would all do it to save our children.

Yes in the heat of the moment but not that calculated way. I didn't ask him to do it. There were other ways to deal with them.

That's not the point. They would have come back, to prove themselves.

How did Father come to tell you what he had done?

Paddy heaves a deep sigh. I think it was by way of an apology.

Apology? What for?

For never having much faith in me, my brother turns to me with a look of weary exasperation. He said it weighed on him that I had suffered that night too, that I had been courageous and done the right thing in protecting my sister. He said he probably should have told me long before that the men had been 'despatched'. That was his word. I asked him what he meant. He told me all then.

Funny kind of apology.

He wasn't going to abase himself before me. It was really a sort of compromise between a confession and an apology. Maybe even an old man's boast. Too late either way to make any difference to me or my feelings about him.

His loss so.

I'm glad you think so, says Paddy. Maybe that whole business poisoned our relationship too. There is a question in his voice and a challenge in his eyes.

Possibly, I concede, meeting his look. When you were sick, in the hospital, I felt sad for the way we had fallen apart.

He drops his eyes then, embarrassed by recollection of last night's outrage, and says, Father was right, that incident shook me too you know.

I'm sure it did. Tim too. He mentioned it when I ran into him before Christmas.

Traumas like that scar our brain cells. They can shape our growth. There's a lot of interesting research on this stuff now.

Are you saying we've grown too far apart to be friends again?

No, he frowns. Not as long as we both make the effort,.

I stretch out my hand and he takes it in his, briefly self-conscious of acting as if we have only just met. Before letting go, however, he says, You'll have to learn to be nicer to Nóirín though.

Of course, I smile weakly then rallying, add, And you to Richard.

Where is the bloody fellow anyway?

He went to buy a paper. He's probably in a café or a pub reading it.

You'd better phone him and tell him to come and bring you home. Is he staying long?

As long as it takes I imagine.

Well, I hope he'll look after you, he says gruffly.

I can look after myself, I retort and swallow the last of the tea. That was nice, I say. Like the hot water and sugar Mother gave us when we were sick.

Yes. He smiles. Sometimes the old remedies are best. Like the slices of bread with butter and sugar. Not that I'd be promoting it now, he laughs, swiftly recalling his public persona.

Chapter Twenty

Is that Siobhán's car? I ask Jean as Richard drives past my house, and the battered Punto parked in front of it, to access the lane.

No response.

I glance around and mime the action of removing the head-phones to the girl.

She complies, raising her eyebrows questioningly, and I repeat the question.

Yes, she nods. She said she'd go for a walk while she was waiting for me.

This has been the first exchange of words in the car since we left the hotel. Richard had arrived shortly after I phoned him and, as Paddy and Nóirín were about to return to Cork, Jean opted to come home with us. To my surprise, and Richard's astonishment, my brother and sister in law embraced me. Paddy even shook hands with Richard, albeit perfunctorily.

He pulls up to let me out before drawing the car in tight to the wall. Jean takes the opportunity to get out too. Tanta remains lying on the back ledge like an old cardie.

While we wait for Richard to park I take Jean's arm for support.

She darts a worried look at me.

I feel a bit dizzy, I explain, then, in an effort to be flip, say, I should have had the breakfast your father offered.

Once again she removes the headphones and I repeat myself.

It was nice, she says.

I am about to go to help Richard who is trying to cajole Tanta from his perch and clip on his lead, when the girl, taking in the scruffy litter-strewn track, says, Is this where it happened?

I nod slowly, Yes.

Her eyes scan the back wall of the garden as if expecting to see a rerun of the assault projected there in the flickering black and white of old news footage.

Like her, I contemplate the crumbling masonry, which houses the echoes of my screams and a cowering fragment of my soul . . . traitorhoortraithoor . . . once more the harsh words grate on my ears the stinking breath fills my nostrils . . . traithoortraitor . . . I try to resist the forced foul intimacy . . . hoortraitorhoor . . . pain blinds me. I swing around to face the girl at my side but neither the rough voices nor my cries reach her ears.

I shudder, desperate to slough off these brutal memories.

There was no CCTV back then, I say, gesturing to the camera that Bernie had insisted the gardaí install. Nor motion sensitive lights.

Most of the occupants of the terrace, absent the Kielys, to be sure, have set these devices on their sheds or houses. Now, every prowling cat and fox is caught in their beam while the birds, sadly deceived by the false dawn, continue to chirrup. Night has all but been abolished.

I can't imagine what it must have been like for you, Jean shudders in vicarious terror. I mean you were about my age then, weren't you?

Yes. Fear streams through my flesh too, not for myself this time but for her. I glimpse the vulnerability masked by her ghostly make-up and nose ring and the instinct to protect her unfurls in my heart. Is this a reflex of the instinct that sent Father out to do murder?

You must have been scared out of your life, she continues. I'd have . . . I don't know . . . It feels horrible even to think about it . . . She spins around as if caught in the vortex of my memory, snatching at its detail. When did Dad and his friend arrive? What did they do? Dad said you—

Richard's stick taps the ground as he approaches from behind and stretches a supportive arm around my waist.

The girl looks put out, her unanswered questions quivering between us.

You go ahead, I say to Richard, taking the house keys from my bag and passing them to him. Let yourself and Siobhán in. We'll follow you in a few minutes,

If you're sure you're okay, he says to me then nods at the girl, whose expression relaxes.

I'm sure, I smile and watch as he and Tanta dwindle down the lane.

Jean follows my gaze a moment before she says in wonderment, Are you still in love with him?

I have to laugh at her frankness. That's a big question. I'm not sure I'm ready to answer it yet.

It's kinda romantic that he came back isn't it? Mum says you must have been really mad at Grandpa or hated him, to get into a relationship with Richard.

Ah now, I say, That's absurd. Your mother knows well that these things aren't always a matter of conscious choice. Richard and I were attracted to one another. He wasn't like the rest of his countrymen who came over in Horse Show week, patronising us as if they were still our colonial masters. We were foolish, or foolhardy, I suppose like most people our age but I imagined I was sophisticated and worldly wise. I cast myself in a melodramatic role believing it was a fated love, with a capital L. The infamous coup de foudre. My friends didn't care for him, which only made me defiant. The Parents were more subtle. They pretended to worry about me being distracted from my studies. Later, they took the line that he wasn't very nice to me.

Yeah, I told Mum I didn't think that was true. I mean I don't get what the big deal was. You weren't going to betray state secrets or anything, she gives an impatient toss of her head.

Exactly so. But you heard what your father said. The assault was a different matter. Those thugs were typical bullies lacking the courage to show themselves in daylight, pumped up with booze and a so-called heroic nationalism, all to impress a girlfriend, who happened to be one of our maids. My 'treachery' was nothing more than a pretext to vent their own petty frustrations.

She frowns, absorbing this information. It goes to show that things like patriotism and nationalism don't actually mean anything. Doesn't it?

I hesitate before replying. Even to me Father's fervid nationalism seemed irrelevant and outmoded. To my surprise he was in favour of our entry into the then EEC, saying we could rely on the French to support us against Britain. When I pointed out we were all to be equal partners in the market he gave me a look that said I was naïve to believe that. Between France and America we would have strong allies if the Brits tried to push us around again. The old alliances are the best, he concluded. His grand-daughter's world is shaped by other loyalties.

They don't any more, I agree. Nationalism was a response to imperialism, another word that has almost been drained of meaning, thankfully, and they were both channels for violence, hatred and brutality. But what will replace them?

Collaboration, cooperation. She asserts. Conservation. We all have to do care for the environment or else nothing will matter.

Ah, yes. I smile appreciatively. This girl is giving me hope.

She circles the space we stand on looking at the ground, seeking long buried clues. Not yet done with the past. Dad says you saved him by hitting one of the men with a rock.

My jaw tightens and my hands clench involuntarily. Yes, I manage to say as nausea rises again in my gorge. My head swims. I look down and see the bloodstained stone nested on a clump of grass, just as it was when Paddy and I returned next day. I feel its heft again in my hands and hear the ugly thud as it connected with the skull of the man who had grappled Paddy to the ground. I remember too how my terror turned to a cold blade of anger, as I calculated the blow, adrenalin pumping through me and the revolting gratification I felt as the man cried out in pain and rolled away off Paddy. Later, back in the house, I discovered specks of blood on my skirt and was disgusted.

Now blood oozes from the stone and collects in a small pool at my feet.

What is it Lena? What are you looking for?

I hear the girl's voice and feel her hand on my arm but am startled nonetheless. I look up. Her face is blurred. I reach for her powdery cheek. Glancing down again I see only a couple of crushed beer cans and the shiny foil from an empty crisp packet. The memory has scuttled back into its hole.

Gathering the bits of myself, I try to sound dismissive. Your father and Tim were very brave.

I think you were too.

Come on, I loop my arm through hers again. Let's move. I'm getting cold standing here.

We begin to walk briskly down the lane.

It's all really weird, Jean says after a few minutes. You know, you see things like that in a movie and it's scary but at the same time you know it's not real. Then it happens to you or someone you know and it makes you feel sick. I don't get why anyone would do stuff like that.

Moral cowardice and feelings of inadequacy mainly. The irony is that they achieved what they claimed to be their aim because they put an end to my friendship with Richard.

That's sad. I mean what harm would it have done to anyone if you had married him?

None that I can see, I shrug. Except maybe to myself and my family. It's not true what your mother says. I'm not sure I'd have been willing to wound my parents even if I didn't agree with them. Life would have been very difficult for me and for my children if my parents disliked or disapproved of my husband.

Then you met Uncle Mossie.

A few years later, yes. Happily. I loved him completely. I think I was happier with him than I could have been with anyone else. I'm sorry you never met him.

Is Muiris like him?

In some ways, yes. He's not as ebullient but he has his father's good sense and kind heart.

Does he know about . . . what you just told me?

No one knew until last night or today. Your father was out of line last night.

Mum says he's not really right since his heart attack. That he gets worked up about things. He was very nervous going on the show. Mum didn't want him to do it.

She was right. It's surely not good for him to get excited.

As we exit the lane onto the avenue, Jean gives herself a little shake and says I'm glad to be out of there. It spooks me now.

Me too, I have to admit. But when people take my parking space I don't have a choice. Bernie's afraid of it too is the problem.

You should carry mace, the girl advises. Did they ever catch those men?

Ah, here it is: the question I dreaded but that had to come. I halt and face her, wondering if she is ready for the whole truth. Paddy would never tell her and would probably be furious at me if he knew I had told her. But we are so far into the disclosure now that I cannot see any merit in denying her the final ugly fact.

She returns my look with one of puzzlement.

I inhale deeply, and, setting my face to the sea again, say, Your father has just told me that your Grandpa killed the men.

Grandpa? That's not possible.

Your father wouldn't make it up. And our father had fought in the Civil War. It probably wasn't the first time he had killed someone.

But that was a long time before, in a war when other people were fighting and he might have been killed too. Those men – that was a personal thing.

Yes, the personal business of a father protecting his child. And the attack was cloaked in a rag of ideology. Your Grandpa didn't like to see his ideals any more than his daughter abused.

We continue in silence, rounding the corner of the terrace.

It's hard to think of, isn't it? She says. Like, I can't picture Dad doing that if it was me.

I reflect on this for a minute. You're right, I say. It is a grim thing to imagine your own family doing such things. Your father would use all the resources of the law to avenge you. Likewise I'd have been satisfied to see them punished, in fact I would like to have seen them made accountable, shown up for the dirty little cowards they were.

How come Grandpa wasn't caught? I mean, people must have looked for whoever killed those men. Their families, friends. Mustn't they?

I can only guess that Father still had friends in the right places. There was unrest in the country. Things can be covered up, blurred, compromised. When the bodies were found, if they were, they might have seemed to be victims of an internal feud. Informers. I'm sorry, I squeeze her arm. It's upsetting. But it's better to get the whole story clear than deliver it in bits and pieces.

Can I tell Pól? She asks timidly.

We have reached the front gate. I pause with my hand on the latch and sigh, I suppose he's virtually one of the family now isn't he?

She nods vigorously. I hope so, although Mum and Dad aren't too keen on him – like you and Richard.

Very well, I say. But no one else. And don't tell your father I told you.

Don't worry, she shakes her head vehemently. I wouldn't say it to anyone.

Good girl.

As if to welcome me home, the moment I open the door the clock chimes, the landline rings, the mobile goes off and Tanta commences to yap.

I pull the mobile out of my bag but as the call is from an unknown number I decide to ignore it. Probably another hackette in search of a scoop.

I'll just see who's calling the landline, I say to Jean. You go and find Siobhán.

She nods and makes to descend to the kitchen.

Brennan's name lights up the screen on the phone.

Yes, Ned, I say wearily.

Lena, sorry if I'm catching you at a bad time but what's a good time I ask myself when I have to tell you that there was someone in here last night. Yes. You see it's never a good time for bad news. Or maybe it's good news. What do you think?

I sink into the chair and pull it up to the desk where I rest my elbows before saying, Run that by me one more time, Ned.

Evidence, there is evidence this morning that there was someone in the office last night.

Did you call the guards?

Not yet. Although she did give me her number, he says suggestively. I think it's our man, so to speak.

Which man? Myles? I shut my eyes and grope for sense. My brain feels like blancmange.

Himself. Yes. You see I was watching the Late Late – that's why I didn't hear the intruder come in, have to turn the volume up these days. By the way, I hope that wasn't you Paddy was talking about?

I'm afraid it was but before we get into his tall tale what was Myles up to? Did you see him?

I hope those scoundrels were caught and given a good hiding.

He pauses but I remain silent so he continues, Yes, as I say, I heard nowt last night. It was only on this morning's round of inspection I noticed that the kettle in the kitchenette was warm. Oh ho, says I to Puss, it didn't boil itself, but just in case I unplugged it. It wasn't only the kettle switched on. The printer was on too. I always switch it off at night and on in the morning – to warm it up for the girls so to speak.

Had anything been printed?

Not that I could see but only someone who knows the run of the place would have gone down there, don't you think?

I suppose so, I muse.

The next bit of evidence so to speak was in your office, well, his now, and once dear Mossie's. Yes, yes, he sighs before resuming. An empty sandwich box in the waste basket. Tuna and sweetcorn, not my favourite. Actually it was Puss who found it. Very odd because there's been no one there for two days and Ivanka empties the baskets every evening. Exhibit number four: the cushions on your, well his now, settee were all piled up at one end, and a dent in the top one as if someone slept there.

That's a bit strange, say I, deciding not to add that it's also all circumstantial and could be attributed to other members of staff using the office to make a call, or to have a nap or a romp and Ivanka not bothering to go near it on the basis that it hadn't been used since she last cleaned it.

Let's keep an open mind for the moment, I add. If you notice anything else over the weekend give me a call and I'll contact the gardaí.

Will do, he says. I'm expecting developments now that the guttersnipe has gone AWOL too.

Who? Geraghty? Are you sure?

No one seems to know where he is. He's not available for comment anyway.

I had a call from DI Nolan this morning, I say, my brain beginning to function again. She says they have evidence that Myles is alive.

Aha! And what could that be only a ransom note.

You could be right. That didn't occur to me.

Typed and printed it out himself here I'd swear. Oho! I think we have him now.

Hold on, I say. You're going too fast for me.

It all adds up, don't you see? He's in a tailspin. Hoping to be caught.

That would be the best thing for him. Or better still, give himself up.

Herself knows well what he's at. Country cute. She's the one gave the story to the Indo too, I'd wager.

The Indo, I begin, recalling Moira Kiely's gloat. I haven't seen it yet – does the story mention Myles?

Yes, Dublin solicitor disparu.

No way, I cry. I'm going to get it now. Thanks Ned. Good bye.

Pip pip, he says.

Replacing the phone with a curse I press my knuckles to the desk and push myself upright, totter slightly then take a deep breath. I need to see the paper immediately. What is that bloody garda playing at? Rosemary must be frantic. I need to talk to her.

She sounds frazzled when she answers the phone and tells me that the Mouse brought the paper to her and is installed again in the house. I ask her to visit me this afternoon, alone.

You don't need to tell Eimear where you're going, I say.

Why? Panic rises in her voice. Is there something the matter? Do you have news?

Let's just say it's a business matter. No need to involve her.

All right, she says grudgingly. She can stay and mind the children.

My instinct is to advise against that but I override it with the thought that at least then we'd know the whereabouts of the vermin. Good idea, say I. See you later.

The two girls are in the kitchen. Jean is brewing coffee, while Siobhán sits at the table tapping a message on her phone. She glances up to acknowledge my greeting.

Tanta stands beside his empty bowl, still yapping. I go into the pantry for his food.

When I return Siobhán puts her phone down and says, That was a random story Paddy told on the Late Late.

Jean glowers at her.

Rambling more like, say I, and turn my attention to the dog.

Is it okay if Siobhán leaves her car outside tonight? Jean asks.

We're going to a gig in town, her friend explains, And there might be alcohol consumed.

And more besides, I think before saying, Sure. Then, with an inspired flash of self-interest, I ask, Would you do me a favour in return please and run to the shop to get me the *Indo*?

Ok, come with me? She glances at Jean who nods agreement.

We climb the stairs together and I take my bag from the hall stand to give them money for the paper.

Keep it, says Siobhán. My treat.

Jean nods assent but I catch an awkward expression crossing her face.

Is there a problem? I ask her.

Yes, she says a shade too quickly. Her hand is on the doorknob when a sudden insight hits me. Do you have enough money for your night out? I ask her.

Yeah, she mumbles and looks down.

Are you sure? Has Geraghty been paying you regularly?

Well that's just it, she says in a despairing burst. He's changed our pay from fortnightly to monthly, and then he said on pay day last week that he's on the point of a big deal and if we held out for another week he'd give us all a bonus.

Behind her Siobhán shifts from foot to foot.

Did he now? And do you have any idea what the deal is?

The girls shake their heads.

He's in Croatia, says Siobhán. That's all we know.

I take a fifty euro note from my purse and hand it to Jean. That's a loan until you get paid. I'm tempted to add, if you get paid but decide not to distress the girl. You didn't tell your parents I take it.

No, she mumbles again, her head swinging sorrowfully. I was going to but then with everything else I didn't want to make a fuss. She looks at me again and says, Thanks a million Lena. I'll give it back to you. I promise.

Very well, off you go. I shut the door behind the girls and bracing myself against it let fly a curse of frustration. I need a drink.

And here is Richard, in the drawing room, pen hovering over the crossword. He has angled an armchair towards the window to catch the light, quite at home with himself.

That took a while, he lays down his paper and pen, and pushes his glasses onto the top of his head.

I go into the dining room and pour myself a large snifter of Courvoisier. Drink? I call.

Not right now, thanks, he replies.

Returning to the drawing room, I sit heavily in Mother's chair. Don't let me distract you. I just need to rest a bit.

Of course, he replaces the glasses and lifts the paper.

I take a swig of my drink before pressing my head into the bay of the winged chair and allowing my eyes to close. Soon, the shadows that had returned a short time ago to rasp and leer at me begin to evaporate. Dorothy was right, I had allowed those men continue to harass me. Even knowing that they were dead might not have freed me of them. It was the shadow of secrecy and shame that haunted me. A hidden self remained trapped in that dark ugly night. I begin to hover, conscious of, but remote from the ambient sounds, the rattle of Richard's newspaper, the scratch of his pen, bird call, a lawnmower, a car alarm, the DART clattering by. Gradually, my heart rate slows, my limbs settle, and I grow calm.

You look worn out, says Richard after a couple of minutes. You should go to bed.

I open one eye slowly and cock my eyebrow at him.

He grins. I don't mean *that*, I mean you need to sleep. You've been through a lot.

Sleep, yes, I murmur. Right now I don't think I have the energy to climb the stairs.

Very well, he bows again to his paper.

Mother liked to do the crossword, I say, closing my eyes again.

I bet she was good at it too, he laughs. She was sharp.

Yes but she never won the competition in the *Sunday Press* which she entered every week.

It must have been rigged, Richard laughs.

Could have been but what annoyed her most was that, when she saw the photos of the winners, she said they didn't deserve to win. Look at the state of her, she'd say, I don't believe she could spell c-a-t, or he's only half in it, vocabulary of a five year old by the looks of him.

I can just see her, Richard laughs. She didn't tolerate fools. Remember when she brought me around the garden? She made a point of telling me that the birdbath came from a Cromwellian estate in Kilkenny. She said, That's what you call restitution.

It was beautiful until a hard frost cracked it. Italian marble wasn't intended for Irish weather.

A pity that.

I think she was testing you, to see how you'd react.

I don't know if I passed. I said it was very elegant.

Ambivalent enough to satisfy her I think. She didn't dislike you. Our situation was the problem. And now I realise that the assault on me must have confirmed their fears for me.

A nerve in his cheek twitches, a tic I recall. I knew, he says, even before your father threatened me that he wouldn't trust me. I could feel it in your friends too, an undercurrent of antipathy. They seemed to make a fence around you, a force field to repel me. You heard Eamon yesterday.

Don't mind that old codger.

I don't but it was symptomatic. Even Ken, last night. I knew he was trying but I could tell it was an effort.

That had more to do with what they thought you had done to me.

His head shakes slowly. He was always like that. Although he made less of an effort in the past. Once he outright told me our relationship wasn't good for you. That I needed to remember who and what your father and his had fought for. He told me to leave you alone.

Ken too? What gave him the right to say that? I ask, bemused and not a little offended that he too would have taken it upon himself to interfere in my life.

He'd had a few drinks. I tried to ignore it. Then I met your father.

How come you didn't tell me what he, what they, said to you?

Because I was pretty sure you'd confront them with it. That would have made matters worse.

Maybe so, I sigh, confused and dazed by these new revelations.

I circle back to Father's inscrutability. Was his action impelled purely by the promptings of love, or was it driven by ancient hatred and an atavistic thirst for revenge which turned those men into proxies for Richard, and the insult to me an insult to him too? Did he confide in Mother, or leave her to guess at it and remain silent? Those questions can never be answered. Strangest of all, when I look back is to realise how throughout that time nothing on the surface of our lives changed. We maintained our exquisite manners. Our home continued to be a model and template of hospitality and genteel civility. But now I see the blood pool once more at my feet, welling up from an underground stream that snakes through the foundations of this house. I cannot admire or respect what Father did for my sake. Such uncompromising determination terrifies me. After he had killed the men what did he feel, a hollow numbness, residual hatred or satisfaction? I open my eyes and look at his empty chair. Were he here I would ask him to detail his act, how he pursued each of the men, whether he declared himself to them, or crept up behind their backs, what account he took of the risk to himself, the consequences for us and Mother had he been caught or killed. I would ask if he regretted what he had done, or was he dogged by it, as I by the shadows of those men.

Father should have told me what he did. Even late in his life. When he told Paddy.

He would not have wanted to add to your hurt, and there was the danger of exposing and incriminating himself.

I ponder the empty chair again for a few minutes before saying, I would have preferred that he told me he loved me than that he would allow anger and hatred to overtake him.

The thirst for vengeance, reprisal, retribution, whatever you want to call it, is hardwired in us. I may work for a peacekeeping organisation but war will never be eradicated. It can only be limited, contained. There will always be people who think something is worth killing for. I think your father and I understood one another. There was no pretence between us and I respected him for that.

I don't think I ever understood him, I sigh. I always felt I wasn't the person he wanted me to be. Or hoped I would be. He put me constantly on my guard. He had a fiery temper. We went in fear of him sometimes.

Much as you may dislike his methods there is some honour or nobility in betraying your own better nature for the good of other people. Don't you think?

I take Richard in, seated there, so avuncular and placid, and try to summon to mind the young man I first knew and place him in the pitch and thrash of battle. Are you haunted by the ones you've killed? I ask him.

Yes, he says, pushing his glasses onto his forehead again, which makes his face appear more vulnerable. Not all the time. Some stay with you longer than others. The worst, though, is remembering your own dead, the ones you failed to save. I know for sure, as the father of a daughter, that your father was eaten up with guilt for what those bastards did to you. Because he had failed to protect you.

From you, say I, recalling Paddy's words.

Probably, yes. He tilts his head. Why are you looking so strangely at me? Have I said something to offend you?

No. No. It's that . . . I glance over his head into the middle distance. Everything looks different now, the past . . . I pause and fumble the words . . . the past and the present. The way I saw things has changed, or the shape of them has changed. And so the present feels unfamiliar. Yes, that's it, unfamiliar.

I'm sorry, he shakes his head. I don't follow.

How could you? I flash him a bleak smile. I'm only beginning to see it myself. Maybe I was more like Father than I pretended. I couldn't talk about what was done to me and he couldn't talk about what he saw or did. You don't either, much, do you?

No. I don't see the point. Brooding on the past doesn't achieve anything. That's not to say it doesn't come back to me or that I have forgotten it but I try to distract myself then, he raises the newspaper. And I can talk to my old colleagues. The ones who are still alive.

I shut my eyes again for a few moments, still trying to align the fragments I have been given piecemeal over the past twenty-four hours. Ah but, here's a missing piece: How come you knew that Paddy knew what Father had done? I ask.

Because he told me.

I sit upright, eyes wide open. He *told* you? When?

Richard folds the paper decisively and lays it on the floor, spreads his hands on his knees and says, I ran into him, in Cardiff.

I don't understand. When was this?

Oh maybe a couple of years after the assault. He was over for a rugby international. I recognised him immediately on the street and greeted him but he blanked me. I knew where the fans stayed so I went to the hotel that night and asked to see him. Naturally, he didn't want to see me. I'm afraid I had to get a bit stroppy with him. All I wanted to know was whether the men had been dealt with. Because if not I was willing to come over and do the job myself. After some persuasion, let's say, he told me, so I thanked him and left.

I take another sip of my drink to steady myself. Poor Paddy, he really did get a going over on my account didn't he?

Yes. The nerve twitches again in Richard's cheek. I probably shouldn't have intimidated him, he continues. But I needed to know. I felt responsible you see.

It wasn't your fault. Those men probably attacked other girls too.

True, but in this instance it was *you* they attacked. I saw red, flaming red. I can be quite detached when I'm doing my job but that was different. It was emotional. I couldn't let it go.

And it never let me go, I say. Now what I can't let go of is how the evil spread from one act. I never imagined there were so many hidden chambers behind the door.

What door?

The one your letter slammed in my face. It's wide open and I see you, Father and Paddy on the other side, interconnected, like a Celtic knot, woven around silence, trying to protect me. My friends were sure you had met someone else, or, worse, that there had been someone else all along. But I wasn't convinced. I never suspected you were in cahoots with my father and brother.

'In cahoots' is putting it a bit strong. I think in a way we were competing to protect you. To prove ourselves.

To one another but not to me. I surprise myself now by laughing. Even the taxi driver that night when we met tried to put me off you. And if I had listened to him you'd have blithely walked home alone.

Alone, yes, but not exactly happily. I would have been beating myself up all the way for being a damned idiot. I wasn't used to forward Irish girls.

And now you're going to tell me I haven't changed.

Well, as you mention it, he concedes. What ever happened to the young man you were with that night?

Gerard? I toss my head. A sad story. It turned out I was right, he did have a lover hidden away, a man. Needless to say, his mother pushed him into marriage but he took off after a year and went abroad. He died in the eighties, like so many others. His parents couldn't protect him from disease.

That's very sad, Richard broods for a moment then says, We seem to have gone backwards like an Italian tank. What now? Is there a forward gear?

I'm stuck in neutral, I say, sketching a helpless smile.

Not good enough, Lena, he says impatiently. I responded to your email, I accepted your invitation, I've told you all I know. We made love. Or was that just sex? Disappointment crosses his expression. Please tell me it wasn't.

I shake my head.

Good, he says. That was . . . you've no idea how I longed for you all those years ago. That was what I wanted to write to you. To say I couldn't get you out of my head, or how desire for you consumed me till I thought I would go crazy. I didn't know how to write it without risking offending you. And then it happened and I was back on Howth with you, as if the intervening years had been swallowed up. It was strange, a kind of doubling as though I was both here and there, acutely alive in the present yet filled with a young man's heart and ardour and intensity. Did you . . . didn't you . . . ?

Yes, I say. Yes I did.

You are still beautiful, he says.

His new tenderness touches me but I can think of no better response than a mere, Thank you.

Where do we go from here, Lee? He persists. I need to know. He lifts the glasses from his head, removes their case from his pocket, sits them into it, snaps it shut and replaces it in his pocket. The pen he clips to his inside breast pocket. His slow, deliberate gestures imply finality.

Chapter Twenty-One

Once again Rosemary Mulvaney sits in my drawing room, tearful and angry, a balled-up tissue in her hand. She has shed the austere black and white of the widow for a pair of jeans and a pale grey sweatshirt with crossed hockey sticks embroidered on the chest. She looks more like herself albeit her face is lined with stress. I have made her a cup of tea and she waits, a trifle impatiently, for me to tell her why I have invited her here.

I'm sorry to have dragged you away from home, I open. But as I explained I needed to see you alone.

You've heard from Myles? She jumps in.

I shake my head. I want to talk about your friend, the M . . . Ms . . . Ms Ní Neachtáin.

Eimear? She looks frightened now. I left her at the house with the kids.

They'll be fine. I say, then join my hands in my lap, gearing up for the disclosure I am bound but loathe to make. The fact is I think she knows more about Myles than she's letting on.

Rosemary cocks her head, sceptically registering my meaning. How? What could she know?

They appear to have been having an affair, I say slowly. I think she used that as a lever to persuade Myles to invest in crocOgold. Or greenGold. But either way it was dross.

And you knew this all along, she gives way to her old anger at me, in need of a target. You knew, she cries, twisting this way and that, caught in the toils of grief and recrimination.

You should have told me. If anything has happened to him, she rails now, I'll hold you responsible. You'll be to blame. It'll be your fault.

I had to be certain before I could say anything.

What if I say I don't believe you? She tosses her head defiantly.

That's your prerogative, I shrug. I have an eyewitness, and I challenged Ms Ní Neachtáin on it yesterday when we left your house. She's a nasty bit of work.

Rosemary bows her head and weeps softly.

I wait in silence while she absorbs the news of this double betrayal, by her husband and friend, my heart brimming with sympathy for her.

I suppose I should have wondered, she says after a few minutes, at the way she suddenly appeared again in my life, all friendly. She looks at me with a bleak expression. I never really liked her in school. She was one of those two-faced girls, you know, sweet as pie when you're with her and bitching about you behind your back. I had no contact with her after we left until a couple of years ago she turned up in a yoga class I go to. She was all over me, as if we'd been best friends in school, saying we must meet for coffee or lunch. Finally I gave in just to put an end to the pestering. She did most of the talking, telling me about the break-up of her marriage and how she was starting a business. Then it turned out she knew John, my brother in law, through work. He started saying how—She breaks off, tilting her head as if she has heard something. Is it possible . . . could the two of them have planned the whole thing? Her mouth falls open with this new realisation.

I'm afraid so, say I. To get clients for Geraghty. And poor Myles fell into the honey trap.

God! How blind I was! She clenches her fists. Especially when Myles talked about the great job she was doing on the office. She renews her weeping, then, looking up sharply, says, It's hideous isn't it?

Yes, I have to confess I got a shock when I saw it.

Do you think she knows where he is? Is this some kind of trick or game? Rosemary springs to her feet, the sports tactician alert now.

That's the trouble, I think she's looking for him too. I'm guessing that's why she's staked out in your house. She wants to prevent him implicating her in any confession or statement he may make. Thing is, the game is up for all of them.

I glance down at the newspaper which I had dropped on the floor when I got up to answer the door. There, just as Brennan said, is a full page spread, follow-up to a front page teaser, devoted to the once ubiquitous but now invisible Mr. Geraghty. The photo of him is superimposed over the studio drawings of Phil the Fluther's eyesores. And in a sneaky bit of editorial juxtaposition, there is a side bar story about the disappearance of Dublin solicitor Myles Mulvaney.

An hour ago Jean and Siobhán had rushed in from the shop gabbling together.

The douche bag's—

The shit's—

Whoa! I put my hands up. Now take a deep breath and tell me slowly what's happened.

The girls glanced at one another and Jean said, He's gone. Geraghty. Our boss.

It's here, look, Siobhán handed me the paper.

According to the story on the front page, two of Geraghty's clients had been looking for the promised dividend on their investment in crocOgold and, tired of being fobbed off, went to Cape Darien to see the site. All they found was a hole in the sand. One of the clients was Donal Sheehy. Geraghty could not be contacted and had not been seen for three days, although no one had reported him missing.

He's gone into hiding, I said, looking over the top of the page at the girls.

Yeah but if these people are after him, said Siobhán, He's in deep shit. And so are we.

What'll happen our jobs, Lena? Jean sucked anxiously on a strand of her hair.

I hesitated before saying, He's sure to turn up but there's obviously something wrong. You girls will have to go to work on Monday morning and take it from there. The police are onto him but it could take a while to establish if there's enough money to refund his investors and pay you, and to get it out of him. It won't be easy for you and your co-workers. Do you have a union?

No, said Siobhán, adding with a panic-stricken look, I have to pay my rent. At least you can stay here, she turned to Jean.

I recalled Felicia's similar cry. Could your parents help you in the short-term?

I suppose so, She looked downcast. But they'll have a fit.

It's not your fault, I said.

Yeah and at least you've a better chance of being kept on, Jean topped her friend's grievance. I'm only there a couple of months.

Steady on, girls. Calm down, I stood up to assert some authority. There's no point arguing about what might or might not happen now. Let's wait and see what Monday brings.

Lena's right, Jean said.

Okay, Siobhán glowered. C'mon, we better go or we'll be late for the others.

While I waited for Rosemary I listened to the message left on my mobile phone by the unknown caller a couple of hours previously. It was a rant from the Mouse warning me not to make unfounded allegations against her, or she would tell the gardaí about Brennan's late night visitors. Not very appropriate in a solicitor's office, she added primly. She was one to talk.

Rosemary dries her eyes now with the crumpled tissue and says, All I want is for Myles to come home.

I know, I say. That's what I want too. Detective Nolan seems very competent. I refrain from sharing Brennan's theory about the nocturnal visitor and the ransom note to avoid raising false hopes, and focus again on the Mouse. You'll have to tread carefully, I warn her. When you go home just tell Eimear she needn't stay, that you'd rather be alone, same as yesterday. The net is closing around them. I'm terribly sorry. It's an awful ordeal for you and the children.

Yes, she commences to weep again, this time with the slow tears of weariness. If I get him back we'll sort it out. Distress troubles her expression. He's probably ashamed. I mean the newspaper, everything. His career is destroyed, isn't it?

I'm afraid so. Let's get him back in one piece first.

As I approach the hall door the bell rings sharp and long. Tanta gets there first, his initial warning bark modulating to an excited yap. Friend not enemy.

I take a quick peek through the spyhole nevertheless and am surprised to see Bernie's face floating in the lens.

Hi, say I, opening the door to her. Is everything all right?

No. No it's not, she speaks brusquely as she steps into the hall. Once in, however, she halts and glances over my shoulder then back to me. Sorry, maybe this isn't a good time.

Stay, I reassure her. My friend is leaving. I turn to Rosemary who nods confirmation and says, Thanks Lena. I'll keep in touch.

Likewise, I say. Bon courage, I touch her arm.

Each of the women steps aside to make way for the other, their gracious smiles touched with rue. I note how alike are the furrows on their cheeks and brows, the dark half-moons beneath their eyes as a wordless empathy passes between them.

When I have closed the door on Rosemary, I turn to Bernie, saying, You worked wonders with Nóirín yesterday. I've never seen her looking so smart.

Thanks, Bernie shrugs with uncharacteristic disinterest. All in a day's work.

We continue in silence to the drawing room, followed by Tanta whose head is lowered as if he too feels the woes of these coming and going women. I resume my post in Mother's chair.

What's up? I ask my neighbour. Aren't you usually in the shop at this time?

Yes, she sighs. I asked Felicia to fill in this afternoon. I had a headache. She glances down at the newspaper where Tanta lies, head on his outstretched paws, eyes flicking from me to Bernie and back again, and says, You've seen it.

The story about crocOgold?

She nods.

A shock for a lot of people I imagine, I hedge, although I hear Moira Kiely crowing in my ear, Rooned. They're rooned.

Yes but not for you, it seems, Bernie challenges me. What about that man? She points to the story about Myles. Isn't that your office? Was he mixed up in this too? That's why the guards were here yesterday isn't it?

I acknowledge her perspicuity with a grimace. I'm guessing it was the terrace spy, Moira Kiely, told her about the gardaí. The Stasi could have made good use of her.

I can't say, I say. I'm not involved in the day to day business of the office any more. But yes, it looks like Myles has got himself into serious trouble. The guards thought I might have some idea of his whereabouts. My main concern is that he is found alive and safe.

She leans back and narrows her eyes, appraising me. Why didn't you trust Geraghty? Did you know something?

I raise my hands defensively. No. I simply thought his promises were too good to be true. Call it gut instinct, I use Mossie's old line. I take it you've been hit?

She bows her head. Everything, she mumbles. Everything's gone.

What? I crane towards her to make sure I have heard aright. Your business? Feargal's?

She inhales deeply and raises a woebegone face to me. I have never seen my chirpy neighbour so discomposed. Her eyes redden now and her cheeks swell, presaging tears. After a few minutes working to control her emotions she repeats, Everything. He – that shit Geraghty – persuaded us to borrow to invest. Short-term he said. Quadruple it in six months. That was nine months ago. Not a penny since. Now I can't raise money to stock the shop. Feargal's the same.

That's unbelievable, Bernie, I exclaim. Please tell me the house is still secure.

The golden bell swings dolefully.

You mean you—I'm so aghast I can't complete the question.

I've just discovered that Feargal used it also as security for the loan.

But he needed your permission to do that, didn't he?

No. He bought it in his name only. I wasn't working at the time.

I bite back the words bloody fool, and ask instead, Was Geraghty involved in your nursing home scheme?

She casts me a guilty look. Yes, the short-term investment in his Cape Darien development was to fund our project. We were toying with calling it Darien House. Phil . . . she gestures to the picture lying on the floor.

I had noticed the similarity in the designs. Did he have a stake in it too?

Oh I've had my fill of him, she gives a wobbly smile. Phoning me morning, noon and night, wanting to know what's happening. Suggesting that we pay him in advance. He's very needy. I've blocked his calls now. I've enough on my plate without mammying him. Oh God, Lena, she plunges her head in her hands. It's all too much. What are we going to do?

I'm afraid there's not a lot you can do at the moment, apart from going to the gardaí. The more information they get the better. There'll have to be a forensic examination of his accounts, all his business dealings. I think this article, I nudge Tanta aside and pick up the paper, is intended to draw more of the people he's cheated out in the open. Maybe you should join forces with them to pursue him. He'll panic and mis-step.

That's what Feargal says, she gulps. A class action.

Yes. If you like I can suggest someone with experience in that area to represent you.

More money, she rolls her eyes.

You're going to need help.

I know. I appreciate the advice. We'll probably have to sell or let the house and move back to Feargal's place in Kiltipper. Or sell everything and emigrate, her distress mounts. Can you imagine? He's seriously suggesting going to Australia. Starting again. You know Feargal, big dreams.

That's a bit drastic, I mollify. I doubt it'll come to that. Geraghty'll be found by the end of the week. I'd say the gardaí have Interpol and everyone else on the job.

I wish I could share the optimism of my own words. I could take a sabre to La Belle Nolan's topknot. Using the press in this way seems lazy and reckless. What happened to on the ground investigation?

I hope so, says Bernie in a defeated tone. I'm sorry, I've taken up too much of your time.

Don't apologise, I say. You have my sympathy, you really do. Don't worry. This fellow'll get his comeuppance.

Yes. She rises to go. I just dread going back to having to scrimp and save and count every penny, she breaks down in tears. It's taken such a long time, so much hard work to get here. We were at our happiest, she sobs. And the children. They won't understand. They're used to having things. I wanted for them to have what I never had. I don't know what to do. Tears course down her face, streaking her make-up and revealing the exhaustion of this determined woman who sees the world she has built for her family slide from under them, leaving them exposed on a teetering ledge.

Don't give up now, Bernie, I say. You're resourceful and strong. You and Feargal both. You'll get through this. I know you will. Go home, splash some cold water on your face and make tea for the kids. Try to keep things as normal as possible for them.

I suppose that's all I can do, she sighs. Feargal will be home soon. Thanks, she reaches up and gives me a quick kiss on the cheek. You're kind, Lena.

I wish I could do more. Let's see what the next few days bring.

Alert to the change in the emotional weather, Tanta raises his front paws to rest on Bernie's legs, looking wistfully up at her. Good boy, she manages to smile through her tears, and pats his head.

Now what? I say to the dog when I have let Bernie out. The silence in the house feels tense and the ticking of the clock, usually reassuring as a heartbeat, has become an anticipatory percussion. My breathing is shallow and short. Nothing for it but to wait, in a vacuum of ignorance and surmise. The dog glances hopefully at his lead dangling from its hook on the hall stand. Good idea, I nod. But I'd better bring the cursed mobile too, that talismanic accessory, less to ward off evil than to keep me apprised of calamity as it unfolds, in the risible conviction that being in the know I can stem its advance.

Strange to think that once upon a time in the last century we didn't have the gadgets and we managed well enough, with the landline and two postal deliveries a day. Now it's got so that people worry if I don't answer the mobile straightaway, Muiris in particular. Since my retirement he has become more solicitous, as if I have crossed a threshold into old age, instead of which I'm looking for new opportunities. Maybe that's what worries him. Perhaps I should have prepared him better for Richard's arrival but it scarcely seemed necessary at his age. Thanks to Paddy's performance last night he is utterly confused. Useless to tell him that unpicking and remaking the shirt changes nothing. I do not regret marrying another suitor. Au contraire. Mossie brought peace to my disordered heart. How do I now pacify the contending currents of my life which is losing the run of itself?

Shortly before he died Mossie urged me not to remain alone, not to grieve for him, not to give myself over to nostalgia and sorrow. As a sign of that wish he even chose what I was to wear at his funeral, a silk cocktail dress aswirl with the colours of the sea. We had made our best and happiest love fresh from swimming in the frisky water, savouring the mingling of its scent and salts with our own, playing with the ribbons of seaweed clinging to our pelts, winkling out the grains of sand secreted in the folds of our flesh, cradling one another as in the swell, senses quickening, fusing, renewing themselves, creaturely, intent, primordial. I never wore the dress again. I couldn't rise to his cheery hopes for me. I have managed to keep my head above water but my limbs are tiring with the effort.

Back in the drawing room I crouch to gather the sheets of newspaper which Tanta has begun to shred on the floor in protest at my not having taken him straight out.

Leave it, I command the dog who scowls at me, a strip of newsprint dangling from his jaw. Ferocious beast, I laugh. Probably the best thing to do with it even if it's not very fulfilling. No meat and a great deal of waffle. But what's this? I hold the front page before me again, taking in the headline which I had passed over in response to Siobhán's angry finger jabbing at the story about Geraghty.

TAOISEACH SEEKS CEAD MILE DOLLARS FROM BOSTON IRISH
Lacey Offers Senate Seat in Return for Disapora Investment at Paddy's Day Do

The photograph illustrating the headline shows a group of smiling men and two women, all accessorised with notes of green, ushering her Laceyship, ablaze in a mint and white striped suit and screaming emerald blouse, through a hotel foyer. I peer more closely at the image without being sure what I am looking for. Myles, perhaps. Or the leprechaun in disguise. The Boston connection is plucking at the back of my mind. Why exactly did the Mouse go there? Is she still in cahoots with Geraghty? Finding no clues in the picture, I turn to the continuing story inside, and find, buried in the last paragraph, a reference to the creation of a school of digital enterprise and entrepreneurship here to be sponsored by the Bostonians. The project will be managed by rain—here the page is ripped. I twist around to retrieve the scrap of paper discarded by Tanta —Bow Holdings. I stare at the name for a few minutes. I've never heard of the company yet it has a familiar look. I pull out the drawer in the side table, releasing a pungent dusty aroma of tobacco from an unfinished pack of Mother's cigarettes, surely stale by now. A lighter and a couple of biros and pencils roll to the front of the drawer. I pick out a biro and, flattening the crossword page on my knee, start to fill the white squares: rainBow. I look at the word for a minute or two then write crocOgold and greenGold. O G B B G O G O B B O G . . . I scurry back to the news story. Yes. There it is: the Bostonian Order of Gaels, BOG. The leprechaun in new raiment. And wasn't it the man in Boston whose balls Myles threatened to break? Now where is the cursed phone when I need it? Nowhere to be seen.

I am about to get out of the chair and go in search of it when I feel a vibration on my buttock. Gotcha, I exclaim as I dig the phone from under the cushion and answer it without looking at the name on the screen.

Yes, I say.

Hello, Lena? I think Eimear suspects something, Rosemary half-whispers.

Is she still there? I find myself lowering my voice too.

No. Yes. Sort of. I told her I wanted a bit of space, like you said and she was very shirty with me. After a while she left in a sulk but she's sitting out there in her car staring at the house. I feel like a prisoner in my own home. It's horrible, she wails. This is torture. When will it be over?

Soon, say I, trying for calmness, although it's far from what I feel. We're all working to resolve this quickly. Have you called Detective Nolan?

No. I don't want to make a big scene. I don't know what to do.

I was about to phone her to see if there are any developments, I fib. I'll tell her about that so and so. She'll probably send someone around from the local station to see how you're doing, mar dhea, which will put the frighteners on your woman.

Thanks Lena. I'm going to close the curtains now. I hate feeling that I'm under surveillance.

Good idea, that'll put her off.

The Mouse is some piece of work, I think. Playing for high stakes or she wouldn't be so persistent. Now for La Belle Nolan.

Yes, Lena, says herself on the first ring.

Ah oh, yes, I fumble with surprise at her promptitude. I've had a couple of thoughts that might help you.

Good, she says. I'm listening.

Well they're hunches and I may be putting two and two together and getting five . . . I cavil before presenting my morsels of amateur deduction.

Thank you, she says, when I finish. Garda Doyle will keep an eye on the office and I'll send someone else around to Mrs. Mulvaney's house. I think we need to talk to Ms Ní Neachtáin again.

Definitely. You should. I'm certain she knows more than she's letting on.

In regards to Mr. Mulvaney, she adds, I'll have to bring him in for questioning and to have a word with him about wasting police time. If, as you suggest, he's involved in fraud or embezzlement we'll need access to his computer and files.

I understand. I'll facilitate you in any way I can, I say. But I'd rather you kept the office name out of the paper.

We'll do our best. I think we'll have a file to send to the DPP soon enough.

Very well, I say. The first priority is to find Myles in one piece, and keep him away from the Ní Neachtáin woman.

I understand. With any luck we'll get him tonight, if Mr. Brennan is right. Have a nice evening.

I'll try, say I.

I should ring Brennan to bring him up to date but I'm not sure I have the energy right now. What's more, if he knows Garda Doyle is staking out the office he'll probably want to invite him in for tea with himself and Puss. I slip the phone into the pocket of my cardigan. Tanta has resumed shredding the newspaper at my feet.

Leave it, I say and bend down to collect the litter. In doing so I spy the dog's old ball which Richard had kicked under Father's chair the night he arrived. Two nights ago. Our little history telescoped into forty-eight hours, and altered in that time, the shirt ripped and refashioned, recollection elided and realigned, bringing the shadows of my unknowing, fed on brooding fears, into the light of a bitter understanding. I will write, yes, a letter, each pen stroke considered as I separate out the strands of my confused feelings, old and new and set them down in carefully chosen words. Then I'll probably tear it up, or burn it, or eat it. For what need has he of my emotional biography? Once it is written it will become another story, set at an angle to my life.

Down on all fours now I reach forward to sweep my hand into narrow space and send the ball rolling across the room. Tanta scampers after it growling.

What on earth are you doing? The sound of Richard's voice startles me and for a second I wonder have I imagined it.

Do you need help? It's him to be sure, still here. A marvel of persistence.

I haul myself up slowly, and brush the dust from my knees. I found Tanta's ball, I explain. Where were you?

I went upstairs to pack my bag but then I thought better of it and lay down on the bed for a nap. I thought what a blithering idiot I would be to walk out after two days when we'd only barely begun to get to know one another again, or maybe really for the first time. We've scarcely been alone since I arrived and when we have we've mostly dwelt on or in the past. The thing of it is I think we could be good together in the future. Look,

he takes a worn leather wallet from his hip pocket. Opening it he eases a piece of paper from one of its flaps. He unfolds the page gently to protect its disintegrating seams, and reveals the *Social and Personal* photograph of the two of us, taken at the Horse Show ball where we met.

You're just an old romantic, I smile. Wait there.

When I return Richard stands at the table in the centre of the room contemplating the photograph which he has spread there.

I lay my matching cutting beside it, and say, Snap!

Amazing, he laughs. Why ever did we keep them?

I'm not sure, I shrug. Love, nostalgia, yearning for something lost, or taken from us. Not from me alone or you alone but a fleeting warm palpable grace that coursed between us. Look at us, I smooth the folds in the matching photos. We were startled by the flash and we took one another's hands. I didn't remember that until I saw the picture then I felt my hand in yours, yours squeezing mine, quite unselfconsciously. We had just met but it didn't feel strange to be standing hands intertwined, taken for a couple. It feels as if everything afterwards was just catching up with that moment.

That all sounds very . . . well . . . you put it well, he says. But if you're right it's been a bloody long and circuitous route to get back to that moment.

Yes but now I realise that moment is long past retrieving. I grieved a long time for that girl, old tears sometimes for what was done to her, taken from her, fresh tears, because she never did vanish. She's still here, the girl in the photo, inviolate. I thought things got lost, broken, died, were supplanted but I know now they don't. They survive in us, with us. We bear them forward.

I open the drawer beside me again and this time take out Mother's lighter. A few turns of the wheel are needed to trigger a small flame.

Wait, what are you doing? Richard cries, reaching to seize the pictures. The picture.

But as the flame begins to sear the faded images and I drop them into the empty grate he relaxes and smiles. You're right.

You see, they're still here, I smile. Watermarked in our cells, along with all the rest. Whatever of good or bad brought us to that moment, and to this one.

And the next? His voice rises on a note of hope.

We'll take it as it comes.

Acknowledgements

I owe my first debt of gratitude to my father, who sadly did not live to see this novel completed. He gave me unstinting love, understanding and encouragement in all that I did but especially my writing. In respect of this novel I am particularly grateful for his vivid memories of Dublin in the 1940s and 1950s.

My sister, Sabine, to whom the book is dedicated, and her husband, Nigel Harris, have provided generous practical and moral support throughout the long gestation of this work.

Meredith Brosnan and Justin Quinn read several drafts of the manuscript and gave me invaluable advice and suggestions which helped to make it a far better novel than I would have achieved alone.

Karin MacArthur painstakingly proofread the manuscript. Her enthusiasm for Lena's story bolstered my confidence in proceeding to publish it.

Rebecca O'Connor and Will Govan of *The Moth* offered me great kindness and hospitality at their idyllic artist's retreat in County Cavan.

Special thanks to Mark Cooney for permission to use his wonderful image, Dreaming Street No. 2 on the cover. You can see more of Mark's work on Instagram at markcooney00.

The thanks I owe to Joe Hennessy, dearest and truest love, are beyond words.

Aisling Maguire was born in Dublin in 1958. She earned a PhD from the National University of Ireland in 1984. Her first novel, *Breaking Out*, was published in 1996 by Blackstaff Press. She has also published short stories, features and book reviews in the national press, international magazines, and journals and anthologies, including *Figures in a Landscape: Writing from Ireland*; *Raven Introductions 4* and *A Very Irish Christmas*. She has worked as a financial journalist, freelance writer and editor, an assistant at the Forum for Peace and Reconciliation and a reporter in the Debates Office of the Irish Parliament.